Infinity's Gateway

INFINITY'S GATEWAY

A NOVEL

JAMES S. PARKER

NEW YORK
LONDON • NASHVILLE • MELBOURNE • VANCOUVER

INFINITY'S GATEWAY

A Novel

Publisher's Note: This novel is a work of fiction. Names, characters, places, and incidents are either products of the author's imagination or used fictitiously. All characters are fictional, and any similarity to people living or dead is purely coincidental.

Published in New York, New York, by Morgan James Publishing. Morgan James is a trademark of Morgan James, LLC. www.MorganJamesPublishing.com

ISBN 9781631951107 paperback
ISBN 9781631951114 eBook
Library of Congress Control Number: 2020934684

Cover and Interior Design by:
Chris Treccani
www.3dogcreative.net

For Margaret
The love of my life

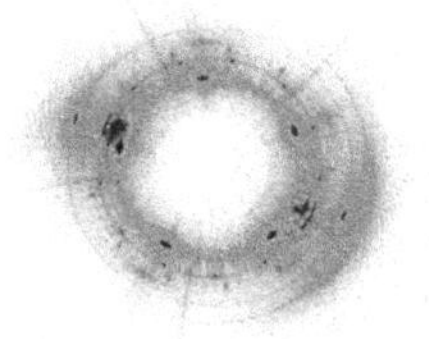

CHAPTER 1
Infinity's Gateway

December 5, 1945

In the blink of an eye, the day morphed from good to terrible. He'd never experienced anything like this before and wasn't handling it well at all. Even though none of this was his fault, the stress was eating him alive, manifesting across his neck and shoulders. But he hardly noticed that compared to what the acid in his stomach was doing to him. Miller swallowed hard, trying to keep from losing his lunch. He knew he'd be the base laughingstock if he lost it and threw up all over his station.

His shift had not started this way, in fact, quite the opposite. The world was good. The Nazis were gone; he was in sunny Florida; and he had a new girlfriend, Sally, the cutest little blonde he'd ever seen. Everything was as it should be. The amount of civilian air travel was continuing to grow, which meant he'd probably have a job if he ever decided to leave the navy. If it hadn't been for the dark clouds building up far to the northeast, there wouldn't have been any clouds in his life. Bad static, however, was another matter, and his ears felt like a dog had chewed them.

Being in the tower put him three stories above the ground. Glancing out the tower windows, he could see the expected weather growing like the tower of Babel in midsky. Although it was moving in fast, it was still a long way away. But it wasn't the approaching storm that had his nerves on fire. For the third time in the last few minutes he checked his watch, then grabbed the duty log and started to skim through it.

About ten or fifteen minutes ago he'd picked up some garbled messages on his radio but couldn't be sure exactly who he'd been listening to. Due to the crazy static, the voices had been so badly broken up that it had been hard to follow. He'd only been able to catch snippets of their conversation, but it was bad, potentially very bad.

The storm didn't look quite like other storms. The static had some undertone harmonics he'd never heard, or maybe just some primal human instinct was connecting with something antihuman. Time suddenly became the enemy. He needed to determine who it was asking for help, but they kept fading in and out. It was frustrating as could be. Fighting the urge to move too quickly, he gently adjusted the dials on his radio, desperately trying to pick up the pilot in trouble.

"Everything all right, Miller?" A simple question, but the pressure of the situation immediately escalated tenfold.

Miller looked up to find the scowling Nordic face of Lieutenant Larsen hovering over his shoulder. Larsen wasn't easy to be around on a good day but would turn into an absolute idiot whenever the smallest of things went wrong. Miller always thought Larsen looked like a Nazi poster child. Unfortunately for Miller, what he'd picked up was not a small thing.

"I don't think so, Lieutenant. Everything had been going just fine, but I think I've picked up someone asking for a compass reading."

"You don't think so?" snapped Lieutenant Larsen. "They either asked for a compass reading or they didn't, which is it?"

"There was a lot of static, sir, and his voice was pretty broken up. The problem, if I heard him correctly, is that it sounded like he said something about possibly having gotten lost after their last turn. I have no idea what that means. At this point I don't even know if it's one of ours, or if I'm picking up civilian noise."

The lieutenant snatched the duty log off his desk, frowning at the pages in front of him. "We've got quite a few planes in the air right now. Could it possibly be ...?"

"Sir, I've got them," said Miller, interrupting the lieutenant.

"Don't just sit there, Miller, put it on the speakers so we can all hear it," said Lieutenant Larsen.

Miller flipped off his headphones and flicked a switch, instantly filling the control tower with bursts of extreme static. That undertone, too smooth for static, was there. Maybe someone else would notice it. Although the voice on the radio didn't sound as if he was panicked, it was clear that things had gotten serious. "This is FT-28. Both of my compasses are out and I'm trying to find Fort Lauderdale, Florida. I am over land, but it's broken. I am sure I'm in the Keys, but I don't know how far down, and I don't know how to get to Fort Lauderdale."

"FT-28," murmured Larsen, "that's Lieutenant Taylor."

At that moment the radio burst to life again. "Lauderdale, this is FT-74, Lieutenant Cox. We have some aircraft out here that are lost. Am requesting immediate assistance."

Lieutenant Larsen picked up the microphone, "FT-28, this is Naval Air Station, Fort Lauderdale. Is your plane equipped with an IFF transmitter?" The only sound in the tower was the constant growling of the almost musical static. All of them waited anxiously for a response. Miller found himself holding his breath, which made him feel even worse.

The lost plane was being flown by Lieutenant Taylor, flight leader of Flight 19, which consisted of five aircraft. Flight 19 was a routine training mission, and according to the duty log, they'd been in the air about two hours. That meant one experienced pilot and four newbies.

"FT-28, I repeat. This is Naval Air Station, Fort Lauderdale. Does your plane have an IFF transmitter on board?" said Lieutenant Larsen. Again, they waited. "Come on, answer the question."

"Sir, I'm not sure I know what an IFF transmitter is," said Miller.

"Friend or Foe, we got them from the Brits. It's the same as a standard YG. If he's got one, and I pray he does, it'll enable us to triangulate his position and we'll be able to bring him home," said Lieutenant Larsen. "Now is not the time, Miller. I'll tell you about it later. Can't believe you don't know that."

Larsen's question to FT-28 went unanswered. They had a lost flight on their hands and for some reason they were having trouble communicating with them. Larsen briefly turned his eyes away from the radio, barking out orders to the other men in the tower, "I want an alert out immediately to all air bases, all aircraft, and all ships, merchant and military. I want to know if anyone out there can see them or reach them by radio. Let them know that the call sign is Flight 19; its team leader is Lieutenant Taylor. His aircraft number is FT-28. Also, send out an emergency alert to Port Everglades alerting them to the situation."

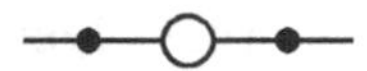

Lieutenant Charles Taylor kept a sharp eye off his port wing, making sure the four other Avengers that made up his team were still in line. "Both my compasses have stopped working. Bossi, are you able to give us our heading?"

Joe Bossi was one of the other four pilots being trained. "Sorry sir, I don't get it, but my compasses have gone nuts. They're jumping all over the place. I can't get a fix." The other three pilots, Powers, Strivers, and Gerber, all chimed in, letting Taylor know that they too were having the same problem.

"They can't all fail at the same time," muttered Taylor, almost to himself.

"Lieutenant, look behind us, hard off the port wing. What in the world is that?" shouted Airman Henson, one of the two crewman onboard Taylor's plane.

Taylor twisted around and looked over his shoulder in the direction the airman had indicated. His stomach turned over as he couldn't believe what he was seeing. It was impossible! A giant wave, or at the very least, an extremely dense wall of clouds, had come out of nowhere and appeared to be racing towards them. Taylor quickly checked his radar, but it too was acting up and he couldn't get a clear reading on anything.

Looking back at the wave again, he experienced a Bible school flashback. *And the Lord went before them by day in a pillar of a cloud, to lead the way, and by night in a pillar of fire, to give them light, to go by day or night.* Perhaps he was witnessing divine intervention.

"Sir, what is happening? Look at the sky. Whatever that thing is it's starting to surround us," said Powers. Powers, youngest of the trainees in tow, couldn't hide the fear in his voice.

"Steady," commanded Taylor. "Stay in formation. We've talked about this before; the weather in this part of the world can change on a dime. We'll maintain our current heading. That should get us through this in short order."

Taylor couldn't take his eyes off the threatening wave of darkness that was forming all around them. He'd never seen anything like this. Whatever was happening, it sure wasn't any kind of storm he'd ever been through. Both compasses were on the fritz, his radar was giving him an electrical light show, and he had no idea which direction they were headed. For the first time in his many years of flying, he had no idea what to do next.

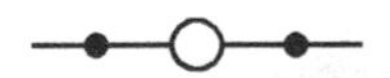

Ensign Breen joined them in the tower and handed a file to Larsen. "Here's the information on the other pilots. Just to give us a better idea of what we're dealing with, I checked, and before takeoff each plane had been fully fueled."

"I guess that's a little good news," said Larsen. "At least we have that going for us. I just don't get it. Flight 19's just conducting a standard navigation and combat training exercise. We've had three other similar missions run earlier today. Did any of them report issues with their radar or their radios?"

"None that I'm aware of, Lieutenant," answered Breen, "and if there had been, I'd know about it. Do you know much about Lieutenant Taylor?"

"He and I have talked a few times. He's not like the hotshot pilots we have strutting around here. He seems like a pretty squared-away sailor, just recently transferred up here from NAS Miami. It's my understanding he'd been a VTB instructor there as well. I've read his file. I'll say this, he's got one impressive record."

"Good to know that we're dealing with an experienced man," said Breen.

"Oh, he's experienced, alright. Taylor completed a combat tour in the Pacific theatre as a torpedo bomber pilot on the aircraft carrier USS Hancock. He scored quite a few kills. Anyone who can consistently take off and land a plane on what is, at best, a moving target floating in the middle of the ocean, qualifies as a good pilot."

"Sir, I don't know what to do," interjected Miller. "I've tried to reach the other pilots that are with Lieutenant Taylor, but I can't get through to any of them. This isn't making any sense. Based on the bits and pieces I'm being able to pick up, they're all having the same equipment failures with their radar and compasses."

Larsen turned to Breen and asked, "How green are the other pilots with Taylor?"

Breen quickly leafed through the file he'd been holding and said, "Looks like they're all reasonably experienced. They've each got close to 300 flying hours, 60 of those hours in the Avenger."

"Then there's no excuse for not being familiar with the equipment on the planes they're flying," said Larsen.

"In fact," added Breen, "that team recently completed three other training missions in this area."

"Are we hearing back from anybody?" shouted Lieutenant Larsen. His frustration with the situation was on full display. He did not want the loss of an entire training flight going down on his record. Miller knew that Larsen was already figuring out who he could blame. A chorus of "no sir" echoed all around him. In Miller's head, the song "Gremlins from the Kremlin" from *Russian Rhapsody* was playing. He was so nervous he almost began humming it.

The minutes continued to drag by with still no word from Flight 19. Finally, Miller looked at the lieutenant and said, "Sir, just picked up a message from Taylor. It's hard to hear him clearly, but he indicated that his IFF transmitter has been activated."

"Finally," said Lieutenant Larsen, breathing a sigh of relief. "Breen, track that signal down. I want to know where those planes are."

Breen sat down in front of one of the consoles and immediately went to work. He tried every trick he knew but could not locate the IFF signal. Breen shouted over to Miller, "Are you sure that's what you heard?"

"Yes sir," replied Miller. "He said it again just a few moments ago."

Breen met Larsen's iron glare. "Sir, I don't know what's going on out there, but we are not getting any IFF signals from anyone. I'll keep monitoring, but if Taylor did turn it on, then we should be picking it up and we're not."

"Does anyone in this tower know what they're doing?" Larsen shouted at the men. "You do know how to triangulate a signal on that thing, don't you, Ensign?"

Breen's eyes turned cold. He gripped the desk with his left hand as hard as he could, fighting the nearly overwhelming urge to throw the young lieutenant down the tower stairs. "Yes sir, I most certainly do. If the lieutenant will remember, I trained you on this equipment."

Larsen ignored Breen's remark, staring out at the ocean. The situation had quickly accelerated from being a frustrating incident to a growing fear that they were going to lose all those men. All the other planes they had in the air had been accounted for. They'd also been able to talk to them. That being the case, he couldn't understand why they couldn't talk to Flight 19. Intermittently, they kept picking up bits and pieces of what the planes that made up Flight 19 were saying to each other, but when they tried to contact them, they couldn't hold on to the signal.

Miller grabbed the lieutenant's arm and flipped off his headphones, turning on the speakers. "We have Taylor, sir!"

The voice they'd come to identify as Lieutenant Taylor said, "We are heading 030 degrees for forty-five minutes, then we will fly north to make sure we are not over the Gulf of Mexico."

Larsen immediately turned to Breen. "Ensign, are you able to get a bearing on them now?"

Breen did all he could with the equipment in front of him, but turned back to Larsen and shook his head. "We are still not picking up their IFF signals, sir. I'm not sure what else we can do."

"Well, I'm not ready to write those men off, Ensign." Larsen moved to Miller's station and picked up the microphone. "FT-28, this is NAS Lauderdale. Turn your radio to broadcast on 4805 kilocycles. Repeat, turn your radio to broadcast on 4805 kilocycles."

Everyone in the tower waited, but the order was not acknowledged. Larsen looked down at Miller, "Stay on 4805 kilocycles. Are we getting anything at all?"

"No sir, just empty air."

Larsen refused to waste more time. While the planes may have taken off fully fueled, the clock was running out on them. "FT-28, switch your radio to Yellow Band, 3000 kilocycles. Repeat, switch your radio to Yellow Band, 3000 kilocycles." Yellow Band was the search and rescue frequency, so Larsen reasoned that there shouldn't be anyone else on that frequency to interfere with them.

This time Taylor responded. "I cannot switch frequencies. I must keep my planes intact."

Had there been room in the tower, Larsen would have been pacing the floor. It was now just before 5:00 p.m. Again he radioed Lieutenant Taylor to turn on his transmitter for YG if he had one. This too was not acknowledged so Larsen had no way of knowing if Taylor had even gotten the message.

Miller had his headphones on, listening closely. "Sir, it's too broken up to put on speaker, but they seem to be changing course."

"Changing course to what?" snapped Larsen. "Are we supposed to guess, Miller?"

"It sounded like they're going to head to 090 degrees due east for at least ten minutes," replied Miller.

Miller thanked God for the tenth time since his enlistment that he wasn't an officer. There were fourteen men in those five TBM torpedo bombers. Logically, based on where they'd supposedly been, going east should take them over Florida. Doing some quick math, Miller guessed that they should have enough fuel to last until 8:00 p.m. That gave them just three hours to find a place to land.

For Miller it had become a contest between his pounding head and the sickness that filled his stomach as to which one was making him feel worse. Before all this started, he'd been hoping to be sharing a couple of beers with Sally at about 8:00 p.m. He knew now that that was not going to happen.

Larsen looked back at Breen, a questioning look on his face. Again, Breen merely shook his head. They still were not able to pick up on the IFF signals, or anything else from the missing planes.

"Lieutenant, what are we going to do?" asked Bossi. Of the four pilots Taylor was training, Bossi was holding it together the best. "Lauderdale keeps asking us to head west, not east, but we can't even tell which direction west is."

"We can't be sure of any direction," chimed in Stivers. "It's strange, even the ocean doesn't look right."

Taylor had precious little to offer his men. Due to the time of day and the bizarre cloud formation that surrounded their planes, he couldn't take a bearing off the sun, which he knew was starting to set. The skies were unlike anything he'd ever seen, and the immense cloud formation continued to steadily close in on them. "Stay together, men. Even if we have to ditch, we're well prepared for it."

Each of the planes carried self-inflating rafts, and the men all wore Mae West life jackets. Nevertheless, setting an Avenger down in the ocean on a clear day was not an option any of them wanted to take on. Trying to do that at night, even with calm seas, was a high-risk proposition at best. But due to the massive clouds that were now engulfing them, they knew all too well that the weather had taken a bad turn. Taylor could only imagine how rough things were going to be in the water below them.

"Tighten up as much as you can," directed Taylor. "Hopefully we'll be over land soon."

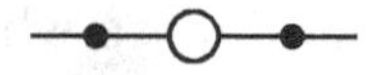

For the next agonizing hour, the tower listened as Flight 19 changed course again. By this time the weather had deteriorated, creating extreme turbulence and unsafe flying conditions. Several ships out on the Atlantic were reporting "tremendous seas," whatever that meant. What little radio contact they'd had with Flight 19 became even more distorted. It was now after six and the sun was nearly gone, taking any hope of visual contact with it.

At twenty minutes past six they received another message from Taylor. "All planes close up tight . . . we'll have to ditch unless landfall . . . when the first plane drops below ten gallons, we all go down together."

It was the last transmission they would hear from Lieutenant Taylor. Miller had been looking at a stupid cardboard Santa someone had stuck up on a support column in the tower. In the years to come, he would often dream about it.

Coordinating with several land radar stations, it was finally determined that Flight 19 was somewhere north of the Bahamas and east of the Florida coast. An hour after Taylor's last message was received a search and rescue Mariner aircraft took off from the Banana River NAS with a thirteen-man crew. Three minutes into the air, the Mariner radioed to its home base that its mission was underway. That was the Mariner's last radio report. Like Flight 19, the Mariner was never heard from again.

The disappearance of Flight 19, along with the Mariner, resulted in one of the largest air and sea searches on record. Hundreds of ships and aircraft combed thousands of square miles of the Atlantic Ocean, the Gulf of Mexico, and remote locations within the interior of Florida. No trace of the bodies or any of the five aircraft was ever found.

There was weeping and heartbreak in fifteen families. Some jobs were lost at the base as headlines momentarily embarrassed the navy, but in January, when Charles de Gaulle resigned, most people forgot. It was a good story for a slow news day, and in the paperback boom of the '70s it got a catchy name, *The Bermuda Triangle.* It got a couple of crappy films and even Mr. Spock narrated *In Search of the Bermuda Triangle* in 1977.

And then we had new scandals, new oddities, new news. It was forgotten except for die-hard geeks, an obscure Catholic order that tracks the strange and unexplainable, the decedents of the tower crew, and of course, fifteen families who have headstones marking empty graves.

Mankind was done with this mystery.

But the mystery was not done with mankind. And this time far more than fifteen families would mourn, and mankind would face a much bigger mystery than any it had seen during its brief run on the planet.

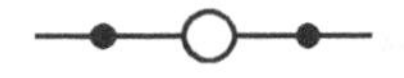

October, Last Year

The rain continued its relentless attack on a ground that had become saturated two days earlier. Admiral William Clarence Fairfax stared out the window from his office at the Pentagon, watching as streams started to appear in places where streams were not meant to be.

The flooding in the area had already caused significant damage and based on the forecasts he'd seen, there didn't appear to be any immediate relief in sight. Once again Mother Nature was reminding the Washington establishment, and not all that subtly, that she would always hold the true power.

It was the sudden silence on the other end of the call that immediately brought him back to that which he was supposed to be focused on. "Admiral, you still there?" asked a demanding voice with what he believed to be a rather exaggerated Maine accent. The senator sounded like a pompous character out of a Stephen King novel.

"Yes, Senator, of course," he replied. "You bleeped out for just a few moments. The weather must be affecting even our communications equipment." This, of course, was not possible, but he was rather confident that the senator, like most of his colleagues up on the hill, wouldn't know that. Secure networks were constructed to be secure, from the weather as well as everything else.

"Then I'm sure I can count on your support. I plan to settle this during the upcoming budget meetings next week. This issue is of the utmost importance to me, as well as to the American citizens we all work for," said the senator, his voice filled with the well-rehearsed sincerity that he usually saved for reelection speeches.

There were times when it took all his years of experience in dealing with politicians, and the strong military discipline that had been pounded into him long ago, to keep the sarcasm out of his voice. He wished that just once the senator could be this passionate about increasing the navy's budget. About getting them the new systems the navy so desperately needed for national defense, or any of the many items on a list that was far too long, a list that had been ignored by this administration and its cronies. But no, that simply didn't line up with the senator's own self-interest.

This "issue of the utmost importance" was about making a minor design change on the uniforms worn by every sailor out there, uniforms that would then be manufactured in the senator's home state. Like almost every other politician he worked with, their highest priority was always on the pork they could bring home. The admiral shook his head in disgust.

"Your interest in this is not lost on me, Senator," replied the admiral. "You have my word that it will get the attention it deserves in my staff meeting this Friday." Before the senator could reply, the admiral signed off saying, "I'll let you know how that goes. Thank you," and hung up.

Admiral Fairfax had spent his entire life in the navy, carrying on a proud family tradition. Well respected by the men he served with, he had a reputation for getting the mission done, whatever it was, using any and all means necessary. Up until the last few years, when he'd been promoted to the Joint Chiefs of Staff, he'd never led from a desk, or the rear, as he thought of it.

Although Admiral Fairfax demanded a great deal from the people in his command each day, he carried in his heart a true compassion for all the sailors working for him. Standing just over six feet tall, he was broad shouldered and had a deep, gravelly voice. His eyes could pierce your soul and in civilian clothes he looked like a hood out of a fifties film. He chose to look tough, and the few folks that had ever crossed him found out his bite was worse than his bark. Although, fortunately, no one had used the metaphor, he was a momma Orca, his sailors were his pups, and the rest of the world was filled with tasty sharks.

At almost the same moment he hung up on the senator, his door burst open and McIntyre, a young African-American lieutenant commander, rushed in, a worried look on his face. Before he could speak Admiral Fairfax held up his hand, signaling the young officer to halt. "Unless they're wearing a military insignia that outranks me, or it's a member of my immediate family, I'm not going to talk to or see anyone. Is that clear?"

One of the legendary stories his men loved to tell new sailors that joined the unit was that the admiral could stop a tsunami with a scowl. The look on the admiral's face gave credence to that story, a look instantly recognized by Lt. Commander McIntyre. "Sir, Captain Ramirez has some very sensitive information concerning national security that requires your immediate presence in the intelligence center. He's in Delta Two operations room."

In fifteen years, Ramirez had never presumed to "summon" the admiral, nor had the captain ever wasted Fairfax's time. A highly competent officer, once, in a very real sense, Ramirez had stopped World War III. Leaving his office, he told another officer on his staff, Commander Benning, to hold all calls. Walking a short distance down the hall, he and the Lt. Commander entered an elevator guarded by two marines. The elevator shot down, taking him to the primary intelligence center within the Pentagon, five stories underground.

As the elevator opened, Fairfax saw several marines guarding the area. These marines were under the command of TOP Nolan O'Conner. A career marine, what the master sergeant lacked in height, he made up for in girth. The size of his arms and chest made it almost impossible to find a uniform that fit. O'Conner and the marines snapped to attention as Fairfax returned their salute. "Good afternoon, Admiral. Captain Ramirez is expecting you, sir," said Sergeant O'Conner.

"Thank you, TOP. Carry on."

The intelligence center was massive, providing housing and all necessities for the three hundred plus people working there. In many ways, it reminded Admiral Fairfax of being on a submarine. The center was completely self-sufficient, containing its own power generators and defense systems. The highly trained people assigned to this post represented all branches of the military, including several from the nation's various intelligence agencies. All the personnel assigned to the intelligence center were given tours of duty that lasted months at a time.

Lt. Commander McIntyre escorted Admiral Fairfax down the hall to the Delta Two operations room, opening the door for him. Once the admiral had gone inside, McIntyre closed the door, staying outside in the hall. Unless otherwise needed, he would wait until it was time to escort the admiral back to his office.

The Delta Two operations room was quite large, containing five large screens configured in a semicircle. One of the screens was used to monitor all ships and aircraft, civilian and military, within a fifty-mile radius of the area defined as the crisis point. The screen next to it, tied into the NSA com center, monitored the communications from all those craft. The third screen targeted the same area but used infrared. At first glance Admiral Fairfax couldn't make out what the other two screens were displaying.

Whatever had happened to require his presence had triggered nearly frantic activity on the part of everyone there. Fairfax could feel the tension in the room. The raised platform in the back, where the admiral had just entered, held a large conference table and a row of analysts off to the right. It overlooked three concentric rows of intelligence officers and analysts, all with multiple computer screens at their individual stations. His arrival went completely unnoticed.

He quickly spotted Captain Ramirez on the phone, standing next to one of the computer consoles near the far end of the conference table. He'd known Ramirez for a long time and the captain had been part of the admiral's team for close to fifteen years. He was known for being able to take the most complex of situations and provide a succinct appraisal with no extraneous detail.

Studying the screen that was monitoring the ships and planes, Admiral Fairfax determined that the area in question was somewhere off the east coast of Florida. Ramirez was unaware that the admiral was now standing directly behind him. "Based on this level of activity, I'm guessing that this is more than just the president suddenly deciding to take a pleasure cruise off the Florida coast," said Admiral Fairfax.

Captain Ramirez turned to greet the admiral, but the look on his face startled Fairfax. Over the years he'd learned that it took a great deal to rattle the captain. That said, the expression deeply etched across Ramirez's face was a mixture of confusion and fear, two traits the captain rarely exhibited. "If only that were the case," said Ramirez, shaking the admiral's hand. "There's something you need to see, sir." Looking at the analyst next to him he said, "Put photo 14 A on screen."

The analyst Ramirez had been standing next to nodded and went to work, hitting the necessary keys on her console. She looked young and Cuban, early thirties max, yet Fairfax knew she had to be one of the best there is or she wouldn't be working here. Ramirez once mentioned to him that her grandfather had been career navy and had started out working in the tower at NAS Lauderdale. There was some wild story involved, but he had forgotten it.

Admiral Fairfax watched the middle screen change images, showing what appeared to be a picture of the ocean from one of their satellites. "Captain, what am I looking at?"

"The coordinates put this section of the ocean as being 135 miles off the coast of Florida, almost directly out from Ft. Lauderdale," answered Ramirez.

"What am I missing? I don't see anything."

"This photo was taken, along with several others, an hour and half ago. Two more of our birds got shots of it, but this one is the clearest."

"Shots of what? All I see is blue water," said the Admiral, wishing that Ramirez would get to the point.

"Ensign Miller, magnify the photo and encircle the object in question."

The screen instantly changed, and the admiral could now see what looked like a dark spot on the surface of the ocean, irregular in form. It appeared to be an angular mass, completely black, but wasn't any kind of craft he'd ever seen. After studying it for a moment he said, "Captain, am

I supposed to guess or are you going to tell me what this is? Come on, it can't be that bad."

"That, sir, is the problem," said Ramirez. It was clear that he was struggling with what to say next. The analysts around them, including Miller, looked to their captain to see how he would proceed. "Admiral, we don't know what this is. Our satellites picked it up and the computers that monitor the feed sent back to the Pentagon immediately went into alarm. We have still pictures and film, but this picture displays the object the best."

"I'm not following you, Captain. You've got the information that the satellites recorded. Surely we can make some level of identification from that. Were there any ships or planes in the area at the time the pictures were taken?"

"There were two ships in the immediate area, both freighters, but they didn't see anything. Also, nothing appeared on their radar. However, that's somewhat inconclusive because both freighters, especially the one closest to it, the *Sea Angel*, reported trouble with their onboard systems," reported Ramirez.

"What kind of trouble?" demanded the admiral, his patience was beginning to wear thin.

"According to the captains on those ships, for a short period of time, nothing worked right. Their radar, the radio, their navigational gear, everything seemed to go haywire. There were also similar problems reported by ships and planes in the nearby area. What's significant is that it seems that the problems they all experienced stopped when this object went away."

"How big is this thing?"

"Its shape fluctuates, but our best measurements put its circumference at covering close to a quarter of a mile," said Ramirez.

The admiral turned to face the captain. "You're telling me there's a craft out there a quarter mile in size and you don't know what it is? Captain, what exactly is going on here?"

"It's not a craft, at least not in the conventional sense. And frankly, we're using the word craft rather loosely. Admiral, we've spent the last hour trying to figure this thing out and the answers we're getting simply don't add up to anything we're familiar with."

"I assume we're tracking it. Where is it now?"

"It was only there for a few minutes, seventeen to be exact. Then it just disappeared. Since then there's not been any trace of it. At present we have two destroyers and one sub in the area, but there's no trace of anything, especially something that size."

"Captain, no offense intended, but that's the most ridiculous report I've ever been given. You're telling me that something that big appeared out of nowhere, hung around long enough to get its picture taken by our birds, and then vanished into thin air!"

"A completely impossible and improbable set of facts. I agree. And yet that's exactly what it did," said Ramirez, "which brings us to the answers we've been able to derive." Again, Ramirez hesitated then said, "Admiral, as best as we can determine, we think it's a hole."

"A hole," repeated Fairfax, his temper beginning to rise. "A hole in what, the ocean?"

"No sir. Every anomalous sighting gets analyzed by our pattern recognition software. The software says it looks like a Feynman diagram."

"You're not helping."

"It's a diagram that shows movement of subatomic particles in space-time."

"That looks a little larger than subatomic."

"The neural net thinks it's not there."

The admiral decided that if this was a Halloween joke, someone was going to be reassigned to Alaska. "Not there?" he asked with an icy cold stare and an ascending tone that commanded everyone's attention in the briefing center. Up until now, no one had ever seen anyone summon the admiral. Even his senior leadership "requested" his presence. "You summoned me to look at something that's not there?"

"No sir. Based on the research that our people have been doing, in coordination with some of the top physicists that we work with, they believe that what we witnessed is potentially a hole in the time fabric. No matter inside of it, no energy inside of it, and perhaps no—I'm not a physicist sir—no time inside it."

The admiral looked closely at Ramirez, and then glanced at the analysts sitting near them. Whatever this thing was, it had them stumped and that just didn't happen. The fear and uncertainty in their eyes was real, more so because, for perhaps the first time in their careers, they didn't know what to do next. Keeping his voice calm, he said, "Captain, can you expand on that for me?"

The admiral had no idea what was coming next. To his way of thinking they had just crossed over to the world of science fiction. He half expected Patrick Stewart to walk into the room dressed in a tight red and black shirt, closely followed by Worf and Mr. Data. Or maybe his alarm would start to ring, and he'd find this had all been just a bad dream.

"I'll give you what we have been able to pull together so far," answered Captain Ramirez. "Much of the science we're talking about here is still theoretical. But based on the data that our satellites were able to capture, there is the possibility that this hole potentially leads, or opens, to other dimensions. As I understand it, years of study have been given to this line of thought by many prominent physicists. It is called the many-worlds interpretation."

"Many-worlds interpretation," repeated the admiral. "Parallel dimensions? What's next, Captain, is Doctor Who going to show up with his phone booth?"

Without thinking, Miller interjected, "Actually, he's just called the doctor." And she bit her lip.

Her remark broke the tension and the admiral stifled a laugh. "Okay, someone made a special effect. They no doubt wanted us to see it. Great psy-op, so why are my senior officers running to the least likely hypothesis?"

"Sir, during the seventeen minutes in which this event occurred, we had close to three hundred other anomalies reported by various people in and around the area. Ships and planes with compasses pointing in odd directions, radios suddenly filled with static, we even had a ham operator in Fort Lauderdale who claims to have received "alien radio" signals. There's also a seismograph reading showing a tremor in the region. All began and ended with this gateway closing."

"Oh, it has a name now." The admiral's voice had turned cold again. Anyone who had served with him knew this tone. They also knew that it was never good to be in the vicinity of the admiral when it showed up. "Regardless of the really bad idea of personifying a possible natural phenomenon, tell me why this is a military issue. Why is your team focused on this instead of NASA or NOAA? I'm sure it's all very interesting, and men in white lab coats may end up building careers on this, but a natural phenomenon is not our problem."

"It's not a natural phenomenon. Admiral, one of my technicians said it best. Miller?"

The young lady, still embarrassed at her Dr. Who remark, said. "Admiral, a uranium atom decaying normally is a natural phenomenon. Several billion of them decaying under forced conditions is Hiroshima."

Then there was a pause.

"Okay, let's say it's not a natural phenomenon, that someone out there is controlling this thing. Who would that be? I sincerely doubt it's the Russians; they're behind us on almost everything from military aircraft to toasters. That only leaves the Chinese and they're too busy trying to steal our stuff."

Ramirez said very carefully, "The energy required to do this is probably not possessed by any nation or corporation. If so, it would be the kind of leap achieved by the Manhattan Project." Ramirez paused long enough to clear his throat before continuing. "Although at this point we do not have anything to definitively tie the two events together, an analyst at the NSA did offer an observation. On December 5th, back in 1945, the navy lost five Avenger torpedo bombers off the coast of Florida. Their disappearance occurred, geographically, in roughly the same place as the object our satellites picked up."

In a flash Admiral Fairfax saw his career ending. This was it. Not Islamic terrorists, not the Chinese, it was going to be the *Weekly World News.* He could see his picture in the checkout lines with a fuzzy map of the Caribbean behind him with a dark triangle pointing north.

"That's enough, Captain!" barked Admiral Fairfax. "Getting questions from our elected officials about the Bermuda Triangle is right in line with the disappointingly low level of expectations I hold for them, but I will not tolerate this kind of nonsense from the best trained people in the world."

"Sir, the NSA analyst wasn't just speculating. As I stated before, the many-worlds interpretation has been seriously researched for years. There are many books and papers out there, all written by experts. By taking and using the data we have just collected, he is saying that there is enough here to suggest that the concept of interdimensional travel just might be possible. Accepting that as a working hypothesis would provide an explanation for many of the craft that have gone missing in this part of the ocean."

Admiral Fairfax was close to losing it. Did he really need to explain to Captain Ramirez that the whole myth about the Bermuda Triangle had been framed years ago by a simple newspaper reporter? Charles Berlitz! He hated the man. Atlantis, the Bermuda Triangle, the Philadelphia Experiment, it wasn't real, it's tripe, they're all works of fiction.

Then it dawned on him as to what he'd just said. He was indeed arguing with the best trained, most intelligent people in the world. None of them would jeopardize their reputations if they didn't firmly believe that they had the data they needed to back this theory up. Ensign Miller was staring at him, dying to say something.

Taking a deep breath, he managed to keep his emotions in check. Looking at Ramirez, he said, "Captain, being the one with the privilege of giving this report to me couldn't have been easy. As always you were direct and to the point. I appreciate that. Continue to work with your team and let's see what they finally determine to be the cause behind this. I'll expect a full report from you tomorrow morning at 08:00 in my office."

"Yes sir, I'll be there."

To the men and women who had watched all of this he nodded and said, "Carry on." Admiral Fairfax then left the intelligence center and returned to his office. Not a deeply religious man, he breathed a silent prayer that they were wrong. They had to be.

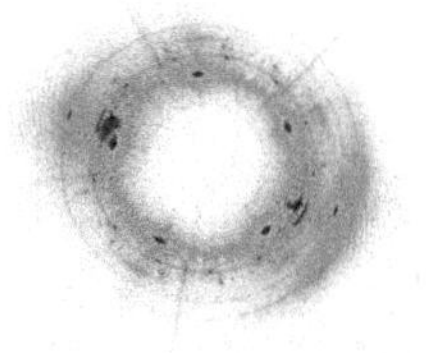

CHAPTER 2

It had been a miserable night for Admiral Fairfax. As the hours dragged on, his mood became progressively worse. Years of experience had taught him that nothing this big could have been kept secret, it just wasn't possible. Word would have leaked out, even if only bits and pieces. A capability this advanced, this game-changing, could simply not remain hidden. Especially when you consider the multitude of intelligence agencies constantly prowling even the most remote back alleys of the world. Today's technology had taken espionage to another level, making it extremely difficult to hide anything, particularly something of this magnitude.

Yet the reality was that something had happened, and that something was very real. Multiple satellites had recorded the event, an event that so far defied any reasonable explanation. Worst of all, it had occurred uncomfortably close to the Florida coast. For anyone to have launched such an event this close to US territorial waters was in and of itself a pretty audacious thing to do. It was also terrifying.

When he was a kid, his father, Captain Fairfax, had drilled into his head the fact that Florida was in danger. The Russians were in Cuba. His grandfather had commanded a carrier during the Cuban Missile Crisis. Now there was this. But this was not how things were supposed to work. Rather than an elite team at the Pentagon working off solid data, it should have been some farmer in Pine Fart, Arkansas seeing a UFO at three in the morning with no radar traces and no sober witnesses. The fact that this event had been so blatant, so in their face, it opened up possibilities that he didn't dare consider.

There were two more items that made him sick to his stomach. This event had been quite public. That meant aerospace companies knew. Academics knew, each inside his or her area, although the meteorologists were probably not talking to the physicists yet. It meant Britain and France and China and Israel and Brazil and Saudi Arabia knew *something.* And secondly, thanks to the internet, and all the things people had access to, everyone from teenage hackers in Ohio on up to other intelligence agencies in the US probably had knowledge of this. And each would have a desire and a spin to deal with the news.

If he hadn't divorced Carolyn, or, more accurately, if Carolyn hadn't divorced him, she would be telling him to get to bed. Lately, more often than not, he found his thoughts going back to when he was married. Truth was he missed Carolyn, missed her terribly.

Despite the confusion and the frustration, Admiral Fairfax had never been one to sit around and wait for developments. Immediately after his meeting with Ramirez, he began to consider the various scenarios they might be facing. Once he had these roughly sketched out in his mind, he then began to determine who he could get to take the lead on such a sensitive operation.

What was that story about Miller? He began googling many-world interpretation, then M-theory. There are eleven dimensions now? What happened to four? Then black holes and white holes and Hawking radiation and "arrow of time." He broke into laughter, "Lions and tigers and bears, oh my."

With operations such as this, there were several risks to be considered. In all probability, this would most likely turn out to be a total waste of time and money. If so, while it would be difficult to explain the loss of said time and money, he knew that that could be easily handled. It was the other end of the spectrum that had him worried. Something like this could also be the precursor to war.

"Do you have an update on Commander Colton?" snapped the admiral, speaking into the intercom on his desk.

"Yes sir," Lt. Commander Flanagan replied. "He's expected to arrive in twenty minutes."

"Good," said Admiral Fairfax. "Have him brought directly to my office."

"Yes sir."

Should worse come to worse, Fairfax knew he'd need a highly trained individual whose loyalty was beyond question. He needed a leader, a man who could follow orders, and yet wasn't afraid to do whatever was necessary to resolve a situation. Brett Colton was the first name that came to mind.

While Colton had extensive combat experience, he was best known for his intelligence work. He'd successfully led several black ops missions comprised of SEALs, CIA, and Naval Intelligence personnel into some of the most dangerous parts of the world. He was as cunning as he was lethal.

Fairfax hit the intercom button on his phone and said, "Flanagan, we have much to do. Please join me in my office."

Lt. Commander Flanagan was a young officer with a promising career. Now in his early thirties, he'd served as an aide to Admiral Fairfax for almost a year and a half and fit into life at the Pentagon better than many of his peers. Standing in front of the admiral's desk he asked, "How can I help, sir?"

"I believe the *USS Eclipse* is docked in Baltimore. As quickly as you can, I need a complete status update on its crew and its readiness to set sail."

"I'll get that together right away. Is there anything else sir?"

"Yes. I need to talk to Captain MacKay. Please track him down and get him on the phone for me," answered the admiral.

"Yes sir, will do." With that he turned and left the admiral, closing the door behind him.

Fairfax had met MacKay a few times and genuinely liked the man. Not only was he completely dependable, but the man could also think on his feet when things got rough. Although his true rank was commander, he carried the title of captain, as far as the public was concerned, being the captain of the *Eclipse*. The *Eclipse*, to say the least, was a very unique ship, especially considering the equipment it carried.

The *USS Eclipse* was an old World War II destroyer that had been rescued from salvage and refitted as a research vessel, supporting various kinds of oceanographic studies. On paper the *Eclipse* was owned by a private US corporation. That corporation helped to fund many of the research missions that were usually cosponsored by organizations such as National Geographic and various universities. But that was only its cover.

Operating far under the radar, the *USS Eclipse* was easily the most advanced research ship of its kind, housing the most current, state-of-the-art equipment, manned and maintained by the US Navy. But what made this ship especially unique was that it housed Argos.

Argos was perhaps the most closely guarded secret in the US military. Years earlier Admiral Fairfax had tried to explain Argos to a congressional budget committee without giving away too many details to a bunch of transient politicians. Keeping it as simple as possible, he described Argos as being a massive computer, loaded with the most sophisticated artificial intelligence available. Its capabilities were nearly endless, and it could run completely independent of any other systems. At sea, or while in port, Argos had its own twenty-four-hour marine security team.

Named for the hundred-eye titan of Greek mythology, it was a combination of linked quantum computers and a vast self-configuring neural net. It could handle regular computation needs at 418 petaflops per second (118 more than the official speed of the world's fastest supercomputer). Argos boasted a neural net that could analyze data like the brain of a young child. It contained artificial curiosity and could correlate more than 665 billion events a second. The admiral had not shared these incredible details with Congress, a body well known for its inability to keep a secret. He could hear a senator beginning his speech with, "I ain't sure about teraflops, but back home we've got plenty of cow flops."

Argos could pull together weather reports, decades of newspaper stories, data from every satellite in the sky, and computer uses all over the planet in seconds. It could watch the Armenian stock exchange and daily experiments at CERN at the same time. One of the scientists that designed it (although Argos had been on its own design team when it reached 30 percent capacity) said that it could even dream. It was created to look for patterns that humans would overlook and then test out hypotheses a million times faster than humans could. There was nothing else on earth even close to Argos.

It had only been about ten minutes when the admiral's door opened, and Lt. Commander Flanagan came back in. "Here are the crew files for the *Eclipse*, as well as the most current maintenance reports. Captain MacKay is updating the ship's readiness report as we speak," he said, laying the files on the admiral's desk.

"Thank you, Flanagan. Where is MacKay now?"

"He's in the briefing room just off the bridge of the *Eclipse*. He's waiting to talk to you. Shall I transfer him in?"

"Please do. Well done, Lt. Commander."

The briefing room on the *Eclipse*, like Admiral Fairfax's office, was a secure location, which meant that even the most sensitive information could be shared without fear of it being intercepted.

Admiral Fairfax picked up the receiver, "Good morning, Captain! Sorry to get you up so early."

"Unfortunately, I was already up, Admiral. My conscience won't let me sleep in like I used to."

Fairfax laughed at that. "Too many of us suffer from that ailment. Captain, I'll get right to the point. We have a rather serious situation on our hands and we're going to need to respond to it immediately. I'll bring you up to speed, at least as much as I can, then I'll let you get started coordinating with all that's being set in motion."

"Not the first time I've received this kind of call, Admiral. We'll make sure that the *Eclipse* is ready when you are."

The call continued for a little more than thirty minutes. He gave MacKay a broad overview of what they were facing but provided few specifics. As Admiral Fairfax hung up the phone, he realized that he was feeling better now than he had for the last twelve hours. Whatever they were facing, he was going to meet it head-on.

The CH-53E Super Stallion helicopter had no sooner touched down when the door was opened by a marine MP. Colton stepped out, returned the young corporal's salute, and followed him inside. "I'm to take you directly to Admiral Fairfax's office, sir," he said.

Colton smiled and said, "This must be serious, I usually don't get door-to-door service."

In his early thirties, and just under six feet tall, Colton's physical appearance could be quite intimidating. Due to the kind of missions he typically commanded, he made it a point to stay in top physical condition, but it was more than just his broad shoulders and rugged features that put people on edge. There was an air about him, a self-assured confidence that let people know he was not someone to be taken lightly. Colton had bright, piercing blue eyes that seemed to be able to drill into a person's soul, eyes that missed nothing. The small scar over his left eye accentuated a sense of danger.

For the past two years Colton had been working out of the Indian Head naval base, not too far from the Pentagon. He'd been on his way to his office when the MPs tracked him down. They quickly ushered him into the helicopter, letting him know that he'd been ordered to report to Fairfax immediately.

The urgency of the situation, however, wasn't all that unusual, and in an offbeat way, he found it mildly amusing. The term "emergency" in Washington was broadly overused. A fender bender with a Russian diplomat did not merit a military response.

Yet, over the past few years, in Colton's opinion, the world had been on a downward spiral, with new enemies popping up almost daily. Considering those circumstances, Admiral Fairfax was the right man to have at the helm. Colton liked and respected the admiral, having worked a few assignments for him before. As flag officers go, Fairfax had kept his ego in check, and kept the best interest of his sailors in the forefront.

When they got to the admiral's office Colton thanked the MP and went inside. He was met by Lt. Commander Flanagan who got up, saluted him, then shook Colton's hand. "My apologies for the way you were rushed over here, Commander, but I'm afraid this is rather urgent."

"Of course, it is," said Colton, the trace of a smile on his face. "The last time I got whisked away to the Pentagon it was also critically important. If memory serves, a congressman had gotten so drunk that he'd left his yacht running, staggered across the dock to the parking lot, and proceeded to pass out in his car. When he woke up, his boat had sailed off along with his girlfriend, a guy who worked at the marina, and a briefcase full of classified documents regarding diplomatic protocol procedures. Yeah, that was some emergency."

Flanagan smiled and said, "I better show you in. Captain Ramirez just arrived and will be joining you and the admiral. May I get you something to drink?"

"No, I'm fine. Let's see whose butt we're saving today," said Colton and went inside. He found Admiral Fairfax at his desk with Captain Ramirez standing next to him, pointing to some photos on the admiral's desk. The aroma of burnt coffee, stale donuts, and nervous tension filled the room.

"Colton, glad you're here," said Admiral Fairfax. "You know Captain Ramirez."

"I do. Good morning, Captain," said Colton.

Fairfax got up and moved over to the conference table. "We have a great deal to discuss in order to bring you up to speed. Captain, would you please brief the commander as to what we are facing?"

Ramirez knew who Colton was, but had never spent much time with him. However, he did know the man's reputation and he wondered just how Colton would respond to all of this. Colton was the kind of man you needed when all else had failed and the enemy was at the gate. He was well known for following his own rules, forget the manual. Ramirez didn't know if this situation merited a man of Colton's temperament. Nevertheless, he quickly walked him through what the satellites had picked up, and based on the data they had, the conclusions that they were now working from.

When Ramirez finished, Colton studied the two men, trying to determine if there was something he'd missed. He was giving it all he had to keep from laughing out loud. *Were they serious?* "Sir, I'm not sure where I fit into this picture. Based on what you've said, there doesn't appear to be any sort of immediate danger. There's very little hard data here to even support the idea of there being any kind of serious threat to us at all. Frankly, if it were anyone else other than the two of you, I'd write this off as simply more Bermuda Triangle nonsense."

"And therein lies a part of the problem," said Admiral Fairfax. "Believe me, we're struggling with the same concerns. The last thing I need is for this to leak that the US Navy is out chasing something we can't explain in the Bermuda Triangle. The media would have a field day. At the same time, we can't ignore it. Our birds picked it up, we have pictures of it, and the best minds we have can't give me a definitive answer as to what that thing is."

"Captain, with the data you do have, is there any indication who might be behind this?" asked Colton.

"No, there isn't," said Ramirez. "This is unlike anything we've ever seen or heard of."

"Captain, thank you," said Fairfax, standing up. "I'm going to go over the next steps with Commander Colton. Please get me a copy of what we have for him to take along." With that Ramirez nodded and left.

Once he'd gone, Fairfax moved over to his credenza and poured some bourbon into a glass. "I don't have any ice, but can I offer you a drink?"

"No sir," said Colton. "Thank you, I'm fine. Sir, with all due respect, I agree that you just can't set this aside, but I still can't see how I can be of any help."

"I'm sending you out on the *Eclipse*, which will leave port first thing tomorrow morning. There may be nothing to this; pretty sure that's what we'll find. But in the event there is something, if it does turn out to be aggressive, then I'm going to need you there to handle it. This is probably for the eggheads, but I'm treating this first as a psy-ops mission."

"Who do you think is staging it?"

"The Russians and the Chinese have the most to gain by showing off a technology we can't even fathom. But even the EU or the Arabs could discredit us. Or if it is interdimensional in origin, it can either have Klaatu stepping forward in peace, which pretty much overturns most religions and even economic systems, or it's Thanos with the Infinity Gauntlet. In short, this is the biggest political event in our times."

"Have you thought that maybe it is the Bermuda Triangle?" Colton managed a smile.

"If it is then that's going to be devastating. Or if some power chose this spot then they're playing some terrible game. I've been reading some classified files on psy-ops we and the Russians did to each other during the Cold War. Also read some stuff that maybe, for all we know, ET is phoning home. I need a political operative there. One with a good kill rate."

"It could be a coincidence," said Colton. "But, in my experience, coincidence is rarely unintentional."

"Well, there is one coincidence. Captain Ramirez has an ensign working for him whose grandfather was on the radar crew when Flight 19 vanished, Ensign Miller. What are the odds on that?"

A more serious look crossed Colton's face. "Like I said, I don't believe in coincidence. You should watch her very carefully."

The room grew cold and quiet for a few seconds. Colton mulled this over, as well as the question of why the admiral had chosen the *Eclipse*.

Colton was familiar with the *Eclipse*. Many accomplishments were credited to the old ship, but with it being a research vessel, he'd never spent any time on her. "Does MacKay still captain the *Eclipse*?" asked Colton.

"He does, and he's expecting you."

"He and I have crossed paths before, good man. Can't imagine too many things he wouldn't be able to handle."

"I agree, but he doesn't have your depth of experience, not by a long shot. I'll be sending orders with you to give to MacKay, letting him know that in the event this turns into a conflict that you, at your discretion, will have the authority to take command of the *Eclipse*."

"You and I both know how well he's going to respond to that," said Colton. "There aren't many sailors I know who would willingly give up command of their ship."

"MacKay's a good officer. He'll understand," said Fairfax. "Now let's get to it. The *Eclipse* is being loaded as we speak with the provisions and equipment that will be needed for this assignment. You'll also be joined by some civilian scientists."

Colton's normal poker face broke a little at that revelation. "Civilians?"

"Yes, some of the finest minds we could pull together on such short notice. The navy doesn't have experts on M-theory or exobiology. Have a seat, Commander; we have a great deal to discuss."

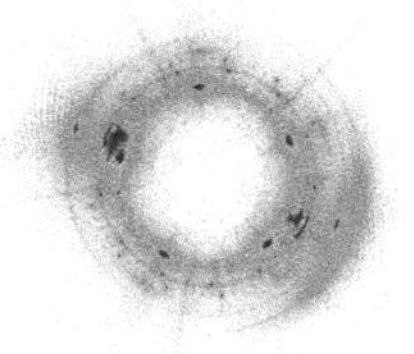

CHAPTER 3

The Harbor Master Bar and Grill had changed very little over the fifty some years it'd stood there, other than the fact you were no longer allowed to smoke inside. Though lightly enforced, new municipal laws had brought that change into effect. Smokers were encouraged to smoke out on the patio, which was nothing more than a twelve-by-twelve, gravel-covered area out behind the bar, next to the dumpster. The "patio" had a few rusted chairs and a long table made of weathered milk crates and a few planks of wood.

Inside the bar the yellow linoleum-covered floor was cracked and faded, and had buckled in a few places, but none of the patrons seemed to notice or care. Many of the neon signs adorning the walls advertised beers no longer in production, but they did produce much of the light inside the windowless establishment. In brief, people came here to drink, not critique the interior design. The food was either fried in the back or received microwave radiation from an improperly shielded oven. There was bad amateur "sea" art and dried nets on the walls and a large poster of an orangutan giving the middle finger.

The Harbor Master catered primarily to dock workers, a few locals, and the crews from commercial ships that frequented the Baltimore harbor. There was also the occasional undercover cop. They usually stood out and were, for the most part, left alone. Unless they were buying drinks, and then they'd be given as much useless information as they wanted.

Harry Turner looked upon the Harbor Master as his office. A retired dockworker, Harry hung out at the bar from dusk to dawn, drinking his way through the day. Well into his sixties, he was terribly thin and wrinkled from a harsh and violent life. His skin was burnt brown from the sun and the little bit of hair he had left looked like dirty strands of rust running across his head.

Harry spent his days talking with various sailors and dockworkers. He'd ask them about the various ships in port, what they contained, and in general, picked up on as many details as he could get. This was his stock in trade. This information, passed on to the gangs who prowled the docks, brought in enough money to keep him in food and drink—mostly drink.

This ended up giving him a broad, as well as unique, insight as to what was taking place on the docks. Each time, when someone began to talk more than they should, Harry moved in quickly to keep the conversation going. For anything that sounded promising, which meant scandalous or illegal, Harry was quick to pick up the check and provide them with as many drinks as necessary to bleed them dry.

Barely getting by otherwise, Harry more than supplemented his meager income from the gangs by passing on tidbits of information he picked up on to a reporter for the *Inside Story*. He'd met the reporter a few years back when a cruise ship made an emergency stop at the docks. There'd been a high-profile murder on board and the police had closed the dock to everyone but essential personnel. The reporter approached Harry, offering him more money than he'd ever seen for his help in getting what he needed. Using his dockworker's ID, Harry was able to sneak on board and take the pictures the reporter so desperately wanted.

Such was the beginning of a beautiful relationship. Over time it became known all along the docks that Harry was the man to see if you had information for sale, even more money for pictures or samples of the stuff that was being smuggled in. Today the winds of greed blew directly into Harry's face.

Dallan Flynn, an old Irishman whom Harry had known for years, came in early that morning and collapsed in a chair at one of the tables near the bar. Flynn was a regular and the barman immediately put a shot glass on the bar and reached for the bottle of Jamison. What drew Harry's attention to him was when he waved off the whiskey and ordered food instead. That simple act, in and of itself, signaled Harry that it would probably be worth his while to spend time with Flynn.

"Off your game this morning Dallan?" asked Harry, taking a chair across from Flynn.

"Don't bother me Harry, it's been a long night and it'll be the same thing again tonight."

"You don't look so good. What have you been up to?"

"Work," said Flynn, "the same back-breaking work you used to do. Second night in a row. We've been loading more cargo onto the *Eclipse* than you can imagine. And it can't be done quick enough to please them either."

The *Eclipse*! This had lottery ticket written all over it. Like most well-kept secrets, everybody knew *something* about it. "I thought the *Eclipse* was scheduled to be in dock for several weeks," said Harry. "It's supposed to be getting some kind of work done on the ship's wiring."

"All I know is that I got called in yesterday and we're still at it," said Flynn. The bartender carried over a plate of eggs, sausage, and potatoes and a bottle of catsup and set it down in front of him. Flynn attacked the plate like he hadn't eaten in days.

"Flynn, you're a man of seniority, experience. How is it you pulled the night shift?"

"That's the only shift there is. Trucks don't even start to roll in until around seven or eight. Then we get to wait while they look the stuff over. We don't even get started until around nine, but then it's straight through till morning."

"Why the delay?" asked Harry. "Seems you're losing an hour waiting around."

"I'll sit and wait there all night if they ask me to. We're on the clock from seven on whether we're working or not, so it don't bother me none. It's double pay."

"Pretty sweet deal if you don't mind becoming a vampire," chuckled Harry.

"Don't laugh, those guys have the warmth of a pack of vampires," said Flynn through a mouth full of eggs, a small piece falling out of his mouth and onto his shirt. "It's almost like working for mob guys, except mob guys are nicer. These guys never smile, none of us are allowed on board the *Eclipse*, and I tell you, I wouldn't want to be the one who crossed them. They're a tough outfit and they're not shy about getting physical."

"The *Eclipse* is just a research vessel," mused Harry. "Strangest thing I've ever seen them load is lab equipment, accompanied by a bunch of nerdy guys. So, what is this stuff they've got you loading?"

"Don't know and I won't be the one asking. Other than having to work all night, I'm pretty happy. I'm being well paid, and I really don't care what they're doing."

Harry thought about this for a few moments. All of this was being done under the cover of night. Whatever it was, someone was going to a great deal of trouble to keep it secret. "Who else is working this with you?"

Flynn looked up at Harry and locked eyes with him. "Leave it alone Harry, you want no part of this. I've seen men like these before. You start nosing into this and you'll get to meet them, up close and personal. From what I've seen, they're short on words, long on actions."

"Alright, alright, no need having you get all worked up. It just strikes me as odd, that's all," said Harry. Time to make a call. This was going to be a big paycheck.

Ricky Favor, his journalist name, leaned back in his chair with his feet propped up on his desk. Favor was not a big man, in fact he was quite short, but what he lacked in stature he made up for in ego. Fighting baldness, what little hair he had he kept greased back, giving him what he thought was a sophisticated look. Favor was trying to determine which of the two pictures he held in his hands would be the most incriminating, have the most impact for his article. Either one of them would end up destroying the guy's marriage, if not more, but that's what you get when you "fall out of Favor." It was his favorite catch line.

The pictures showed the guy, stark naked, with two young ladies, who were also naked. But more importantly, they were both underage. Ricky's target was the general manager of one of the snootier country clubs in the Baltimore area. Ricky had given him the opportunity to avoid this kind of notoriety. He'd tried to talk reason to the guy, even offering him the chance to buy his way out, to keep these pictures from appearing in his paper, *Inside Story*. But no, the guy had to act like a bigshot, got in Ricky's face, threatened him, and then had his security guy bounce him out of his office. Literally.

The guy's response to this really hadn't surprised Ricky, but this prick was a bully and Ricky hated bullies. Ricardo Favaria, Ricky's real name, had gotten his fill of being bullied growing up. Unfortunately for him, all through school he'd been too small to fight back. It wasn't until after he graduated that he discovered the power of the pen.

Everyone has secrets, and those secrets quickly became the source of Ricky's way of making a living. It was Ricky's mentor who taught him that once you'd learned the secrets a person held sacred, you owned them. Well, here was one bully whose secret was going to take him down. He sat there, smiling to himself as he toyed with the idea of even sending the negatives to the cops. Then his phone rang.

"Favor here."

"Mr. Favor, it's me, Harry, from down on the docks."

"Like I don't recognize that raspy voice of yours," said Ricky. "You got something good for me today Harry?"

"Yeah, I sure do Mr. Favor, and it's big, real big," said Harry, looking over his shoulder. He was using the payphone back by the restrooms at the Harbor Master. "I think you might wanna come down here. I can meet you at the bar."

"Let's talk a little first," said Ricky. "Last time you hustled me down there it turned out to be a bust. You remember that? I wasted half a day. Give me a little of what you got, and we'll see."

Harry licked his lips trying to think of what to say next. He really needed the money, but if he gave away too much, he'd have nothing to bargain with. "It's about the *Eclipse.*"

Ricky put the pictures down and sat up in his chair. "What about the *Eclipse*? You told me it'd be in dock for some time to come. If it has already pulled out, I'm going to be very, very disappointed and that, my friend, will not be a good thing for you."

"No, no, it's still here, but that's why we need to talk. There are things happening down here you don't want to miss. It looks like they're getting ready to head out, but they're only loading at night."

Favor looked at his watch, glancing back at the two pictures lying on his desk. After a few moments he said, "Okay Harry, I'm coming down. This had better be worth it."

"Oh, it is, Mr. Favor, really," stammered Harry. "And you'll have my money, right?"

"Don't I always? If it's as big as you're making it out to be, you'll be well taken care of," said Ricky. "See you in an hour."

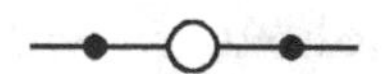

Most of the ordinance and equipment had been brought on board the past two nights. Captain MacKay had his crew working at a feverish pace to get everything set up, secured and ready to go. Despite the rush, they hadn't broken anything too important. Tonight, the final shipment of the supplies would arrive, along with the guests that would be sailing with them. But it wasn't the civilian scientists he was thinking about. His curiosity was piqued by the guy from Naval Intelligence, Brett Colton.

Over the years, he'd run across Colton a couple of times, always in places that no one in their right mind would ever want to go to. Colton's reputation was very interesting, at least within the intelligence community. While he had run some of the most dangerous, as well as intricate operations the navy had ever taken on, he was not well liked by most of the top brass at the Pentagon. A commander in rank, Colton openly and happily shared his opinion of the officers who acted more like Washington bureaucrats than like the military personnel they were supposed to be.

A bit of a lady's man, Colton had the rugged good looks that drew women to him. Although Colton had grown up in a traditional military family, he *liked* being a spy. He *liked* prying into things, taking crazy risks. Once he had spray painted his name on the bedroom wall of a North Korean official. He literally introduced himself to a three-star general as "My name is Colton, Brett Colton." There was swagger and there was Colton.

So why in Heaven's name was a guy like Colton being assigned to the *Eclipse*? As far as MacKay knew, this was going to be just like several other trips they'd made, boring. Their new orders were to take a bunch of civilian researchers out to sea to study some variance, some anomaly that the boys in the Pentagon couldn't explain, and then bring them back in one piece. You don't need James Bond with you to accomplish something this mundane.

That said, the *Eclipse* was also part of the intelligence community within the navy, but very few people knew that. On the books, the *Eclipse* was privately owned and operated, but its crew was all navy, carefully selected, and the ship had enough firepower to defend it if attacked or provoked. To the public, the *Eclipse* was an old World War II destroyer that had been retrofitted as a top-of-the-line scientific research vessel. But that was just its cover. It also had Argos on board.

MacKay was not comfortable with Argos at all. One of the most closely guarded secrets in the navy, it came with its own marine security detail watching over it twenty-four hours a day. Argos, about the size of a small travel trailer, was housed in the forward hold. It had been explained to McKay that it was the most advanced computer system of its kind with artificial intelligence.

In short, it could think on its own. As MacKay understood it, the process was progressive, meaning that the more things that Argos was tasked with, the quicker its ability to reason grew, and that growth was exponential. Argos had been brought on board the *Eclipse* five months ago along with a team of technicians to monitor it. It wasn't MacKay's area, but the results produced by Argos were supposedly making everyone happy. Everyone except MacKay.

What bothered MacKay, whether his concerns were rational or not, were memories from the movie *2001: A Space Odyssey*. He'd watched the film years ago and worried that he now might get to live part of it. The film was set in space, on a spaceship carrying out some extended mission. They too had a computer on board, very similar to Argos, named Hal. Hal also had the capability to think on its own and could even converse with the crew. For MacKay, the thing that worried him was the part of the story where things did not end well for the astronauts that Hal was supposed to have been taking care of, all thanks to Hal.

Argos acted as if the crew was there to serve its every whim, at times even asking for things. Once it asked if the *Eclipse* could anchor over a submerged cable in the Atlantic. Once *it* had sent MacKay an email telling him to check out a certain sailor's locker. The guy had speed. It ran a continuous interactive program for the crew; it could beat you at chess and even act as therapist. He discovered that more than a few of his crew had spilled their guts to it.

One day it did card tricks. It would print out a prediction and then get a sailor to shuffle the deck any way they could think of, and then pick a card. It was right 90 percent of the time. So, MacKay had tried to cheat. He asked Father Donatelli for a saint's card. St. Dennis in fact. He stuck it in the deck and then pulled it out. The technician reading the printout nearly went nuts. Argos had printed out "Your card is St. Dennis." MacKay told the tech that Argos had cheated by spying on him, but the tech said that wasn't possible. He said Argos was dealing with some quantum foam probabilities, whatever that meant. As far as MacKay was concerned, the machine cheated and manipulated humans. Father Donatelli had called somebody in Rome about it.

The orders to prepare to set sail had been signed by Admiral Fairfax and had arrived about an hour after their talk. MacKay greatly admired the admiral. Fairfax, for the majority of his career, had led from the front and had earned the respect he was given. The orders MacKay had received for this trip were straightforward, and not all that unusual. The *Eclipse* was to take on enough supplies to last several weeks and would be joined by seven civilian scientists, two of which were prominent enough that even MacKay had heard of them. So again, why Colton?

MacKay let go with a small sigh. You'd think that after all these years of having worked in a part of the navy that dealt with secrets that he'd be used to it by now. Still, it rankled him to be kept in the dark, and if he was certain of anything, it was that he was being kept in the dark. The pieces just didn't fit together.

US Marine Lieutenant Tanner stepped on to the bridge, interrupting MacKay's thoughts. Captain MacKay looked up from the charts he'd been studying, happy for the interruption. "Afternoon Lieutenant. How are things?"

"We may have a problem, sir," answered Tanner. Tanner looked like something out of the NFL. Right at six foot three, Tanner weighed in at a modest 260 pounds, with very little body fat. He proudly sported a crew cut and had a jagged scar that spread across the jawline on the left side of his face. MacKay didn't know how he had gotten that scar but wondered what the other guy looked like. Dressed in civilian clothes, he came across as the kind of guy you wouldn't want to mess with. "That barfly up at the Harbor Master has been hanging around down on the pier and he's been asking questions to anyone he can get close to."

"Yeah, I know who you mean. What's his name?" mused Captain MacKay. "Harry! That's it. He's pretty much a harmless old guy. Our people certainly aren't going to say anything to him, and as far as the workmen we've been using, none of them know anything. They haven't even been allowed on board."

"True, but the word is that he's tied into one of those scum ball reporters for the *Inside Story*," said Tanner. Tanner was second in command of the marine detail on board the *Eclipse* and oversaw security while in port.

"Ah yes, I remember now. Tried to sneak on board and got knocked on his can by Seaman Pritchard. *Inside Story*'s the bottom of the birdcage paper he works for. Claimed we were hiding mermaids in the hold, or some such nonsense. I rather doubt that too many people take that paper seriously."

"Agreed, but that's not the problem, sir. I had two of my men go up to the Harbor Master, just to see if they could find out what the scuttlebutt is. In brief, our midnight deliveries have stirred up some interest. Just as they were getting ready to leave, that reporter, Ricky Favor, showed up," said Tanner.

MacKay frowned at the mention of the name, trying to remember where he'd heard it. "He's the reporter we were just talking about, right?"

"Yes sir, he's the one," said Tanner. "Favor sat down with Harry and they talked for quite a while."

"Were our guys able to hear what they were saying?"

"No sir, they couldn't get close enough. But we just learned that Favor has chartered the *Wave Runner*, that forty-two-foot fishing yacht on the other side of the bay. The word is he plans to follow us when we leave to see what we're up to," said Tanner.

"Well, we can't have that, can we?" said Captain MacKay. He turned to one of his men on the bridge, "Petty Officer Briggs, get me Admiral Fairfax on the phone. I need to let him, and Commander Colton, know what we've learned."

"Is there anything you want us to do, sir?" asked Tanner.

"Alert the crew. If we see Favor near the ship, I want him watched, carefully. We know what he's capable of," said MacKay. "Tonight, on the docks, I want you to strongly reinforce the idea that it's in the best interest of everyone's health not to hang around people like Harry, and especially people like Favor. Any questions, Lieutenant?"

Tanner grinned at the prospect. "No sir, happy to pass along that message." With that he turned and left the bridge.

"Sir, I have Admiral Fairfax."

"Thank you, Briggs," said MacKay, taking the receiver from him. "Good afternoon sir. I wanted to bring you up to speed on a situation we may have here." Captain MacKay quickly told the admiral about Harry and the reporter, Favor, and that it might cause a problem when they pulled out.

"It's bad form for me to shoot them out of the water, so I thought you might have a more subtle course of action," said MacKay. He listened carefully, then smiled and said, "Very good, sir. I look forward to the commander joining us."

Captain MacKay handed the receiver back to the sailor, stepped outside the bridge and leaned on the railing, looking out over the pier. In short, the admiral had told him to let Colton handle the reporter. MacKay smiled, saying to himself, "Not a good time to be Ricky Favor."

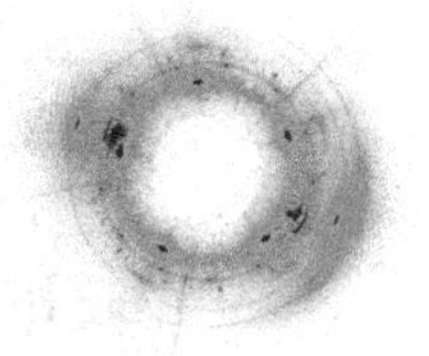

CHAPTER 4

It was a beautiful morning, the sun just barely peeking over the eastern horizon as the *Eclipse* weighed anchor and prepared to leave port. As they pulled away from the pier, Commander Colton joined MacKay on the bridge. The commander had come aboard the day before, but surprisingly, MacKay had seen little of him. Although Colton had been very nice, he explained that he had a great deal to do before they pulled out. That worked well for MacKay as he, too, had plenty to take care of.

Colton immediately went to work, making it a point to meet and get to know each of the officers on board, as well as the scientists that had been invited to join this mission. But of all the people on the *Eclipse*, he spent the most time with Lieutenant Nandin Sahir, the navy specialist in charge of Argos. MacKay would like to have been a fly on the wall for those talks. But then, for his own peace of mind, he was probably better off not having heard those discussions. He had learned that through the years that sometimes it's better not to know.

As with the first time they met, it amazed MacKay that Colton didn't look the way someone would envision a guy with his reputation. Most people would have expected Colton to look more like Errol Flynn as he'd appeared in *Captain Blood*. He couldn't have been further off.

Dressed in civilian clothes, he looked like most of the other men on the ship and did nothing to draw attention to himself. MacKay knew that he'd attended Annapolis, graduating with honors with degrees in Navel Architecture & Marine Engineering and History. A native of Maine, he'd grown up around the ocean his entire life. All in all, he was a good, capable man and MacKay was pleased to have him aboard.

If you really want to keep a secret, make it look like you're keeping a *different* secret. Following the pattern MacKay had already established, Commander Colton had several crates, all labeled top secret, loaded on deck by regular dockhands the night before they left. He paid them in cash, and with Tanner standing menacingly behind him, told them to say nothing to anyone. He then made sure they were off two hours before the bars closed. Lastly he also asked for their prayers, since they were leaving before dawn, and if any of them spoke Portuguese. He needed a translator. The seeds were sown.

As expected, their early morning departure didn't go unnoticed. Across the bay one of the crew on the *Wave Runner* watched as the *Eclipse* prepared to head out to sea. Putting his binoculars aside, he went below deck to the captain's quarters, softly knocking on the door. "The *Eclipse* is pulling out, Captain."

After a couple of moments, the door opened. It was clear that Captain Madox had been asleep, or more likely passed out, as the cabin reeked of booze. "Get the rest of the crew up and prepare to set sail. Oh, and wake our guest up. I know he's a pain, but he's paying the freight on this and I'm pretty sure he's going to want to see all there is to see."

"Aye, aye, Skipper," answered the crewman. Leaving the Captain's quarters, he continued down the hallway to the cabin Favor had been given. The guy was a prick, no doubt about it, but the money was crazy good, which probably worked out best for Favor. Had the money been any less, well, Favor wouldn't be the first guy to "accidently" fall overboard.

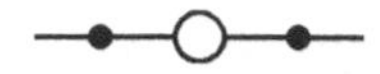

It didn't take the *Eclipse* long to clear the Baltimore harbor, heading due east out into the Atlantic. Colton walked over to the young sailor manning the radar. "We're expecting guests, but they'll probably stay at a distance. Keep me apprised as soon as you spot anyone who might be trailing us."

"Yes sir," answered the young sailor. This was Abner Hatfield's second voyage on the *Eclipse* and he wanted to make sure he carried out his duties to the letter. One of the youngest members of the crew, Hatfield was rail thin with bright red hair covering his head. He looked more like a computer programmer than a hardened man of the sea. MacKay had noticed that over the years, as their systems continued to become more and more sophisticated, that too many of his crew were beginning to look like Hatfield.

"Guests?" queried MacKay. "My guess is that you're referring to the reporter."

"Perhaps, you never know who you'll come across on the high seas," said Colton, winking at MacKay. "As to Mr. Favor, he's probably lost interest in us. I'm just being careful. Truth is I have no idea what we're going to find out there, but whatever it is, I want to be sure we do it without anyone else watching," said Colton.

"Understood, but we've had some experience with Favor before," said MacKay. "Giving up is not something he's known for. The guy's like a leech. He's the worst of the worst when it comes to reporters, and that takes some doing. He plays fast and loose with the truth and doesn't believe that laws apply to him in his quest to deliver the almighty story. 'The public has a right to know!' Can't begin to tell you just how much that excuse sets me off."

Colton laughed at this and sipped his coffee. "I've run into a few of those guys myself. Like you, I have little patience for them. If Mr. Favor does make an appearance, I'm confident the situation will remedy itself."

That didn't make any sense to MacKay, but as they'd obviously beaten that horse to death, he moved on. "What are we doing out here, Commander? We've taken on enough supplies and ordinance to support a small army, and we've never had all three labs filled to overflowing with equipment."

Colton shrugged, and then motioned the captain to follow him outside the bridge. Leaning on the railing, Colton stared out to sea. MacKay took advantage of being outside and proceeded to light up his pipe. His father had given him the yellowed meerschaum pipe when he first joined the navy, a long, long time ago. He'd told him that a pipe continues to get better with age and gives a man time to think. MacKay had become so attached to it that he couldn't imagine being without it.

"A few days ago, our satellites picked up something at the exact coordinates we're heading for off the coast of Florida. Assuming the data is correct, whatever they saw was massive. It only appeared for a short period of time then vanished."

"We can't possibly be the first ship to respond to this," said MacKay.

"We aren't. The navy had two ships and a sub on location in less than an hour, but they couldn't find a thing. Those ships held their position for two days. At no time did their instruments come up with anything out of the ordinary."

MacKay bowed his head in disbelief. "This sounds like more typical BS regarding the Bermuda Triangle. Things don't just appear and then disappear, not when they're big enough to trigger our birds."

"Hard to argue. Now, let me add a little more to what I've told you," said Colton. "At the time of the incident, there were two civilian freighters in the immediate area. Their radar, their radio, all their equipment either quit working or went haywire. So yes, I'd say it does sound remarkably like a Bermuda Triangle story."

Colton looked him over and made a quick assessment. "MacKay, I don't like keeping secrets from someone I'm working with and need to trust. You on my side?"

Captain MacKay said, "We both know each other's record. I'm on the navy's side."

Colton chuckled. "I've done quite a few operations, some we keep secret from the navy. Then there are those we keep secret from other agencies. We're keeping this one secret from everyone. Here are a couple more things I can share with you. A handful of academics working on-site at the Pentagon, not political guys, but actual physicists, met with the admiral regarding this event.

"When that meeting ended, Admiral Fairfax was close to losing it. Either he's abnormally stressed out about this or he's lost his mind, in which case we're all in trouble. MacKay, you immediately connected the dots to the Bermuda Triangle. If any of this gets out, others will jump to the same conclusion and it will be just one more crazy, sensationalized scandal for the tabloids. More than likely, it's some foreign power creating something that looks like the Bermuda Triangle. Or who knows? Maybe there is something out there. Either way the press goes nuts."

"So, there is a plan in place to stop him?" asked MacKay.

Colton's eyes seemed to brighten a little as a smile crossed his face. "I'd say we're ready, although I personally liked your idea to simply blow him out of the water. Unfortunately, the admiral didn't buy in to your recommendation."

MacKay thought that through for a moment, shook his head, and said, "There has to be more to the story than what you've told me. Based on all that we brought aboard, as well as the civilians who've joined us, this mission is costing a small fortune. And then, Commander, there's you."

Colton looked at MacKay in a questioning way, raising one eyebrow. He knew MacKay was sharp. He had a shrewd mind and the experience to see through the lies. The gray hair around his temples seemed to help accentuate his authority as captain, although he really didn't need any help in that area. MacKay had a strong build and had proven on more than one occasion to be good to have with you in a fight.

"This is far from your cup of tea. Now, unless there's an eminent threat bearing down on us that you haven't shared with me, your being here just doesn't make any sense."

"Captain MacKay, I argued that very point with the admiral," said Colton, resuming his gaze out on the calm seas they were gliding through. "I truly can't tell you why I've been assigned to this mission, but I've also learned not to argue with Fairfax once he's made a decision."

"He didn't give you any kind of explanation at all?" said MacKay. It really wasn't unusual to get orders you didn't fully understand, especially where black ops were concerned. And nowhere in military training is there ever a situation where it is okay to question orders. In fact, quite the opposite. The discipline drummed into each sailor's head was to unquestioningly obey orders the instant they were given. MacKay knew that this was more likely a question of "need to know," an expression he'd come to loathe over the years.

"The primary problem is that no one even has a good guess as to what that thing was. Personally, and it wouldn't be the first time, I wouldn't be the least bit surprised to find out that the whole thing was some kind of giant systems error. Nevertheless, with the navy not knowing what to expect, I've been directed to tag along."

Reaching into his pocket, Colton pulled out a sealed envelope with MacKay's name on it. "Guess there's no better time than now for me to give this to you," said Colton.

MacKay took the envelope, opened it, and read the one-page document inside. His face clouded over, even though he saw that it was signed by Admiral Fairfax. "I don't understand."

"If this turns into a fight, or we find something that turns aggressive, it will be my privilege to put those orders into effect. Captain, you know my background. And just so you'll know, I read your file as well. It's very impressive. So, it will all come down to my discretion. That said, unless you become physically incapable of running this ship, I have no plans to relieve you of your command."

"Anything else?"

"Isn't that enough?" answered Colton. "No, that's everything I know. My opinion, Captain? We're chasing some kind of computer anomaly that we will have no way of proving."

MacKay nodded. "Sounds like the navy. What's in the crates you had loaded?"

Colton smiled "My props. You can't put on a good show without props."

Before MacKay could respond, crewman Hatfield stuck his head out the door and said, "Commander, I believe we may have that company you referred to."

The *Wave Runner* was keeping its distance, allowing the *Eclipse* to stay well out in front of them, just on the horizon. Favor had nearly hurt himself getting out of bed when the crewman told him that the *Eclipse* was pulling out. Now he stood next to the captain, watching the *Eclipse* through a pair of binoculars. Although the sea was very calm, Favor was on his third nondrowsy Dramamine.

"Really not clear on what you're planning to do, but you do know how much of a long shot this is, don't you?" asked Captain Madox.

"You've been well paid, Captain. Just do as I tell you and keep that ship in sight," said Favor, not bothering to lower the binoculars.

Captain Madox laughed a little and said, "We don't mind taking your money, but there are some simple facts that I don't want you to lose sight of. I pointed these out to you back at the dock. I'm just making sure they haven't slipped your mind."

"Alright, Captain," sighed Favor. "Let it out. You got something you'd like to say again?"

"Frankly, Mr. Favor, I do. In fact, there are a few items I'd like to go over with you. First, we have no idea where they're headed, or how long it's going to take them to get there. We have enough provisions and fuel for about four days and even that's a bit of a stretch. Second, that ship was once a navy destroyer. While I have no idea what they've done to upgrade her engines, I promise you they can out run us any time they set their mind to it. So, tell me, what's going on? What's so special about that ship?"

"There's more to the *Eclipse* than meets the eye, Captain. I'm sure of it. It's portrayed as just another research ship, but from what I've been able to pick up, that's just a cover story. The information that I've been given is that they're involved in all kinds of secret stuff, stuff no one would want to see in the papers."

"You talking government or criminal stuff? There are a few people out there that I have no intention of pissing off," said Madox.

"I'm not really sure, but I'm betting government stuff. Unless I'm wrong, and that rarely happens, the *Eclipse* handles all kinds of secret projects, things you'd see in the *X-Files*."

"I don't know what you're talking about," said Madox, his hands tightening on the helm. He was beginning to realize just how big of a nut job he'd teamed up with. The money had been too appealing; he should have asked more questions.

"Captain, it's not important whether you understand or not. My instructions were quite simple. Stay in range of the *Eclipse* so that I can get pictures of whomever it is they have on board. If I can just get a look at some of the equipment they're using I'll be able to get some idea of what they're up to. All I need is one piece of leverage, something they don't want released to the public, and I'll finally have them right where I want them."

"It's your business Mr. Favor, but I've known a few blackmailers in my time and things didn't end well for them. Man can get himself killed doing this kind of work."

Crossing his arms across his narrow chest, Favor tried to take on what he thought was a very macho pose. "I'm not a blackmailer. I'm a journalist. You run your little boat; leave the tough work to me."

It was almost more than Madox could do to keep from bursting out laughing. Favor looked about as tough as a kitten. "Alright, I'll do my part and keep the *Eclipse* way out in front of me, just like you ordered. But how do you plan to pull this off? With them so far away, how are you going to get the pictures you want from way back here?"

"We live in a marvelous age of technology, Captain. You really need to get caught up. The reason I'm having us stay this far back is because if we get too close, they'll spot us and get suspicious. By staying this far back I'm hoping they'll forget we're even here," said Favor.

For Madox this confirmed that Favor was even more naïve than he imagined. Whether the *Eclipse* was manned by the good guys or the bad guys, you can bet your bottom dollar they wouldn't lose track of a ship that was trailing them. "Okay, but that doesn't answer my question as to how you're going to get pictures if we're so far away."

"Those three boxes I brought on board contain the best drones money can buy, fully equipped with high resolution cameras. We'll be able to get as many pictures as I want, and they won't even know what's going on."

Captain Madox thought about that for a moment and nodded. "Might work, but I'm telling you now. If they spot your flying cameras and start shooting, at the drones or at us, I'm turning my 'little boat' around and heading for shore. We clear?"

"Or what, you'll throw me overboard?" asked Favor.

"Something like that," said Madox.

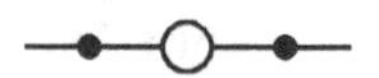

A little over an hour had passed since Hatfield had alerted Colton to the fact that it appeared someone might be following them. Oddly, Colton didn't seem to be all that concerned. He thanked the sailor and asked him to keep them posted. He then stepped back outside and using his sat phone, made a short call. He then joined MacKay back on the bridge as they continued due east into the Atlantic.

Finally, MacKay asked, "So what are we going to do with our little buddy back there?"

"We'll just let things play out," said Colton. "We both know that things are not always as they seem to be. Patience Captain, patience."

A little more than twenty minutes passed when Hatfield turned in his chair and said, "Commander, we may have more of a problem than we thought."

Colton and MacKay stepped over to the radar station and looked at the monitor. "What do we have, Mr. Hatfield?" asked MacKay.

Hatfield pointed to a dot on the screen. "This is the ship that has been with us since we left Baltimore. He hasn't gotten any closer to us, but he also hasn't lost any ground. But now there's more, look at this."

The young crewman pointed to two other dots on the screen. Both were approaching the *Eclipse*, one from the north and one from the south. "They appear to be coming right at us," said MacKay.

"They are, sir, and at a very fast pace. If they hold their course, they should intercept us in about fifteen minutes," said Hatfield, his voice not doing too good of a job at hiding the nervousness he felt.

MacKay picked up a pair of binoculars and stepped outside, followed by Colton. "What are your thoughts on this Colton? I would never have guessed that they'd make a direct run at us. What can they possibly hope to achieve?"

Colton studied one of the approaching ships through some binoculars for a few moments, but didn't seem to be disturbed by this turn of events at all. Setting the binoculars down he smiled and said, "Captain, would you please have Captain Garrett and Lieutenant Tanner join us on the bridge immediately?"

"Do you really think we need marines on the bridge?" asked Mercer.

"I want them to make sure their men are ready for what's about to happen," said Colton.

"And what exactly would that be, Mr. Colton?" asked Captain MacKay.

"The *Eclipse*, Captain, is about to be boarded."

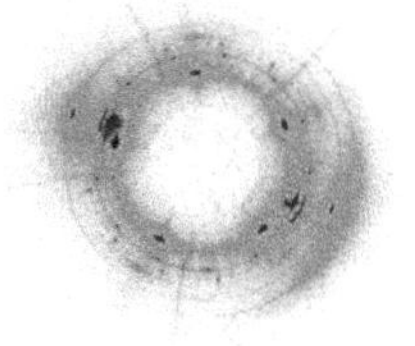

CHAPTER 5

One of the crewmen that Madox had assigned to help keep an eye on the *Eclipse* joined him on the bridge and said, "Captain, not sure what's going on, but take a look at this." He handed Madox a pair of binoculars and directed his attention to a point off the port side. "No idea who that is, but they're closing fast, heading directly towards the *Eclipse*."

It took Madox a moment to focus in on the ship, but it was too far away for him to get a good look. "Do you know where Favor is?"

"Last I saw him he was busy unpacking one of those boxes he brought aboard."

"Better let him know what's going on," said Madox. "It may be nothing, but in case I'm ... Madox stopped midsentence as something caught his eye off the starboard side. It looked like another ship, and it too was racing toward the *Eclipse*. Raising the binoculars, he studied this new arrival for a few seconds. "Get Favor up here on the double. Whatever is going on, I don't like the looks of it."

"Aye, aye, Skipper."

Madox had a bad feeling about this in the pit of his stomach. He hoped that these two ships bearing down on the *Eclipse* were strictly interested in the *Eclipse*. His fear was that the *Eclipse* had called in reinforcements to take care of them. What had that idiot of a reporter gotten him into?

Favor raced back to the bridge as fast as he could. Madox pointed to the two ships closing in on the *Eclipse*. "We're too far away for us to identify them, but I'd say the *Eclipse* is about to have visitors."

"Yes! This is the break I was hoping for," said Favor, almost jumping with excitement. "Full speed ahead, Captain. Get us as close as you can."

"That might not be a good idea," answered Madox. "If the *Eclipse* is up to no good, and those ships are friends of theirs, there's a chance that they were called in to persuade us to stop following them."

"You are such a simpleton. The *Eclipse* doesn't even know we exist. Speed it up, Captain! Now! I want to get as close as we can as fast as we can so that I don't miss anything. And I do mean close. I'll be in the back getting one of the drones ready to go."

Although this went against every instinct he had, Madox moved the throttle forward, pushing the *Wave Runner* as fast as she could go. Fortunately, the sea had stayed remarkably calm, which helped their progress. It wasn't as if they weren't armed, but, if push came to shove, it was three against one and Madox hated those odds.

Five minutes passed, and the *Wave Runner* was rapidly gaining on the *Eclipse*, but so were the other two ships that seemed to have the *Eclipse* hemmed in. As best he could make out, it appeared that their quarry had come to a full stop. They were now less than a half mile from the *Eclipse* and closing fast when suddenly a loud, wailing siren erupted from behind them.

Their focus had been so centered on the *Eclipse* that they hadn't paid any attention as to who might be coming after them. The siren continued to blast out over and over again. The crewman manning the radio turned to Madox and said, "Sir, we're being ordered to come to a full stop."

"Who's ordering us?" asked Madox, trying to get a look behind them.

"US Coast Guard, and they don't sound happy."

Madox had no idea what was going on, but he quickly complied, pulling back on the throttle. Walking over to the radio operator's station he told the crewman, "Let the coast guard know that we are coming to a full stop and will await further instructions from them. Then alert the crew. I don't know where this is going, but clearly we've done something to attract their attention."

Madox stepped outside the bridge and watched as the coast guard rapidly approached. Favor nearly flew up the ladder to the bridge, his face red with rage. "Why are you stopping? I want to get as close to the *Eclipse* as we can!" he shouted.

Nodding his head toward the coast guard ship, Madox asked, "Did you not hear that siren behind us? We've been ordered by the coast guard to stop immediately."

"I don't care what they've ordered. What do you think they're going to do, shoot you out of the water? Now get this antique moving, Captain, that's an order!"

Madox laughed, but there was no humor in his voice. Madox towered over Favor and was fighting the urge to bust him in the mouth. Grabbing the man's shirt with both hands, Madox shoved him hard up against the wall. "You have less than two minutes to tell me what this is all about. I know you've been holding out on me and I'm not going down for something you're mixed up in."

Favor tried to break away from Madox, but he was easily overmatched. "I know as much about this as you do," said Favor, his fear of Madox evident in his voice. "But don't you see, it was like I was telling you, the *Eclipse* is up to no good. Why else would the coast guard be here?"

Madox glared at the reporter. "You had better hope on your mother's life you're telling me the truth."

"Please, if you won't go any closer, at least let me launch my drone," pleaded Favor. "All I need are some pictures and we'll have accomplished what I set out to do."

Before Madox could decide, the same crewman who had alerted him to the approaching ships came up to him and said, "Captain, this is starting to look pretty serious."

Madox released Favor, took the binoculars from the crewman, and focused in on the *Eclipse*. "What have I missed?"

"Both of those ships are coast guard. The one off the port side is keeping its distance from the *Eclipse* and has its guns trained on her. The other one lowered a boat and sent over a boarding party. See, on the starboard side, they're in the process of boarding her right now."

Madox now had a much better view. He could see two coast guard officers aboard the *Eclipse* and they appeared to be shouting at someone. The *Eclipse* had obviously not resisted, but that would have been a stupid thing to try. "Captain, the coast guard just radioed over that we are to stand by to be boarded."

Handing the binoculars back to the crewman, he said, "Tell them we're standing by." Turning to Favor, who hadn't moved an inch, he said. "Stay right where you are. You launch that drone now and they're likely to open up on us."

Favor nodded his head, but inside he was dying. The *Eclipse* was finally getting its day of reckoning and he was missing out on the whole thing.

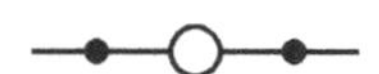

From the bridge, MacKay and Colton watched as the coast guard ship rapidly approached the *Eclipse*. They had been joined by Marine Captain Casey Garrett, officer in charge of the marine unit on board the *Eclipse*, and Jarek Tanner, her second in command. They'd also been joined by Father Ryan Donatelli, the ship's chaplain.

"Father Ryan," said Colton, "glad you joined us. I'm guessing that, under the circumstances, you feel we may be in need of prayer." Colton certainly had nothing against prayer. He'd called on God for help many times, but he also believed that God was more apt to help those who helped themselves. More than one man of the cloth had told Colton that that was completely wrong, but Colton just couldn't buy in to the idea that the God of the universe truly expected his people to just sit around and do nothing. His whole career was a complete contradiction of that notion.

Father Ryan Donatelli had served in the navy as a chaplain for close to twelve years. Although not that tall, he was thick chested and looked more like a boxer than a man of the cloth. "This man's navy is always in need of prayer, Mr. Colton, some of us more than others."

Colton smiled at this. "Glad to have you with us, Father. We're going to need all the help we can get."

"Gentlemen? Somebody want to fill us in on why we're being boarded by the Coast Guard?" asked Captain Garrett.

"At this point you know as much as we do, Captain," said MacKay. "That is unless our guest, Commander Colton, isn't sharing everything he knows."

Turning to Colton, Garrett said, "Sir, our job is to protect this ship, but more importantly, to protect Argos at all costs. Do you know what this is all about?"

Colton, glancing over at Garrett, experienced the same feelings he'd felt the first time they'd met. In his time, Colton had served with several marines, but Garrett didn't look like any marine he'd ever seen. Quite young to be a captain, she was about five-and-a-half feet tall and weighed in at probably 120 pounds, soaking wet. Her hair was dark brown with subtle, auburn highlights, although Colton didn't know if those were natural. But most startling of all was her figure. She had a build that would attract the attention of any man with a pulse. Colton knew that his appraisal of her was completely unprofessional, but facts were facts. Captain Garrett was a stunningly attractive woman. Physical appearance aside, Captain Garrett was highly decorated, had seen her share of action, and was probably one of the best shots on board.

"Just make sure that you and Mr. Tanner make it clear for your men to stand down. They are not to interfere with the boarding party in any way. Understood, Captain?"

"My marines will do as ordered, Commander, but understand this, we will not allow the area containing Argos to be breached. Not by anyone," speaking deliberately and looking at each member on the bridge for acknowledgement.

"Captain, no one here is going to try and circumvent your orders," said Colton, a small smile spreading across his face. "I'm pretty sure Argos will not be in any jeopardy."

"Commander," Garrett glared contemptuously, "I can assure you that Argos will not be in any jeopardy."

Garrett clearly didn't appreciate the commander's cavalier attitude. Although she knew a little of his reputation regarding black ops, at this point she was anything but impressed. He acted like just another arrogant Pentagon bureaucrat. She'd seen too many of these hotshots in action before. And too often it was left to the marines to clean up the messes they created.

The Coast Guard boarded the *Eclipse* and quickly spread out tactically along the deck, taking up strategic positions that were quite visible. Lieutenant Commander Mercer met the Coast Guard officer in charge and escorted him, and two of his men, to the bridge.

"I'm captain of the *Eclipse*," said MacKay. "How can we be of service to the Coast Guard?"

"Lieutenant Washington, sir," the tall, African-American officer said, saluting MacKay. "I'm looking for Commander Colton."

"This is Commander Colton," said MacKay. "Is there a problem, Lieutenant?"

"Yes sir, as I understand it, there most certainly is," answered Washington. Looking directly at MacKay he said, "We've been sent here to take this ship into custody."

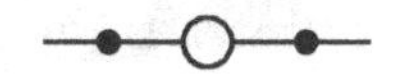

Seamus Donovan was the closest thing to a first mate that you'd find aboard the *Wave Runner*. Thin and wiry, over the years his skin had been burnt brown by the sun, completely bleaching out his hair. He'd worked with Madox for twelve years and Madox always felt better having Seamus aboard. More than fifteen years his senior, Seamus looked upon his captain as the son he'd never had, or at least ever fessed up to. Seamus yelled up to Madox, "Here they come, Skipper."

"Help them aboard Seamus, and stay close. A couple of our boys aren't all that sharp, and until someone explains to me what's going on, the last thing I need is for one of our men to do something stupid. We don't want to get branded with a reputation we don't deserve."

Donovan thought this was hilarious and burst out with his distinct wheezing laugh. Was Madox really worried about what one of the crew might do? When you considered all the shady things the *Wave Runner* had been involved in over the years, it was funny to find Madox suddenly concerned about getting a bad reputation. This tale alone was certain to get him a few rounds of free drinks!

The Coast Guard's boarding craft pulled up alongside the *Wave Runner* and Seamus directed the crew to help them secure the small boat. A very rough-looking lieutenant, accompanied by eight sailors, climbed aboard. All were heavily armed, and stern faced. They quickly spread out, taking up defensive positions, like what the other Coast Guard team had done on the *Eclipse*. Madox had left Favor on the bridge, hopefully safely out of the way, and was there to welcome them.

"Are you the captain of this ship?" asked the Lieutenant as Madox approached him.

"I am Lieutenant, Captain Tommy Madox. What seems to be the problem?" he said, extending his hand, which the lieutenant ignored.

"I'm Lieutenant Grimm. From this point forward, you will answer my questions and follow any directions I give you to the letter. Is that understood?"

"Certainly Lieutenant, we have no reason not to cooperate with the Coast Guard."

"Good. How many crew and passengers do you have aboard, Captain Madox?"

"I have fifteen crew and one passenger," said Madox.

"Be certain of those numbers, Captain. We mean to search this vessel and if I come up with a different total we're going to have a problem."

Madox looked at Donovan, "That's an accurate count, isn't it?"

"Yes sir."

"Very good," said the lieutenant. "I want all of your men brought up on deck immediately."

"Of course, but would you mind telling us why you've boarded us in the first place?"

Lieutenant Grimm stared at him for a moment, then turned his gaze briefly towards the *Eclipse*. "We'll get to that Captain, you can count on it. Now, get your crew and your passengers up on deck."

"Seamus, round up the crew." Seamus nodded and moved off towards the ladder leading up to the bridge.

"Hold it," order Lieutenant Grimm. "Where's he going?"

"Our intercom is up on the bridge. He's going to use it so that we can comply with your order."

"Estrada, Hoover," barked Lieutenant Grimm. Two tall, well-built coastguardsmen stepped forward. "Please accompany this crewman so that there won't be any confusion regarding my orders."

"Aye, aye, sir," responded the two petty officers in unison.

The three men headed off to the bridge while Grimm waited in silence with Captain Madox. Within two minutes the crew, as well as Favor, had joined them on deck. "Ensign Walker, take your men and begin your search."

"We're on it, Lieutenant," said Walker.

It was only then that Madox noticed that Ensign Walker was a woman, and a reasonably attractive woman at that. *How did I miss her?* Madox thought to himself. *I'm not that old.*

"Make sure you scan everything thoroughly with those Geigers," directed Lieutenant Grimm.

"Yes sir," said Walker. Three of the Coast Guard crewmen stayed on deck with Lieutenant Grimm, while the rest spread out through the ship.

"Who are your passengers, Captain?" asked Lieutenant Grimm.

"As I said, we have just the one," said Madox, motioning Favor to join them. "This is Ricky Favor. He chartered this trip."

"Do you have identification, Mr. Favor?"

"Absolutely," answered Favor, reaching into his pocket. He handed Grimm his press credentials.

Grimm studied them for a moment, and then placed them in one of his shirt pockets. "Those are some rather sophisticated drones sitting over there. Are they yours, Mr. Favor, or do these belong to you, Captain Madox?" asked Grimm.

"I'm with the *Inside Story*. The drones are mine. I use them for aerial shots to illustrate the stories I write. What I don't understand is why you've stopped us. We haven't done anything wrong."

"The *Inside Story*. Yes, I'm familiar with your paper," said Grimm. "Based on the few articles I've see accredited to your publication, I'm guessing that an imaginative guy like you has already come up with two or three headline-capturing reasons as to why you've been stopped. But before we get into that, tell me, what kind of dirt could you possibly expect to dig up out here? Does this so-called story have anything to do with the *Eclipse*?"

"The story is my own business. I don't see any reason why I have to tell you anything. I know my rights," said Favor. He'd had some success with this line of defense in the past, so it seemed like the right time to trot it out.

Grimm smiled down at Favor. "I, too, am aware of your rights. Hopefully, for your sake, you are as fluent in maritime law as you think you are and how your actions at sea might affect the very rights you're referencing." Turning to Madox he said, "Are you and the *Eclipse* working together?"

"What? Working with the *Eclipse*?"

"Stalling for time isn't going to help you, Captain. Don't play dumb with me. We've been tracking you for miles and you've stayed directly on course, right in line behind the *Eclipse*."

"No, we are not connected with the *Eclipse* in any way," stammered Madox. "We have been keeping the same course, true, but that's it."

"So, your following them has just been out of idle curiosity, or has your keeping the same course as the *Eclipse* been one of those amazing coincidences that happens all the time?" said Grimm. At that point his radio beeped, interrupting him. Grimm listened for a moment then said, "Search harder, Ensign. You find anything that looks out of place, tear it apart. I don't think these men are being completely straightforward with us."

"Alright, alright," said Favor, stepping toward Grimm. "I can explain, but can you please tell us what this is all about? You have my press credentials, so that should prove to you who I am. And as Captain Madox said, we are not in any way connected to the *Eclipse*, but we are following it."

Grimm gave Madox a hard look, "Would have been in your best interest to have opened with that, Captain," then looked back at Favor. "Why are you following the *Eclipse*?"

"The *Eclipse* is known for doing research on various things, a lot of which is kept way under wraps, and very far away from the public eye."

"I'm listening, Mr. Favor, but that doesn't tell me why you're here," said Grimm.

"A couple of days ago I got word from one of my informants that the *Eclipse* was going out to examine an old World War ll German sub that someone recently located. Apparently, the sub's in pretty deep water. The word is that this U-boat was carrying secret German weapons to be used against the United States but was sunk before it could get close enough to our coast to launch them. Frankly, my plan was to scoop everyone else on this story. I was going to use the drones to get pictures so that the guys on the *Eclipse* wouldn't be able to refute the story."

"That's very interesting," said Grimm. "Just about what I'd expect from a writer. Madox, is he telling the truth?"

Before Madox could reply, the faint sound of two shots rang out from the direction of the *Eclipse.* Seconds later Grimm's radio began to beep. Ensign Walker and her team appeared back on deck at the same time. Grimm turned and talked into the radio, but neither Favor nor Madox could make out what he was saying. Grimm stopped talking and said, "Ensign, there have been developments on the *Eclipse.* Keep everyone here on deck. I'll rejoin you shortly."

As Grimm moved away from the men gathered on deck, Ensign Walker moved to where he'd been standing. "Everyone remain calm, keep your hands where we can see them, and do not talk to anyone."

"Ensign, please, why can't someone tell us what's going on?" asked Favor.

Walker looked at Favor as if he were something that had just crawled out from under a rock. "I just directed you to stay quiet. I won't repeat myself again. Do you understand?"

Favor nodded. For the first time since the Coast Guard had boarded them he started to get worried. The *Eclipse* was obviously mixed up in something major-league bad to have attracted this kind of attention, but what could it be? And was it something so bad that they'd all be arrested for being associated with the *Eclipse*, an association that didn't exist?

The next few minutes felt like an eternity to Favor, Madox, and his crew. Finally, Lieutenant Grimm came back, but his demeanor had lightened considerably. "Captain Madox, we now have a better handle on things and it appears that you and your ship are not involved."

"Glad to hear you say that," said Madox, his relief clear to see.

"So, what's all this been about?" pressed Favor, "What did they do? And why did you think that we were involved?"

Grimm mulled that over for a moment. "All I can tell you is that several law enforcement agencies have been searching for a rather large quantity of stolen illegal substances. Those substances have been found on board the *Eclipse.* We have also apprehended two of the primary suspects in regard to that theft. Based on what we now know, it's been determined that neither you, nor your ship, are involved."

"What happens now?" asked Favor.

"The *Eclipse* is now in the custody of the US Coast Guard and will be escorted north to the Indian Head naval base in Washington. As to the *Wave Runner*, we'll be following you back to port."

"Hold on," protested Favor. "You just said we've been cleared. Why do we have to go back?"

"Let's just say that for the time being, this area is not safe. It turns out that the *Eclipse* was to have rendezvoused with another ship. I can assure you that the people they'd planned to meet up with are the last people you'd ever want to cross," said Grimm. "Also, based on the rumors you picked up from your contacts, Mr. Favor, there are some NCIS agents waiting to talk with you when we get back. I'll be handing your press credentials over to them."

"My sources are confidential," said Favor. "I don't have to give them up or tell anyone anything about them!"

Grimm smiled and said, "I'll let you take that up with them, Mr. Favor. This involves national security. I'm sure they'll appreciate your wisdom and insights into the law as much as I have."

Madox gave orders for the crew to get back to their stations. He and Favor watched as the Coast Guard boarding party prepared to return to their ship. Grimm was the last to board their small craft.

"Captain Madox," said Grimm, "we'll be following you back. So as quickly as you can, make ready, turn this boat around, and head back to port. Understand that we're doing this for your protection." He started to climb over the railing to leave the *Wave Runner*, stopped, and looked at Favor. "This is an active criminal investigation. Should any of those drones be launched, they'll be shot out of the sky and you'll be arrested. We appreciate your cooperation."

Favor returned to the bridge with Captain Madox. He couldn't believe what was happening. There had to be some way to skirt around the orders he'd just been given, but he couldn't think of anything. The frustration he felt burned within him, rapidly turning into rage. He watched as off in the distance the two Coast Guard ships sailed away, taking the *Eclipse* north to their base. Favor screamed in frustration, slamming his fist into the wall.

"Something bothering you?" asked Captain Madox as he turned the *Wave Runner* around. Although he managed to keep the smile off his face, the sarcasm in his voice was obvious to everyone but Favor.

"I was right. The *Eclipse* is dirty and what do I have to show for it? Nothing! The stupid Coast Guard just robbed me of probably one of the biggest stories of the year!"

"The 'stupid' Coast Guard just saved your life, as well as the rest of ours," said Madox. "Do you really think the people the *Eclipse* was getting ready to meet with would have just stood there and smiled for your stupid drone as it took their picture? You would have gotten us all killed."

Favor hadn't heard a word that Madox said. His mind was still racing, trying to figure out any possible way to salvage his story. Then it hit him. "Captain, I need to use your radio."

"For what?"

"I need to contact my people back at my office. They may think they've won, but they clearly don't know who they're dealing with," snapped Favor.

Madox shook his head. Some people just don't know when to quit. "Seamus, please take Mr. Favor down to the radio room."

Seamus winked at Madox. "Will do, Skipper. This way, Favor."

The "radio room" on the *Wave Runner* consisted of two shelves in the galley. Favor couldn't determine which smelled worse, the open garbage can by the door or the odor coming from a large pot cooking on the stove.

A crewman put the call through for Favor, then handed him the mic. Favor waited impatiently until the crewman and Seamus stepped away, leaving him alone. He barked at the receptionist to put him through to Frank Bannister, senior editor at the *Inside Story*. Favor quickly brought him up to speed on all that had just taken place.

"Geigers," said Bannister. "So, whatever they were looking for was hot, radioactive hot."

"This is huge, Frank, I'm telling you, and we have to act fast. It looks like I'm going to be tied up for a while with some navy cops, but I can handle that. I need you to get a crew up to the Indian Head naval base ASAP with the best photographers and camera equipment we have. This is front-page stuff, Frank, and everyone is gonna want to buy these shots from us! This has been a long time coming and I want pictures of them bringing the *Eclipse* in. It'll be the greatest perp walk ever!

"Got it, we're all over it. Favor, you've outdone yourself! Call me if you need for me to get Mickey down there to help you." Mickey Hart headed up the paper's legal team. He and Favor got along well as they shared a similarly low level of ethics.

"You're the best, Frank," said Favor. "I'll call you as soon as I can."

Favor put the receiver down and stepped back out on deck. Squinting his eyes, he scanned the Atlantic, looking for his quarry. Finally, far off on the horizon, he caught site of the *Eclipse* being taken in by the two Coast Guard ships. They were almost out of sight.

"Got you, you arrogant bastard," muttered Favor to himself. Although things clearly had not turned out the way he would have liked, he was still going to get the story. Favor imagined himself on all the morning talk shows, telling how he'd bravely and defiantly stood up for his rights, refusing to back down to anyone. Ricky Favor was about to become famous! Pulitzer famous!

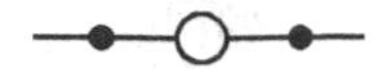

The *Eclipse* and their Coast Guard escorts moved slowly north. The boarding party had departed, and Colton stood on main deck, back at the stern, watching as the *Wave Runner* was escorted back to the Baltimore harbor. His plan had worked beautifully. This was one report he knew Admiral Fairfax would enjoy reading.

"For a moment there I thought Captain Garret was going to shoot you."

Colton looked behind him and smiled as Father Ryan joined him. "Guess it was rather touch and go there for a few moments."

"The captain is a fine officer," noted Father Ryan. "Not sure it's a good idea to get on her bad side."

"I don't disagree, Father, it's just that, other than MacKay, I haven't worked with these people before. I had to make sure that everyone played their part the right way," said Colton. "From my perspective, the marines were the only wild card in the deck. I had to make sure they wouldn't start defending a hill that really wasn't even being threatened. I'll talk with her, Tanner too."

Father Ryan was intrigued by Colton. The men and women who lived in his world of black ops were a rare and special breed. They truly walked to the beat of their own drum. "None of us know very much about this mission. Fortunately, for most of us, having been in the military for some time, we're accustomed to that. Need to know, I get it. But on the *Eclipse,* you have a seasoned, strong, and capable crew backing you up, Commander," said Father Ryan. "I should think that gaining their trust would be one of your priorities."

"Trust is effervescent, but loyalty is firm. They don't need to trust me, just love the US. Me? I'm a scary guy that knows too much. For example, Father Donatelli, aren't you in the Order of St. Cyprian? The Vatican's X-File priests? I know you're not a ninja turtle."

Colton's knowledge of the Order of St. Cyprian caught Father Donatelli off guard. Very few people knew this. He'd not even told the navy. His order was very powerful, but secret, and was never openly discussed. Images flashed through his mind, things he witnessed over the years, things his order was sworn to defend against. Demons, creatures that stalked humans for their very souls, the dark ones that waged war against the Church. "You continue to surprise me, Commander."

The *Wave Runner* was almost out of sight. Colton's gaze remained fixed on the small ship as it sailed back to port. "To your point, Father, once this little ruse is complete, and we finally get underway to our true destination, I plan to have a briefing with the officers, as well as the civilians that we have with us. I'd like for you to be there when I do."

At that moment crewman Hatfield approached Colton, handing him a folded sheet of paper. "This just came in for you, Commander. Captain MacKay asked me to bring it to you right away."

"Thank you, sailor," said Colton, taking the paper from him. "You did well spotting the ship that was trailing us. Keep up the good work. And tell Captain MacKay I appreciate him getting this to me."

"Will do. Thank you, Commander."

As Colton read the note, the trace of a smile crossed his face. "Good news?" asked Father Ryan.

"When Tanner learned that the press was sniffing around the *Eclipse*, he informed MacKay, who then called Admiral Fairfax. Due to the sensitivity of this mission, we had to take the press out of the picture, especially a sleazy rag like the *Inside Story*."

"If memory serves, MacKay's first instinct was to sink them."

Colton chuckled at that. "I know, the admiral told me. However, laws being what they are, we decided upon a different course of action. The reporters on that ship were given a front-row seat to watch as the Coast Guard stopped us, boarded the *Eclipse*, and proceeded to arrest the lot of us. They too were boarded and were initially accused of being in collusion with us."

"And what dastardly deed are we supposed to have committed?" asked Father Ryan. "I'll guess human trafficking and drug running."

"Please, Father, give credit where credit is due. I'm far more imaginative than just having us pose as everyday, run-of-the-mill, drug runners. The Coast Guard made sure that the crew of the *Wave Runner* knew that the team searching their ship was using Geiger counters. After we fired off the two shots to add even more excitement to the show, the Coast Guard officer on the *Wave Runner* received a call on his radio, absolving the crew of that ship of all guilt. The stolen radioactive substances had been recovered, and arrests had been made. A happy ending for everyone."

"Now I understand why you made it clear to Garrett and Tanner to have their team stand down. Those two shots fired by that Coast Guard officer would have attracted a rather eager and aggressive crowd. That would not have been good."

"It would not," said Colton. "Despite all this, the message that sailor just brought to me confirms that the reporters trailing us have not given up."

"You're kidding! I appreciate their tenacity, but what can they do now? Seems to me they've been taken out of the picture."

"The Coast Guard told them that the *Eclipse* is being taken to the Indian Head naval base in Washington. The message I just received is courtesy of our friends at the NSA. We made sure that all the *Wave Runner*'s radio transmissions were closely monitored. Once the Coast Guard left and they turned around to head back in, one of the reporters called the paper's office. He told their boss all that happened. They are now working frantically to get photographers to that base to get pictures of the *Eclipse* being brought in."

"That should keep them busy for a while," said Father Ryan. "Too bad that your ruse will be over when the *Eclipse* doesn't show up," said Father Ryan.

"Father, Father, Father," teased Ryan, "you are still refusing to appreciate my subtle genius. Late this evening the *Eclipse*, or at least a ship posing as the *Eclipse*, will be brought in by these two Coast Guard cutters. The phony *Eclipse* will be taken to a covered and secure dock at Indian Head. They'll get some pictures, but only of a silhouette, and even that will be from a long way off. My guess is that they'll spend at least a few weeks digging into this before they begin to suspect they've been had."

Father Ryan slapped Colton on the shoulder, smiling from ear to ear. "Glorious! Simply glorious! Commander, I'm looking forward to the day when we can play poker. You can't be this good all the time."

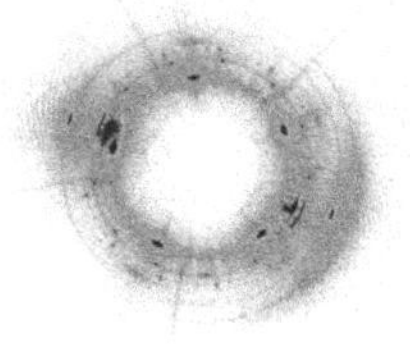

CHAPTER 6

"Lt. Commander, it appears that we are close to being finished," said Admiral Fairfax as he thumbed through the report he'd be presenting to the armed services committee tomorrow. "They're not going to understand half of what I'm showing to them anyway. I'll need eighteen copies of these, all bound and pretty for our brothers and sisters on the Hill."

"Sir, I'm sure you recall that two members serving on the committee are veterans," said Lt. Commander Flanagan. Although he was pretty sure the admiral already knew this, he didn't want his boss getting broadsided by anyone.

"Yes, if I'm not mistaken, both army; not an Annapolis graduate to be found. Congressman Burke was an officer in procurement and Congresswoman Wilkes served in recruitment, neither one of them making it above the rank of captain." Smiling at his young aide he said, "I think I can handle them."

"Last month Congressman Wilkes asked several questions regarding the *Eclipse* and its current mission. I imagine she'll be expecting an update."

Fairfax glanced at his watch. "Heh, so am I. I've got a call coming up in about fifteen minutes with Commander Colton. Hopefully, he'll be able to give me something I can use."

"In a way, the weekly reports have been interesting," said Flanagan. "Thanks to Argos and the civilian scientists on board, they've made some pretty interesting observations. Unfortunately, they haven't made any progress determining what caused the initial disturbance."

"Flanagan, in one or two sentences you've summed up nearly eight weeks of work costing more tax dollars than I'm willing to admit to," said Fairfax as he leaned back in his chair, running his fingers through his hair with both hands. "It's been a total bust. But the problem is that we just couldn't afford to sit here and ignore it. But not one of those hypocrites on the Hill will ever see it that way. They always act so righteous when it comes to money being spent, unless, of course, it's tax dollars being directed to their districts. They're always more than ready to send the pork back home."

"How much longer will the *Eclipse* be out there?" asked Flanagan.

"I'll be giving Colton the good news today. Either they find something in the next week or we're terminating the mission. Captain Ramirez and I have discussed this at length and his team hasn't been able to find any other options. We certainly can't leave them out there indefinitely, and yet we're no closer to understanding what happened than when this whole mess got started. It's frustrating and worrisome all in the same breath."

"It was my understanding that Argos, early on, did discover an anomaly that showed great promise," said Flanagan.

"It did, first couple of days they were there. Argos reported finding remnants of an energy source that it couldn't identify, or locate, but levels were off the charts in the sense of its strength. Dr. Meinhard and his team dug into it, but by day three not even Argos could find any trace of it."

"It's especially surprising that Argos couldn't determine what it was," said Flanagan. "It's my understanding that Argos is years beyond anything else we have."

"That thing is supposed to be the most advanced computer system of its kind in the world. It too cost an astronomical amount of money, and it drew a complete blank. Lieutenant Sahir did his best, but he couldn't coax anything else out of Argos. It couldn't determine where the energy source had come from, or what it consisted of. However, it did put forth a very illuminating hypothesis. It concluded that whatever was causing this, the actual source was being shielded." Fairfax gave a small laugh and said, "Nowadays, even the computers make up excuses as to why they can't produce answers."

"I didn't see anything more regarding the strength of the energy source they did pick up. Was Argos able to firm up any measurements?"

"It's one of the main reasons we've kept the *Eclipse* out there for as long as we have. I don't have the technical jargon handy, but based on the measurements Argos was able to make, think of the bomb that hit Hiroshima times forty. That in itself scared Ramirez and his team half to death, and I came close to asking for a meeting all the way up to and including the White House. But since then no one has been able to find a thing."

Ensign Flanagan stood up to leave. "As soon as Commander Colton's call comes in I'll route it to you."

"Thank you, Lt. Commander."

The relationship between Fairfax and Flanagan had started years ago. Fairfax knew that it was unusual for someone of his rank to be as open with a junior officer as he was with Flanagan, but the young officer had earned his respect. Fairfax saw him as more than just a trusted aide, but as probably being the man to sit in his chair one day.

Fairfax, Ramirez, and his team knew that there had been something there, but despite their best efforts, they'd not been able to find it, or for that matter, even come up with a good guess as to what it had been. And based on what facts they did have, it was clearly something they desperately needed to find. It had been caught on film by more than one satellite; its size far exceeded any ship they were aware of; and apparently it could generate a level of energy that, if weaponized, would be lethal to a vast area of Florida's coast. On the other hand, sadly, there were the practical realities. The mission was costing the navy a small fortune and they had nothing to show for it. It was time to bring the *Eclipse* home. Financially they couldn't justify leaving it at sea.

The intercom on the admiral's desk buzzed and he hit the button. "Yes?"

"I have Commander Colton, sir. He's on line three," said Flanagan.

"Thank you. Please see that I'm not disturbed."

Hitting the button for line three, Admiral Fairfax said, "Good afternoon, Colton. How are things on the *Eclipse*?"

"At this point I'd say the only one enjoying the cruise is Argos, and I'm pretty sure he's getting bored too, assuming of course that he is a he, and is even capable of being bored. The only item of significance to update you on took place a couple of days ago. Captain MacKay decided to redirect our course, and the ship is now following a figure eight pattern. We'd been going around in a circle for so long he reasoned that we might be in jeopardy of creating a whirlpool."

"Have any civilian craft spotted you?"

"I don't think so. The crew does a pretty good job of monitoring the area. When it looks like another ship might get close to us, MacKay just moves us out of the way until they've passed."

"Remember those reporters that tried following you out to sea? They ended up staking out the base for nearly seven weeks before throwing in the towel. All in all, it was very entertaining. Captain Ramirez won the pool we had going. Now, in regard to your mission, do you have anything new to report?"

"Admiral, the short answer is no. The only abnormality that's been observed, and I'm all but certain about this, is that Father Ryan cheats at cards. No one's consistently that lucky."

"He is good. Should have warned you about him," said Fairfax. "How are our civilian friends holding up?"

"They're more than ready to go home, but on the other hand, they've taken full advantage of their time on the *Eclipse*, as well as the limited access they've had to Argos. They've run a few pretty interesting experiments, but they're not used to being cooped up like this. It's beginning to take its toll. I haven't had to call in Garrett's marines yet, but there have been a few rather intense disagreements."

"We all know that being at sea without an end date in sight creates its own kind of stress," said Fairfax, "especially your first time out. I don't care what kind of ship you're on, as time goes by it seems to get smaller and smaller."

"Other than that, I'd say that overall morale is good. Two days ago, we were resupplied, so from a food and drink standpoint, we're good." Colton paused for a moment then said, "Admiral, there's no easy way to say this, but I think we're wasting our time out here. I've looked at the pictures and films that our birds took many times over. While I know something had to have happened to trigger their response, whatever might have been here is long gone. I really don't think there's anything for us to find,"

"Commander, keep in mind that the data we do have does not point to any kind of natural phenomena that we can identify. In addition to the pictures taken by our satellites, there's also the energy reading that Argos picked up on when you first arrived at your present position. The levels on that reading were staggering. They were so strong that we can't even come up with a good guess as to what the source for them might have been. But, unfortunately, like everything else about this insane mission, we haven't been able to find any additional evidence, nothing tangible that we can point to."

The line went silent. Colton knew that Fairfax was not waiting on a response from him. The admiral was merely voicing his frustrations, but frankly, Colton had a few of his own. This was not his kind of mission. He had never been an academic, and, after having spent this much time with several of them in close proximity, he harbored no interest in ever becoming an academic, or frankly, ever speaking to one again. Most of them could give lessons in righteous arrogance.

But the most frustrating part for Colton was that he hadn't been able to contribute anything to the mission. Sitting around and waiting for something to happen was not how he'd been trained, nor was it the way he normally carried out his duties. Why was he even out here? Had it not been for his daily attempts to beat Argos at chess, his personal mission to figure out exactly how Father Ryan was cheating him at poker, and his constant baiting of Captain Garrett as to why the Marine Corp truly is subpar to the rest of the navy, he'd have lost his mind.

The pregnant pause in their conversation was finally broken by Fairfax. "One more week, Commander. Push that team as hard as you can to come up with something, anything, but if they come up empty, bring them home. I'll have orders communicated to MacKay, but he'll be waiting on you to make the final call as to whether the *Eclipse* will return to port or will stay in position. Any questions, Commander?"

"No sir," answered Colton. "That's pretty straightforward."

"Colton, something's going on out there, something big. It's imperative that we find out what it is, or I believe in my heart that at some point in time it's going to come back and bite us, and we can't afford to let that happen.

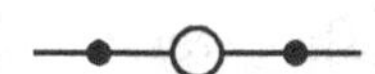

Captain MacKay was on his third cup of coffee when Colton entered the mess hall. Dressed in shorts, T-shirt, and running shoes, it was obvious that Colton had just finished working out.

"My guess is that you were demonstrating to Captain Garrett that the navy can do more push-ups than the marines."

"I'm afraid to go down that road. Based on what I've seen of her, I'm pretty sure she could easily hold her own against any man on this ship. Mind if I join you?" asked Colton.

"Not if you sit downwind of me," said MacKay.

"Now you're starting to sound like Garrett," said Colton as he got his coffee and loaded it up with creamer.

"You've been riding her pretty hard, but then, she's been doing a rather good job of handing it right back to you. You boil it all down and I think the two of you are more alike than either of you are willing to admit. From my seat in the stands, I'd also say that you've taken more than a casual interest in our young captain," said MacKay.

"Blasphemy!" said Colton, pretending to be shocked. "Keep that up and I'll report you to Father Ryan."

"Me thinks the lady, you in this case, doth protest too much," said MacKay, smiling from ear to ear.

Colton smiled, but shook his head, "Anything more than a professional relationship at this point in time would not be a wise move. That said, you've been to Quantico. How many marine captains have you ever seen that looked like that? I'll probably never meet him, but kudos to her recruiting officer."

"Any updates from our science team?" asked MacKay. "Lieutenant Sahir let me know that Dr. Chudzik and Dr. Meinhard spent quite a while putting a great deal of data into Argos last night."

"Not yet. I typically get my daily briefing from Dr. Meinhard right after dinner. It's fascinating to watch. It can take him up to a full hour just to tell me they got zero, and yet it leaves me feeling impressed with all they've accomplished. If his present gig doesn't work out, there's a career in politics just waiting for him. Argos asked them to shoot craps for eight hours and logged each roll. I think Argos is cracking up too."

A voice behind Colton said, "Excuse me, sir. I've had this waiting for you."

Colton looked up to see the smiling face of Hezekiah "Cookie" Abebe. Hezekiah was at least six foot six and Colton knew easily tipped the scale at 320 pounds plus. When he first met Hezekiah, he'd guessed that he was meeting either Captain Garrett or Jarek Tanner, one of the ship's two marine officers. But he couldn't have been more mistaken. Rather than being a highly trained, tough-as-nails, elite marine officer, Hezekiah was the head cook on board. And he was very, very good at what he did.

"Exactly what is that concoction, Cookie?" asked Captain MacKay. "I've been meaning to ask you that for weeks."

"It's what you should have every morning," answered Hezekiah. "It is a protein shake with fresh fruit and vegetables."

"No thanks," said MacKay. "I like food I can chew."

"You should try it for a few days," said Colton. "It'll make a new man out of you. Come on, Captain. I've converted Garrett and half her men to having this for breakfast. It's much better for your heart than that plate of sausage and eggs you're wolfing down, and it'll also help you burn off some fat. Hezekiah has drunk these for years. Isn't that right?"

"It's how I keep my girlish figure," answered Hezekiah as he walked off laughing, his distinct baritone chortle filling the room.

Once Hezekiah had stepped back into the kitchen, Colton leaned forward, and in a quiet voice said, "The man is a magician. A couple of years ago I started drinking these breakfast shakes. Good for me or not, frankly it was a bland way to start the day. So, when I came on board the *Eclipse*, I asked Hezekiah if he would make this for me every morning. I told him the ingredients and he gave me that bone-rattling laugh of his and said, "Sure." The next morning, when I showed up in the mess hall, he handed me my shake. Tasted better than anything I'd ever put together. That's when he told me he too had been drinking these for years, but, over time, had improved upon the recipe. I'm telling you, the breakfast shakes he makes are addictive."

"Yeah, well, I'll give it some thought," said MacKay. "So, we have what, three days left? Doesn't look like the dream team is going to be able to find our mystery blob."

"Mystery blob?"

"What do you call it? I saw the pictures, even watched the film our birds took. It doesn't look like anything I've ever seen and doesn't seem to hold its shape all that well. It may have mass, but it doesn't have form. Hence, I call it a blob."

"Sadly, that's as good as anything they've come up with and that's with Argos backing them up. I'm going to get cleaned up, then spend a few minutes with Lieutenant Sahir. Our time out here is going to come under close scrutiny from the finance weenies back at the Pentagon, and for Admiral Fairfax's sake, I want to make sure we've tried everything there is to try."

"I'd ask you to say hi to Argos for me, but it probably already knows I'm going to say that," said MacKay. "I don't care for that machine. It gets under my skin."

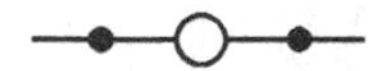

To say that the security around Argos was tight would have been an understatement at best. Two heavily armed marines stood guard beside the solid steel door leading into the area where Argos was housed. Anyone wishing to enter had to identify themselves to the guards, who would then relay the request to enter to Lieutenant Sahir whose office was next to Argos.

Once the approval was given, the door was unlocked from the inside and the visitor would enter a small, six-by-six area. It was a mantrap. Here the visitor was met by a second steel door that had a bulletproof glass porthole at eye level. At this point, the person seeking to enter went through two more security checks. Similar to human scanning devices found in most US airports, the individual was scanned for weapons. Additionally, visual identification was made via the porthole before the visitor could enter.

Argos was situated in the center of one of the high-ceilinged holds with workstations positioned all around it. Lieutenant Sahir had the only office, but its walls were made of glass, giving him visibility to Argos at all times. In addition to the marine unit detailed to protect Argos, Sahir had four very talented senior computer technicians who supported him with Argos' maintenance and care.

It was one of these technicians that led Colton to Sahir's office. "You've got to let me in on how you got the budget for this level of security," said Colton, teasing the young lieutenant.

"Pretty amazing, isn't it?" said Sahir. "The interesting point to all of this is that if push came to shove, Argos would probably be more effective at protecting us."

Colton stared at the massive computer. "Are you saying it has defensive capabilities?"

Sahir got up from his desk and stood next to Colton. "You can't think of Argo as just being a larger, more advanced computer. It's hard to put into words, but comparing Argos to other computers of its kind that contain artificial intelligence is like comparing the heat generated from a single match to the heat produced by a volcanic eruption. They're just not in the same league."

"It's that advanced," said Colton, almost to himself. "How is that even possible?"

"That's a long story, but I will share with you one little fun fact that I am certain you'll never forget. After we got to a certain point in the process, Argos actively participated in its own development." Colton just stared at him, a disbelieving look on his face. "I know, it's hard to wrap your mind around such a concept," continued Sahir. "Let's just say we should be glad that Argos works for us."

"The work is why I'm here," said Colton. "Lieutenant, you were given more of a complete briefing as to why we're out here than most of the people on this ship. You've had the lead in working with Meinhard and his team. Not to put too fine a point on it, but so far we've failed to produce anything that will help to determine what it was that our birds picked up."

"Other than the data from the satellites, you're correct, we haven't found anything that could account for it," said Sahir. His stance was not defensive in the slightest, his tone a mere statement of fact. "Everyone did get rather anxious at the energy readings that Argos picked up initially, but in truth, we really don't even know if the two are connected."

"Were you able to get anything else out of Argos on those readings?" asked Colton.

"No. We couldn't find anything that would help us to pinpoint what the source behind those energy readings could have been. That, in and of itself, is nearly impossible. Energy levels that high don't just appear out of thin air."

"Could Argos have made a mistake? I mean, computer errors do happen all the time."

Sahir's smile at Colton's question was not the kind of smile anyone wanted. It was the smile an adult gives to a small child when they say something that's stupid, but the child has no idea just how absolutely stupid it is. "No sir, it was not a mistake. For every piece of data that Argos produces, there are more than a thousand failsafe procedures run against them before they're released. If Argos tells you the sun won't shine tomorrow, it's a safe bet you won't need your Ray-Bans."

"Argos doesn't theorize like humans do. It runs millions of simulations that are quantum-entangled with real-world energy fluctuations. It can't make a guess. It's saying the energy it detected wasn't part of this world, then it was, then it wasn't again. It says that the laws of thermodynamics were broken for several minutes. It has no idea why. It's like saying magic pixie dust came and left."

Colton stared at Sahir, then said, "Lieutenant, we have very little time left. I want you to get with Meinhard and his associates and see what we can pull together. I have no interest in returning to port empty-handed."

"I understand, Commander, and will do my best," answered Sahir. "I too have a great deal of respect for Admiral Fairfax, but we cannot be expected to deliver on things that are simply not here," said Sahir, then he gave a big sigh. "That said, I'll see what we have and hope that it will make do."

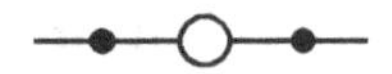

Before Colton left Sahir's area, he stopped and took a long look at Argos. He knew that like everything else the military had, this massive pile of circuitry could be used for good in several ways. But experience had taught him that the blade always cuts both ways. While he didn't share MacKay's nearly superstitious dread of Argos, Sahir's intimation that this machine could defend itself did create another element of concern that Colton had never considered.

The day passed by slowly and about thirty minutes before dinner Colton returned to his cabin. He'd been up on the main deck, watching the sun as it started to go down. The imagery it created was spectacular, spreading its final colors of the day across the dark water. As he turned to leave, he spotted Father Ryan and the ship's doctor, Lieutenant Commander Piers Severin, on the deck above him. They too had been admiring Mother Nature's evening light show. Father Ryan smiled and waved to him with his cigar in hand.

Colton took advantage of the few minutes he had to stretch out on his bunk. After dinner he'd have his usual long and drawn-out meeting with Meinhard, where it would be explained to him in mind-numbing detail why they'd once again come up empty. For reasons that Colton did not understand, Meinhard had kept a strict code of formality between them. Perhaps that's why he didn't trust him.

After his briefing with Meinhard, and he was looking forward to this, he'd be having another go at Father Ryan at the poker table. Earlier in the day Father Ryan had informed him that, surprisingly, Captain Garrett would be joining them. Colton knew in his heart that she was doing it just to goad him while cheering for the priest. Tanner and Dr. Severin, the game's other two regulars, would also be playing.

But tonight, would be different. Colton decided to mix it up, breaking his own rules. He planned to purposely sit with his back to the hatch (a special ops no-no), cut the deck light, and raise on everything no matter what he was holding. Reckless, yes, but nothing else had worked, so why not. In fact, he —

The ship's alarm shattered the silence of his cabin, repeatedly blaring out its nerve-shredding wail. Over the ship's intercom he heard, "General quarters. General quarters. This is the bridge, all personnel to their stations. This is not a drill."

Colton hit the floor running, making his way to the bridge. He was always amazed at how quickly crews were able to respond, getting to their individual stations in seconds, all without running over each other. He entered the bridge to find MacKay and Lt. Commander Mercer leaning over the radar, closely examining the display. Their stunned expressions were deadly serious.

"What's going on?" asked Colton.

"We're not sure," answered MacKay. "It appears that we have a giant wave rising up just to the south of us." Turning to Mercer he asked, "Does the forward lookout have a visual on this?"

"I'll check and see," answered Mercer, moving over to the communications console.

"A rogue wave? From the south?" asked Colton. "Has there been any seismic activity in the area?"

MacKay picked up a phone and tapped in five numbers. "Sahir, this is MacKay. Is Argos picking this up?" MacKay waited, and Colton watched as the captain's face turned pale. "Keep me informed if it starts to get closer."

"What did he say?" asked Colton.

"Argos lit up like a Christmas tree. Remember the energy readings it took when we first arrived here? Well, they're back, and the energy levels Argos is picking up now dwarf the previous readings. Sahir's first guess was that someone had set off a nuclear bomb, but Argos dismissed that idea as being too small."

"Captain, it appears to be spreading," said the crewman manning the radar station, his voice tight and strained.

"Spreading?" said MacKay, returning to the radar screen. Both he and Colton watched as a bright yellow line seemed to be starting to encircle the *Eclipse*.

"Yes sir," answered the crewman. "It appears to be forming around us.

"Mr. Mercer, any word from the forward lookout?" shouted MacKay.

"No visual on the wave, sir, but he reports that something is starting to black out the sky."

"That's nuts," said MacKay. "I don't even know what that means."

"He says that whatever this is, as it gets bigger, the stars start to blur and then completely vanish. It's as if there's a wall forming around us," said Mercer.

Colton grabbed some binoculars and bolted out the door. The forward lookout had been right. Whatever was going on was blacking out the evening sky. Colton rushed back inside and shouted, "Get Fairfax on the phone immediately."

"What's going on, Colton?" challenged MacKay. "Do you know what this is?"

"I know as much as you do, but if the energy levels are truly as high as Argos is reporting, then we are probably in serious trouble. We need to warn Admiral Fairfax that this thing is back in all its glory."

Another crewman shouted out, "Captain, all of our weapons systems just came on line."

"How did that happen?" shouted MacKay.

Mercer held out a phone to Mackay. "I've got Sahir on the line. He's telling me that Argos just activated our weapons systems. His team is actively working to override that action."

"Crazy machine is trying to take over the ship," muttered MacKay, taking the phone from Mercer. "Sahir, we'll address this later. Does Argos have any idea as to what we're facing?"

"Commander Colton," said a crewman, "I've got Admiral Fairfax on the phone for you, sir."

Colton grabbed the phone from the crewman. "Admiral, I may not have much time, but the energy levels that Argos picked up weeks ago is back and even higher than before. There's also some kind of wall, or force, which we can't identify, surrounding the *Eclipse*."

Admiral Fairfax pointed at Lt. Commander Flanagan, who had joined him in his office, and said, "Alert Captain Ramirez and his team that the *Eclipse* is in trouble. Get all ships in the area out to their location immediately. Then advise all our defense aircraft that are in the area to proceed to the *Eclipse* at full speed. I want all NSA and satellite intel from the last hour sent to Captain Ramirez immediately. Once you have all that working, get word to the Chairman of the Joint Chiefs and the Secretary of Defense advising them that I'll be briefing them in the next ten minutes." Turning back to the phone he said, "Colton, your signal is breaking up, but I got the gist of it. What's happening?"

All Fairfax could hear were several bursts of static, intermingled with words. ". . . completely surrounded, we can't . . . everything is blurring, even our . . . ocean has gone . . .

The line had gone dead and Admiral Fairfax slammed down the receiver. Springing up from his desk he took off to join Captain Ramirez, his mind racing, trying to grasp all the implications around what was happening to the *Eclipse*. As he ran down the hall he prayed that this was not the start of another war.

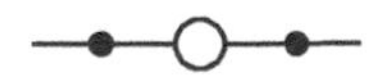

Colton was having trouble hearing the admiral. The bridge was in chaos as none of the ship's systems were responding. "Admiral, this wall, or force, has us completely surrounded, we can't see beyond a hundred yards," Colton shouted into the phone. "Everything is blurring, even our systems have stopped functioning. The ocean has gone completely still."

The bridge of the *Eclipse* was the only thing that Colton could see clearly. Something was happening to him. He could hear the crew around him, but their words sounded chopped up, he was only hearing every other syllable, making it impossible to understand what was being said. It wasn't the unnatural silence that blanketed the *Eclipse* that was keeping him from hearing. Meaning was melting in his mind. The sky, the ocean, all blended into one swirling mass that was rapidly closing in on them. Time wasn't going in the normal course, and his soul was dizzy.

Colton dropped the phone and waited for the inevitable. Suddenly he became extremely light-headed and grabbed onto the wall for support. Then, without warning, the deck seemed to drop beneath his feet as the *Eclipse* and all those aboard slipped into darkness.

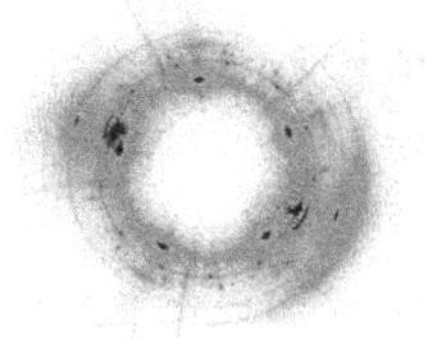

CHAPTER 7

"What's the status on those Hornets?" snapped Ramirez.

"They should be approaching the last reported position of the *Eclipse* in seven-and-a-half minutes sir," answered Miller. She'd been monitoring the *Eclipse* for the last twenty minutes. Once again it had been the satellites that had first picked up on the problem, probably even before the *Eclipse* knew there was anything going on.

She now had the Hornets on her radar, watching as they rapidly closed in. The Boeing F/A 18 E/F Super Hornets were the premier attack fighters flown by the navy and Miller marveled at their capabilities. Armed to the teeth, the Hornets could hit an enemy with devastating impact with airspeed of Mach 1.8. Miller couldn't even imagine being in something going that fast. But this time, unfortunately, it wasn't going to be fast enough. A little over two minutes ago the *Eclipse* had vanished from her screen.

The potential loss of the *Eclipse* made her sick to her stomach. The only thing she could think of that could have taken out a ship like the *Eclipse* that quickly would be a catastrophic explosion. The implications of that alone terrified and saddened her.

The door to the situation room burst open and Ramirez watched as Admiral Fairfax rushed in. Ramirez turned his attention back to the multiple screens in front of him. "It's not good, Admiral."

"I was just talking to Colton when his signal broke up," said Fairfax. "Have we lost all communication links?"

"Sir," said Ramirez, briefly hesitating, "it appears that we have lost the *Eclipse*."

The short statement hit Fairfax hard, confirming his worst fears. "I need more than that, Captain. What happened?"

"Once again, we're not sure. The anomaly that started this whole mission suddenly reappeared. One of our birds picked it up and alerted us to the situation. Right on the heels of that, we received communications from Argos. It had begun to pick up the same energy readings that it had recorded weeks ago when they first arrived. This time, however, the readings were multiples higher than the readings it had previously recorded."

"How is that even possible? From what? Was there some kind of explosion?"

"No sir. Apparently, Lieutenant Sahir thought the same as you, but Argos immediately confirmed that the energy source was not from any kind of explosion, or ordnance, that we're familiar with."

"I don't understand," said Fairfax. "You say the energy levels were significantly higher? Something that powerful just can't materialize and come at us from out of thin air. Was Argos able to pinpoint the source of the energy?"

"At first Argos reported that the *Eclipse* was right on top of it, whatever *it* is. Then Argos corrected its initial report, indicating that the source had repositioned, forming up all around them. As to identifying what it was, or what was creating this enormous amount of energy, there were no definitive readings. Not long after that, all communications with Argos went silent. My guess would be that your call with Commander Colton ended at the same time.

"Sir, the Hornets have just arrived at the *Eclipse*'s last known position," reported Miller.

"Have they spotted the ship?" asked Fairfax.

"No sir. They've made three passes and there is no sign of the *Eclipse*. It's dark, so they're having trouble getting a visual, but they have not been able to pick the ship up on any of their equipment. They're going to start running a grid pattern to see what they can find."

Fairfax looked at Ramirez and asked, "Do we have any other ships in the area?"

"At present we have two cruisers en route. Shall I alert the Coast Guard?"

"Yes, immediately," said Fairfax. "Get everything we have out there. I want that ship found!"

"Miller, contact the Coast Guard," said Ramirez. "Give them the last known coordinates of the *Eclipse* and let them know that we have a ship in trouble." He then turned to Admiral Fairfax. The admiral stood there, staring at one of the large screens in front of him, but Ramirez didn't think he was seeing it. Nothing in the room now seemed very real.

"Admiral," said Ramirez, softly. A couple seconds passed before Fairfax acknowledged Ramirez. "I need a word with you sir."

Fairfax nodded his acceptance and followed Captain Ramirez to a small conference room off to the side. "Would you like some coffee, sir?"

"I'm already having trouble sleeping, Captain. Coffee's the last thing I need."

Ramirez gave a grim smile to his commanding officer. "Understood. Have a seat, Admiral. This may take a while."

"No, I think I need to take this standing up," said Admiral Fairfax. "If what you're about to tell me is half as bad as I've already guessed, then we're in trouble. So please, Captain, tell me what you know."

"There's no way to paint a good picture on this," began Ramirez. "Although our analysis is in its preliminary stage, we're all but certain it's the same phenomenon that we recorded two months ago. It occurred in practically the same location and data we've collected matches up almost identically to what we collected and analyzed the first time."

"Do we have any guess as to what we are dealing with?"

"There's been nonstop, detailed analysis taking place on the data ever since we first collected it, as well as the energy readings that Argos took when the *Eclipse* first arrived on scene. Despite that, we have nothing definitive that we can point to. Everything we collected was fed into Argos. Although I know this is hard to accept, our most probable hypothesis is still the many-worlds theory that was originally suggested," said Ramirez.

"Your 'hole in the ocean' theory," said Fairfax, fighting to keep his frustration, and especially his temper, reigned in.

"Not really a hole, sir. Think of it as being more of an entrance, or gateway, if you will, into another dimension."

"You cannot possibly expect us to go to the White House and report to the president, let alone the Joint Chiefs, that we just lost one of our best equipped, most well-armed, black ops ships to a hole in the time fabric. Oh, and by the way, the ship we lost just happens to contain Argos. If we're lucky we'll be locked up in an insane asylum without the courtesy of a hearing."

"As always, sir, I will be proud to accompany you when you give this report. Together we'll be able to walk them through, in detail, the data that has led us to this conclusion. Data, I might add, that has been confirmed and reinforced by Argos. The results of our research are indisputable."

"Very brave of you, Captain. Hate to have to drag you down with me." Fairfax turned and began to pace back and forth, his head bowed in thought. "When the *Eclipse* arrived on the scene, was the phenomenon still active? Were we still picking up the same data?"

"No sir," answered Ramirez. "When the *Eclipse* first arrived, things were all clear, except for traces of the high energy levels that Argos detected. However, those energy levels quickly dissipated."

"So, to be clear, it seems that we may have two separate events going on in the same area. Coincidence, maybe, but still two separate events. Unless we can prove that the phenomenon and the energy levels are connected, wouldn't that put a bit of a chink into your many-worlds hypothesis, Captain?"

"As I mentioned earlier, we have continually fed all the data we've collected, along with the analysis we've completed, into Argos. We've been as thorough as possible, but even so, didn't want to leave any stone unturned. We wanted to see what conclusions Argos would draw from the same material. We also asked Argos if the energy levels could be connected to the phenomenon in any way."

"And?" demanded Fairfax. His gut told him he wasn't going to like the answer. The good news, if there was any, was that at least Argos would provide a nonbiased, strong level of credibility to the theory they'd settled in on.

"Argos confirmed our findings. In fact, Argos determined that to open such a gateway, it would take an extreme amount of consistent energy to make it functional. Argos surmised that the energy readings it picked up were probably residual energy traces left over from the initial event. Tonight, the phenomenon and the energy levels reappeared at the same time. There's no doubt sir, the two events are most definitely tied together."

A light tapping at the door interrupted them. Ramirez got up and opened it. Miller looked at him and said, "Sir, we have an update for you."

"What is it Miller," snapped Admiral Fairfax.

"One of our two cruisers is now on the scene. The captain just reported that they've not been able to find anything regarding the *Eclipse*. We've also completed our first pass at the data from the two satellites that recorded the entire event. One moment the *Eclipse* is there and then it seems to fade from sight."

"Our birds were able to maintain a visual on the *Eclipse*?" asked Fairfax, finding that hard to believe.

"Via infrared, yes sir, they were. The *Eclipse* has a very distinct heat signature," answered Miller.

"So, what are you saying?" growled Fairfax.

"Sir, we're not quite sure how to interpret the data we have. I mean, we don't know if this is good news or bad news, but so far we haven't been able to find any evidence that the *Eclipse* was even there," said Miller.

"Miller, that's ridiculous," snapped Fairfax, "I'm in no mood for riddles. The *Eclipse* was there. We know that. Get to the point."

"For the *Eclipse* to have just vanished from our screens like it did, we were expecting the worst. There could be no other explanation. But instead of finding evidence of the *Eclipse's* destruction, there's nothing there. There's no oil slick, no debris, nothing that would point to something catastrophic having happened. The search is just getting started, but all things considered, we thought this was a rather significant development."

"Thank you, Miller," said Captain Ramirez. "Return to your post and keep us informed as soon as you get any other updates."

Fairfax stayed where he was, staring at Ramirez. "I guess I'm being a little slow on the uptake, but is Miller suggesting that the *Eclipse* and her crew are okay? I pray to God that's true, I want it more than anything, but ships that size do not just vanish."

Ramirez had walked over and picked up the phone on the conference table. "Miller, forward the infrared feeds from the satellites into the conference room." Ramirez waited for a moment and then said, "Yes, from both satellites. Thank you."

"What are you looking to find?"

"For the moment, I want to see what Miller and the team saw. For all my years in the navy, I've never watched a ship simply vanish."

Ramirez worked at a rapid pace with the keyboard in front of him. The large monitor in the room lit up. The feed was dated, time stamped, and gave the exact coordinates. The screen was dark except for a cylindrical form that had variations in color ranging from dark orange, to red, to a deep, purplish red. "That would be the *Eclipse*," said Ramirez.

"What's causing the bright red coloration midship?" asked Fairfax.

"The *Eclipse* is nuclear powered. That would be the reactor you're seeing."

The screen suddenly began to brighten, giving the appearance that the waters directly under and around the perimeter of the *Eclipse* were on fire, glowing with a bright, orange-yellow tone.

"It was an explosion," muttered Fairfax. "Look at that."

As the two men watched, captivated by what they were seeing, the light began to expand outward from the *Eclipse*, growing in brightness and morphing into a tight ring around the ship of nearly pure, white light, speckled with faint traces of pale yellow. The ring of light continued to brighten, growing in strength. The monitor then appeared to blink. The brightness of the ring diminished significantly but held the same white-hot color as it had before.

"What just happened?" asked Fairfax.

"All of our satellites have the capability to take pictures of anything out there, including the sun. To protect the cameras from being damaged, they have filters especially designed to kick in and filter out light if it becomes too strong. One of those lenses just activated."

"And Argos was measuring all of this?"

"Yes sir. As we discussed, Argos immediately sent the new readings to us and they were impossibly high."

"How could that be?" While the question may have been somewhat rhetorical, Fairfax would have given anything for an answer.

The light continued to grow, spreading out within the circle, closing in on the *Eclipse*. Soon the *Eclipse* was totally enveloped by the light. The infrared signature of the *Eclipse* could still be seen but was beginning to grow fainter. For a few more seconds everything remained the same. Then it happened. Ramirez and Fairfax watched as the *Eclipse* slowly faded from view.

Once the ship had completely disappeared, the light that had engulfed it retreated back to the ring that had surrounded the *Eclipse*. Then it too began to fade and was soon gone. All that was left now was a black screen.

Fairfax dropped down into a chair, continuing to stare at the monitor. "What just happened?" his voice barely above a whisper.

"I don't know, sir. At this point I can only speculate," said Ramirez. He, too, was as shocked and numbed as the admiral by what he'd just witnessed.

"Speculate."

Ramirez cleared his throat. He needed water badly. "My guess, and that's all this is, is that one of two things happened to the *Eclipse*. Either that ship, and all aboard, were disintegrated by a powerful explosion, or . . . ." Ramirez stopped; it was too fantastic even for him. To talk about it and theorize was one thing. To actually see it happen brought a chilling reality to him that he wasn't ready to accept.

"Or what, Captain?"

"Or we just watched one of the finest ships in this man's navy pass through a portal into another dimension," answered Ramirez. "May God be with them."

The gentle rocking of the ship let Colton know that he hadn't yet left the land of the living. For some reason his eyes were shut and at first, he couldn't remember where he was. Surprisingly, he was still standing. Upon opening his eyes, he found that he had a death grip on the wall and just as tight of a grip on the navigation console in front of him.

The pain in his head was intense. It kept pounding away, so bad that it felt like his head was getting ready to split down the middle. Colton's stomach was in equally bad shape, feeling just like it had the day after he'd graduated from SEAL Qualification Training Class 348. But he was alive!

Things had changed, he could feel it, but couldn't grasp exactly what had changed. Slowly, his mind began to sift through things. The air was thicker, far more humid than it had been, laced with a strong, pungent odor that wasn't helping his stomach at all. His mind struggled to nail what could be causing this smell, but he just couldn't identify it. It was then he noticed the chaos around him.

If he'd blacked out, it had only been for a few moments. It was still night. The storm, or whatever that had been, had passed, and the *Eclipse* now rested in relatively calm waters. MacKay was on the floor, sitting with his back to the helm. There was a small cut above his left eye, the blood having stained his uniform. He, too, was just coming out of it and looked up at Colton. "What happened?"

Although not yet that steady on his own two feet, Colton leaned over and helped MacKay up off the floor. As best as he could tell, everyone on the bridge had sustained some kind of injury. Like him and the captain, the rest of the crew on the bridge were just coming around, all of them acting dazed and disoriented. "I have no idea. One minute we're about to be wiped out by a monstrous wave and the next thing I know the sea is as calm as a bathtub," replied Colton.

"My head is killing me," said MacKay. Reaching up, he gently touched the cut on his forehead, winced, and left it alone. Looking around the bridge, it was easy to see that several of his men had been bounced around. He asked if anyone was seriously injured, but other than some minor cuts and bruises, everyone was okay. Hatfield, the sonar operator, was cradling his left arm. Looking at Colton, MacKay said, "You don't look so good, Commander."

"Back at you. But then, you didn't look all that good when I first came on board," Colton said, trying to craft a smile. "My head feels like it's splitting in half."

Petty Officer Hatfield had ridden the storm out at his station. Somehow, he'd kept himself from being thrown out of his chair, but had nonetheless injured his arm. Although his head throbbed like everyone else's, and his arm ached terribly, he was distracted by something much more disturbing, something that didn't make any sense at all. Hatfield's expression drew Colton's attention and watched as the young sailor fought one-handed with the various dials and controls in front of him.

"Mr. Mercer, you in one piece?" asked MacKay of his first officer.

"I think so sir, but my head feels like a new recruit returning from his first shore leave. Apparently, my head hit the deck hard, but it doesn't seem to have broken the skin."

"Good. It appears we're all in one piece. Get me status reports from all stations. I've no idea what that thing was, but it seems to have left us intact. Find out how many casualties we've sustained and get me an update on our operational status. Dr. Severin is going to be a very busy guy over the next several hours."

"Aye, aye, Skipper," said Mercer.

Colton walked over to Hatfield and stood behind the young crewman. "Problem, Petty Officer Hatfield?"

The young crewman didn't take his eyes away from the screens in front of him. "Sir, I'm just not sure. It looks like our sonar, as well as even our navigational controls, are totally hosed."

"What's going on?" asked MacKay, joining the two men.

"Sir, I don't get it. When that wave came at us we were in four thousand feet of water. The readings I'm getting now say that the bottom is only seven hundred feet below us. I don't see how that's possible. Could we have been carried by that wave into much shallower water?"

"I rather doubt that," answered MacKay. "It has to be your instruments. Have you run a system check?"

"Yes sir, twice. I've even rebooted the entire system and I keep getting the same readings."

"Stay with it, Petty Officer Hatfield. Let me know what you find." Picking up the phone, he entered Sahir's number. It took several rings before Sahir answered. He didn't sound good at all. In fact, he sounded as if he was barely hanging on, slight traces of panic evident in his voice. "Mr. Sahir, is everything all right in your area?"

"No sir, I mean, yes sir, my team is okay, although crewman Hightower fell, and it appears may have broken her arm. She's on her way to sick bay. We have some other minor injuries, but that's about it," said Sahir.

"You don't sound like yourself," said MacKay. "What's going on down there?"

"Sir, Argos has completely shut down! That's never happened before and frankly, sir, it's not supposed to be able to happen. Ever. Under any circumstances. We're trying to get it back on line, but something has either destroyed its programing or caused Argos to shut itself down, both of which are nearly impossible scenarios."

MacKay looked at Colton and said, "You need to hear this. We may have lost Argos." He put the call on speaker, replacing the phone in its cradle. "How could this happen?"

"If it turns out that something shut Argos down, then, at least for now, I'm as in the dark as you are. There are no external forces out there, at least none we're aware of, that could accomplish that. As systems go, Argos is as close to being impregnable as you can get."

"And yet, here we are," said Colton. "So, if Argos turned itself off, why would it do that?"

"That would only occur under the most extreme circumstances and would be a defensive move if it were to implement such a protocol."

"Defense against what?" asked MacKay. "You just told me that Argos is impregnable. Has your area been breached?"

"No sir, nothing like that," said Sahir. "If somehow Argos became, overloaded, for lack of a better word, with data at such an immense level that the feed could potentially damage Argos, then, strictly as a defensive move, Argos would take itself off-line."

MacKay stared at the phone for a moment. Computer systems were not his long suit. "Update me as soon as you can."

Colton shrugged his shoulders. "The only possibility that Sahir gave us as being practical is that somehow it became 'overloaded'?" Colton smiled at MacKay. "Didn't think a computer could do that, but it sounds like our impregnable Argos may have fainted."

Before MacKay could reply, Mercer joined the two men. "We had seventeen crewmen injured. Fortunately, only three of the injuries are serious. Severin believes that they'll recover, but they're out of action for quite a few days. In addition to that, we have two men missing. I have a search of the ship already underway. Regarding the ship itself, as you said, we seem to be in one piece but many of our systems don't seem to be functioning properly."

"Explain," said MacKay.

"For starters, as Hatfield pointed out, we're now in much shallower water than before that wave washed over us. Also, we were well over a hundred miles from shore, but now we're picking up a giant landmass just six hundred yards to starboard. To top everything else off, it appears that all our communications are dead," said Mercer.

"Dead?" queried Colton.

"Yes sir, at least that's how it looks. We have not been able to reach anyone on the radio, and we also haven't been able to get any feeds from our satellites. What's even stranger is that we aren't even able to pick up anything on regular radio, I'm talking nothing on any of the AM or FM bands."

"Well, whatever the wave was comprised of, it seems to have fried our communications gear," said MacKay.

"Not sure if this is good news or bad news, but that's not it. We immediately ran a system check on our communications gear and they all check out as being undamaged. But then you try to use them, and they don't function as they should. Had they been fried, as you suggested, you would not have been able to have the call you just had with Sahir. For some reason, we're cut off from everything outside this ship. I just can't tell you why."

"The landmass to starboard," said Colton. "Have you been able to identify it?"

"Without the satellites, no, we've not been able to do that. At first, I thought we'd strayed into some small, isolated island, but radar indicates otherwise. From the size of it, we could be right off the coast of Florida."

"Gentleman, I need some fresh air. Would you join me outside?" asked MacKay.

Colton and Mercer followed MacKay outside the bridge and all three men stared off into the inky blackness. In the distance they could see the faint silhouette of land, but not one light pierced the darkness. The air was thick with humidity and the same odor that had assaulted Colton as he came to was even more pronounced.

"Well," said Mercer, "wherever we are, it doesn't look like anybody's home."

"I wonder if the same thing that is affecting our communications gear could have knocked out the power on the mainland," said Colton. "It scares me to think of the possibilities, but the facts we're facing are starting to lead me to some pretty serious conclusions."

"What are you suggesting?" asked MacKay.

Colton gave a small smile, but there was no humor in it. "You know what I'm suggesting. It's why we're standing outside. We may be at war. We may have encountered the effects of a first strike, which would account for the loss of all communications, as well as the mainland being completely blacked out. That might also explain why Argos was 'overloaded.' "

MacKay nodded his agreement. "That was my first thought. Once Sahir gets Argos back up and running we'll check for radiation levels in the air."

"Our compasses are still working," said Mercer. "Shall I plot a course to take us back to base?"

"That's going to be tough to do if we can't figure out exactly where we are, and at the moment, that does seem to be in question," said Colton. "And if we are at war, then there's a good chance that our base no longer exists. I recommend waiting until we can at least get Argos back up and see what information we can pull from it."

Everyone who signed up for the military had trained for this very day. But no one, in their darkest nightmares, ever expected it to happen. Nuclear war was a no-win option for anyone.

MacKay sighed deeply, leaned back against the wall, and gazed up into the night sky. There was a thick mist in the air, but the breeze around them occasionally made it give way, allowing them to clearly see the star-filled sky. "Can't recall the last time I've seen the sky this bright. Even as a kid, I used to love going out on a summer's night and seeing how many constellations I could pick . . . ." his voice, rather suddenly, trailed off.

Colton looked over at MacKay and was shocked to see the look on his face. It was one of pure, unadulterated fear and confusion. "Captain, are you all right?"

MacKay could not pull his eyes away from the night sky. "It's wrong," he whispered. "This can't be. It's all wrong."

He'd started to slide down the wall, but Colton got to him in time to keep him from falling to the deck. "It's okay; we'll get you down to sick bay."

MacKay, getting his legs back under him, jerked his arm away from Colton. "I don't need a doctor," he nearly shouted. "I need someone to explain to me what is going on around here. Look at it! Can't you see?"

"What is it?" said Colton. "What am I missing?" Colton's training had prepared him to face the unexpected, to be ready no matter what happened. Too many times he'd seen people break down when the pressure was on. He knew how much of a threat those people posed to themselves and to the mission. Even though it would be completely out of character for him, Colton feared that MacKay may have reached his limit.

"It's the stars," answered MacKay. Mercer was also staring intently into the sky. The realization of what MacKay had seen hit him with the same staggering impact. "They're all wrong."

"This can't be," said Mercer, more to himself than anyone.

"MacKay," snapped Colton, "tell me what you're seeing."

MacKay finally broke away and looked Colton in the eye, struggling to control his emotions. "The stars aren't where they're supposed to be. It's not possible, but they're not. Mr. Colton, I don't recognize this sky."

"I don't understand," said Colton.

"Neither do we, Colton," said Mercer, "but that's not our sky."

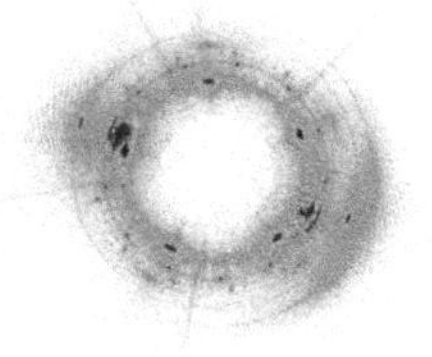

CHAPTER 8

The sun was just starting to breach the horizon as the senior officers gathered in the briefing room just off the bridge. There was a slate color to the world, something unreal. It was a somber crowd, many of them looking like they'd just come from a bar fight. The wave, or whatever it was that hit them, had tossed the crew around, resulting in several injuries. To his credit, despite a deep cut across his forearm, Hezekiah had already brought in coffee for them in two large thermoses. Except for Colton and Garrett, who were leaning against the wall, everyone was seated around the table.

MacKay stood at the head of the conference table. Despite the ventilation, the air was thick, the humidity terrible. A heavy rain had settled over the ship. He didn't have much in the way of information to share with his team and he prayed their training would see them through. No one had relevant experience, but quite a few had seen combat. He had to convince them they could handle this, whatever the hell this was.

"It's good to be standing here with you this morning," said MacKay. "There were a few times last night when I wasn't sure how things were going to turn out. I can tell you this; Hezekiah's coffee has never tasted so good." They all smiled at this, a few giving way to quiet laughter.

"I know that each of you have questions. Clearly, we have a great deal to discuss, so we'll get right to it. Although what we experienced may indeed have been the first strike in a war, as many of us have already speculated, we really don't know if that's true. It falls to each of you to keep your teams focused. I cannot stress the importance of that enough. It is imperative that the sailors serving under you do not start to panic over pure speculation. We'll soon know what happened, and at that time we will face head-on whatever it is we're up against.

"Dr. Severin, would you please give us an update on casualties?" Dr. Severin stayed seated. Remarkably he was one of the few officers who had not been injured. Severin, easily in his late forties, made a point of eating right and staying in shape. His business was health, and therefore, he felt a need to practice what he preached.

There were several papers piled in front of him, but he didn't refer to them once. "Close to two-thirds of the crew sustained a broad spectrum of injuries, but none, fortunately, are in any way life threatening. Sadly, it appears that we may have lost two of the crew. Initially we had two men missing. One has been found, crewman Harris. He fell and landed behind one of the engines, striking his head against the support braces. I'm sorry to report that crewman Harris died from his injuries. The second crewmember, Ensign Nadir, is still missing. The last time he was seen, he'd stepped outside to smoke a cigarette."

"Thank you, Doctor," said MacKay. With the medical report finished, he wasn't exactly sure how to proceed. MacKay had been in tight situations before—this was not his first rodeo—but he'd never found himself at a loss for words. The problem this time was that there were so many unknowns, and the facts they did have didn't make any sense. The significant change in the climate, their sudden proximity to land, and the depth of the water beneath them was vastly different from where they'd been. All of this was so fantastic that he really didn't know where to begin. And that list didn't include the impossible positioning of the stars he'd witnessed in the sky above them. That alone scared him to his core.

So, as experience had taught him, when in doubt, trust in the basics, delegate. "Mr. Colton, would you care to give the crew an update as to where things stand?"

Colton could see the frustration in MacKay's face. These were his people. He was their leader. Many of them had served under him for years, and they'd all come to trust him. So how do you stand up in front of your crew and tell them that not only do you have no idea what happened, but what you do know is so impossibly fantastic that none of it makes sense?

Colton moved to where MacKay had been standing, looking at the anxious faces in front of him. There was an air, a sense of strength about Colton that was hard to define. Leading teams in dangerous situations came naturally to him, his presence alone exuding a sense of calm in even the darkest of times. He was a man that others instantly trusted, someone they instinctively knew they could rely on.

"Thank you, Captain. What we first thought was a rogue wave heading straight at us turned out to be some kind of massive energy wave that, for lack of a better explanation, engulfed the *Eclipse*. That said, we're only guessing that it was an energy wave, and that's primarily based on how it affected many of our systems. The blackouts, the nausea, and the terrible headaches that almost all of us experienced we believe were due to this wave, but we don't yet know why."

Dr. Severin interjected at this point. "I guess I should say that the good news, as far as we can tell, is that there aren't any long-term, negative effects from this. However, should any of the people in your command start to have recurring issues, get them to sick bay right away."

Colton continued, his voice strong, steady, confident, providing a calm that was desperately needed. "As crazy as things have been up to now, here are the facts as we know them. Unfortunately, they're going to create more questions than they answer. Prior to the wave hitting us we were in more than four thousand feet of water. The ocean floor now lies just seven hundred feet beneath us. We were roughly 120 miles off the coast of Florida. There now appears to be a very large landmass six hundred yards to port. Six hundred yards! We went from being at sea to suddenly almost being docked."

"Excuse me, Commander, but how is any of this possible?" asked Lieutenant Tanner. "Could we have blacked out long enough to have drifted that far from our previous position?"

"Of all the crewmen we've talked to, we don't think anyone was out for longer than maybe thirty seconds," said Dr. Severin. "In fact, there were a small number of crewmen who didn't black out at all, but they're now suffering significant inner ear problems, causing them to have issues with balance."

"Both are good questions, Lieutenant," said Colton, "questions that we will find answers for. We have also lost all communications with our satellites and have not been able to reach anyone, civilian or military. At this point we're not even able to pick up any normal radio bands. This too is all but impossible, and yet that's the position in which we find ourselves."

There was more, but Colton paused long enough to let all of this settle in. While he was doing his best to calmly communicate their situation, he was all but convinced that they were at war. There were very few alternatives that he could think of that would explain at least some of what they'd experienced. But perhaps the hardest fact to understand, the hardest fact to explain, was yet to come.

"I'm afraid there's one more fun fact I need to share with you. This would have passed right by me but was spotted by the captain and Mr. Mercer. It seems that even the stars have shifted. Captain, I'll let you explain this one."

MacKay stood there slightly nodding his head. It was the posture of a man who'd witnessed an accident but couldn't wrap his mind around the horror he'd just seen. "Afraid there's not much more that I can say to elaborate on what Mr. Colton has just shared with you. Thanks to my dad and my grandfather, as a teenager I was able to navigate my way home just by using the stars. At Annapolis, I studied astronomy in far more depth.

All I can tell you is that the night sky that we saw after that wave passed over us is not the sky I'm used to seeing."

"I'm not sure I understand what you're saying," said Father Ryan. "Do you mean it's completely different, or just looks different as if we were suddenly in a different hemisphere?"

MacKay looked at Father Ryan a couple of moments before answering. "Mr. Mercer and I were equally shocked. What I'm trying to say is that it is completely different, which I know isn't possible, but it is. To put it another way, I've never seen that sky before, which tells me that I have no idea where we are. Hopefully, if we can get Argos back on line, we'll get some help in figuring all this out."

Years of listening to confessions told Father Ryan that the captain suspected more than he was admitting to.

The room went silent, everyone struggling with their own thoughts, trying to reign in the fear that was coursing through them. Just as MacKay was doing, they too would be sharing all this information with their people. As hard as it had hit them, they could only imagine how their teams would react. A gnawing sense of loss and uncertainty began to set in.

"Finally, there is one last item I want to cover with you and it doesn't leave this room," said Colton. "When Admiral Fairfax assigned me to this mission, it was a real shot in the dark. Neither he, nor his staff, had any idea of what we might find. In the event we did encounter hostile activity, the admiral gave written orders to Captain MacKay and myself stating that at my discretion, I would take over command of the *Eclipse*."

The expressions on the faces looking back at him ran the gambit from shock to barely concealed anger. "You're taking command?" said Garrett, her voice hard and cold. "So, is this your way of telling us that we're caught up in the middle of some crazy black ops mission? Tell us, Commander, what is going on here?"

"Captain," snapped MacKay, "you are addressing a senior officer. You will show the appropriate respect at all times."

Colton raised his hands to quiet the room. "The reason I'm sharing this with you is so that from here on out there won't be any secrets between us. A very wise man told me how strong and talented the crew of the *Eclipse* is. He told me that not only should I trust you, but that I should do all I can to earn your trust. So, I'm being as open and transparent as I can. Under the circumstances I want you to know all that I know."

"What the commander is telling you is completely accurate," said MacKay. "Also, I agreed with him that this is something you needed to know."

"So, sir, if I may ask, are you taking command? To be 'transparent,' is this some kind of black ops that we've stumbled into?" asked Lieutenant Tanner, backing up Garrett.

"Things have been moving so fast that Captain MacKay and I haven't had too much time to talk," answered Colton. "However, in answer to your questions, no, I have no intention of taking command of the *Eclipse*. As to whether this is tied to a secret operation, frankly, I wish it were. At least then we'd have some idea as to what is going on. However, and I do want what I'm about to say to be clear and understood by all, for all activity that we may engage in ashore, I will be in command. Any questions?"

"Thank you, Commander," said Father Ryan. "Your candor is greatly appreciated. Captain, on a different note, have we heard anything from any of our other ships?"

"No. As I stated earlier, we have not been able to establish communications with anyone, military or civilian. Frankly, we're not even sure where we are, so until we get more information we're holding our position," said MacKay. "Mr. Sahir, do you have a status update on Argos?"

"The good news is that Argos took itself off-line as a defensive measure," said Sahir. "Fortunately, as best as we've been able to determine, it did not sustain any damage. Argos is in Orientation Mode."

Colton asked, "What does that mean?"

"Argos maintains a dynamic world simulation. In other words, Argos stays up-to-date with the world on a ten-minute basis. It monitors radio, TV, the World Wide Web, and various other indices of the world. Just as you are aware of nearly a trillion signals a minute in your body, Argos is aware of a sextillion signals a minute from all over the world."

Colton shook his head no; he wasn't following.

Sahir sighed and tried another tack. "Let's say you wake up. It's two hours after you were supposed to be at work. You have a massive headache. A memory of hanging out at a cheap airport bar, and beside you is another human being covered in a sheet. You're not sure if it's a known lover, a one-night stand, etc. You have a theory, based on your past, whether it's male or female. You are fairly sure the mystery guest is alive. So, you lie very still and try to figure out what's going on. You are in Orientation Mode."

Colton grinned. Some folks laughed out loud. It was the first tension-breaking moment in several hours.

Colton asked, "So how long does Orientation Mode last?"

Sahir's voice was a little high when he answered. "About ten seconds. We tried simulating a fake news scenario. We fed Argos the 1938 broadcast of *War of the Worlds*. Argos went into Orientation Mode for fourteen seconds and then told us we were running a test based on a historical hoax, possible from the period preceding World War II."

"Well, good," said Father Ryan. "The machine isn't going to let us put one over on it. What's your next step?"

"Judging from the depth of Argos' abilities," answered Sahir, "it would be more interesting to determine who Mr. Colton picked up in that airport bar."

This prompted sincere laughter. Except from Colton.

"Mr. Sahir, please tell us what you've found," directed Colton. His voice was low, almost neutral in tone, and yet there was a faint, unmistakable edge to it. The tension continued to eat away at everyone.

"Oh, yes sir, be happy to. We're having trouble understanding all the data, but we've made progress on some of the information that we were able to get from Argos, information that it gathered just before it shut down. As described by Captain MacKay, we were engulfed by some kind of energy wave."

"My guess would be that we experienced some level of nuclear event," said Garrett. Colton noticed the bruising along the side of her face, just below her eye, spreading out along her jaw. Even with the injury Colton had trouble viewing her as a rough, tough marine captain. It wasn't that he doubted her capabilities. She was just too attractive. It was distracting. "That could potentially explain the issues we've been having with our electronic systems."

"That was our first thought as well," said Sahir. "But when you look at how high the energy levels were, it's clear that we were wrong. We can't even begin to guess at what generated that energy wave, but the levels it reached were several multiples higher than any nuclear weapon the United States has in its arsenal."

"I don't understand how that can even be possible," said MacKay. "If something that strong hit us, how is it that we're still here talking about it?"

Before Sahir could respond to Captain MacKay, Colton said, "Lieutenant, is that everything you have? You said you were having trouble understanding all the data. It's important, no matter how odd it may be, that you do not leave anything out. Please tell us everything you've found, then we'll discuss your findings."

"Hopefully my team and I will know more later today, but we're scrambling for answers. We are only just now beginning to develop a working hypothesis as to what might have caused Argos to shut down," said Sahir. Like the rest of them, the whole event had him just as rattled. He didn't have the answers and it was clear that what he did have scared him to death. "Frankly, none of us have ever seen anything like this before."

"Lieutenant, we're not attacking you," said Father Ryan soothingly, trying to take some of the pressure off Sahir. The tension in the room had become palpable. "Like you, we're trying to come to grips with all this and at the present, you are our best source of information."

Sahir looked at the priest, nodded, and continued. "What we are calling an energy wave is at best a misnomer. It was far more than the burst of energy you would expect from the detonation of a bomb. This thing was extremely powerful and yet seems to have been controlled. It was able to maintain extremely high levels of energy at a constant rate, and at the same time hammered everything and everyone on this ship with data probes at speeds that we can't even measure. That thing was scanning us, probing us from stem to stern repeatedly at impossible speeds. That is why Argos turned itself off. Simply put, it was too much for it to handle. And folks, Argos is the best our world has to offer. At least we thought it was."

The impact of what Sahir said hit hard. The information he shared was frightening, and like so many other things, created even more questions. He couldn't have presented more unsettling news if he'd tried.

"I'm not following you," said MacKay. "For that matter, I didn't understand half of what you just said. But I do understand that whatever it was is bigger than anything we've got, it hit us, and yet we're still here. Again, how can that be? Or perhaps now would be a good time for Father Ryan to give us as much detail as he can about purgatory."

"Excuse me for interrupting again, but I'm not sure it was a weapon," mused Colton. MacKay looked at him, waiting for him to explain.

"Not a weapon?" said Tanner, almost shouting. "Our communications are shot. We have no idea where we are. We're told that whatever hit us was too overwhelming, too intense for the most sophisticated computer on the planet. And to wrap it all up, for all intents and purposes, we've been effectively taken out of action. If that's not a weapon, then what the hell was it?" said Tanner.

"Everyone in this room is military. So, every one of us knows that the weapons we've been trained on are designed to do one of two things, kill people or break things. Yet neither of those things happened. Yes, we've sustained casualties, but unless I'm mistaken, those were due to our falling as we blacked out. The casualties were accidental. While our systems went off-line, as best we can tell, they've not been damaged and are fully functional. As weapons go, it would be the gentlest weapon I've ever heard of."

"And our communications gear, our navigation systems? Did they black out too?" pressed Tanner.

"In their own way, yes," answered Colton. "Practically everything we have on this ship, radar, navigation, everything went nuts when that wave hit us. But the systems weren't destroyed. The *Eclipse* is still in one piece. I'll agree that it was very disruptive. It's left us in one terrible spot, but I've never heard of any weapon designed to do that. And it's especially hard to imagine anyone using such a weapon as its choice for a first strike against an enemy as powerful as the United States. When you add in the sustained energy levels that Sahir shared with us, you can make a pretty compelling argument that this wasn't meant to hurt us."

"Then what was it supposed to do?" asked Tanner. "What was that thing?" Most of the wind had been taken out of his sails, but like the rest of them, he didn't want to stop pushing. He wanted answers.

"Let me share with you an embarrassing event from my past," said Colton. "I was married once. Briefly. Our first night was spent in a hotel in Trenton, New Jersey. While my wife and I were getting acquainted, six of my friends, with some 'borrowed' heavy equipment, picked up my Volkswagen, moved it six miles to a baseball diamond, and built a snowman family around it. When my wife and I started looking for our car after breakfast, the first thousand thoughts we had didn't involve snowmen, public parks, or that my best man's uncle leased heavy equipment. Our thoughts centered around malicious car theft."

"Are you saying we're being pranked?" asked Father Ryan.

"No, Padre. I'm saying we haven't figured out our blind spots. That means there's a good chance that it's not a weapon, but something that we haven't even considered."

"Mr. Mercer," called Petty Officer Briggs, "the port watch has spotted something."

Mercer moved over to the communications station that Briggs was monitoring. Briggs had been constantly scanning the airwaves to see if he could lock on to broadcasts from anywhere. Low levels of static and silence were all that he could find. "Have you been able to pick anything up yet?"

"No sir, it's nuts. I'm hardly even getting any static. This is really weird. The airwaves are completely silent. There's nothing out there," answered Briggs. "I'll keep trying."

Mercer took the receiver from him. "This is Mercer. What have you got?"

"Sir, you need to step outside the bridge and listen to this. The fog over there is still so thick that I can't see anything, but it sounds like there's one heck of a fight going on."

Handing the receiver back to Briggs, Mercer quickly stepped outside. The railing was wet from the mist and the high humidity, but he used it for support. Leaning against it, he tried focusing in on the distant shore through his binoculars. There the mist was even heavier, creating a thick, wet blanket hugging the ground. As the sun continued to rise, he began to be able to pick out a few trees here and there.

It wasn't long before he too could hear what the port watch had reported. Even though they were parked about a quarter mile offshore, he could hear screams emanating over and over again. It sounded like more than one creature screaming, but he had no way of being sure. One thing he did know was that it didn't sound human. Some of the screams were so intense that he was confident that something was being killed.

"That's been going on for about five minutes," said Petty Officer Klimek. Mercer had not heard the young seaman approach and it startled him. Klimek, in his midtwenties, was tall and lanky, with tattoos running up his right arm.

"It doesn't sound human," said Mercer, "but then I'm not sure I've ever heard an animal make a sound like that." He continued to stare at the shore, trying to catch a glimpse of what was going on.

"Whatever's happening over there, I think it's starting to settle down. About ten minutes ago it was even louder, and there were at least two or three different creatures crying out," said Klimek. "I didn't have any way of recording it, so I called to alert you. The screams are so strange, so loud, it would be pretty hard to describe."

"Well, wherever we are, we now know that there are critters ashore. And from the sound of it, I'd say rather large critters. Get back to your post, Klimek," directed Mercer. "You spot anything at all, let me know immediately.

"Aye, aye, sir," said Klimek.

Briggs looked intently at Mercer as he rejoined them on the bridge. The look on Mercer's face was a mixture of concern and confusion. "Shall I call the captain?"

Mercer gave it a moment's thought, then slowly shook his head. "No, I can't do that to him. Why add one more thing to the list of stuff we can't explain?"

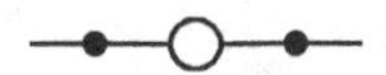

"Until we know otherwise, we will be operating at general quarters as if we are at war," said MacKay. "Captain Garrett, as OIC I'll ask you to coordinate with Mr. Mercer. I want the crew fully armed and I want two-man patrols to get started immediately. Sahir, as soon as you can, launch some drones and send them ashore. I want to know where we are."

"I'll join Sahir and give him a hand," said Colton. "Between Argos and the drones, we should be able to start piecing this thing together rather quickly."

"Does anyone have anything else to report before we get back to work?" asked MacKay.

"I do," said Colton. "Father Ryan, I'd like to ask you to visit with as many of the crew as you can, along with the civilians on board."

Father Ryan knew that this was a direct order and not a request, but he appreciated the way Colton approached it. He too was concerned about the crew and how all of this would affect them. "Commander, I was already planning to do that very thing."

"Good. I want us to stay as close as possible to the mood of the crew. No matter how well people are trained, everyone reacts differently under stress. The goal is to be able to address any issues that may come up as quickly as we can," said Colton.

"Commander, generally speaking, I'm not a pessimistic man, but I need for every one of you officers to stay sharp and watch your people closely as possible," said Father Ryan. "The military training that our people have been given will help them a great deal, but at the end of the day, they're still people. Depression will become as big of a problem as any enemy we may face. If it does turn out that we're as isolated as it seems, then the separation from their loved ones, the not knowing, the worry that they'll never get back, I'm afraid that depression will become a big problem for us, probably sooner than you'd expect. It has been my experience that we humans tend to shut down in the face of the unknown."

"Thank you, Father, we'll all keep a close watch," said MacKay. "Alright, let's get to it."

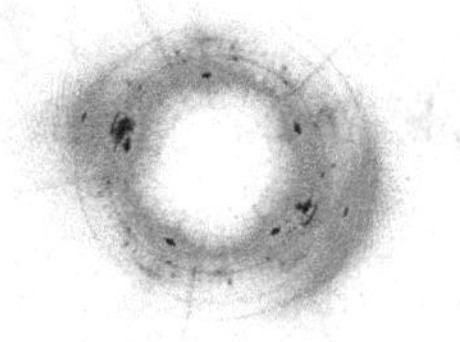

CHAPTER 9

A crew operating at general quarters is a crew with a lot to do. With the threat of war hanging over their heads, things that would normally have been routine now became infused with an unspoken level of anxiety. That morning everyone on the *Eclipse* was at their station, making sure everything on board was in tip-top shape in anticipation of being pulled into a fight. They all knew that this constant state of preparation could mean the difference between life and death.

Dr. Meinhard, although first loudly objecting to having his team being ordered around, reluctantly pitched in and helped the crew with several of the electronic systems that had been acting up ever since the wave had hit them. Personally, he felt that this kind of labor was beneath him. However, his low opinion of the military quickly brought him to the conclusion that things wouldn't get back on track without him.

Colton, who had a fair amount of experience tinkering with drones, worked closely with Sahir's team to get the drones prepped and in the air. Dr. Brennan, a member of Meinhard's team, worked to further fine-tune the cameras attached to the drones. As this was one of his areas of expertise, the fine-tuning that he applied helped to greatly enhance the pictures they'd be sending back.

The patrols ordered by Captain MacKay were in full swing. Despite the advanced scanning systems housed on the *Eclipse*, both MacKay and

Colton agreed that human intelligence was just as important. Looking down from the bridge, Mercer spotted the two men walking patrol on the starboard side of the ship. As sailors go, they were practically polar opposites and their differences made them comical to look at. Mercer smiled and turned away.

Hans Magnor, a thirty-eight-year navy veteran, stood barely over five feet tall. Over the years he'd gradually put on more weight than a man of his stature should carry, but he could still keep pace with most of the young sailors he served with. The navy had taken Magnor all over the world and he was quite willing to share his stories about the things he'd experienced with anyone who would listen. Unfortunately, for those sailors serving with Magnor, he tended to share the same stories over and over again.

He was more than opinionated, very old school, and played host to a naturally grumpy demeanor. Despite all this, he was a crew favorite and surprisingly got along with almost everyone. Affectionately he was known as "Skipper."

His patrol partner towered over him, standing at just under six foot five. Barrel chested and well-muscled, Blaine Dempsey was in his late twenties and looked more like a lineman for the NFL. Naturally quiet, he was the perfect audience for Magnor. Dempsey had served in the navy for a little more than two years. During that time, he'd proven himself to be one of the best, hence his deployment on the *Eclipse*. As they walked along, the subject at hand was their current predicament and whether they were actually lost.

"I'm telling you, this is nothing," growled Skipper. "A ship like the *Eclipse* can do a lot of things but getting lost isn't one of them. We're also not at war The whole thing is ridiculous."

"I don't know, Skipper. Not so sure you're right about this," said Dempsey. "An hour ago, I ran into Hightower. She told me about the briefing she and her team got from Sahir and it sounded like they're pretty sure we just survived the first strike in a major war."

"If this is a war, then it's the most peaceful war I've ever been in. I swear you plebes are starting to jump at your own shadows."

"Well that wave that hit us sure as hell wasn't a shadow," said Dempsey.

"Look, the ocean is a vast and mysterious place. There's a lot out there we don't understand. Ever since man first put to sea there have been all kinds of unexplainable things happen," said Skipper. Glancing at the young sailor, Skipper studied his victim and tried to keep his face as stern as possible. *If you can't pick on the young ones, who can you pick on?* "On the other hand, and I hadn't thought much about this, we are officially in the Bermuda Triangle. Maybe we should be on the lookout for the kraken?"

"Knock it off, Skipper. We both know that's one of the biggest myths there ever was. All I'm saying is that I've been watching and listening to the officers and they're worried. More worried than usual."

"Officers worry all the time," sneered Skipper. "Sometimes I think they're paid to worry. If it weren't for men like us, this whole place would go to rot. The truly sad part, if you want my opinion, is that all they're really worried about is making admiral, confused as to which hind end to kiss next."

"So why do they have us on full alert?" pressed Dempsey. "They didn't do that for nothing."

"Will you stop whining like some little girl? You've got nothing to worry about, believe me. This isn't bad. But do you want to know what is bad? Did I ever tell you about that time in the Indian Ocean when the sun didn't come up? Now that was bad." Dempsey just shook his head and smiled to himself. He let his hand skip atop the railing as they walked along, bracing himself for another unbelievable Skipper tale.

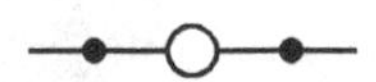

It had two moods, hungry and angry-hungry. Something new was in its territory, so it was angry-hungry. Its rival had a shell, and parts of it smelled like flesh, so those were the parts to seek out. The soft parts were all above the waterline.

Cautiously he glided through the warm water, staying close to the surface, alert to anything that could pose a threat. He could feel the odd vibrations from this new creature as they coursed through the water. The closer he got, the stronger the vibrations became. They told him that whatever had ventured into his waters was big. But that didn't matter. He'd killed other creatures larger than himself, many, many times. Rather than feel fear about the situation, the intrusion angered him, and the anger spurred him on, increasing the speed of his approach. He could smell it now, and he was hungry.

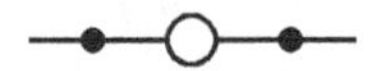

The amazing amount of sea life moving in and out beneath the ship amazed Hatfield. The sonar monitors at his station displayed an unusually large amount of fish for the Atlantic, assuming, of course, they were still in the Atlantic. Ever since the wave of energy had passed over them, their world had completely changed.

Hatfield had pointed this out to Commander Mercer, both men in awe over the extraordinary abundance of sea life. School after school of fish, all living in tight proximity, filled the sea around them. Although Hatfield couldn't say exactly what kind of fish they were looking at, the schools of fish produced distinct signatures on his monitor, especially by the way they moved.

What surprised him most was the number of large fish inhabiting the area. These, without a doubt, were predators. Their presence provided him with all the information he needed to decide that he wouldn't be doing any diving off the side of the ship. A twelve-foot something had just passed under them, and for all the right reasons, had been dominating his attention since he spotted it.

His attention was now drawn to this new and much larger creature coming at them at a remarkable rate of speed. It was huge, close to forty feet in length. He first thought that a small submarine was heading right at them, but the signature kept changing in such a way that he determined that it couldn't be any kind of sub he'd ever heard of. Further, it didn't move like a sub. Could it be two or three large fish swimming together? Then, suddenly, its rate of approach dramatically increased. He couldn't take any chances.

"Mr. Mercer, you need to take a look at this."

"What have we got?" asked Mercer, standing behind him and looking at the monitors.

"I'm not sure, but it's big and it's headed directly towards us."

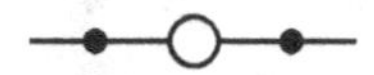

Self-preservation finally slowed the creature down. Scars running across its back gave evidence of previous fights, fights that could have gone either way. While these injuries had not made him any less aggressive, they had taught him to size up his prey before rushing in headfirst. Raising his large head, barely breaking the water's surface, he gazed at the large ship in front him. Of course, he had no idea what a ship was. Not moving, it appeared to be just another large rock. But there were things moving on the rock, two that he could see. Small creatures were tasty creatures.

Diving down away from the surface, his broad back briefly broke through the surface, the sun reflecting off it. Leveling off in about twenty feet of water, he moved towards the ship, a blood lust driving him forward. He'd take one more quick look before attacking, just to pinpoint his prey's location. His attack would take these creatures utterly by surprise, ensuring his victory.

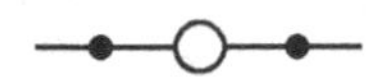

". . . and it was then I knew that if there was to be any bit of hope, I was going to have to be the one to step in," said Skipper, finally coming to the climactic moment in his story. "You see they hadn't thought to . . ." Skipper stopped, his voice trailing off. As they walked along, he'd been looking out across the ocean while recalling a different day on a different body of water. But something unexpected had appeared in the water and it broke his concentration.

"Come on Skipper," said Dempsey. "You can't leave me hanging like this. What hadn't they thought of?"

Skipper stopped where he was. Gripping the rail, he stared as hard as he could at the spot in the water where he'd seen the creature. He knew it hadn't been a whale; the coloration was all wrong. Plus, whales don't have heads, at least not like the one he'd just seen. True, he'd only gotten a glimpse of it, but it was strange enough to completely capture his attention. This thing, whatever it was, had a tapering snout and eyes that were as black as a demon's. What in the world had he just seen?

"Hey, Skipper, what are you looking at?" asked Dempsey.

"Keep your pants on," growled Skipper. "I thought I saw something."

"If you're trying to suck me in with a 'got you,' I'm not falling for it. Plus, keep in mind, those really piss me off. So, understand, if you go ahead and try one, I will throw you overboard."

The surface of the water remained calm, but Skipper wasn't ready to continue their patrol. "Shut up. I need to give this a minute."

Dempsey smiled as he leaned against the railing, his back to the ocean. He studied Skipper's face but couldn't find an ounce of subterfuge in it. "Okay, we'll take a break, but I'm on to you, Skipper. You're not going to get me to fall for any of your nonsense."

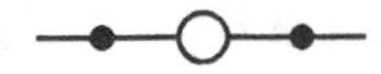

"Looks like it stopped," said Mercer.

"You're right. It's just sitting there."

"The length is right, but it's not shaped anything like a sub," said Mercer. He reached for his clipboard to see who was on patrol on the starboard deck. Dempsey and Magnor, both good men.

"Sir, it's moving again and it's almost on top of us."

"Mr. Briggs, get Dempsey and Magnor on the radio, now. Sound battle stations."

"On it, sir," said Briggs as he reached for the receiver.

Dempsey waited as patiently as he could but knew that they had to keep moving. "Skipper, don't you think you're carrying this a little too . . ." It was at that moment the creature burst upwards from the calm waters. Dempsey caught sight of the huge head on the long, snakelike neck out of the corner of his eye. On instinct, he grabbed Skipper, pushing him as hard as he could to get him out of the way.

Off balance, Skipper hit the deck hard, his head striking one of the steel bolts holding the railing to the deck. The creature's long neck slammed into the railing as Dempsey whirled around to face his attacker. With amazing speed, its jaws clamped down on Dempsey, striking with the force of a steel trap, its long, pointed teeth sinking deep into his upper torso, nearly cutting him in half.

The odor from the creature, along with the gore from Dempsey's shredded body, was overwhelming. Looking up from the deck, Skipper tried to focus in on what was happening, but his vision was blurred due to the blood pouring from his injured head. His own blood, as well as the blood and guts that showered the deck from Dempsey's corpse, partially blinded him. Clumsily pulling his sidearm, Skipper fired wildly, but the creature had already lifted Dempsey's lifeless body from the deck and pulled him down beneath the waves.

At the same moment the creature attacked, the ship's alarm split the air, signaling the crew that an attack was imminent. The horror of what he had seen, his head injury, and the loud, pulsating wail of the ship's siren, was more than he could handle. Skipper's pistol slipped from his hand and he slumped down onto the deck, losing consciousness.

MacKay and Colton had just left Sahir and were on their way back to the bridge when they heard the ship's alarm followed by two shots. Colton immediately radioed Mercer, "What have we got?"

"We believe the starboard patrol has been attacked. Garrett and her men are on their way. I've also alerted sick bay," said Mercer.

Turning to MacKay, Colton said, "Starboard patrol's been hit. Let's go."

Due to the tight quarters, it can be hard to run on a ship, but Colton took off down the passageway with surprising speed and nearly flew up the steep stairs to the next deck. MacKay did his best to keep up with him but had no chance of matching his pace. Colton ran out onto deck, quickly spotting Garrett and two of her men back near the bow of the ship. He had no idea what had happened, but the marines were scanning the water, their M27 automatic rifles at the ready. Garrett was on her radio, a nine-millimeter Glock in her hand. Behind her he saw the body.

As he got closer, Colton could see that the deck was covered in blood, as were parts of the railing. A corpsman had just arrived and was already at work attending to the fallen sailor. "What happened?" asked Colton.

"We're not sure," said Garrett. "Hatfield spotted what he thought might have been a small sub heading towards us. He and Mr. Mercer studied the monitor, but were puzzled by its odd shape, as well as the way it moved. Mercer doesn't know what attacked us, but he's convinced that it wasn't a sub."

At that point MacKay, Dr. Severin, and another corpsman arrived. "Mateo, how is he?" asked Severin, addressing a young corpsman.

"Looks like he took a pretty hard hit to the head, just above his left eye. Other than that, I haven't found any other injuries," answered Mateo.

"Let's get him down to sick bay," said Severin, nodding to the corpsman holding a stretcher.

"He's still alive?" exclaimed Colton, shocked that he'd survived what had obviously been an extremely violent attack.

"You're surprised?" said Severin.

"Aren't you?" said Colton. "Look at this place. I've seen slaughterhouses with less blood on the floor."

"The blood's not all his, Commander," said Garrett. Severin followed the corpsmen as they carried the man away. "The two crewmen on starboard patrol were Magnor and Dempsey. The wounded sailor is Magnor. At this point there's no sign of Dempsey, but we believe that whatever attacked them pulled Dempsey over the side."

Colton studied the deck more closely. Where there wasn't blood, there was water. It was clear to see that something had come up out of the ocean and attacked the two sailors. A nine-foot section of the iron railing had been pushed in; three of the bolts holding it to the deck stripped, ripped away from the deck. Colton couldn't imagine the weight of the creature or the sheer brute force it must have taken to inflict this kind of damage.

The deck was nearly fifteen feet above the surface of the water. What would be big enough to do this much damage and be able to launch itself high enough to reach the men? Colton's radio beeped. It was Mercer, but before he could say anything Colton asked, "Do you have any idea at all what attacked these two men?"

"No, but stay alert. It may strike again. We're still tracking it. At the moment it appears to be resting right below us, around three hundred feet down," replied Mercer. "The blood in the water is attracting other predators to us. Looking at the monitor I'd say there's a feeding frenzy going on down there."

Colton looked at Garrett and MacKay and said, "Whatever that thing is, it's still here. Mercer tells me they're tracking it and it's right below us." Talking back into the radio he said, "I can't think of too many fish that can breach this far out of the water. Are you able to tell if it's some kind of shark?"

"Colton, I don't know what that thing is, but I can tell you this, it's no shark. That thing is nearly forty feet long. Maybe a giant squid. At this point I can't even give you an educated guess as to what we are dealing with."

"There was no sign of Dempsey?" asked MacKay.

"No sir," said Garrett. "We just happened to be close by. We heard shots and by the time we got here we found one sailor on the deck, blood everywhere, and there was still a fair amount of blood in the water when we looked down. Most of it has since dissipated."

"Mercer says the thing they're tracking is forty feet long," said Colton. "Other than a whale, I have no idea what this could be."

"A whale didn't do this," muttered MacKay, staring at the water.

Colton and Garrett's radios beeped loudly. Garrett quickly pressed the "receive" button. Go ahead." Garrett listened as Mercer was shouting into the radio. Colton couldn't understand what he was saying, but the urgency was audible, and it clearly had an impact on Garrett.

Garrett yelled out, "Everyone, get back from this railing. That thing is coming back, and we are obviously vulnerable here."

Rather than run inside, Colton pulled out his Glock and positioned himself at the railing. The two marines quickly grabbed MacKay, pulling him back inside the ship. As they went by, Garrett grabbed one of her men by the arm. "Marine, give me that grenade."

The marine didn't hesitate and handed the grenade to Garrett. "Get back, Commander. Do you really think you're going to stop something that big with a pistol?"

They both stood at the railing, looking down into the water, waiting for the creature to reappear. The water was reasonably clear, giving them fair visibility down to about fifteen or twenty feet. Whatever was about to happen, it would be on them almost before they could react.

Garrett spotted the enormous bulk charging straight up at them. Colton saw it too but couldn't believe his own eyes. Pulling the pin, Garrett dropped the grenade into the water. As she turned to get away, she grabbed on to Colton and pushed him into the wall of the ship. They both went down, bouncing across the deck. Two seconds later the blast erupted from the sea behind them. Colton and Garrett quickly got up and moved back to the railing, but there wasn't anything there. The creature was nowhere in sight.

Garrett was already back on the radio with Mercer. As she clicked off she moved up to the railing and stood next to Colton. "We don't know if the grenade hurt it, or just scared the hell out of it, but Mercer said that whatever it is it's now moving away from us." They both continued to stare at the water, the broken bodies of other fish killed in the explosion floated to the surface. It wasn't long before the other fish in the area began to feast on their bodies.

"This is insane," said Colton. "Do you have any idea what that could have been?" The two of them stood there, holding on to the railing, their adrenaline-filled bodies just starting to calm down. Colton looked over at her. Obviously cool under fire, it was clear that Garrett was made of very tough stuff. "Captain, you handled that very well. All I could think of was that I wanted a piece of that thing. Guess I didn't think things through too clearly."

Garrett looked at Colton, smiled, and shrugged her shoulders. "I'm a marine. It's what we do. Besides, with you being a high profile 'spook squid' officer and all, there was no way I could leave you alone. If you'd so much as gotten your hair messed up, I'd be the one getting the blame. I'd also get a grilling for letting you run off and do something that stupid in the first place."

Colton smiled at her. "It is so comforting to know how much you care about my safety, Captain. Who knew? It just may be worthwhile having some marines on board after all."

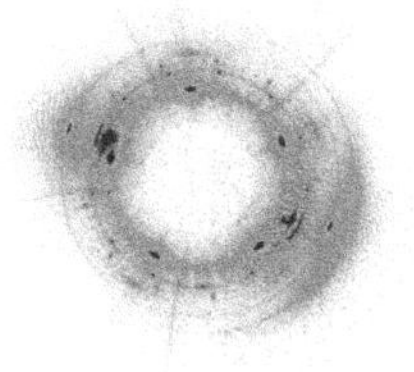

CHAPTER 10

MacKay was just hanging up the phone in the conference room, located behind the bridge, when Colton joined him. Nearly three hours had passed since the two sailors had been attacked, and once again the ship was a beehive of activity. The creature had not returned, which most of the crew took as good news. Despite their efforts, they'd not been able to find any trace of Dempsey. "How's Skipper doing?" asked MacKay.

"Hard to tell. Severin says he's got a serious concussion, but at this point he expects him to recover. Unfortunately, he's so out of it we haven't been able to question him to see if he can shed any light on what he might have seen," said Colton.

"With a head injury that serious, we may never get anything useful out of him."

"That's pretty much what Severin is thinking," said Colton. "Between the concussion and the shock of the whole incident, there's a good chance he won't be able to remember a thing."

"It's the not knowing that really eats away at you," said MacKay. "I know that this will start to make me sound like the Skipper, with all his tales of sea monsters, but I'm beginning to wonder if there might actually be some truth to some of his wild stories."

Colton grinned at MacKay. "Are we afraid of sea serpents now? If you'd like to borrow it, I've got a small flashlight in my cabin you can use for a night-light."

"I would, but then what would you use? Look, after all we've been through during the last twenty-four hours, I'm not ruling anything out."

"On a more proactive note, Mercer is getting the submersibles ready to launch. They'll not only give us a better look at what's down there, but will also be taking water samples. Hopefully, once we analyze those samples, they'll also help to give us a better idea as to where we are," said Colton. "Who's got the bridge?"

"Lieutenant Gallo," said MacKay. "He's been with me for a couple of years. Good officer."

"He and I have really only talked in passing," said Colton. "I need to spend some more time with him. Any updates from Sahir?"

"That was Sahir I was just talking to. He's not sure, but we may have just experienced our second attack."

"What happened?" asked Colton.

"Of the three drones we sent out, only two made it back. There's a thick shroud of fog that hugs the ground over there, so much so that it makes visibility almost impossible. Maybe some of it will burn off later in the day, but so far, it's not showing any signs of doing that. Anyway, the sailor piloting the missing drone came across places where the fog reached as high as two hundred feet into the sky. The drone had already passed through some similar patches of fog and hadn't experienced any problems. Then, it entered another patch, and suddenly went off-line. He has no idea what happened to it," explained MacKay.

"Not sure that's evidence of an attack. It's possible that it just connected with a tree," said Colton.

"Agreed, but that's the puzzling part. Those things are equipped with navigational radar. We sent one of the drones up the coast, and a second one in the opposite direction, looking for harbors, coastal villages, any sign of life. This particular drone was the only one we flew directly into the interior. Everything was going along just fine and then boom, it was gone. As with the other two drones, the feed from its systems was being fed directly into Argos. This enabled us to check and we confirmed that the drone's radar hadn't detected anything in its flight path."

"Are they getting any signals from it?" asked Colton.

"It had only been about twenty seconds into the fogbank when the pilot lost all contact. Sahir said that they're still getting intermittent signals from its locater beacon, but even that's off and on. Whatever it ran into, it took it down hard. Sahir's getting the pictures from all three drones loaded. We should be able to look at them in a few minutes. They're also working with Argos on its analysis," said MacKay.

It suddenly dawned on Colton as to what MacKay had said. "Argos is on line?" asked Colton. That would be a spot of good news.

"Sahir told me it's in Deep Data mode," said MacKay. "It's running the protocols for initial activation. Sahir offered a more detailed explanation, but I knew it wouldn't make it any clearer for me."

"I've asked Captain Garrett, Dr. Chudzik, and Father Ryan to join us," said MacKay.

"That's a rather eclectic group," said Colton.

"Amongst her other accomplishments, Chudzik also has a background in botany. I want her to get a good look at the plant life over there. Mercer and I still believe we're somewhere in the Caribbean, but we need all the info we can get."

"I like her," said Colton. "She's a sharp lady, yet she doesn't carry that academic chip on her shoulder like some of the others we have on board."

"Wouldn't have known she even had an interest in plants, but I ran into her talking with Hezekiah in the mess hall a few weeks ago. They were in a very deep discussion on the exact herbs, and of course quantities, to be used in making an authentic marinara sauce. First time I've ever seen Hezekiah struggling to hold his ground in his own kitchen. She was nice about it but was quite intent on showing him the error of his ways," said MacKay.

"I'd have paid big bucks to watch that," said Colton, laughing and picturing the whole thing in his mind. Hezekiah was the size of a small mountain. Dr. Chudzik weighed in at just over a hundred pounds soaking wet. Going forward his pet name for her would be *The Chihuahua*. Of course, he also knew he'd never call her that to her face, a secret he had learned during his first marriage. "I'm glad you asked Father Ryan to join us."

"His role on this ship is becoming more critical with each passing hour," said MacKay. "As if our potentially being at war, and not knowing where we are, isn't enough, we had that terrible attack on Skipper and Dempsey. All combined I have a crew that is very on edge. Father Ryan's been at it almost nonstop, continually making the rounds. I don't know what he's saying to folks, but so far it seems to be working. He's doing a really good job in calming everyone down."

"I've had dealings with priests before in various parts of the world, some good, some not so good," said Colton, "but I have to say, I'm impressed with Father Ryan. Man has depth to him. Of course, you'll never be able to convince me that he doesn't cheat at cards, but other than that, I'm glad he's with us."

"So how much do you owe him?" asked MacKay. It was the first time since the wave hit them that he came close to smiling.

"More than I should."

"During your briefing with the admiral, didn't he warn you about playing cards with Father Ryan?"

Before Colton could respond there was a knock on the door. Colton opened it to find Captain Garrett and Dr. Chudzik deep in conversation. Hezekiah stood patiently behind them, balancing two trays of food. "Can't work on an empty stomach," said Hezekiah, placing the trays of food in the center of the table.

"This looks good, Cookie. Much appreciated," said Captain MacKay. As Hezekiah turned to leave, Colton saw him exchange smiles with Dr. Chudzik. He was glad that she'd made friends with someone outside of

Meinhard's little self-contained gaggle of scientists. Of all the hardships Colton had endured during his time in the navy, he honestly believed he'd turn homicidal if he were ever sequestered with that group for more than an hour.

"Please dig in," said MacKay, gesturing towards the food. "We're waiting for Sahir to get the pictures from the drones loaded, and I've also asked Father Ryan to join us."

About ten minutes later Father Ryan rushed into the room. "My apologies, I'm running a few steps behind today."

"Join us. We were just grabbing a bite," said Colton.

"So how are things going from your perspective, Father?" asked MacKay.

"Surprisingly well, Captain," answered Father Ryan. "When you consider all that we've been through, especially with the horrific attack on those two sailors, I'm impressed with how well this crew is actually handling things. Believe me, I've been attached to other commands that wouldn't have held together half as well."

"Thank you, I appreciate that," said MacKay. "Things have been coming at us so fast that I haven't been able to give the amount of focus to the crew that I want to."

"Stopped by sick bay on my way up here," said Father Ryan, stuffing half a sandwich into his mouth at the same time.

"Is there an update on Skipper?" asked Colton.

Father Ryan swallowed some water before answering. "Skipper's been drifting in and out of consciousness, which Severin says is a good sign."

"Has he said anything?"

"No, not really," said Father Ryan. "He mumbles things, but nothing that makes any sense. Started shouting at one point, scared the piss out of a young corpsman."

"Father, this could be important. He's the only witness we have. What did he shout?" pressed Colton.

"Like I said, most of it has been nonsense. He's asked for Dempsey a couple of times. When he shouted he was calling for help, telling someone to 'get it away' from him. Two or three times he's mumbled something that sounded like 'it's a kraken, it's a kraken.' Not much there to help us, I'm afraid."

"Perhaps," said Colton. "Perhaps not." Getting up, he looked at MacKay and reached for the phone. "On second thought, I think I'll be hanging on to that night-light for a while. Father, I'll be blunt. I know it's not public knowledge, but if you remember, I am aware that you are in the Order of St. Cyprian."

Father Ryan's demeanor didn't change, but his eyes hardened. "Despite what the internet says, or what you may believe, we are not the Vatican's X-Files, as so many quaintly put it. I know some members of our order specialize in exorcisms and oddities. But for me, I'm just a simple priest."

"But you could call on unusual advice?" said Colton.

"I could, and I will, assuming we ever resume communications outside this ship. In truth, I wish my old friend Father Collin were here with us."

Colton dialed the number for sick bay, which was immediately answered by a corpsman. "This is commander Colton. I need to talk to Dr. Severin."

"Commander, how can I help you?" said Dr. Severin, coming on the line.

"I'm calling about Magnor," said Colton. "Father Ryan says that he's regained consciousness a couple of times."

"Well, let's say he's headed in that direction. He's been trying to talk, has even yelled out once or twice, but he doesn't really know where he is. Think of it as someone talking in their sleep, but in this case, they're having a really bad dream. While it is encouraging, he's not made it back to us yet."

"Doctor, I want a corpsman beside him at all times. No matter how crazy the things he says may sound, I want every word written down. Is that understood?"

"Yes, Commander, I understand. Not sure how much help it's going to be, but you obviously think it's important, so we'll make it happen. My hope is that by this time tomorrow he'll have regained full consciousness."

"Thank you, Doctor," said Colton, and then hung up.

"You're not really putting any stock into that kraken business, are you?" asked Father Ryan.

"No, not in so many words," said Colton. "Thing is, we don't know what attacked them. We do know it was big enough to reach the deck fifteen feet above the surface, smash in at least ten feet of iron railing, and from the looks of it, managed to carry off one of our crew without having to try too hard. No, I don't think anyone has released the kraken. But at the same time, I still can't even hazard a guess as to what it could have been."

"That's the problem, Father," said MacKay, the weariness apparent in his voice. "We don't know what we're dealing with, where we are, or why we are not able to reach anyone."

"Father, I agree with what they are saying," said Garrett. "Had I not seen the amount of blood sprayed all over that deck, and the damage that thing did to the railing, I'd say that all this is taking things a little too far. Unfortunately, we're dealing with so many unknowns that until we have some hard facts, we can't afford to rule anything out. No krakens, of course, but like the commander, I am keeping an open mind." Looking at Colton, she said, "I do have a question though."

"Go ahead, Captain," said Colton.

"You sleep with a night-light?"

Before Colton could respond, trying to keep the smile off his face, MacKay said, "That's another story for another time. All three of the drones sent back live feeds to Sahir and his team. The pictures we're about to see have been taken from one of those feeds. They are from the drone that we flew eastwards up the coast. Rather than sit here and watch all the footage, the pictures we'll be viewing were taken fifteen seconds apart from each other. Should we spot something interesting, then there's more footage available for us to review." MacKay worked with the computer for a few seconds before the first picture appeared on the large screen on the wall.

"I trust that the entire feed is being reviewed," said Garrett.

"Most certainly, by Argos as well as by analysts on Sahir's team," said MacKay. "It's a very thorough process. Also, I think you should know that one of the drones didn't make it back. We don't believe it was shot at, but we're hoping the footage it sent back will give us a better idea as to what happened."

For the next hour and a half they closely studied the pictures, one by one. The ground fog turned out to be as thick as reported, never really giving them a clear glimpse of the land. They did see a few places that would serve as a natural harbor, but there was no sign of anyone living in these inlets. Dr. Chudzik had them pause a few times, looking closely at some of the fauna. Colton was intrigued by the amount of notes she was taking.

They were close to finishing with the first set of pictures when Garrett spotted something. "Wait! Go back to the previous picture. There, in the upper left-hand corner, just to the side of that large bush. What is that?"

The mist had cleared enough in this shot so that they could see land, but it was still hazy at best. Looking closely at the point where Garrett had directed them, they all spotted it at practically the same time. "Is that a leg?" asked Father Ryan.

"It sure looks like it," said Garrett, "but it's certainly not human. It looks more like an alligator's leg, only bigger, with more girth."

"I know we're not sure of where we are, but we certainly can't be in Indonesia," Colton muttered quietly, more to himself than to anyone else.

"Did you say something, Commander?" asked MacKay.

"Just thinking out loud," answered Colton, his eyes locked on the picture. "A couple of years back I went on an expedition with a couple friends of mine to what is called the Lesser Sunda Islands, which is part of

Indonesia. This can't be right, but as I'm looking at this picture I'll swear it looks a little bit . . . ."

"Like a Komodo dragon," said Garrett, cutting him off. "But how is that possible? We've been taken way off course, I understand that, but it's not possible that we've ended up on the other side of the planet, is it?"

"No," answered MacKay. "That is highly unlikely."

"I've written down the ID number on the photo," said Chudzik. "I'll get with Sahir's team to see just how much they can do to enhance the image."

"How big do Komodo dragons get?" asked Father Ryan.

"We saw a few that were at least nine or ten feet long," said Colton. "They're bigger than you'd want them to be."

The next set of pictures was from the drone that had moved westward along the coast. As before, they found some inlets that would serve well as a harbor, one rather large, but still no signs that anyone had ever lived there.

About halfway through they stopped to look at a picture that showed a big disturbance in the sand leading down to the ocean. "Looks like that happened recently," said MacKay, squinting his eyes to get a better look. "My guess would be early this morning."

"What could have caused that?" asked Father Ryan.

"The drag marks look like someone ran some kind of craft out of the ocean and up on to the beach," said Colton. "As to what caused the gouges in the sand near that bush I have no idea. Whatever it was, it then appears to have returned to the sea. There, to the right, those drag marks are like the other ones and lead back into the water."

"Perhaps it was some kind of seal?" ventured Father Ryan.

"That would be one big seal," said Dr. Chudzik. "No, more likely a whale, but it couldn't have gone that far out of the water. I've seen films of killer whales bursting out of the water going after seals, and they do come up on sand, but not nearly that far away from the water. They'd be stuck on the beach if they ever did get that far."

The third and final batch of pictures was from the drone that had disappeared. It had gone directly into the interior and had sent back some fascinating shots. It showed that the land was heavily forested, with several significant outcroppings of rock here and there. This suggested that there were also some deep ravines, or even small valleys, but the ground fog made it impossible to tell.

On occasion there would be three to six consecutive pictures of almost pure grayish white. These were the times when the drone would enter a patch of fog. As they came to the end of the pictures, they could see some tall trees starting to break through the fog with what appeared to be tall cliffs off to the left. "The next five pictures are the last that this drone sent before it went down," said MacKay.

The first picture was half haze, half whiteout as it entered the fog. The next two showed nothing other than the typical grayish-white fog they'd gotten used to seeing. The fourth, however, was very intriguing. While still engulfed in the grayish-white soup, there was something dark covering about a third of the lens.

It was hard to make out exactly what they were looking at. Whatever was covering the lens was dark gray and seemed to have some kind of pattern running across it. Its outer edge was sharp and distinct with small points sticking out here and there. Along the edge, near the middle, was a knob, or lump, which caused the edge to angle in more so on that side than the other.

"Oh good," sighed Colton. "More questions without answers. Anyone want to take a stab at what that is?"

"Hang on," said MacKay. "Let's look at the last picture."

The final picture was dark, but they could make out what looked like branches and leaves. "There you have it," said MacKay. "The crazy thing ran into something that knocked it out of the sky. Our final picture is our drone crashing down through a tree."

"Captain, I wouldn't conclude at this point that it ran into something," said Colton. "It's quite possible that something intentionally ran into it."

"Not disagreeing with you, Commander, but what makes you say that?" asked Garrett.

"These drones are very sophisticated, some of the best I've worked with. As we discussed earlier, they are equipped with navigational radar. Sahir's pilots are not new at this and they would have most probably seen something coming up on the radar if there'd been anything in the area," said Colton.

MacKay had put the next to last picture back up on the screen. They all stared at it, searching for an answer.

"That could very easily be a branch. Perhaps it got snagged by a stray branch that just wasn't big enough to be caught by the radar," said Father Ryan.

"Possible," said MacKay, "but those little birds of ours are pretty tough."

"Speaking of birds," said Dr. Chudzik, as she got up and headed towards the screen. "Look at these little points running all along the edge, these three in particular. I'm going to see if either Sahir or Dr. Brennan can do anything to enhance this photo, but in my opinion, those look like feathers."

Garrett smiled at this. "Are you suggesting that one of Sahir's little birds got whacked by a bigger bird? I apologize," Garrett said quickly. "I'm not making fun of your theory. It's just that I do know a little bit about these drones, and it would take a good-sized bird to be able to take one of them down. That bird would have to be in line with the ginormous seal Father Ryan suggested was terrorizing the beach in one of the earlier pictures."

Father Ryan chuckled at this. "Doctor, I do believe we have both been insulted. On the other hand, I agree that those do look like feathers. If it inadvertently ran into a flock of large birds in that patch of fog, would that have been enough to bring it down?"

"Yes," said Colton slowly, "but that too is unlikely. I don't want to keep harping on the same point, but the navigational gear on those drones, in all likelihood, would have picked up a flock of anything big enough to threaten it."

"Well, I think we've done all the damage we can do here," said MacKay, standing up and stretching. "Let's get these photos that we've earmarked enhanced, look at the rest of the footage we have when these photos were taken, and see if Sahir and his team can find anything else. Thank you. I appreciate everyone's time with this."

Garrett took off, letting them know that she'd be bringing Lieutenant Tanner up to speed. Father Ryan left with Dr. Chudzik, both on their way down to talk with Dr. Brennan, while Colton stayed behind with Captain MacKay.

"Your thoughts, Commander?" asked MacKay.

"I'd hoped to have better intel before acting, but I think it's time we sent a landing party ashore for a better look. Due to the poor visibility, we may have flown over entire villages and not seen a thing. Like you, I believe that we must be somewhere in the Caribbean. It's just a question of where. Nevertheless, we need to find out firsthand what's over there."

MacKay nodded his head. "Yeah, that makes the most sense. I trust you'll be leading the team."

"Of course," answered Colton. "I'll pull together an operational plan with the personnel I'll need and discuss it with you after dinner."

"You'll want to go in very well armed, Commander," cautioned MacKay. "Again, I'm not trying to take over for Magnor and his crazy stories, but something is wrong here, very wrong. The last thing I want is for you to run into more than you can handle."

Colton grinned from ear to ear. "We'll be okay, Captain. To be completely honest with you, I can't wait to get back on solid ground. I've been on this ship too long. No offense."

"None taken," said MacKay. "I almost envy you. Almost."

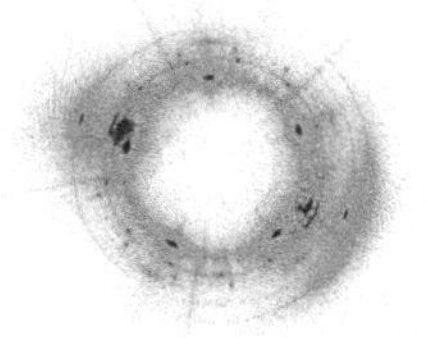

CHAPTER 11

Having just left Garrett and her team at the armory as they prepared for their presunrise departure, Colton joined Lt. Commander Mercer in the captain's conference room, just off the bridge. He and Mercer began to once again go over the small amount of intelligence their team had been able to collect. They also discussed the mission, focusing on its goals and timeframes. Both men realized that the *Eclipse* wouldn't be able to give them much in the way of support.

"Sahir will have two drones in the air, monitoring your progress as best as he can. His team will also be helping with radio communications. We believe that you should have a range of roughly twenty-five to thirty miles, but we don't know what you'll be facing," said Mercer. "There are things, of course, that could negatively affect transmission."

"You're referring to things like broken terrain," said Colton.

"Exactly, that would be one possibility. Deep canyons, certain metallic alloys in rocks, atmospheric conditions, take your choice. All of it could play a role in how strong of a signal you'll be able to maintain," said Mercer. "This is a lot harder to do without the satellites."

"Good thing we have the drones," said Colton. Shaking his head in quiet disbelief, he looked up at Mercer and said, "All of this still doesn't make any sense to me. It is so hard to wrap my head around the possibility that the world just experienced something so catastrophic that all our satellites have been completely knocked out. That even basic AM and FM radio is gone. I don't know what's happened to us, but I'm having more and more trouble buying into the 'first strike' theory."

"Wish I had the answers for you," said Mercer. "Fortunately the crew is handling all of this surprisingly well, but we're all desperate for answers."

"The good news," said Colton, "is that Argos hasn't picked up any unusual levels of radiation in the atmosphere. Both Sahir and Meinhard's team agree that that pretty much rules out a nuclear strike."

"Don't take this the wrong way, because I'm not disagreeing with you, that is good news," said Mercer, "but what does that leave? What other power on earth could have taken out our satellites and all communications as quickly and completely as it obviously has?"

Colton managed a small smile. "Like you, I have no idea. When I hear that all of this has even stumped Argos, I know it's time for me to stop trying to figure it out. Hopefully, once we go ashore and meet with a few of the locals, we'll have more information to work with."

"Here's hoping you get lucky," said Mercer.

"Luck?" said Father Ryan as he joined them in the conference room. "That is very disappointing to hear. Is luck all you've got to offer, Mr. Mercer? Personally, I'm looking to a far greater power for answers," said Father Ryan.

"Forgive me, Father. What was I thinking?" said Mercer, smiling at the priest. "If you two will excuse me, there are still a couple of things that I need to finish up before you and your team shove off."

As Mercer left, Father Ryan took a chair across from Colton. "No offense to Mr. Mercer, but this actually works out quite well. I was hoping to get a few minutes alone with you."

Colton looked up from the report he'd been reading, arching an eyebrow at Father Ryan. "Are you here to finally own up to your evil ways at poker? Not trying to tell you your own business, but confession is good for the soul."

"Evil ways? Not at all. When it comes to games of chance, I'm blessed with an abundance of natural talent. No, I want to talk to you about all that has happened."

"Alright," said Colton. "What can I do for you?"

"Let's start with how you feel about all of this," answered Father Ryan. "Scuttlebutt around the ship ranges from nuclear annihilation to us being yet another victim of the Bermuda Triangle."

Colton leaned back in his chair and stretched his arms above his head. "Fortunately, we don't have to worry about either one of those. There is zero evidence to support nuclear activity, praise God, and the Bermuda Triangle doesn't exist. It's just a fun tale that people like to tell."

"That's good to hear, very reassuring," said Father Ryan.

But Father Ryan wasn't finished by a long shot. His eyes closely studied Colton's face, almost as if he were examining some odd creature they'd just pulled up from the sea. The two men stared at each other for a few more moments, then Colton asked, "Is there something else you'd like to talk about? The only time I ever see you this serious is when you're cheating me at cards."

Father Ryan smiled at that. "Again, Commander, you cannot blame me for how poorly you play poker. A wiser man would have stopped playing and cut his losses after the first couple of weeks. But then, that's not who you are, is it? I've learned a great deal about you, Mr. Colton. By sitting across from you at the poker table to the way you duped those miserable reporters. You're an interesting man in that you refuse to quit. You won't back down, no matter what the odds."

Colton held his hands out to his sides, palms up in mock surrender. "Not my fault, Father. It's a reflexive response that has been pounded into me due to years of intense training."

"No, that's not it," said Father Ryan. "It runs much deeper than that. You're not the kind to accept losing, ever. You will keep going at something until you've beaten it, or it kills you. Which is an excellent trait for a highly trained Navy SEAL. And, based on the success you've had, I'd say it's working for you. But will that headstrong, win-at-all-costs attitude be the right course of action, the right tactic, for whatever it is we are presently facing?"

"I'm afraid I'm not following you," said Colton, his face a mask, revealing nothing.

"Think about what is happening. For the first time in our adult lives, we are facing the complete unknown. We don't know where we are. We don't know what's happened to us, or how we got here. And we have no idea what's waiting for you and Captain Garrett's team on shore."

"Father, facing the unknown is kind of what we do in black ops, and we do it all the time. I'm not sure how this is all that different from any other mission."

"Commander, please, I've been in this man's navy for some time and I'm not ignorant regarding black ops. But you are missing my point. Think back on your previous missions. True, each time you've faced certain unknowns, like, how many men does the enemy have? Could they possibly know we're coming? What if the intel we have is all wrong? But what we have going on here is so far different from anything that either you, or those marines, have ever faced.

"On your past missions, you at least knew where you were. Afghanistan, North Korea, wherever, you knew about the country, its people, and had a pretty good understanding of what you were up against. The circumstances of what we are now facing are 180 degrees away from that.

"For all of us, this is far more than just not knowing where we are, or what's happened to us," continued Father Ryan. "We've taken casualties, lost crew members. The stories of what attacked those two sailors are becoming more fantastic by the minute. This whole crazy thing is one big unknown, and it is the unknown that can be the most devastating, fear-inducing element that I can think of."

"I'm going to be perfectly frank with you, Father," said Colton, trying to keep a serious look on his face. "This has got to be the worst pep talk I've ever received before setting out on a mission."

Father Ryan's expression didn't change, and he ignored Colton's sarcasm. "Commander, of all the people on this ship, it is imperative for you to understand what I'm talking about, to recognize the difference between what you've gone up against in the past, versus what you're facing now. This is as different as night and day."

Now it was Colton's turn to study the priest. Father Ryan's face was redder than usual, and he appeared to be short of breath, as if he'd just run up some stairs. He also noticed that the priest's hands were slightly trembling. "Where are you going with this, Father?"

"In just a few hours you and your team depart and none of us have any idea what is waiting for you over there in that mist. You're going to need more than just the luck Mr. Mercer wished for you and a never-say-die attitude."

"And what would that be, Father? What is it that I need?"

"That's the piece about you I'm not yet clear on," said Father Ryan. He seemed uncertain as to what to say next. "A few minutes ago, when you told me that there was absolutely no evidence of nuclear activity, you said, '*praise God.*' Did you mean that, or was it just an expression?"

"Ah, okay," said Colton, "now I get it. You want to know if I believe in God."

"That's part of it, yes. I want to know exactly where Commander Brett Colton stands with God. Is it just a casual, yes, I believe, but I spend little to no time fooling with it? Or do you have a true and growing relationship with God? Without hesitation, I can tell you that many of the best leaders I've worked with in the military fall into the second category," said Father Ryan.

"Father, with all due respect, I'm still not clear what you are asking, or why," snapped Colton, his temper starting to rise to the surface. "My training, for the most part, has been to kill bad guys and destroy things. We don't know what's happened to us, but even though it wasn't nuclear activity, I cannot rule out enemy action. So, until I know differently, my mindset is that I'll be going into enemy territory. This will not be a casual walk in the park. Does that clear things up for you?"

"Good to know, but no, that's not what I'm asking. I want to know if you know how to turn to God for help? It's more than just believing. It's trusting in God, asking for guidance," said Father Ryan, his voice getting a little louder, matching Colton's demeanor. "I'm not sure you know how important this is. Do you have any concept of the power of prayer? All of us, not just Garrett and those marines, all of us need a strong, confident leader who's not afraid to turn to the Almighty for help. A leader who trusts in Him. If you do not trust in God, Commander, then you're turning your back on the most powerful, most significant force for good there is. He will hear you; He will help you. All you have to do is ask. And believe me, before this is over, you're going to need His help."

"Fortune-telling, Father, or is this actual prophecy?"

Father Ryan started to get up from his chair. His face paled a little, but he held himself in check. At first, he glared at Colton, but then turned his eyes away and stared down at the table. Colton had never doubted Father Ryan's passion about his faith, but up until today he had never seen this side of him. Then it dawned on him. Father Ryan wasn't angry at him; he was frightened, and that, in and of itself, revealed a great deal to Colton.

"I haven't shared this with anyone," said Father Ryan. His voice had dropped dramatically, now just above a whisper. "Yet I knew I had to talk to you before you left. This is going to sound crazy, but it doesn't matter. I need to tell you about this." He continued to stare at the table.

"You can trust me, Father. What's going on?"

"You've pointedly mentioned, more than once, that I belong to an order that is cloaked in secrecy. To be precise, it is Ordo Sancti Cypriani. We're not the weirdos that we're portrayed as being, but we all have some level, some ability with premonition, a sixth sense for all intents and purposes. Did you know that there was a priestly order in Rome before the coming of Christ? The Etruscans were quite good at prophecy. So, the early Church didn't view dream divination as silly. One just had to be cognizant as to the origination of your dreams. Was it God reaching out, or the enemy and his demonic hordes?" said Father Ryan.

"You've lost me. What are you trying to say?"

"I've had dreams, visions, whatever you want to call them. They started two days before that energy wave washed over us. Each one has been so clear, so vivid, I really can't describe it, but they're unlike anything I've ever experienced. They start without warning and hit me at different times, and not just when I'm asleep. Each time these visions have occurred, they are so completely overwhelming, that when they're over, I am utterly exhausted. Although I'm at peace with God, I know in my heart that there are terrible tasks facing me."

"What tasks? What have you seen in these visions that scares you?"

"Commander, let me just say that our being here is no accident. We, the *Eclipse*, and this crew have been brought here for a very specific reason. A tremendous responsibility has been placed on us."

"Father, please, I'm not making light of what you are saying," said Colton. He wasn't sure how to respond, but he knew he had to tread carefully. Father Ryan wouldn't be sharing, wouldn't be opening up with something as personal as this if he didn't believe there was more to it than just some weird kind of dreams.

"I'm nowhere near as close to understanding God, theology, any of this as you are. However, I do believe in what you just said, that there is a definitive reason for our being here. When I was a kid, I heard it at home and in church all the time, God has a plan. It's been my experience that He's not too big on sharing exactly what that plan is; guess He sees it as need to know. I'm okay with that. What I want to know is what is it about these visions that you've been having that have you so on edge?"

Father Ryan finally looked up, staring directly into Colton's eyes. "My fear is that I will fail Him, that I won't be strong enough to do my part in all of this when my time of trial arrives. There will be sacrifice, Mr. Colton, terrible sacrifice. I've seen it and it's not just about me. These visions have been about you as well, and you will not be able to bring us through this on your own. That's why it is so important to me that I know where you stand with God. In the event I fail, I need to know that there will be someone else here to do my part. So, Commander, do you trust in the Lord?"

It was obvious that Father Ryan wasn't going to give him any of the details as to what he'd seen in his visions. At the same time, Colton knew that he was not the kind of man easily rattled. Father Ryan had served in combat, had two purple hearts to prove it, one of which was for running into a cross fire to rescue a wounded soldier. Father Ryan was anything but a coward. If he truly was having visions, if visions simply weren't a case of his being overwhelmed like the rest of the crew, then whatever they were revealing to him had to be devastating. They'd obviously done a number on him.

"Don't hold this against me, but God and I really don't talk on a regular basis," answered Colton. "That's more on me than Him. But if it's any comfort to you, when things get rough, I do believe He has my six."

Father Ryan nodded his head. "Okay. Lots of room for growth, but it's a start. I'll be seeing the team off, along with Captain MacKay. But before we wrap things up here, thank you for talking with me. I'd also like to pray with you."

"Father, you really haven't told me what you saw in those visions. Before I leave, is there anything I can do to help you?"

"No, not at the moment. In some ways, I'd like to be going with you, but for now I'm needed here," said Father Ryan. "Just know that God is with you. Let us pray."

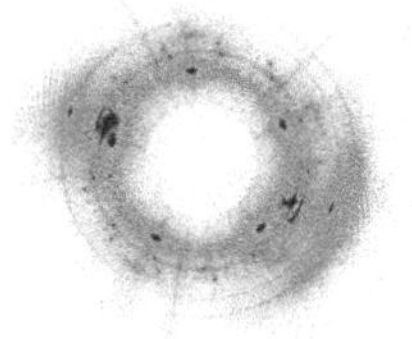

CHAPTER 12

"Corporal, get those boats secured and out of sight," directed Colton, his voice just about a whisper. He estimated they still had about thirty to forty minutes before sunrise. Colton planned to do all he could to keep the element of surprise on their side. Looking at Garrett, he said, "We'll leave two men here to watch our backs. Make sure they keep in contact with Tanner at regular intervals. If they're attacked, we'll be the closest thing they have for backup."

The trip from the *Eclipse* to the shore took very little time and went without incident, but not without some very tense moments. About halfway to shore, Hatfield radioed Colton that they might have a problem. What appeared to be a very big fish, close to fourteen feet, was heading directly towards them.

Colton alerted his team. Opening the throttles, they pushed their small boats as hard as they possibly could, but it quickly became apparent that they were not going to reach the shore in time. Hatfield's voice bordered on hysteria as he let Colton know that the thing was nearly on top of them and moving fast. With guns drawn and ready, each of them peered into the water, hoping to drive it off before it could attack.

Corporal Lee shouted out as he spotted the creature near the rear of his boat. He and Colton watched as a black, massive form passed underneath them. The creature quickly turned and started to head back towards them.

Then, for some reason, it turned and swam off. Colton breathed a sigh of relief. Considering the damage that had been done to the *Eclipse*, he knew that their small landing crafts would not have withstood an assault.

The smell was the worst. Two parts Louisiana swamp, one part open sewer. But despite the humidity, the stinky air was surprisingly easy to breathe, almost energizing.

The *Eclipse* had moved eastward, taking them a little more than a mile up the coast, enabling Colton and his team to take advantage of one of the inlets their drones had spotted the previous day. Using night-finder headgear, they hadn't seen anyone on the shore as they approached or in the inlet as they landed. The water in the inlet turned out to be rather shallow and surprisingly warm. As far as they could tell in the predawn light, there was no sign of anyone ever having used this place.

Yesterday evening, just after dinner, Colton had called a meeting to discuss the details regarding the shore party. In addition to Captain MacKay and Lt. Commander Mercer, he was joined by Captain Garrett, Lieutenant Tanner, Drs. Meinhard and Chudzik, and Father Ryan in the captain's briefing room.

The plan was rather simple. The *Eclipse* would sail up the coast that night, taking up position across from the inlet he'd decided to use. Choosing one of the tighter inlets they'd seen from the pictures, Colton reasoned they'd have less chance of running into a sizable number of natives. Colton, of course, would lead the landing party, with Captain Garrett acting as second-in-command. They'd be taking twelve of her marines with them.

Once on land, they would move inward, the goal being to find some locals, and, as gently as possible, figure out where they were. His decision to use this inlet also had secondary motives. Something over there had taken out one of their drones. Despite Sahir's team's best efforts, assisted by Dr. Brennan and Dr. Chudzik, they still had no idea what had happened to it. Even Argos drew a blank, which was a little unsettling. Argos did, however, confirm Dr. Chudzik's theory that what they'd been looking at had indeed been feathers.

The downed drone continued to send out intermittent signals from its locater beacon, but these signals were becoming less and less frequent. Colton wanted to get a close look at it to see if they could determine what had knocked it out of the sky. He still struggled with the concept of a huge bird being able to take down one of those drones. But, as with everything else about this place, it defied explanation, so why not throw in a gigantic, drone-killing peacock? Or was it a roc or a thunderbird?

The landing team pushed off from the *Eclipse* roughly an hour before sunrise. As they might be landing in hostile territory, they were well provisioned and heavily armed. Sahir launched two of his drones at the same time to give whatever assistance he could from the air, also enabling communications with the shore party. While the drones may not be able to penetrate the ground hugging mist, they would be able to easily spot any approaching boats or aircraft. Or rocs.

"Everyone down!" hissed Private Hill, quickly moving over to Colton and Garrett. "Other side of the inlet, just to the left of that tall palm tree, something moved."

"What did you see, Private?" asked Garrett.

"Pretty sure it was an animal, but I only caught a glimpse of it as it moved away. All I saw was its backside."

"So long as it didn't have a license plate attached to it," said Colton. "How big was it?"

"Sir, from what I could see it was either a small hippo or a really big hog. Grew up hunting wild boar in Texas. They are as aggressive as it gets."

"Alright, Private, "said Garrett. "Keep your eyes open.

Corporal Lee motioned to Colton and Garrett, and the entire team stepped just inside the tree line for cover. "Privates Shaw and Fuller will stay here to guard the boats. We're ready to move out."

"Very good," nodded Colton. "Private Hill thinks he may have spotted some wild boar over there," said Colton, pointing across the water. "I want you and Hill's keen eyes to take the point. Captain, I'll follow close behind them. You deploy the rest of the men. Corporal, let's move out."

Even this close to the shore, the mist rolling out from the jungle limited their visibility, keeping it to less than thirty or forty feet. As they set off into the jungle, they found the vegetation to be thick and wet, but they were still able to make steady progress. Between the mist that moved and swirled around, combined with the wet foliage, it didn't take long before all of them were soaking wet. The grunts and howls of various kinds of animals filled the air, but other than the one random hog sighting by Private Hill, they hadn't seen any animals.

No matter how hard they tried, the thick vegetation made it impossible for them to move quietly as they continued to press forward. Even though the mist in certain areas became less dense, they were still moving at a much slower pace than they wanted. The limited visibility also forced them to be extra cautious. The last thing any of them wanted to do was to accidentally bump into an opposing force.

About thirty minutes in, Corporal Lee came across a small game trail. The path was hard packed and rather tight, with the jungle pressing in on both sides. The good news was that the path headed in the general direction of where they'd pinpointed the drone's locater beacon to be transmitting from.

Colton signaled Corporal Lee to follow it. They'd stay with it until it changed direction. This made the going much easier and they were able to modestly increase their pace, but the conditions were miserable. It seemed as if they'd dropped into an entomologist's nightmare. The deer flies were huge and plentiful. There was also some kind of beetle that looked like a green ladybug and bit like a mosquito.

Private Hill, who was leading the team, suddenly halted, dropped to a firing position on one knee, and aimed his rifle straight ahead. Corporal Lee signaled everyone else and they immediately brought their weapons up, ready to fire.

Hill then began to backtrack, but never took his eyes off the trail in front of him. Colton and Corporal Lee advanced and were soon next to him. "What is it, Private?" asked Colton.

The young private was clearly shaken. "I'm not sure, sir, but it's about twenty yards in front of us, off to the right side."

"Another hog sighting, Hill?" said Colton, a trace of a smile on his face.

"No sir," said Hill, his voice a little shaky. "Too many legs."

"Explain yourself, Private," snapped Corporal Lee.

"It looked to be about two-and-a-half feet in length, black with brown splotches, and a whole lotta legs. It scurried off the path real fast before I could get a clear view of what it was," answered Hill.

"Now I've spent a fair amount of time in the jungle," said Colton, "but I can't think of too many animals that match that description."

"Wasn't an animal, sir," said Hill. "Insect."

"An insect two-and-a-half feet long?" said Corporal Lee. "You think maybe you're stretching things a little bit, Private?"

"Like I said earlier, sir, I grew up in Texas. Grew up with some mighty big critters. Spiders, scorpions, centipedes, all of them bigger than you'd want them to be. But the thing I just saw put all of them to shame."

"I'll take the point," said Colton. "Hill, you stay close to me and when we get to the spot where your insect was, point it out to me."

"Sir, I know it sounds crazy, but I also know what I saw," said Hill. "Be real careful."

"Count on it," said Colton.

The three men moved out with Colton about five steps in front of them. The rest of the squad followed, each of them keeping a close watch for anything that moved. Hill quickly caught up with Colton just as they approached the place where the thing had been. He and Corporal Lee looked around, studying the ground.

"Over here," whispered Corporal Lee, pointing to the ground. "As miserable as this mist and the humidity is, there is one good thing you can say about it. It keeps things muddy enough that everything leaves tracks. Look at this."

Colton and Hill studied the ground. Leading from one side of the trail to the other were little holes in the mud that looked like someone had punctured the ground repeatedly with a pencil. "For all of my years of hunting and tracking, I've never seen anything that would make those kinds of tracks," said Hill.

"I have," said Colton, "but we're too far from the beach and there are too many holes. Crabs moving across the sand can leave tracks like that, but it looks like this thing has cornered the market on legs."

Raising his weapon, Colton stepped off the trail and into the jungle, following the tracks. They continued deeper into the undergrowth, but after about fifteen feet disappeared into some rocks and thorn-covered plants. Whatever had made those tracks had disappeared into the jungle, but it added a new level of apprehension in Colton. He wasn't a big fan of bugs in the first place, but to have one the size of a small dog walking around made the hairs on the back of his neck stand up.

Returning to the trail, Colton said, "Whatever it was, it's gone now. Private, lead on. Corporal Lee, pass the word to everyone to watch the bushes alongside the trail. Anything that big has got to have an appetite."

As they moved deeper into the jungle, they soon noticed that the trees were getting taller, their girth much thicker. This also started to diminish the amount of undergrowth. The game trail gradually led them downhill, bringing them to a stream with a slow but steady current. Close to twenty feet wide, there was no way to judge the depth of the stream's murky brown water.

Colton, Garrett, and Lee studied the stream, trying to see if there was a better place to cross. They could see where the game trail came out of the water on the other side. "My guess is that the water's as shallow here as it's going to be anywhere else," said Corporal Lee. "Which is probably why this path is where it is. The animals figured it out long before we got here."

Garrett nodded her agreement. "What is that smell?" she asked, looking around.

The odor was strong, putrid, and sickly sweet. It was like someone had mixed cheap perfume with urine. "Wondered that myself. Reminds me of my former mother-in-law," said Colton. Looking around, he quickly located the source. "I think it's coming from that flower downstream," said Colton, pointing to a huge flower with large petals that appeared to be half submerged, near the opposite shore, about twenty-five feet away. "On the other hand, I'm not sure that's a flower. That thing is massive. And look at the petals. Have you ever seen a flower with petals like that?"

There was only the one blossom, but based on the potency of its scent, one was enough. The flower gave off an odor that was overpowering, saturating the area around it.

The blossom was nearly three feet across, its multiple leaves extending out flat, much like long, oval-shaped lily pads, all floating on the current. The center of the blossom was submerged. At the point where the petals emerged from the stream they were very broad and thick, quickly tapering to long, sharp, dagger like points. The petals were off-white with several yellowish-orange bulbs attached to each of them.

The reeds along the edge of the stream, just a few feet away from the flower, suddenly parted. A large lizard stuck its head out, its snout in the air. The three of them quickly knelt behind a small shrub, signaling for the rest of the men to take cover. "What is that?" asked Corporal Lee.

"I don't know," whispered Colton, "but it's certainly not a Komodo dragon."

"It almost looks like a Nile monitor, but on steroids. I've never seen one anywhere near that big," said Garrett.

They watched as the lizard approached the water. It kept its long, narrow snout in the air, its nostrils flared, seemingly drawn to the odor from this strange flower. Its long, forked tongue darted in and out in rapid succession. The lizard moved cautiously as it drew closer to the flower.

All they could see were its head, its shoulders, and its front legs. The lizard's skin had black, brown, and speckled gray lines running down its neck, continuing towards its back. Its legs were thick, like the one Garrett had spotted in the photo, with four thick, curved claws on each foot.

Gingerly stepping into the water, the lizard approached the flower, wading in between two of the petals. Turning its head at an angle, it reached out and started to nibble on one of the bulbs on the broad section of the petal. Taking the bulb into its mouth, the lizard moved further into the very shallow water.

Without warning, the stream erupted with the force and violence of a small explosion. The petal the lizard had been chewing on, along with the petal next to it, rapidly closed in on the lizard, latching on and wrapping around its body. A piercing scream from the lizard filled the air as the dagger like points on the end of the petals were thrust into its torso. The flower closed in on itself with more and more petals attacking the lizard, steadily drawing it into the center of the blossom.

The submerged center of the blossom burst from the water, opening and revealing row after row of what looked like hook-shaped teeth. The lizard struggled frantically, trying to escape, but Colton knew that it didn't have a chance. This fight had been over before it began.

The three of them watched as the lizard's head and upper body were pulled into the waiting teeth. The remaining petals closed in over the struggling lizard, forming an oblong ball. Then the entire blossom disappeared beneath the water. As quickly as it had started, it was over, the whole battle taking less than a minute. Silence reigned over the stream, the current smoothing over the turbulent water.

"What the hell was that?" asked Lee, not taking his eyes from the water.

Like Lee, Colton and Garrett continued to stare at the part of the stream where the flower had been. "If that's a plant," said Colton, "then it's the granddaddy of all Venus flytraps."

"Lee, check the area, up and downstream from here. I want to know if there are any more of those flower things in this area."

Lee motioned for Privates Diaz and Logan. He quickly gave them their orders and the two men moved out, carefully watching each step. Colton took their primary radio from Private Bannister and told MacKay, Meinhard, and Tanner what they'd just witnessed.

"You sure that thing was a plant?" asked MacKay.

"Judging strictly on appearance, yes," answered Colton. "But I don't know too many plants that can pull down a nine-foot lizard and have it for lunch."

"We'll alert Shaw and Fuller," said Tanner.

"Good, they can't take anything for granted based on looks," said Colton. "We're out." Turning off the radio, he handed it back to Private Bannister.

Diaz and Logan had returned and were talking with Garrett and Corporal Lee. "It appears that that's the only one of its kind around here. At least there weren't any that could be seen," said Garrett as Colton joined them. "Based on what we just witnessed, I'm not sure what our next move should be. Do we go ahead, try to wade across that stream, or do we run the risk of making some noise by pulling down a couple of trees to build a bridge?"

"Not all that anxious to give away our position," said Colton, "but I share your concern." Handing his rifle, his handheld radio, and his backpack to Corporal Lee, he turned to Private Hill and said, "Private, give me the rappelling line."

Private Hill lowered his own backpack to the ground and got the rappelling line Colton asked him for. Colton took the rope and wrapped it around his chest and shoulders in an X-type pattern, then wrapped it around his waist.

"Sir, you shouldn't be doing this," said Corporal Lee. "We'll handle the crossing."

"Thank you, Corporal, but I'll take the lead. Like you said, this looks like a good place to cross," said Colton. "There are tracks there and there that appear to be fresh and I can see some on the other side of the stream that look to be equally recent. There are always predators near the water, but this particular place obviously gets a lot of use, so it's probably as safe a crossing point as we're going to find."

"With all due respect, sir, how much do you know about tracking?" asked Private Hill.

"Not a great deal, but probably enough to stay in the conversation," said Colton.

"Then you'll have noticed that those prints are not only big, but those two indentations indicate that whatever it was that passed this way does not have retractable claws," said Hill, squatting down and pointing to the tracks he'd referenced.

"Can you tell what kind of tracks those are, Private?" asked Garrett.

"No sir, but based on their size, it was either one heck of a big dog, a good-sized bear, or another one of those lizards like the one that just became plant food. And look at those over there. As deep as those tracks are down by the water, I'd say it could have been that lizard's bigger brother."

"Corporal, I want you and two of your men to keep this line taut," directed Colton. "Anything starts to pull me under, I'm counting on you to get me out of there."

As Corporal Lee and Privates Hill and Logan gripped the rope, Garrett pulled her pistol out, chambering a round. "What exactly are you planning to do with that?" asked Colton, a smirk spreading across his face. "If something under the water does grab me, are you planning to just start shooting and hope you hit something?"

"That would be rather silly, don't you think, Commander?" said Garrett. "No, I'm just going to make sure that you don't suffer."

Colton stared at Garrett for a moment, not sure if she was being serious. Shaking his head, he moved down the steep bank to the edge of the stream. Before stepping in, he once again studied the stream as carefully as he could, looking for any sign of something hiding in the water. He took an equally hard look at the trees and bushes on the other side.

The fog was thick, but as best he could tell, there wasn't anything over there waiting for him. With pistol in hand, he stepped into the warm water and started to wade across. "There's some mud on the bottom, but it's mostly rock," reported Colton. "Don't keep the line too taut, Corporal, I have no plans to linger in this stream."

The current wasn't strong enough to be an issue and the water turned out to be rather shallow, the deepest part staying well below his waist. Colton crossed the stream without incident. He looked to see if he'd picked up any leeches, or any other unwanted creatures. Unwrapping the rope from around his body, he tightly secured it to a tree. He then signaled for the rest of them to cross. Hill and Logan came across next, bringing Colton's gear with them. They then took up defensive positions. The rest of the team followed, with Corporal Lee bringing up the rear.

The game trail continued into the jungle, snaking its way through the trees, but generally kept them heading in the right direction based on the drone's locater beacon. The day was turning hot and even though the mist never let up, they soon began to somewhat dry out from their forge across the stream. The terrain started to become rockier with large boulders strewn across the ground, the trees getting thicker and taller. The biting insects seemed to thin out.

They soon found themselves running parallel to a bluff, the cliff face towering upwards into the mist. On occasion the sun would break through, giving filtered light in some of the small clearings they passed through. Three times now they'd stopped as large creatures bolted away from them, but hidden by the thick foliage, they weren't able to get a clear look at any of them. The air was saturated with numerous scents and odors, all combining into something that reinforced Colton's earlier assessment, comparing it to a Louisiana swamp that had gone bad. It was not appealing in any way, shape, or form.

Corporal Lee's fist shot up into the air and he dropped to one knee, signaling the rest of them to stop and take cover. Colton had spotted the problem at the same time as Lee and moved up next to him. Ahead of them, up in one of the taller trees, or possibly on the cliff face, something had reflected the sun. None of them moved, watching and listening.

With Privates Diaz and Johnson watching their rear, Captain Garrett carefully moved up to join Colton and Lee. Lee was looking through binoculars and soon found what he was looking for. Handing the binoculars to Colton, he pointed about two-thirds up one of the trees that was almost touching the cliff.

"What is it?" asked Garrett as Colton studied it through the binoculars.

"Not sure, sir," answered Corporal Lee. "It's up in that tree and it's got some size to it. It may be a blind of sorts."

"Sniper?" asked Garrett.

"That's my concern," said Lee.

"Captain, take a look and see if you can figure out what that is," said Colton, handing her the binoculars. "There's definitely something up there, but I can't make it out."

Garrett soon spotted what they'd been looking at, but the mist, along with the branches and leaves from the surrounding trees, kept her from getting a good look. "I can't tell what that is either. How did you even spot it? It's so well hidden."

"The sun reflected off something," answered Lee. "My first thought was a rifle scope."

"I saw it too," said Colton. "Corporal, take Hill with you. See if you can get a better look."

Corporal Lee and Private Hill advanced, taking full advantage of the available cover. Colton soon lost sight of them. The waiting was terrible. Conditions being what they were, if the two men were in trouble, Colton would have no way of knowing.

About twenty minutes later, Private Hill returned. "Corporal says it's okay to advance. There's something stuck, high up, in one of the larger trees. We're not sure, but it may be lodged into that rock face as well."

They all followed Hill and soon found Corporal Lee at the base of a huge tree, the trunk at least fifteen feet in diameter. "It appears to be about fifty or sixty feet up. Still not sure what it is, but it's not moving. What's interesting is that it doesn't look natural."

"What do you mean, Corporal?" asked Garrett.

"Whatever it is, I don't think it was put there by nature. I've done the best I can from here to get a good look at it, but it appears to be camouflaged. I can't tell where it ends, and the tree begins."

"Any tree climbers in the group?" asked Colton.

Lee smiled at this. "Yes sir, I'm pretty good at it and Logan can climb anything."

"Okay," said Colton, "let's see what's up there."

Lee and Logan made ready for the ascent, both connecting rappelling lines to harnesses they'd brought. Taking only light weapons with them, they started up the massive tree. Not too far off in the distance, a loud growl could be heard, but none of them could tell if the animal that'd made it was heading towards them, or away from them. The team waited as the two men continued to climb. It was slow going, but they soon made it to the thing they'd spotted.

After a few minutes, they started back down. The descent was far easier than the climb up and they both seemed to be far more relaxed. As soon as he was back on the ground, Lee went to Colton and Garrett to report.

"It's a plane," said Lee, "or at least what's left of it. The wings are gone, but a good part of the fuselage is still there. My guess is that the sun reflected off a small piece of glass from the cockpit. The strange part is that it'll probably be there forever."

"Tree sap, sir," chimed in Logan. "Don't know how long it's been up there, but it's completely covered in amber-colored tree sap. Looks to be at least an inch or two thick."

"Any sign of human remains?" asked Garrett.

"No sir," said Lee. "And it's not a civilian craft. Sir, that plane is one of ours. Looks like an old navy plane."

"Are you sure?" asked Colton.

"Yes sir, but it's very old," said Lee. "It not only looks old, but for the tree sap to have coated it the way it did, I'd say it's been up there for at least forty or fifty years."

Logan handed Colton a small piece of paper. "We got lucky. Not only could we read the numbers on the side of the plane, I was also able to get these numbers off a part of the engine. The fuselage was torn away from most of the engine, and the sap that covered it is crystal clear. Not only that, but when you look at it from just the right angle, the sap magnifies things."

"Bannister," said Colton, studying the numbers from the plane that Logan had given him. "I need that radio."

"Could you tell if it had been shot down?" asked Garrett.

"There's not enough left up there to really figure out what happened," said Corporal Lee. "All what's left is about eight or nine feet of plane. That said, I didn't see any holes in it. Did you, Logan?"

"No sir, not a one. Not sure how it ended up in that tree, but I didn't see any signs that it'd been shot down or on fire when it came down."

Colton gave the numbers off the plane to MacKay. Meinhard took them and called Sahir so that he could run them through Argos. "So far, we haven't seen a soul," said Colton. "We're hearing all kinds of wildlife. Some of it sounds like its coming from some good-sized animals, but we haven't come across any of them yet."

"Good to hear, Commander," said MacKay. "Watch yourself."

Garrett told the men that they'd be taking a fifteen-minute break. Lookouts were posted, and the rest of the men sat down. "Certainly didn't expect to find a plane wreck up in one of these trees," said Garrett.

"Neither did I," said Colton. "Although in one way, finding that plane is a bit of a relief. At least we know someone has been here before us." Colton was now able to let go of some of the crazier thoughts that he'd been entertaining. Sadly, the time they were spending waiting on an answer from the *Eclipse* was the last time he would think of things as being wholly sane.

They heard the radio beep and Bannister brought it to Colton. "It's Captain MacKay, sir. He wants to talk with you."

"Thank you," said Colton, taking the radio from him. "What's going on, Captain?"

"That's what I was getting ready to ask you, Commander. You wouldn't be trying to pull one over on us, would you?"

Colton looked at Garrett, a puzzled expression on this face. "Not sure I'm following you, Captain. What are you talking about?"

"The numbers on that plane you found, would you please give them to me again?"

"Certainly," said Colton, reaching into his pocket and pulling out the crumpled piece of paper. "Here goes," he said, reading them to him once again.

The radio stayed silent for a moment, then MacKay came back on. "This is on the level, right, Colton?"

"Captain, what's wrong?" said Colton.

"The plane you found disappeared back in 1945 from the Fort Lauderdale Naval Air Base."

"Okay," said Colton. "What's so strange about that?"

"That plane was part of Flight 19," said MacKay. "It, and four other planes just like it, was on a training mission. They took off from Fort Lauderdale and once they were in the air, everything seemed to go wrong. Radios, navigational equipment, everything stopped working like it was supposed to. The men on the ground tried everything they could think of, but Flight 19 never returned. All five planes disappeared. There were no bodies, no wreckage, no oil spills, nothing. They all disappeared in the Bermuda Triangle. It's the case all the wackado Bermuda Triangle types mention. That's what's so strange."

Colton looked at Garrett, trying to make sense out of what MacKay had just said. "This is nuts. Where are we?" In Colton's mind he thought, *Wait a minute; we're going to be heroes. We just solved one of the biggest mysteries of the Bermuda Triangle.* The thought brought a smile to Colton's face. Then his brain said, *Or we're in hell.*

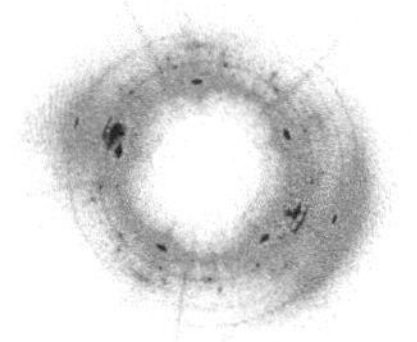

CHAPTER 13

"Over the last twenty-four hours, thanks to the efforts of everyone in this room, we've been able to pull together a great deal of data," said Sahir. Dr. Meinhard, along with Dr. Brennan and Dr. Chudzik, were anxious to get their hands on the analysis Sahir and his team had been frantically working to complete. Meinhard had been quite vocal in his objections about having to wait. He made it clear that he felt his team to be far superior to Sahir's, and because of that they should have been allowed to participate in all that Sahir's team was doing. He even went so far as to lodge a formal complaint with MacKay. Captain MacKay filed the complaint in the appropriate receptacle.

Except for Sahir, they'd all grabbed a quick lunch and were now gathered in the small conference room connected to Sahir's office, in the same secure area as Argos. Sahir was particularly glad that Lt. Commander Mercer had been able to join them. Sahir knew that he'd be depending on Mercer for direction regarding their next steps.

"The data from the drones sent out to study the landmass, as well as from the submersibles launched by Lt. Commander Mercer, has been reviewed by my team. That data was also automatically downloaded into Argos. The information, as well as the conclusions I'm about to go over with you, have all been verified by Argos," said Sahir, setting the stage for what he knew was going to be a very difficult meeting.

"What about the shots we took of the night sky?" asked Mercer. "Were you able to get an explanation for what's going on there?"

"I must have missed out on that one," said Dr. Brennan. "Is there some question regarding the stars?"

"Yes, there most certainly is," answered Mercer. "Captain MacKay and I first noticed it right after that wave of energy rolled over us. Let me just say that nothing is where it's supposed to be. It's completely wrong."

"I'm not following you," continued Dr. Brennan. "When you tell us that nothing is where it's supposed to be, what exactly are you saying?"

"I really don't know how to put it any plainer," said Mercer. "I've studied the stars for years; Captain MacKay even more than I have. That night, not long after that wave hit us, Captain MacKay, Colton, and I all stepped outside the bridge for a breath of fresh air. It was MacKay who first spotted it, drawing my attention to the sky. We looked for the North Star, the Big Dipper, and Polaris. They weren't there, or rather they weren't where they're supposed to be. Polaris goes in a big circle every twenty-six thousand years and it wasn't even close to where you'd normally see it."

"So, you're saying we're twenty-six thousand years in the future?" asked Dr. Brennan.

"No, that's not what I'm saying at all. Think of the change as being much more dramatic. When we went inside it was summer and when we stepped back out, it was winter. But, . . ." Mercer paused, "it wasn't the next winter. Polaris is easy to spot. It's our location to the constellation of Hercules that measures Deep Time."

"Deep Time?" scoffed Meinhard. "This is sounding more like deep manure."

Mercer inhaled deeply, doing his best to ignore Meinhard's rudeness. "The sun is a star that circles around the galactic core once every fifty thousand years. The galaxy itself is moving away from other galaxies, although there's some speculation as to the speed. There are, however, constants in the universe. As humans, we're just used to the small ones such as the earth rotates once a day, goes around the sun in a year, the magnetic field is aligned in a certain way, so forth and so on. We don't need the big ones."

"So exactly what are you trying to tell us?" asked Dr. Chudzik.

"All I'm saying is that on top of everything else we can't explain, the position of the stars above has added to the confusion. That said, I'm going to turn this briefing back to Mr. Sahir."

"I'd like to start with the drones we flew up and down the coast, as well as the one we sent into the interior," said Sahir. "Unfortunately, as far as we can tell, the ground fog, or haze, stays in place throughout the day. It never burned off like we hoped it would. So, due to that, the drones couldn't give us too much in the way of usable data. Dr. Chudzik, however, did give us some additional items to dig into, based on some of the plants she was able to get a clear look at and identify."

"I'm afraid identify is a little too strong. What I gave to Mr. Sahir was more in the neighborhood of being several good guesses," said Chudzik. "A few of the plants that I took note of appear to be very similar to some species of plants growing in Hawaii, as well as some other islands in the South Pacific. But, to be completely straightforward, due to the limited visibility, it's hard to be sure."

"Initially, we were not able to identify any of the plants from the pictures," said Sahir. "We also tried to determine our location by mapping the coastline and feeding that into Argos. Amazingly, even Argos came up empty on the plants as well as the coastline."

"You said 'initially.' I'm guessing that you have been able to identify some of the plants after all," said Dr. Brennan.

"We think so," said Sahir. "Interestingly, our being able to identify them is tied in to the analysis of the night sky. That is what ended up opening the door for us. But again, if I may, I'll come back to that."

"Please, Lieutenant, are you trying to be deliberately obtuse, or are you just too scattered to present your findings in a coherent manner?" barked Meinhard, sitting up in his chair, raising his high-pitched voice for emphasis. "Were you able to identify them or not?"

Before he could respond, Mercer interjected himself into the exchange. "Dr. Meinhard, I have to assume that you have achieved some level of accomplishment in your given field, or you wouldn't be on this ship. I respect that. But so long as you are on board the *Eclipse*, you will show the proper respect to its crew. I've served with Lieutenant Sahir for three years and he is a very intelligent and capable officer. I am confident that we will get a very thorough and complete briefing from him. I'm equally confident that he is giving us that briefing in the manner he believes will present the data in the clearest light. Do you understand what I'm saying to you, Doctor?"

It was clear that Dr. Meinhard was not used to being reprimanded. He'd also, on many occasions, made it equally clear that he held himself above and apart from the military personnel serving on the *Eclipse*, which made Mercer's reprimand a square pill for him to swallow. His face flushed, turning a dark pink, but he managed to hold himself in check. Meinhard's sense of self-preservation recognized that Lt. Commander Mercer was not a man he wanted to challenge. At least not today.

"Yes," mumbled Dr. Meinhard begrudgingly. "I understand. My apologies, Mr. Sahir."

"I appreciate that, Dr. Meinhard," said Sahir. "And I do understand your frustration. It is the same frustration that we experienced. It wasn't until we had enough pieces of the puzzle that we were finally able to draw our conclusions, and then we had them verified by Argos. Please bear with me, Doctor. We will get there. All of this is very important. It is also important to remember that Argos is not an all-knowing god. It just correlates more content than we do."

"As many of you now know, the *Eclipse* is a very special ship," Mercer interjected. "It has capabilities far and above any other ship in the navy, Argos being the primary differentiator. When Lieutenant Sahir informed me that Argos could identify the shorelines mapped by the drones, I offered to send up HAPS."

"Is that another kind of drone?" asked Dr. Chudzik.

"I'd never heard of it either," said Sahir, "much less that we had them on board."

"You're exactly right, Dr. Chudzik," answered Mercer. "It is another kind of drone. In fact, it's the latest in drone technology. HAPS stands for High Altitude Pseudo Satellite. Not sure if you're a Star Trek fan or not, but it looks a great deal like a Klingon bird of prey."

Having been chastised by Mercer, Meinhard refused to participate in the conversation. Even though he was dying of curiosity, he refused to ask about HAPS' capabilities. The expression on his face was that of an insolent, pouting child, glaring at anyone who caught his eye. Dr. Brennan, on the other hand, was as curious about this as Dr. Chudzik. "Can you tell us how HAPS is different from the other drones we sent up?"

"Absolutely," said Mercer. "Dr. Brennan, you'll especially appreciate this. The HAPS drone can provide high-resolution imagery down to six-inch resolution."

"From what height?" asked Dr. Brennan.

"HAPS can reach heights higher than seventy thousand feet, which gives it the capability of seeing more than 250 miles to the horizon and provide imagery in excess of 386 square miles. It's an amazing piece of machinery."

"That's incredible," said Dr. Brennan.

"The good news is that it is powered by the sun, so, if need be, it can stay in the air for a long time."

"How long?" asked Dr. Chudzik.

"Close to forty-five days," answered Mercer. "Thanks to HAPS, we were able to map a considerable amount of the coastline, all of which was sent to Sahir's team."

"Which we immediately fed into Argos," said Sahir. "We also examined the data we collected from the submersibles. Not only did we get pictures of the marine life, but they also gathered several samples of the water at various depths. As with the plants highlighted by Dr. Chudzik, initially we couldn't identify any of the fish that had been photographed."

At Sahir's use of the word "initially" again, Meinhard sighed audibly, rolling his eyes in disgust. Everyone ignored him.

"From a microbiology standpoint, we were equally stumped. Dr. Curra, of your team, was nice enough to review our findings, but he couldn't come up with any answers either. It was around that time we received the findings that Argos provided by combining the pictures we took of the night sky, along with the mapping of the coastline provided by HAPS. At first, we didn't believe the findings, but as all of you understand, it would be rather a waste of time to challenge Argos. I'm not sure it can make a mistake."

"Finally," muttered Dr. Meinhard, "Some hard facts. So, where are we, or should I say, when are we? I mean, that's what you're saying, right, time travel?"

"We don't know," answered Sahir. This earned him dark looks from Mercer, as well as Meinhard, who got out of his chair and started pacing in the back of the conference room. Clearly it was not the answer any of them had anticipated. "But it did give us the new set of parameters we needed to complete our research."

"What kind of parameters?" asked Dr. Chudzik. She was being as nice as she could be, but at this point everyone's patience was wearing razor thin. Even her voice had a cold edge to it.

"Time parameters," answered Sahir. While it may have appeared to the casual observer that Sahir was enjoying himself, nothing could have been further from the truth. Yes, Sahir and his team had the data and were ready to give their conclusions to the scientists on board, as well as to Captain MacKay and his officers. But, at the same time, Sahir was extremely apprehensive about sharing this information. In short, what he had to tell them was simply crazy. Had it not been for all the other unexplainable things that had happened to them, he would have dismissed their findings out of hand, Argos or no Argos.

"Once we recalibrated, using the new time parameters, we were finally able to identify seven of the plants and close to fifteen of the fish photographed by the submersibles," said Sahir.

"Hold on, Lieutenant," said Mercer. "Are you telling me that Argos still couldn't determine where we are even with the hundreds of miles of coastline mapped out by HAPS? That's not possible."

"Argos has given us a theoretical location," said Sahir, choosing his words carefully. "But it's not any place that any of us are familiar with."

"You've been able to identify several of the plants," said Dr. Brennan, "as well as quite a few of the fish, but the best you can get out of Argos is a 'theoretical' location, a location you refuse to name?"

"I'm not refusing to name anything, Doctor," said Sahir. "As far as I know, it doesn't have a name. Look, the reason we couldn't identify the plants, or any of the fish at first glance, is that they are all supposed to be extinct. And I don't mean recently extinct. I'm talking millions of years extinct. Tens of millions."

Mercer pushed his chair back from the table. "Mr. Sahir, I'm starting to recognize the slow speech of an old-fashioned country doctor. It took my dad's doctor twenty minutes to tell him he had Stage IV cancer. Just how bad are your team's findings?"

Sahir dreaded what he was about to say, but he had no choice. Despite his paralyzing fear of going anywhere near a jungle, right now he would have given anything to have gone ashore with Colton and Garrett. "Based on the pictures we fed into Argos of the night sky, as well as the data sent to us from HAPS, with 75 percent accuracy Argos has determined that we are on earth."

"That was never in question, Lieutenant Sahir," Mercer nearly shouted. "I want to know where and when on earth?"

"Again, based on the location of the stars, the coastal mapping, and backed up by the extinct fauna and marine life, Argos has determined that we are on earth as it existed roughly sixty-five million years ago. Due to continental drift, the world's landmasses looked very different then.

Yes, we're close to land, but that's the best we can tell you. If Argos hadn't confirmed all this, I wouldn't believe it either."

The room went completely silent.

"Stupid question, but you're positive there's no mistake about this," said Mercer, his voice betraying the fear that coursed through him.

"Argos is not theorizing, nor does Argos make hypothesis on its own. It answers the questions we ask. Argos says it looks like we are on earth sixty-five million years ago."

Mercer looked at the three scientists. Slowly nodding their agreement, they were still trying to wrap their minds around the information they'd just been given. Sahir looked like he was going to be sick.

"None of this leaves this room," said Mercer. "Lieutenant, your team is confined to this area until further notice."

"Yes sir," said Sahir, his voice just about a whisper.

Mercer didn't move, staring down at his hands. Finally, he leaned forward and picked up the phone sitting in the middle of the conference table. "Captain, we need for you to join us." Mercer listened for a few moments, and then said, "No sir, it would be best if you joined us here."

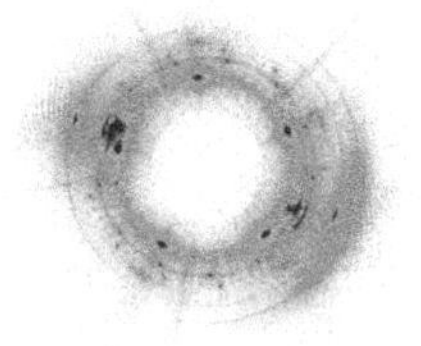

CHAPTER 14

The shore party continued to penetrate deeper into the interior, following the signal from the downed drone as best they could. Although the locater signal was becoming less and less frequent, as well as weaker in strength, they had been able to establish a pretty good bearing on where it had come down.

The sounds from the inhabitants of this jungle were new and strange to all of them, ranging from piercing, gut-wrenching howls to fierce screams and the anguished cries of battle. This unsettling symphony of nature surrounded them, but so far, they hadn't seen anything too extraordinary. That is, if you chose to overlook that flower thing that attacked and killed the lizard. The scene of that fast and lethal attack kept playing over and over in Colton's mind, and try as he might, he couldn't let it go.

The only other item of curiosity that bothered him was when Garrett pointed out the lack of birds. None of them had seen a single bird since they'd set foot on shore, nor had they heard anything that remotely sounded like a bird. At one point a large shadow raced over a partial clearing, but none of them had been able to see what had caused it. Corporal Lee suggested that perhaps they were staying high in the treetops, the dense vegetation keeping them out of sight. Whatever the reason, it simply added one more thing to the list of unanswered questions.

The discovery of the plane had certainly been surprising, but Colton reasoned that maybe it would finally help to put to rest all the Bermuda Triangle nonsense. Like everything else in the world, there was always a natural explanation for why things happened, although he knew Father Ryan would never agree with that assessment. Father Ryan needed mystery; it was the source of his energy.

He'd read a great deal about Flight 19 years ago while at the academy. The tremendous amount of time and manpower that had gone into the search for those planes had been the largest to date by the US military. Obviously, they'd all been looking in the wrong place.

A wry smile passed across Colton's face. He realized that even though one of the planes from Flight 19 had now been found, the navy was no closer to knowing where it had disappeared to than they'd been in 1945. Although not one of their crew had said it out loud, they all realized that they too were as lost as the plane they'd just found. They had joined the lost, rather than bringing the lost to the found.

The terrain thinned out as they headed uphill. While the jungle remained reasonably dense, they were starting to see more and more rock outcroppings that appeared to have erupted out of the earth centuries ago. The tall rock face that had been to their right stayed parallel to the course they were following.

The game trail they'd been following veered off to the left, cutting through a patch of thick bushes with wicked thorns along the edges of the leaves. Suddenly Colton could hear something coming his way at fast pace, and he realized he'd lost sight of Private Hill and Corporal Lee. By instinct he brought his rifle up, clicking the safety off, all in one fluid movement. Private Hill, a little out of breath, burst into sight, running towards him.

"Sir, we've found something up ahead," he said, keeping his voice just above a whisper. "Corporal Lee is there waiting for us. Turns out, we're not alone is this jungle."

"What have you found?" asked Colton, dropping his voice to match Hill's.

"There's no one there right now, but I've never seen anything like this. I'm guessing it's a monument of some kind, but that's all I can tell you," said Hill.

Garrett, with her men deployed, joined Hill and Colton to see what had happened. "It seems that Private Hill and Corporal Lee have come across some ruins," Colton explained, a bit exasperated with Hill. The way the private was acting, it was as if they'd come across an enemy force.

"Sir, they're not ruins," said Hill. "I mean, they're not new, but they look like they're in pretty good shape, and the grounds around them are beautiful, like a park. Maybe it's a religious thing, I don't know."

"Alright," said Colton, "let's take a look. Captain, tell everyone to stay alert and be ready."

Hill turned and took off at a slow trot. Colton, along with the rest of the team, followed Hill and they soon came upon Lee, crouched down behind a small boulder. "It's up ahead, sir, just beyond that small rise. Talk about out of place, wait till you see this."

"Did you see anyone?" asked Garrett.

"No sir, but they can't be far away. The grounds around this thing are too well kept. Someone keeps the area nicely trimmed."

Colton turned and motioned for Private Bannister to join them. "Captain, I'm going to take these three men with me and see what we have. If Lee is right, let's not let anyone come up behind us. If there's trouble, depending on their strength, we may need to make a quick retreat."

"Be careful, Colton," said Garrett. "We're not exactly dealing from a position of strength here, so before you start shooting everything that moves, try diplomacy."

"An easygoing guy like me?" said Colton, smiling broadly. "Diplomacy is always my first choice, especially when their gun is bigger than mine."

Leading the way, Colton set out, slowly advancing up the small rise, all four of them listening for the slightest sound that would let them know that there were potential enemies close by. The normal sounds of the jungle that they'd become used to droned on. Dropping to his knees, he slowly stuck his head over the edge of the rise. Just as Corporal Lee had said, what lay before him was totally out of place.

The jungle opened, giving way to a perfect, circular area covering at least an acre and a half. Just inside the perimeter of the circle stood three eight-sided pillars of stone, each, he estimated, to be thirty feet in height. On the sides of the pillars were all kinds of symbols, covering every square inch, all the symbols unfamiliar to him. The three pillars were spread out along the edges of the circle, forming a triangular area in which nothing grew. The ground inside the triangle was completely bare, with not even one blade of grass growing.

In the center of the triangle were three more eight-sided pillars, but these appeared to be only around nine feet in height, all three with rounded tops. They too were positioned in such a way as to form another triangle and were covered with what appeared to be the same kinds of symbols. What really amazed him was how perfectly manicured the grounds within the circle were maintained. How did the gardeners even get in there? Did they drop in?

"Amazing," Colton muttered under his breath. "I've played golf courses not this well cared for."

"What did you say, Commander?" asked Lee, who was right next to Colton, but up until now had gone unnoticed.

"Nothing, Corporal," answered Colton. "What is this place?" Turning to Private Bannister, he said, "Private, take pictures of this and shoot them back to the *Eclipse.* Let's see what they can make of it."

"On it, sir," said Bannister.

"Private Hill, let Captain Garrett know that it is okay for her and her team to advance. She needs to see this." Hill turned and started back down the trail.

"What is that sound?" said Corporal Hill. "It's kinda like bees, lots of bees."

"I hear it too," said Colton, "but no, it's not bees. It rather sounds like electrical current, that sound you hear when you walk under massive power lines."

"Sir, I've sent the pictures back to the ship," reported Bannister.

"Thank you, Private," said Colton. "Can either of you identify the symbols on those pillars?"

Before they could answer, Captain Garrett crawled up beside them. "I've got the men deployed in a defensive grid," she told Colton, then caught sight at what they were staring at. "What is that? That's not English, Russian, or Chinese."

"Your guess is as good as mine," said Colton. "Time we took a closer look. Private Bannister, you will accompany Captain Garrett and me. Shoot as many pictures as you can, including some close-ups on those symbols. Just be careful where you walk. We have no idea what this place is. Corporal, in the event anything should happen to us, take the men and get back to the ship. Is that understood?"

"Yes sir, it is, but don't you think it would be better if Private Hill and I first took a look around?"

"Unfortunately, we must be cognizant of the time," said Colton. "We'll be spending the night in this jungle and we're going to want to try and find some place far more secure than this to make camp before the sun sets. Considering the animals we keep hearing, not to mention the things we glimpsed crawling along the ground, we need to find a place that is far more defensible. I don't want to get caught in the open when the predators come out."

"He's right, Corporal," said Garrett. "We're going to run out of daylight all too soon. Let's get this done."

Garrett got up and led the three of them as they cautiously moved forward. The edge of the circle was so fine it could have been cut with a knife. Not a single plant from the surrounding jungle encroached on the area at all. Another item that didn't make sense. Within the circle the ground was covered with a grass that was very fine, not all that different from what you'd see on a golf course green.

Colton went up to the closest pillar and after studying it for a moment, took a chance and lightly touched it with the back of his hand. The pillar appeared to be a type of stone, one that resembled granite and yet was quite different in its texture. His attempt to interpret the symbols came up empty. As far as he was concerned they might as well have been Mayan hieroglyphs, completely undecipherable.

"These three pillars come to a point at the top; the shorter ones are rounded. Wonder if there's a reason for that?" said Garrett, her question almost rhetorical.

"Let's check out the smaller triangle. Those pillars look to be made of a different kind of rock," said Colton. Bannister continued to take pictures as they moved towards the center of the circle. "As well kept as this place is, there's absolutely no sign that anybody ever comes here."

"The humming sound is getting louder," said Garrett. "I think it's coming from those three smaller pillars."

The smaller pillars were darker than their larger cousins but were covered with similar markings. The humming sound was its loudest here, so whatever power was being generated, this was where it was focused. The area inside the smaller triangle appeared to be one triangular slab of stone, highly polished, so much so that it reflected things around it.

Taking a small tin of rations out of his backpack, Colton said, "Everyone step back. Let's see if anything happens when I do this." He lightly tossed the small tin, striking one of the pillars. The tin merely bounced off and landed on the ground. No sparks. No flashes of light. Nothing.

"That was rather anticlimactic," said Garrett. "What were you expecting?"

"I'll take anticlimactic any time I can get it," said Colton as he leaned down to pick up the tin. As he leaned over he put his left hand on the small pillar to steady himself. The moment he touched it, the three pillars seemed to come to life. The humming sound became louder and the three pillars were slowly encased in a light-blue light, starting at their base and gradually working its way to the top.

All three of them quickly stepped back and were watching as the light seemed to gather in strength at the top of each pillar. Three beams of light, one from each pillar, shot out, meeting in midair in the center of the triangle. There the light briefly formed into a small globe of soft blue light before being transformed into what looked like a highly detailed map of some kind. Made up of varying shades of green, there were also numerous streams and what appeared to be rock outcrops. There were also a few red dots in certain places and two dark blue dots.

"Bannister," Colton whispered, "you getting this?"

Like the rest of them, this had taken Bannister by surprise. He quickly started clicking away. The image held steady. For a hologram, it was extremely clear and detailed.

"Is that a map?" asked Colton.

"That would be my guess," said Garrett. "This is amazing." Then, as suddenly as it had appeared, the hologram went away and the blue light encasing the pillars slowly faded.

"Bannister, get these pictures back to the *Eclipse* as quickly as you can," ordered Colton. Once again he closely studied the three pillars, trying to understand what the symbols might represent. "I wonder if you get the same image every time. Or does it make a difference as to which pillar you touch?"

Before they could experiment with this they heard Corporal Lee calling to them. Although he was keeping his voice as low as possible, there was an intensity about his tone. Reluctantly, they turned around and left the circled area. Private Diaz was standing there with the corporal. "Sir, I know this is an important find, but we may have a problem heading our way," said Diaz.

"What is it, Diaz?" snapped Colton. Privates Diaz and Johnson had been tasked with guarding their flank.

"At first only Johnson noticed it, but then I heard it too. We held back for a few minutes and waited, but we didn't see anything. For a little while we thought it had gone away, but now it's back again," explained Diaz.

"What's back again?" asked Corporal Lee.

"That's just it, sir, we don't know," said Diaz. "It's big. You can tell by the sounds it makes moving through the trees and the bushes. But it hasn't gotten close enough for us to get a look at it. Johnson has spent more time in the woods than I have, but we're pretty sure something is stalking us."

At that moment, Logan, who had been sent on up ahead to see if there was a village in the area, returned to the unit, moving as quietly as he could through the trees. "About thirty, forty yards ahead we got a very deep ravine. I tried, but with the mist and all the foliage I couldn't see the bottom. The good news is that I did spot a tree growing out of the rock face on our side of the ravine, about twenty feet down. Sir, we may have found the drone."

The radio Bannister was carrying beeped, and Bannister handed it to Colton. "Captain MacKay, sir."

"I trust you got the pictures we sent to you," said Colton.

"Sahir and his team are working on that now," answered MacKay. "At first pass, Argos has come up empty. Considering how dense the jungle is where you are, it's amazing how pristine that area looks. Have you discovered anything else?"

"Well, we have good news and we have bad news," said Colton. "Private Logan thinks he may have found the drone just up ahead. That's good. The bad news is that Privates Diaz and Johnson think something may be stalking us."

"Stalked by who?" MacKay's voice was not as clear as it had been earlier when they'd found the remnants of that plane up in the tree. Colton wondered if the circular area behind him was in any way interfering with the signal.

"At this point, we don't know," said Colton. "We'll get back to you." Colton handed the radio back to Bannister. "Any ideas what it is that you think is on our trail?"

"No sir," replied Diaz. "But, as I was saying, from the sound of it, it's bigger than you'd want it to be. It's a good guess that it's a predator."

Garrett looked to Colton to see how he wanted to proceed. "Diaz, rejoin Johnson. Keep a sharp lookout, but stay close to the rest of us," said Colton. "Logan, lead on. Show us what you've found."

It took very little time before they arrived at the ravine. As Logan had described, due to the mist they could barely see the other side, which looked to be at least eighty to ninety feet across. The bottom of the ravine was as shrouded in mist as the rest of the area. The trees had somewhat thinned out near the ravine's edge. To their left the jungle looked as thick and menacing as it had since they'd left the beach. To their right the ground rose up steeply, the foliage much thinner, and the ground covered with boulders of all sizes.

Logan motioned to Colton, and he and Garrett joined the private as he pointed down into the ravine. There was the tree he'd told them about, and it did appear to be growing out of the rock face. "Looks like the drone is wedged into the branches, but from here I can't be sure," said Private Logan.

Colton pulled out a small pair of binoculars from his pack and focused in on the tree. There was certainly something lodged in its branches, but the foliage was too thick, and the mist blurred his vision. "I don't get it. In college I couldn't keep a Wandering Jew alive. Here we have trees growing out of rocks."

"Corporal," said Garrett, "I want a defensive perimeter set up in those rocks." Corporal Lee nodded and headed off, directing the men as he went. Garrett then took out some small binoculars and she too peered down at the tree.

"Are you seeing what I'm seeing?" asked Colton.

"Good job, Logan," said Garrett. "There's something down there, alright. Whether it's our drone, or part of another plane from Flight 19, you really can't tell from here. Shall I have Lee and Logan go down there and take a look?"

"No," said Colton, taking off his backpack. "I'll go down with Logan. If it is the drone, I want to get a close look at it."

Private Bannister walked up to Colton while Logan was setting up the rappelling lines. "Sir, I have Captain MacKay for you again, but it's a little broken up. I've tried boosting the signal, but it's still in and out."

Taking the radio from Bannister, Colton said, "Colton here. How are things back at the ship?"

The signal had weakened and Colton had to listen carefully. "We have new information. You and your . . ." MacKay went away for a few seconds. ". . . in serious danger if this information is correct."

"Having trouble hearing you Captain, please repeat."

Once again MacKay's words were jumbled, but Colton was able to hear enough of what MacKay was trying to tell him to know that his team was in danger. Colton guessed that Argos had been able to decipher the symbols on those pillars. "Understood," said Colton. "We believe we've located the drone. Once we examine it, we'll head back to the *Eclipse*."

The radio went silent and Colton didn't know whether MacKay had heard him or not. A few moments later MacKay's voice came through stronger and clearer. "Argos helped us to boost the signal. You said you've located the drone."

"We think so," answered Colton. "We're getting ready to take a closer look."

"Commander, the situation has changed. We are not under attack but believe your team may be in extreme jeopardy. Whether it's the drone or something else you've found, it doesn't matter. I strongly advise that you return to the ship now. Do you copy?"

"Loud and clear, Captain. I take it you were able to translate the symbols on those pillars."

"No. Argos, Sahir, and even Meinhard's team are still pounding away at that. Just get your team together and get out of there."

"We'll make short work of this and head back," said Colton.

"What do you think that's all about?" asked Garrett.

"No idea, but MacKay's a pretty tough guy," answered Colton. "If something has him spooked, then it's probably a good idea to act with caution. Looks like Diaz and Johnson might be right about our stalker. Keep a tight watch while we're gone."

"Sir, the rappelling lines are ready," said Private Logan.

Corporal Lee joined them and told Garrett, "Sir, the men have been deployed." Then, looking at Colton, he said, "Begging your pardon, sir, but wouldn't it be better if I accompanied Logan over the side to have a look at that thing? It's what we do, and I'd hate to see you get hurt, Commander."

Colton smiled at this, putting on the harness and attaching himself to one of the lines. "There you go again. Just how fragile do I look to you, Corporal?"

"No sir, it's not that, it's just that if anything were to . . ."

"It's okay, Corporal," said Colton. "I do appreciate your concern, but like you, I've done this before. Garrett, keep an eye out. Something took that drone down. Now, considering what Diaz and Johnson think is coming up behind us, along with the warning from MacKay, it's no longer a question of whether or not we're alone."

Colton and Logan stepped back off the edge of the ravine and began to work their way down. Apart from their sidearm, they'd left their weapons and backpacks with Corporal Lee. This side of the ravine was nearly vertical, but the rock face was riddled with cracks and holes, providing them several good footholds as they descended.

They soon came to the tree. "Stay where you are, Private," directed Colton. "I'm going to lower myself into the branches and see what we have."

"Here. You might need this, sir," said Logan, pulling a machete from its sheath and handing it to Colton. "Keep an eye out for critters. They like to hide in the top of trees, picking off unwary prey."

"Comforting thought, Logan. Thank you for that," said Colton, half glaring at the young private. "Keep your eyes open as well. You're right, it's hard to tell what kinds of creatures may call this rock face home."

The machete was razor sharp and it didn't take Colton long to open a space wide enough for him to enter. Slowly he lowered himself into the foliage and there, to his right, he saw where a few branches had been splintered and cracked in half. About twelve feet further down he found the drone, wedged tightly between two thick branches.

"Good eye, Logan," called Colton. "It's the drone. I'm going to look it over, then we'll head back up." Colton was careful not to get his line tangled in the mass of branches that surrounded him. The trunk of the tree was nearly covered with sap, and he did his best not to get it on his boots.

Colton carefully made it to one of the thick branches holding up the drone. It had come to its final resting place right side up, which would have helped Colton tremendously if he'd had the need to open it. Fortunately, that wasn't going to be necessary. Colton could see the deep scratch marks across its top and one side had been completely smashed in. It didn't take much in the way of deductive reasoning to see that something had attacked the drone and knocked it out of the sky.

"You doing okay, Commander?" asked Logan.

Colton snapped several pictures of the drone, then said, "On my way up, Private."

Minutes later Colton climbed out of the tree and back onto the rock face next to Private Logan. "Alright, let's head back up. We've seen what we came to see," said Colton.

The words had no sooner left his mouth when a terrible screeching roar filled the air above them. Acting on reflex, both the men pulled themselves into the rock face, frantically looking around to see what was attacking them.

The roar was quickly followed by shots from automatic weapons. Diaz and Johnson's stalker had arrived. Whatever was going on, Garrett and her team were clearly under attack. "I'll lead, you watch our back," said Colton, handing the machete back to Logan. He then started the vertical climb back up as quickly as he could.

Once again, the high-pitched roar drowned out everything else around them. The strength and intensity of the roar filled Colton with a dread he'd not felt in a long time. He couldn't even begin to imagine the kind of creature that could make such a strong, bone-chilling sound. Visions of the lizard-eating flower raced through his mind.

As Colton neared the lip of the cliff, he could hear, off in the distance, other creatures roaring in response. Whatever it was, there were apparently more of them in the area. A herd, a flock? Cautiously, he pulled himself up and over the edge of the cliff, and staying close to the ground, scooted up behind the two trees they'd tied off on. Lying on his back, he released the climbing harness and rolled over to the small bush where Corporal Lee had left their packs and rifles.

For the moment, all was quiet. The shooting had stopped. The air was thick with the smell of gunpowder and smoke from the marine's weapons. Colton reasoned that whatever it was that had attacked them had either been killed or fled the area. Logan lay next to him on the ground, his rifle in hand. Colton motioned for him to stay down as he slowly got to his knees to see what was going on.

He quickly spotted Garrett and her command. They'd taken position up in the rocks about twenty yards away from him. Colton could see the corpsman kneeling behind one of the larger boulders, frantically at work. The team had at least one man down.

Colton quickly surveyed the ground in front of the marines, leading away from them to the edge of the jungle. Off to the right, there was a fair amount of orange-red blood on two of the smaller rocks. Whoever had attacked them had paid a high price. Colton hoped that it had been enough and that the fight was over.

For the moment, the small clearing in front of them was empty, but the jungle bore evidence that something huge had been there. Several bushes, as well as a couple of small trees, had been knocked over and crushed into the ground. Many of the larger leaves, and a few of the trees, had been shredded by bullets.

Garrett caught sight of him and motioned for Colton to join them, but to keep an eye on the tree line. Before they could communicate any further, the quiet was shattered by multiple roars, the same bone-rattling sound that Colton had heard hanging from the rappelling lines.

Although their attackers were some distance away from them, the sounds of snapping branches and crunching made it clear that they were coming at them hard and fast. Colton still didn't have a clue as to what they were facing, but he sure wasn't going to stand there and wait to see what it was.

Grabbing their packs, Colton and Logan took off at a dead run to join the marines, now spread out amongst the rocks. Logan moved on over to help cover the corpsman, while Colton took cover next to Garrett.

Staring intensely into the forest, Colton cocked his rifle and shouted, "How big of a force are we facing?"

"In the first assault, there was only one of them," said Garrett.

The fact that there'd been only one attacker took Colton by surprise. This did not line up with the area of devastation he was staring at. Once again, he studied the kill zone in front of him. Other than the ground being torn up, there was no sign of any enemy bodies. "Only one?" said Colton, trying to understand what had happened. "Where is it? I heard at least thirty shots. Not even marines can miss a target with that heavy of a barrage."

"And that's the bad news," said Garrett. "We didn't miss. Our bullets just didn't seem to have much of an impact on it." Garrett turned to her men and shouted, "Aim at the chest, dead center and pour it on. As soon as it breaks from the trees, launch grenades."

"It?" asked Colton. "Captain, what exactly attacked you?"

Garrett's voice broke. This tough, well-trained, intelligent woman could not find the words. Colton couldn't believe the fear, mixed with un-spilled tears in her eyes. "I don't know! Godzilla? Maybe dragons from the Game of Thrones? I've never seen anything like it. A monster, we're killing monsters, sir."

At that moment, the creature burst through the tree line, charging directly at them. Colton was stunned. He couldn't move, his legs frozen to the spot where he was standing, his mind trying to comprehend the creature in front of him.

It was at least sixteen feet tall, standing upright on two legs. Its arm like appendages had curved claws the size of garden sickles, and it moved with the agility of a cat. Opening its mouth, it once again roared its challenge at them, revealing rows of dagger length teeth, each three to four inches long. Its skin, although bloodied in some areas, was a blend of colors that would easily keep it concealed in the thick jungle.

Colton's mind tried to deny the nightmare bearing down on him, but the terrifying truth was that they were being attacked by some type of dinosaur. Impossible. Ludicrous. Horribly real.

The marines immediately opened fire, all of them targeting its chest. At the same time three grenades were thrown at the beast, two passing harmlessly by, exploding in the bushes behind it. The third one, however, fell short and the creature stepped on the grenade just as it went off.

The bullets had dug a hole in the creature's chest and when the grenade detonated, the creature's left leg erupted in pieces of flesh, blood, and gore. A scream of terrible agony erupted from its throat. The creature crashed to the ground, but continued to reach for them, clawing at the air.

At that moment, four more of the same type of dinosaurs burst from the tree line, one of which was very close to them, off to the right, having nearly flanked them. Garrett's men immediately started to withdraw, tightening their position as the creatures charged their line. Logan and the corpsman dragged the wounded marine further up into the rocks.

The creature closest to them was smaller than the others, maybe ten feet tall, but just as aggressive, just as deadly. In three quick strides, it was almost on top of Corporal Lee, snapping at him with rows of nightmarish teeth. Lee dove out of the way, barely avoiding the snapping jaws, but when he hit the ground, the impact caused his rifle to fly from his hands. The creature's hot and rotten breath nearly choked the young marine and he would remember it as the smell of death for the rest of his life.

The creature's momentum carried it forward a few more steps and it now stood between Corporal Lee and the rest of the command. Lee stayed low, crawling away, desperately trying to find some place to hide. The other three dinosaurs had moved forward, pausing at the creature lying on the ground as if unsure what to do next. Fear and hunger ruled their big eyes, an expression no mammal ever wore.

One of them lowered its head, sniffing the fallen dinosaur, nudging it with its nose. After a couple of moments, it raised its head and gave a terrifying roar, a roar filled with rage. Colton expected them to attack, but instead they clawed the ground, lowering their heads and studied their prey more closely. This temporary pause gave the marines time to reposition for the attack they knew was coming.

Colton ran over, placing himself directly in front of the dinosaur that had attacked Corporal Lee. Shouting and waving his hands in the air, he tried to distract the creature as Lee continued to belly crawl away, putting as much distance as possible between himself and the creature. "Reload," shouted Garrett. "We have to take down the one by Corporal Lee."

"Sir, we are running really low on ammo," shouted Diaz. "It takes too many bullets to knock those walking nightmares down."

"Colton, back up, you're too close," yelled Garrett, her eyes glued to the other three creatures who continued to mill around the fallen dinosaur.

"When those three start to advance, hit them with more grenades," ordered Colton. "Diaz is right, we don't have enough ammo to do the job." Colton had a nearly full clip in his rifle but had only one remaining spare clip before he too would be out. His pistol, he knew, would have little effect. "Continue to pull back. Our only chance is to take cover in the larger boulders."

The stench was almost overwhelming. It was an odor that Colton had experienced on a much smaller level in the zoo reptile house decades ago in a saner world. How many of these things were there? He almost giggled at a wildly inappropriate thought. What was the genre, a "stink of dinosaurs?" A "fart of death dealers?"

His mind flashed back to Flight 19. He prayed that the pilot had died quickly and mercifully in the crash. To have faced one of these creatures with 1945 armaments, and possibly being injured and alone, was too terrible to consider.

The creature in front of Colton tilted its head, now staring directly at him. Slowly it started to advance towards him, its head lowered, its mouth partially open. The only good thing about this was that it didn't seem to be aware that Corporal Lee was lying in the rocks behind it, nearly helpless. As it advanced on Colton, its jaws began to open. Colton started to inch backwards, doing his best to keep pace with the creature.

But the ground was covered with sticks and small gravel shaped rocks. As Colton moved backwards, he was doing his best not to trip and fall. Suddenly the creature lunged its head forward, roaring at Colton. Involuntarily Colton stepped backwards too quickly, his foot coming down on a thin, flat rock that slide out from under him. Having had his full weight on the rock, it threw him off balance. Colton landed hard on the flat of his back, nearly knocking the breath out of him. The fear that rushed through him was more intense than the pain of his fall.

The creature raised its head, roaring in victory, its prey lying before it. The strength of its roar gave the other three creatures what they needed to advance. They too roared as they approached the doomed command. It was a roar of victory. Colton raised his rifle, taking aim at the creature's throat, but knew his situation was nearly hopeless. Four of the marines pulled the pins on their grenades, waiting on Garrett's command to launch as the creatures charged.

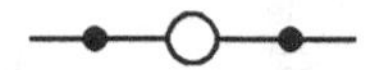

"Argos confirmed that the sounds we heard are gunshots and most probably grenades," said Mercer as he hung up the phone. "We have two armed drones prepared to launch. Shall I give the order?"

"Stand by," said MacKay. "I want to help Colton and those marines as much as you do. But there's no point in sending another drone in over the interior. The mist hasn't lightened up, so we'd have very limited visibility. Even if we already had one in position, we'd be firing blind."

"Don't those things have heat sensors, or something like that?" asked Father Ryan. He'd joined them on the bridge not long after Colton and his team had pushed off.

"Yes, Father, they do. But we still wouldn't know who to target. We're not able to distinguish between the heat signatures from our team and the force attacking them."

They thought they heard another explosion. Then everything went silent. They waited, but try as they might, they couldn't hear anything else. MacKay picked up the phone and called Sahir. "Is Argos still picking up sounds from the battle?"

"Just a moment, Captain," said Sahir. MacKay could hear Sahir's team working in the background. "No sir, everything has stopped."

"Try getting them on the radio again. Argos was able to boost the signal last time. Have it do it again."

"On it, Captain," said Sahir. "Stand by."

Waiting for Sahir to get back to them was agonizing. The only thing they could hear now was the gentle pounding of the surf and the occasional eerie cry from the jungle.

It had only been two minutes, but MacKay had taken all he could take. Just as he reached for the phone, it buzzed. "What have you got?" he barked into the receiver.

"We've not been able to reach them. Argos has even further strengthened the signal, but they're not responding. However, it's important to keep in mind that despite what Argos has been able to accomplish, there could be several reasons why they're not answering," said Sahir.

"Thank you, Lieutenant," said MacKay. "Keep trying and let me know the minute you hear from them."

MacKay put down the receiver and motioned for Mercer and Father Ryan to join him outside the bridge. Resting his arms on the railing, he stared at the jungle in front of them. "If there was ever a time for prayer, Father, this is it."

Father Ryan put his hand on MacKay's shoulder. "Way ahead of you, Callum, way ahead of you."

"Mr. Mercer, launch both drones. At this point I'm ready to do anything I can to help those men."

"Will do, sir," said Mercer, and he left the bridge.

"We all knew how high the risk was sending them in, and that was before Argos determined that we were no longer in our world, so to speak. Based on what we now know it's hard to guess what they're facing."

Father Ryan stood next to MacKay, deep in thought. "Based on everything I've read, and the things you've shared with me, Colton is a tough guy to kill. I wouldn't write him off just yet."

"Agreed," sighed Captain MacKay. "I'm trying to stay positive, but this whole thing is just so impossibly bizarre that I really don't know what to think anymore. How did we get here? And more importantly, how do we get back?"

"The crew is going to be asking the same questions, if they aren't already," Father Ryan said quietly. "We're going to have to be ready for that."

"I know," said MacKay, sighing deeply. "It's been eating at me ever since Sahir briefed me on their findings. Oh well, as they say, one dragon at a time."

Mercer returned to the bridge, joining the two men. "Both drones are away and should reach the estimated location of the battle in about seven minutes. Argos provided us with the navigational headings."

Once again, they were forced to wait. For all his years in the navy, for MacKay there was nothing worse than waiting to find out if your crew was all right.

It was Petty Officer Briggs who came and got the captain. "Sir, I have Lieutenant Sahir for you."

Glancing at Father Ryan and Mercer, MacKay reentered the bridge and picked up the receiver. "What do you have, Lieutenant?"

MacKay listened to what Sahir had to say and his facial expression stayed the same, but Father Ryan noticed his knuckles turning white as he gripped the phone. When Sahir finished MacKay just stood there for a couple of moments. "Stay on it, Mr. Sahir. Let me know if you find anything else."

Hanging up the phone he turned to Father Ryan and Lt. Commander Mercer. He cleared his throat and said, "Neither drone was able to pick up any human heat signatures. In fact, the entire area was devoid of life."

Everything was quiet except for Father Ryan. Apparently, his order still used Latin for some things.

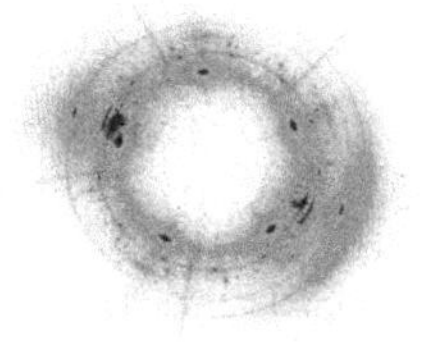

CHAPTER 15

Colton's eyes locked onto the creature standing in front of him. Its huge, wet, black eyes glared back, slowly closing the gap between them. It was only about twenty feet away from him, but Colton held his fire. Taking careful aim, he took deep breaths, doing all that he could do to keep his hands from shaking. No margin for error.

The creature took two more steps toward him, strands of saliva spilling from its tooth-lined jaws, its rotten breath choking him. Colton began to put steady pressure on the trigger of his rifle, still trying to steady his aim. His talk with Father Ryan flashed through his mind. He breathed a silent prayer that he wouldn't miss. Perhaps he could put enough rounds into its neck, all in the same spot, tearing the creature's throat out.

Then, for some reason, the air seemed to ripple, blurring his vision. Colton blinked his eyes, desperately trying to clear them, but he still couldn't see clearly. Is this what panic is like? Were his senses shutting down? The air had taken on the appearance of the concentric circles, just like what you see when you throw a rock into a pond, completely distorting the reflection of everything around it.

As suddenly as it had started, the rippling stopped, and his eyes cleared, but it didn't last for more than a couple of seconds. Once again, the air started to ripple, but this time it was far more pronounced than before, completely blurring his field of vision. Colton quickly looked to his right for Garrett and her men. He was getting ready to yell for help but realized that everyone had stopped firing their weapons. Whatever was happening, it was affecting everyone in the same manner.

Colton's eyes darted back to the creature that had been standing over him to find that it too seemed to be having problems. Rather than attacking him, it had backed away and was now making its way towards the other dinosaurs. Raising himself up on one arm, he saw that all the dinosaurs were moving off towards the jungle. The air cleared, but only momentarily before the third rippling wave washed across the area. This time, however, it was accompanied by a soft, bluish-white light that covered the entire area.

The light, for some inexplicable reason, was comforting. Colton's hands stopped shaking and he found that he was suddenly able to breathe normally. The paralyzing fear that had nearly taken over his mind and body no longer held him in its grip. Searching for the source of the light, Colton gazed up into the sky. As startling as his first glimpse of the dinosaurs had been, that was nothing compared to what he was seeing now. In fairness, he had prayed. Maybe it was an angel.

A huge, egg-shaped ball of nearly pure white light hovered above them. Its edges were indistinct, constantly changing in a gentle, flowing motion. Try as he might, it was hard to get a clear look at this thing as it was so intensely bright. It was no different than trying to look at the sun. Nevertheless, Colton continued to take brief glimpses at the object, trying to figure out what this could possibly be.

He continued to steal brief glimpses of the object. Colton could see that there appeared to be some kind of a large, multifaceted object rotating inside the egg. With almost regular intervals, Colton caught a glimpse of seemingly hard edges and corners of this object as it pierced through the sides of light, only to quickly disappear again within it. He had absolutely no clue as to what he was looking at. Worse, he didn't know if he and his team were now facing some new kind of threat.

The egg-shaped light didn't move at all, holding its current position, hovering directly over them. Colton estimated that it couldn't have been more than two hundred feet off the ground. Its dimensions were close to 120 feet in height, with a girth, at its widest point, being close to fifty feet. The bluish-white light covering the area radiated from this thing.

The realization that everything had gone deathly silent finally registered in Colton's mind. Everything had gone completely silent. There were absolutely no sounds coming from the dinosaurs, his team, or the jungle. Even the egg-shaped craft, or light, or whatever it was hovering above him, operated with absolutely no sound.

Colton sat up and once again looked at Garrett and rest of the marines. Finding his voice, he yelled out, "Hold your position; cease fire. Do nothing that can be taken as a hostile act." He was surprised at how loud his voice sounded in the absolute silence that dominated the area.

Standing up, he carefully moved forward, not making any sudden moves, and helped Corporal Lee to his feet. Together they slowly made their way back to where Garrett and her soldiers were standing. "Do you have any idea what is going on here?" asked Garrett, never taking her eyes off the dinosaurs that had grouped together at the edge of the jungle.

Two of the men were mouthing prayers. One of them was recommending himself to Mary, full of grace. The other was mumbling something repeatedly, but it was unintelligible.

"No, Captain, I do not," answered Colton. "Who is the wounded man?"

"Private Lockridge," said Garrett. "At first only one of those creatures attacked us, but it charged out of the jungle so fast we had almost no time to react. One of its claws caught Lockridge across the chest and dug into one of his legs. Then it swung its tail around, slamming it into Private Blake, knocking him into those trees over there. I don't know if he's dead or alive."

Colton was getting ready to go and look for Blake when beams of light-blue light shot down from the egg, encompassing the heads of each of the dinosaurs in front of them. The beams were quite dense, so much so that you couldn't see through them. As they watched this, they could see white, star like flashes of light glide through the beams, softly penetrating the heads of the dinosaurs.

This didn't last long before the dinosaurs turned and left the area, melting back in to the thick jungle from which they'd emerged. Despite the unexplained calmness that had already settled over him, their departure brought a sigh of relief from Colton. Just ten minutes ago he'd expected to be killed by one of those creatures. Now he didn't know what to expect.

"Sir, I need help over here," shouted Corpsman Payne. "Lockridge is still losing blood, and if I don't stop the bleeding soon, he's not going to make it."

"Stay where you are and stay alert," Garrett ordered the rest of her men as she quickly made her way over to Payne. Colton followed right behind her and couldn't believe that Lockridge was still breathing. It was plain to see just how serious his wounds were, and it was nothing short of a miracle that Payne had been able to keep him alive this long.

Without warning, a beam of the same light-blue light shot down, landing on Payne's head, completely encompassing his head and shoulders. Almost on reflex, Colton and Garrett pulled their pistols, aiming up at the egg above them. "Payne, are you all right?" shouted Colton. "What's happening?"

Payne didn't respond. He stood completely still, as if frozen in place. Colton saw the star like flashes of light descending onto his head. As it had been with the dinosaurs, the beam was so dense that he couldn't see Payne's head, but, at the same time, he didn't appear to be suffering.

"Payne," shouted Garrett, "are you all right?"

Then the beam of light lifted off Payne and he looked at both officers. He was smiling, smiling as if he'd just won the lottery. "It's okay, I'm all right. We're all going to be all right."

Before either of them could say anything, Corporal Lee said, "Captain, look up, Something is happening."

A small, blue sphere emerged from beneath the egg. It hovered there for just a few seconds. It then silently moved toward Payne, landing softly on the rocks in front of him. It wasn't there long before it lifted off, returning to the egg-shaped craft above them, but it had left something behind. On the rock where it had landed now sat what looked like a small, rectangular crystal box. It too glowed with the same bluish white light.

Payne started to move toward it, but Colton cut him off. "Stay away from that, Private. We don't know what that is."

Ignoring Colton's order, Payne brushed by him and knelt beside the box, carefully opening its lid. Inside was a dark blue gel. "It's okay sir, they told me all about this. It's medicine. It will help Lockridge."

"How can you know that? Who told you about it?" demanded Garrett.

"I can't explain it," said Payne, "but when that light shown down on me, it was the most relaxing, comforting thing I've ever experienced. I felt like I was back home with my family, just as happy as I could be and completely at peace. Then they told me that they were going to send me some medicine that will help Private Lockridge. Sir, they knew his name! All I have to do to help him is to apply this gel to his wounds."

"They?" said Colton. "Did you hear more than one voice?"

"Again sir, I just can't explain it, but I didn't hear any voices," said Payne. "Yet somehow they were able to tell me that this would help him. What I mean is that I didn't actually hear any words, but it couldn't have been any plainer to me than the way we're talking now."

"We can't use that stuff until we know more about it and figure out what's going on here," said Garrett. "For all we know it will kill him."

"I agree there is certainly risk, but I don't believe it will hurt him," said Colton. "Whatever that thing is up there, it just saved our lives. If they wanted us dead, they could have just let the dinosaurs finish us off."

Garrett started to respond, but Payne cut her off. "Sir, if I don't do something fast, Lockridge is going to die. There's nothing more that I can do. This gel, whatever it's made of, is all I've got. We have to try it."

Colton wasn't anxious to overrule Garrett in front of her men, but he knew time was of the essence. He looked at Garrett, giving her the chance to respond.

Nodding her head, she said, "Do it. It seems to be our only alternative."

Payne picked up the box and carried it over to where Lockridge was lying on the ground. He then began to apply the gel to his wounds. Although Lockridge had lost consciousness, his body responded to the gel. As Payne put it on his chest wound, his whole body seemed to spasm, rising off the ground.

"Is it hurting him?" demanded Garrett, standing right next to Payne.

"Hard to tell, Captain. He obviously feels it, but I have no way of knowing if it's a good or a bad feeling. I can tell you this much. That gel is very cold. It's the only cold thing I've experienced since we've been here."

Colton looked down at the gel, then up at the craft that still hovered above them. "Private Bannister," said Colton, "see if you can raise the ship on the radio."

Bannister pulled out the radio from his backpack and went to work, trying to reach the *Eclipse*. "There doesn't seem to be anything wrong with the radio, sir, but I'm not getting any response from the ship. For that matter, I'm not even picking up any static."

A worried look crossed Garrett's face. Garrett looked up at the craft and then, in hushed tones, said, "It's blocking our communications. Not a good sign."

"Yes and no, Captain," said Colton. "It could go either way. Whatever or whoever that is above us, they just saved our butts. They're also obviously more advanced than we are. Blocking our communications could be just their way to keep us from doing something stupid."

"Who is they, Commander?" asked Garrett. "That's what I'm struggling with. We have the most advanced military equipment, the most advanced technology of any country on the planet. Just who do you think this is?"

"Captain, you're talking to a guy who just got attacked by dinosaurs, creatures supposed to have been extinct for millions of years. Then, right on the heels of that, I get saved from the dinosaurs by a craft using technology that I haven't even heard anyone hint at. At this point I'm willing to believe they're angels. Even though I just experienced all of this firsthand, actually saw it all transpire with my own eyes, I'm still having trouble believing that any of it even happened. Captain, I have no idea who this is or where we are. Unfortunately, at this point, the next move is theirs, not ours."

Payne finished applying the gel to Private Lockridge and was monitoring his condition. As Colton waited for him to report, he noticed for the first time that his arm was bleeding from the fall he'd taken on the rocks. Looking around, he saw that some of the other men had also sustained small injuries. Looking back at the gel, he muttered, "Well, in for a penny, in for a pound."

Colton dipped his hand in the gel, taking a very small amount. Payne had understated its temperature. It was beyond cold, nearly numbing his hand. He applied the gel to the cut on his arm. Garrett watched him do this but did nothing to try and stop him. He looked at her for a moment then looked back at his arm.

The gel's temperature didn't vary. Even on his skin, it stayed cold, terribly cold, almost to the point of being painful. He now understood the reaction that Lockridge had had to the gel, conscious or not. If anyone had smeared this across his chest, he too would have had a rather pronounced reaction.

His wound, as well as the skin around it, immediately went numb. He grimaced at this, but it was not so much from pain as much as from the shock of how intensely cold this stuff was. Staring at the cut on his arm, he watched in amazement as the cold finally started to subside and the wound began to close. Not only did the gel act like stitches, but it also brought almost immediate relief from the pain.

He looked at Garrett, held up his arm so that she could clearly see what the gel had done, and she nodded her head in agreement. "For any of you that are hurt, if you'd like to use this gel, it seems to work quite quickly."

The men looked at each other, but they were still apprehensive. While the gel appeared to have helped Colton's arm, none of them were anxious to become another guinea pig. "I'm not going to order any of you to do this," said Colton, "but I want you to consider your circumstances. We are deep in a jungle that is obviously filled with plants and animals that we have no knowledge of. Additionally, at least for the time being, we are cut off from the ship and therefore have limited medical supplies. If you've got an open wound, I would encourage each of you to try this gel before infection, or something worse that we know nothing about, sets in."

As this thought sunk in, the men, one by one, walked over and began to apply the gel to a host of wounds they hadn't complained about. Colton stood next to Garrett, looking down at Lockridge. "How's he doing, Payne?"

"He's still in bad shape," said Payne, "but that's primarily due to a loss of blood. However, and this is hard to believe, he's beginning to stabilize. The bleeding has stopped, and his pulse is stronger than it was before I put the gel on. I don't know what this stuff is, but we need to get as much of it as we can."

"Captain, I don't know what's going to happen next with our new friend," said Colton, "but I'm going to see if I can find Private Blake. Based on the size of that dinosaur, the force of the impact of getting hit with its tail had to have been significant. I'm not optimistic."

"I'll do that Commander. It's my responsibility," said Garrett. "I shouldn't have waited this long."

"Don't be too hard on yourself, Captain," said Colton. "Between being attacked by prehistoric nightmares and then a guest appearance from something out of the *Twilight Zon*e, it's fair to say that we've been somewhat distracted. Stay here with the men. Get with Bannister. Tell him to keep trying to reach the ship every ten minutes or so."

"And if he gets through," said Garrett, "what am I supposed to tell them?"

For the first time in the last few hours Colton managed a smile. "That's why I'm leaving you here, and I'm going to go look for Private Blake. Without sounding like we've completely lost our minds, I have no idea what to say to them."

Colton then moved away from the marines and repositioned himself almost directly under the egg-shaped craft. Then he slowly took off his gun belt that held his holstered weapon, and gently laid it on the ground. Without turning he said, "Corporal Lee, Private Hill, I want you to slowly walk over here and join me. Don't make any sudden moves."

The two men followed Colton's instructions and stood beside him. "Okay. Now slowly and carefully take off your rifles and your gun belts and lay them on the ground. All things considered, I don't think they'd be much use to us against that thing anyway, if it came down to it."

"What about the creatures that attacked us?" asked Hill. "How do we know they won't come back? I know our weapons didn't seem to slow them down too much, but I'd feel a whole lot better having mine with me."

"So long as that craft is hovering above us, I'm guessing we're safe," said Colton. "It clearly has some level of control over them. Corporal Lee, I want you to lead us to where you think we might find Private Blake but take your time. Private Hill and I will flank you to give us as broad of a search area as we can."

The men moved forward towards the jungle at a slow but steady pace, heading to the area where they hoped to find Private Blake. Colton continued to look up and over his shoulder, but the craft didn't move. It was only when they reached the edge of the jungle that they could see that the bluish-white light extended some distance into the trees.

Still, not knowing what may be lurking in the undergrowth, they cautiously moved forward, searching for the missing private. Colton hoped that the influence that the craft had over the dinosaurs extended to any other meat-eating creatures that might be in the neighborhood. It was Private Hill who found him.

"Commander, Corporal Lee, over here." Hill was staring down at the ground next to a broad, vine-covered tree. Colton and Lee quickly joined him, but as Colton had feared, they were too late. Private Blake's neck had been broken, as well as one of his legs that sprawled away from the body at an impossible angle. Corporal Lee checked for a pulse anyway, confirming what they already knew.

Colton stepped forward and started to lean over to pick up the private's body, but Hill stopped him. "If you don't mind, sir, I'd prefer the honor of returning him to our squad."

Colton nodded his agreement and Private Hill and Corporal Lee picked up Blake's body. Private Hill then lifted the body up over his shoulder and started to make his way back. Corporal Lee walked beside Private Hill, Colton bringing up the rear. He continued to glance up at the craft, as well as keeping an eye on the jungle.

Although he was reasonably certain that so long as the craft stayed with them they were safe, there was no point in getting careless. His mind began to shift gears to start focusing on a new set of concerns. What did this craft want with them? Was it strictly being a Good Samaritan, or was there a much different agenda? Would it let them return to the *Eclipse*, and if so, could they even make it through the jungle, considering the predators roaming this land?

Garrett and her men watched as they approached. Many of them had bowed their heads, a couple dropping down on one knee. The silence that dominated the area took on a very somber mood. They'd lost a man, a brother, along with another one of their team seriously wounded. If the craft said it was God, or from the gods, the men were ready to believe. Colton thought this was a bad thing. He didn't know what he would say. The gel was still healing him, but this was not like anything he'd ever experienced. Then he had one last thought. What if the thing above them was rewiring him, altering his mind? Then all thought stopped.

Just as Colton was getting ready to call out to Garrett to get the men ready to move out, a light-blue beam shot down, covering Colton's head and shoulders. He couldn't see or hear anything around him, but at the same time he didn't feel any fear. Once again, a level of comfort flooded over him. He waited to see what would happen next. It was then that his world began to change forever.

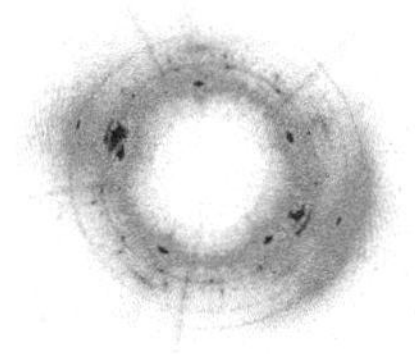

CHAPTER 16

A dark, greenish-black wall of storm clouds towered into the sky, looming across the horizon. Hurricane weather. The team on the bridge had been monitoring this developing storm, waiting to see what would happen. Five minutes ago, the winds had altered their course and the storm was now rapidly bearing down on the *Eclipse*.

Strong gusts had already started to pick up. MacKay knew that they would not be able to ride out the approaching storm this close to shore, not in such shallow waters. The problem was that Colton's team, or at least what was left of it, was still on shore and he didn't plan on abandoning any of them.

"Sir, Lieutenant Tanner reporting as ordered."

"At ease, Lieutenant," said MacKay. "I trust you've been briefed."

"Yes sir, by both Mr. Mercer and Lieutenant Sahir," answered Tanner. "Sir, I would like to volunteer to lead the relief party to go into the jungle and extract the landing party. We can be ready to go in ten minutes."

"I appreciate your enthusiasm, Lieutenant, and I wish it were that simple. Your request is denied. We have not been able to reestablish contact with anyone on Commander Colton's team. While I don't relish the idea of leaving any of my crew behind, putting more of our people at risk is most certainly not the answer. However, regarding the team that went ashore, I believe they left two men near the beach to guard the landing craft. Is that correct?"

"Yes sir, Privates Shaw and Fuller."

"Have you been in communication with them?"

"Yes sir," answered Tanner. "They're still in position. As to any possible threats, they haven't seen anyone. They did report that a couple of large animals came close to where they've taken cover, but they never really were able to get a clear look at them."

"Sadly, we have limited options. Lieutenant, please know that I don't like this, but here's what we're going to do. We are going to order Shaw and Fuller to return to the ship immediately. The weather is growing worse by the minute and unless they move out now, we won't be able to wait for them."

"Sir, with all due respect, we don't know what has happened to the rest of the landing party," complained Lieutenant Tanner. "For all we know, their radio has been damaged and they simply have no other way of reaching us. Without verification of their demise, we can't just leave them behind."

"Lieutenant, I'm not in the habit of explaining my orders, I'm used to having them obeyed. I appreciate your feelings on this and they are not all that different from my own. The drones, due to the atmospheric conditions on shore, have been of little use to us. However, we can use them for more than just visual surveillance. When we flew them over the position that Argos directed us to, the drones were not able to pick up any heat signatures indicating that our people were still alive. It's not the answer we wanted, but we have to deal with it."

"Again sir, with all due respect to Argos and Lieutenant Sahir, the information that we have gathered is anything but complete. The drones, as well as Argos, are simple machines," argued Tanner.

"There's nothing 'simple' about Argos, Lieutenant."

"Be that as it may, you said it yourself. The atmospheric conditions on shore have complicated our mission," continued Tanner. "For all we know it's blocking their heat signatures as well as taking out the radio. And that's just one possibility. When the drones flew over, our people could have been taking cover beneath some rocks. Most of the rocks we're seeing are red granite, which can shield heat and EM force very well. That, or something else like that, could have interfered with the readings the drones took. We don't have enough intel to go on and I refuse to just write them off."

"No one is writing anyone off," growled MacKay. "I'm dealing with a set of facts, and whether I like those facts or not, they're all I have. Let me sum this up for you. No matter what the reason may be, we've lost contact with the landing party. The drones have failed to pick up their heat signatures. And now, on top of everything else, a storm is bearing down on this ship, and due to that, we must move the *Eclipse* into deeper waters. Even if they were recently slain, we'd still get some heat patterns. So, either they're hiding, or swallowed by something big and cold, or out of the area."

"Sir, I understand all that. What I'm suggesting is that I lead a few more men ashore, reinforce Shaw and Fuller, and establish a base camp to work from. True, the storm will be on us soon, but that's not a problem. My men have been wet before. This way we'll be in place when Colton and Garrett do make it back, and we'll be able to provide any assistance they may need."

MacKay studied the young marine for a few moments, and then shook his head. "No, Lieutenant, that's not what we're going to do. Under normal conditions I would consider your arguments more closely. Unfortunately, the things that are happening here are anything but normal conditions. Somehow, we are now on an Earth that existed millions of years ago, filled with an animal population that is extremely aggressive, not to mention carnivorous."

"Sir, I'm not even sure I believe all that. It's too . . ."

MacKay cut him off, holding up his hand. "That will be all, Lieutenant. I called you here to join Mr. Mercer and me, along with Dr. Meinhard and two of his team, to discuss how we're going to get Shaw and Fuller back to the ship. Rough seas aside, I'm afraid we have some even bigger challenges to overcome."

With that, MacKay turned and went into the conference room directly off the bridge. Tanner took a deep breath and followed close behind him. Garrett was his commanding officer, and those were his men, stuck somewhere out there in that godforsaken jungle. It went against everything in his fiber to even consider leaving them behind. Colton, that CIA spook, has led them into some kind of time war, or maybe it's some new kind of drug that makes MKUltra look sissified.

Mr. Mercer stood at the head of the table, watching Dr. Meinhard as he fixed himself a cup of coffee. Mercer had never seen someone use as much sugar in a single cup of coffee as Meinhard did. Six teaspoons! Wonder where you get sugar in the Cretaceous period? Dr. Chudzik and Dr. Brennan were sitting down, talking quietly. Mercer nodded at MacKay and relinquished his position, taking a seat next to Dr. Brennan.

"If everyone will be seated, we have very little time," said Captain MacKay. Looking at the three scientists he said, "I appreciate your help with this. As you know, we have two of our landing team on the beach, and we need to get them back to the ship ASAP. Dr. Brennan, who has been working closely with some of my people, has identified several predators in the water surrounding us."

Dr. Brennan nodded and gave a modest smile. "Paleontology started out merely as a hobby. Never imagined in my wildest dreams that it would end up having a practical use."

"The men we have on the beach will be using lightweight boats with powerful outboard motors to return to the ship. We estimate that they'll have to cover at least a hundred yards or more of open water to get back to the *Eclipse*. One of the problems that we're facing is that due to the oncoming storm, the winds are now much stronger than when they first went ashore, and the sea is getting choppier by the moment. Hence, due to the weather, this will not only slow them down, but will also hinder their maneuverability," explained MacKay. "Here's my question. Of the predators you've identified, do you believe any of them pose a threat to these men?"

Dr. Brennan slowly nodded and said, "Captain, as Dr. Chudzik and I were just discussing, all that we truly know of these creatures comes from the fossils that have been collected over the past several decades. We're continually learning that what we thought to be true of a given specimen's looks, habits, and diet, later turns out to be wrong, as more current information is discovered."

"What is your point, Doctor?" said MacKay.

"For me to tell you how these creatures will behave, or how they will respond to changes in their environment, such as the small craft your men will be using, will simply be nothing more than hypotheses. We just don't have many hard facts to go by. Due to the sediment in which the fossils have been collected, we have learned a fair amount about the environments in which they lived, but again, this doesn't tell us how they reacted to things in that environment. In short, most of what we claim to know about dinosaurs is based on presumption. Our theories have been derived from what we know of the reptiles and marine animals that live in our own jungles and oceans. If all I had was the skull of a grizzly, I couldn't tell you if the bear would run from gunfire or attack. And that's a life-form much more like us."

MacKay nodded, trying to contain his impatience. First Tanner, now Dr. Brennen. For the two men stuck on the beach, the clock was rapidly ticking down. All he wanted was some simple, concise answers to what he thought were straightforward questions. He didn't have the time for detailed explanations, or the arguments he kept getting. "We appreciate that, Dr. Brennan, but frankly, you're all we've got. So, to my question, will these men be at risk from any of the predators that you've spotted?"

Dr. Brennan picked up on the intensity boiling just beneath the surface of MacKay's demeanor. "Yes, Captain, they most certainly will."

"Very well. I want you to describe what these predators look like, their size, and the best idea you have as to how to protect our men," said MacKay.

Brennan remained seated and said, "Judging by the pictures our cameras have taken, as well as what we've tracked on the sonar, the primary predator that we need to worry about is the Elasmosaurus platyurus. The name Elasmosaurus means 'plated reptile.' They were likely one of the most vicious marine predators to roam the seas during the late Cretaceous period."

Mercer, trying to not smile, looked at MacKay and shook his head. "Doctor, we know nothing about the animal you just named," said MacKay. "What can you tell us?"

"Let me show," he said, pulling out his tablet and turning it on. "Mr. Sahir helped me to set this up; it's tied directly into Argos." Brennan typed a few commands into the tablet, then after a moment, handed it to Captain MacKay. "That picture was done by the Carnegie Museum of Natural History. It's as accurate of a rendering of what those things were supposed to have looked like that you can find."

Taking the tablet back from MacKay, he once again went to work on it, smiled, and handed it back to the captain. "Those two pictures were taken just off the starboard side of the ship yesterday. As big as that thing is, unfortunately, they get bigger. If you take a close look at it, it's impressive how close the rendering came in comparison to the actual photo. I hope to one day share this with the people at the museum," said Dr. Brennen.

"I'm sure they'll feel wonderful," muttered Lieutenant Tanner, glaring at Dr. Brennan. "Just how big is that thing and how do we kill it?"

"We're all but certain that this is the animal that killed that poor sailor the first day we arrived here," said Dr. Chudzik. "Like so many marine animals, their sense of smell and hearing probably far exceeds anything that we have. We believe that the *Eclipse*, being the size that it is, sent enough noise through the water to draw the platyurus in. To the best of our knowledge, they're not pack animals and it probably thought that another predator had invaded its territory."

"That's why we believe that it attacked. It may have just been hungry, but we think it was trying to scare us off," said Dr. Brennan. "The one in those pictures is close to forty feet long and probably weighs in at around 4,700 pounds."

The platyurus' head sat on a very long neck that connected to a bulky body with four huge fins that enabled it to move rapidly through the water. Its tail, compared to the rest of its body, was surprisingly short. "Their teeth are quite long and the platyurus' mouth has often been described as 'sharp fanged.' While there were certainly many other predators in the ocean in those days, the Elasmosaurus platyurus was near the top of the food chain," said Dr. Brennan, as calmly as if he were lecturing a class full of college kids.

"Not hard to understand the damage done to the railing along that deck, is it?" said Mr. Mercer quietly. "You get something that big, moving fast enough to jettison out of the water, shooting up high enough to reach that deck with its jaws, and it's going to leave a mark."

"Slamming into the side of the ship, as it obviously did," said Captain MacKay, "could it have hurt itself? The impact had to have been incredible. It destroyed twelve feet of iron railing."

Dr. Brennan shrugged. "I doubt that it even felt it. It attacked, killed its prey, or at least one of its prey, and was rewarded with a meal. We believe that's the reason it's still here swimming around is because the *Eclipse* hasn't moved on. We're still in its territory, which is pissing it off, and it'll most probably stay around until we've left."

"Why didn't those sailors see it coming?" asked Tanner. "I've seen pictures of these things before and they almost always have their neck and head sticking up out of the water."

Dr. Brennan chuckled at this. "Yes, that is the popular rendering, much like the Loch Ness Monster. It makes it look dramatic. The truth is that we believe that their necks would have been fairly rigid. Although they're usually pictured that way, it is impossible for them to hold their head high above the surface of the ocean in a swanlike posture. They can't physically do that. It stalked us, approached from under the surface, and then shot up out of the water, attacking the two sailors."

"Lieutenant, if you look at the two pictures we took, you'll see what Dr. Brennan is saying," said Dr. Chudzik. "There's very little curvature in its neck."

"Alright, good information. We now know what we are up against," said MacKay. "So how do we defend against this thing?"

"We have plenty of grenades on board," said Tanner. "We could launch several of them all at once, saturating the water, killing anything that's out there. Once that's done we have Shaw and Fuller launch their craft and get back as fast as they can."

"That would not be advisable, Lieutenant," said Dr. Brennan.

"Why is that?" asked Captain MacKay. "I'm not wild about slaughtering a bunch of fish, but I'm going to do whatever it takes to get those two men back here safely."

"We all share in that common goal, I assure you," said Meinhard, sighing deeply. He had been unusually quiet throughout the entire briefing. "But employing such ham-handed methods would end in disaster. If you want to get your sailors back, we're going to need to employ a little more brainpower, and far less brawn."

"They're marines, not sailors," growled Tanner, gripping the table with both hands and doing his best not to knock Meinhard off his chair. The man could probably piss off a saint, given the opportunity.

"Under the right circumstances, your idea might work, Mr. Tanner," said Dr. Brennan, inserting as much diplomacy into the conversation as he could. "The problem is that we have to move quickly. At this point in time, we don't know where the platyurus is. By killing all those fish, we'd end up putting a great deal of blood in the water, which would certainly draw it in. And maybe his friends."

"It is no different than pouring chum into the water," said Mercer. "I get it. So, what do we do?"

"I would suggest we try using sound waves," said Dr. Brennan. "We could lower speakers into the water and send out large booms, coordinating this action as your men approach the ship. The vibrations should make most of the marine life around us scatter, as they'll think that something much bigger is now in the area."

"You think that will scare this monster off?" asked Captain MacKay.

Dr. Brennan thought for a moment, then shook his head. "No, I don't. But I believe it may buy us the time we need to get those men back."

The room turned quiet. All eyes were on MacKay. "Any other ideas?" he asked. No one else had anything to offer.

"Very well, then," said MacKay. "Dr. Brennan, work with Mr. Sahir and get everything you need ready to create these loud noises in the water. Mr. Mercer will see to it that you get complete cooperation."

Dr. Brennan nodded and Dr. Chudzik said, "I'll help as well."

"Thank you, Doctor," said Captain MacKay. "Lieutenant Tanner, position your three best snipers at different positions along the ship to cover those men. If they get the opportunity, and that creature breaks the surface, I want them to take the shot. Headshots, Lieutenant, that's what I believe it's going to take. I'll be on the bridge. In twenty minutes, I'm recalling those men, so let's get moving."

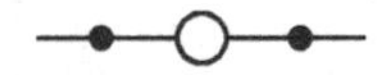

The radio started to buzz. Private Shaw, who was closest to it, scooted over on his stomach to answer it. "Private Shaw, over."

"Private, this is Captain MacKay. I want you and Private Fuller to get one of the boats ready and be prepared to head back to the *Eclipse* in ten minutes. Do you copy?"

"Yes sir, but Captain Garrett and the Commander have not yet returned," replied Private Shaw.

"We understand, but we need you back on the ship before this storm breaks," said MacKay. "Is Private Fuller with you?"

"Yes sir, he's right here," said Shaw. He looked at Fuller, thinking hard. He didn't like the sound of this and was trying to think of anything that would buy them more time. "Sir, we'll get the boat ready, but it's going to take us at least thirty minutes, if not more, to gather up and load all of the equipment."

"Leave it," barked MacKay. "Private, you have ten minutes, and then you and Fuller are going to launch one of those boats. Am I making myself clear?"

"Sir, yes sir," said Private Shaw. He barely stopped himself from saluting the radio. MacKay could be intimidating when he wanted to be.

Fuller was looking at him. "What was that?"

"You're not going to like this," said Shaw. "We've been ordered to pull out."

"What about the captain, the men?"

"You know as much as I do," said Shaw. "We need to get moving. Captain MacKay doesn't sound like he is in a very patient mood."

MacKay grabbed the phone as it started to buzz. "Mercer here, sir. We are ready and standing by. Argos will be sending out deep, baritone sounds as soon as their craft hits the open water. It'll also be sending out whale sounds."

"Whale sounds?" said MacKay.

"It was Dr. Meinhard's suggestion, and it may actually be a good idea. Whales are the biggest marine animal there is, or, at least, will be, and because it's bigger, the sound may help to scare that thing off. I still can't pronounce its name."

"Platyurus," said MacKay. "I'm not a highly trained scientist, but this doesn't make any sense to me. How is a platyurus from sixty-five million years ago supposed to know what a whale is? And on top of that, how would it know if an animal that doesn't even exist is bigger than he is?"

"Can't explain it, but it's not all that different from what big game hunters do on safari. At night, they sprinkle elephant piss all around the perimeter of their camp. It helps to keep lions and other night stalkers away. Just from the smell alone, animals can tell that it's bigger than they are."

"Alright, whatever it takes," said MacKay, shaking his head. "Tanner has his marine snipers in place, so here we go. We'll give them two minutes to launch the boat, then start the music."

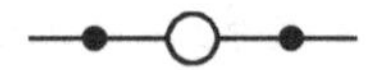

"Private Shaw reporting. We're ready to launch."

"Very good, Private, well done," said MacKay. "I want both of you to keep a sharp eye out and be ready to use your rifles. We believe there may be a large marine predator in the water that's been stalking us. It is big enough to do significant damage to your boat. We're going to give you as much cover as we can, but we need you to push your boat as hard as you can and get back here as quickly as possible."

"What kind of predator would that be?" asked Shaw. "Do you mean some kind of shark?"

"No, it's very different from that, but just as deadly. Now move out, Private."

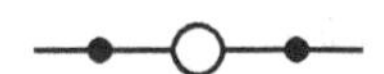

MacKay turned and addressed the bridge. "We are trying to get two of our marines back to the ship. Hatfield, you've been working with Dr. Brennan and you know all too well that there are large predators in the area. Keep a close watch and let me know the first sign you see of anything big approaching us or the small craft that our marines will be using.

"Aye, aye sir," responded Hatfield. He'd not only been working with Dr. Brennan, but he'd also seen several more of the pictures they'd taken of the terrifying things swimming around the ship, more pictures than even MacKay had seen. The pictures had flat out given him nightmares to the point that he felt nervous just being on the *Eclipse.* He couldn't begin to imagine the utter terror he'd be feeling if he were with those two marines, knowing what lay beneath the waves between the beach and the ship.

Using his binoculars, MacKay watched the small craft exit the inlet they'd been using as a landing site. They were just beginning to head out into open water. Using his radio, MacKay said, "Mr. Mercer, they are on their way. Start the music. Mr. Tanner, have your men keep a sharp lookout for anything that moves."

The winds had continued to increase and were blowing hard against the marines' small craft. The waves crashing onto the beach had grown, so much so, that at first, MacKay feared they'd be swamped by the rough water. Three times he lost sight of them, thinking they'd been taken under, only to see their small boat burst up over the water. He could just make out the two men, struggling to keep their boat on course, while hanging on to keep from being thrown into the sea. It was evident that if they were attacked they wouldn't be able to put up much of a fight.

"Sir, it's back and it is heading right for us," said Seaman Hatfield.

"Range?" asked Lieutenant Gallo.

"Two hundred twenty yards and closing rapidly," replied Hatfield. "At the rate it's moving, it'll easily get to us before the marines do."

"Mr. Mercer, how are we doing with the bursts of sound?" MacKay shouted into his radio. "We have company and its heading right for us."

"We've picked up the creature's course and we're adjusting the speakers, turning them more towards the beast and increasing the volume."

"Get it done, Mr. Mercer; we have to buy those men more time." MacKay turned his attention back to the marines. He didn't make a sound, but inwardly groaned. They weren't making much progress. The waves and the wind kept pushing them back.

"The creature has slowed down," reported Hatfield. "It appears to be swimming in circles, but the patterns are very irregular."

Shaw and Fuller were now far enough out from the beach that the waves breaking on the shore were no longer as much of an issue. They were finally starting to make better time. The craft they were in was especially built for this kind of work and continued to plow its way through the large swells. As best as MacKay could make out, Fuller had tied himself to the boat, freeing up both hands so that he could use his rifle if necessary.

"Sir, it's moving again, heading towards us, but at a slower pace. It's heading down into deeper water," reported Hatfield. Lieutenant Gallo stood next to Hatfield, making sure that his reports were accurate.

Up until a about an hour ago, MacKay might have taken this as good news. Unfortunately, he now knew that this was not a good sign, not good at all. Dr. Brennan had explained that from what they understood, when a platyurus attacks, quite often it comes straight up at its prey from below.

"Keep your eyes sharp, Hatfield," ordered MacKay. Picking up the radio, he said, "Shaw, Fuller, can either of you read me?"

"Aye, aye, Skipper. You're coming in loud and clear."

"Who is this?" asked MacKay. The noise of the wind and the ocean combined had nearly drowned them out.

"Private Fuller, sir."

"Fuller, there is a large marine animal the size of a small whale headed your way. The minute you see it, open fire. Did you read me?"

"Yes sir, we'll be ready."

MacKay didn't want to take his eyes off the small boat, but he needed to see where the creature was in relation to his men. Crossing over to Hatfield, he leaned over the young sailor's shoulder. "Where is it?"

Pointing to the screen in front of him, Hatfield indicated one of the white spots. "That's him. He's not far now, although the good news is that he's really slowed down. If he holds true to his present course, he'll be right under us in about five minutes."

MacKay grabbed the radio. "Mr. Mercer, that thing is almost on us. He'll be directly under us in just a few minutes. Crank up the volume as much as you can!"

Turning back to the window, he could see that the small boat was now about thirty yards out. The marines were hanging on as best they could as the waves tossed them all over the place. MacKay realized that even once they pulled alongside the *Eclipse*, it was going to be a struggle to get them safely on board.

Setting down the binoculars, MacKay prepared to leave the bridge. "Mr. Gallo, you have the bridge. Hatfield, keep me informed as to what that thing does, good or bad." MacKay rushed down the steep stairs and ran as fast as he could to the rear of the ship. Less than three minutes later he emerged onto the lower deck to see Tanner and several sailors and marines already in position, waiting to pull the two men on board.

MacKay watched as Shaw desperately battled against the waves, trying to bring the small boat next to the *Eclipse.* As soon as they were close enough, Fuller threw a rope to one of the sailors. Despite the strong gusts of wind that seemed to be deliberately working against them, the sailor snagged it on the first try. He, along with two other sailors, began to pull the two marines towards them. MacKay clicked on his radio. "Hatfield, where is it? Has it moved?"

A split second later the question was answered for him as the sea erupted in violence. The creature's head, with its gapping jaws, burst through the waves, smashing into the rear of the small craft, lifting it out of the water. The impact of the platyurus sent Shaw flying out of the small boat and towards the ship. He slammed into the side of the *Eclipse*, as well as part of the deck railing before falling unconscious into the sea.

Fuller had not fared much better. His body half in the water, he hung from the side of his boat. A sudden swell raised him and the boat up and the crew tried to grab hold of him, just missing his outstretched hand. Fuller fell backwards, following the boat as it crashed back down into waves. MacKay could see that Fuller's right arm and shoulder were still tied to the side of his craft. Using his left hand, Fuller frantically fought with the knot, trying to break free.

Only seconds had passed when the creature struck again. Shooting out of the water, it lunged at the *Eclipse*, snapping at the sailors standing near the edge of the deck. Its wide jaws slashed the arm of one of the men, while its head rammed into another, sending the man flying into the metal wall behind him. MacKay and another sailor grabbed the sailor with the slashed arm just before he fell over the side and into the sea. There was now blood in the water.

As the creature slipped back beneath the surface, one of Tanner's marines jumped into the boat, knife in hand, and began to cut away at the rope holding Fuller in place. At almost the same time, MacKay saw Lieutenant Tanner dive headfirst into the water next to the *Eclipse*. Rushing back to the railing, MacKay looked down, pistol in hand, ready to do whatever he could to help. It wasn't long before Tanner resurfaced, holding on to the unconscious Private Shaw. Grabbing onto a rope, the sailors quickly pulled the two men in, hauling them out of the water.

But the creature was not yet finished. Its next attack was far more successful. Hitting the small craft with tremendous force, the creature's jaws closed with a vicelike grip onto the rear corner of the boat. The terrible force behind the creature's bite punctured the bottom of the boat and tore jagged openings into its side. The marine who had been helping Fuller was thrown from the small craft. Spinning head over heels, he landed in the water about twenty feet from the *Eclipse*. Slightly dazed, he started to swim towards the *Eclipse*. He didn't get very far. The creature's jaws appeared on both sides of the marine, closed, and pulled him under.

The men continued battling the surging waves, trying to pull the boat in, but it was becoming more and more difficult as the damaged craft rapidly filled with water. Fuller's arm was still not free of the ropes holding him to the small craft. The creature reemerged, once again biting into the rear of the sinking boat. Fighting to keep from sliding into the creature's snapping jaws, Fuller gave it all he had to break free. The creature, focused on the boat, kept trying to pull it down beneath the waves, and the bow started to rise up out of the water.

Keeping its jaws tightly locked, the creature dropped beneath the waves, its tremendous strength taking the boat and Fuller with it. The waves quickly closed in over where the doomed craft had been. MacKay couldn't believe what he'd just witnessed. He didn't know what to do. He felt like he was going to throw up. The navy had trained him to do almost everything, but it had not prepared him for something like this.

Suddenly, Private Fuller's head broke the surface and he began to inch his way towards the ship, but it was clear to see that he was having trouble. His arm was still tied to part of the boat. Two more sailors dove in, grabbed him, and got him back to the *Eclipse*. Just as they pulled him onto the deck, the creature shot up out of the water one last time.

Opening its mouth, it let loose with a terribly shrill roar and lunged at the men, making one last grab for any of them it could reach. The creature splashed down into the water, drenching the rescue team standing near the railing. Now that the two marines were safely on board, several sailors rushed to the railing and began to pour round after round of rifle fire into the dark gray water.

Mercer joined them on the deck, along with several corpsmen, and started directing them to get the wounded men to sick bay. It was only then that MacKay noticed Tanner sitting on the deck, his back against the wall, his legs splayed out in front of him. MacKay rushed over and squatted down next to him. "Lieutenant, are you all right?"

Tanner looked at MacKay and nodded. "Yes sir, I'm fine. I watched it get Private Franks. There was nothing I could do. What was that thing?"

"What you just did has to be one of the bravest things I've ever seen," said MacKay, helping the young lieutenant to his feet.

"I've never been so terrified in my life," said Tanner, his voice so low it was hard to hear him.

MacKay turned to Mercer and said, "Get him to sick bay. I think he's going into shock."

"Wait," said Tanner, jerking away from Mercer, turning on MacKay. "What are we going to do? If there are monsters like that thing living in those jungles, then Captain Garrett and my men need my help, all our help. They can't possibly make it back against creatures like that, not alone. They don't stand a chance!"

"Stand down, Lieutenant, there's nothing we can do for them, at least not now. I want Dr. Severin to look at you. That's an order."

MacKay watched as Mercer walked away with the limping Tanner. He still couldn't believe that Tanner had dove into the water with that monster trying to kill them. Smiling to himself, he silently acknowledged that marines are definitely a unique breed. Thank heaven they're on our side!

Clicking his radio on, he said, "Mr. Gallo, get us out to sea as fast as you can. We have recovered the two marines and they are on their way to sick bay."

Turning off his radio, MacKay noticed that his hands were trembling, and he felt slightly out of breath. It was then he realized that he too was experiencing his own kind of shock. He couldn't remember a nightmare as bad as what he and his crew had just gone through. Walking back to the bridge, he made a silent vow. As soon as the storm was gone, they'd be back and do everything in their power to help Colton and those marines.

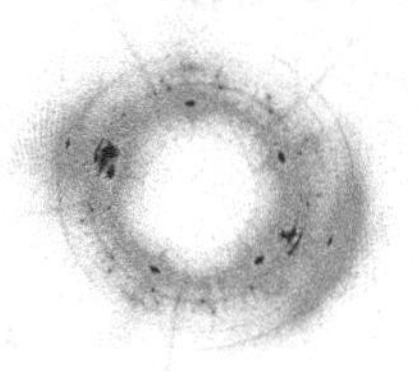

CHAPTER 17

Although Colton didn't know what was happening to him, oddly, he was completely at ease. The sensation was like what he'd experienced years ago, in a sensory deprivation tank. The only difference now was that rather than his surroundings being completely black, they were filled with a soft, undulating blue light. It was like floating in a cloudless sky. A deep euphoria filled him.

Considering all he'd just gone through, culminating with the finding of Blake's body, the way he felt didn't sync up in any way with what he'd just experienced. The roller coaster of extreme levels of fear and sorrow that had consumed him mere seconds ago were gone. Instead he felt a strong sense of peace, the horrors of the jungle miles away, left behind. He was in a place of safety. Then, listening closely, he began to hear something, words possibly, but this too was different. Someone was communicating with him, the words steadily growing in volume, and yet he wasn't hearing them in the traditional sense. The words were going directly into his mind. This new mode of communication broadened its scope, filling his mind with new concepts and information about the world around him.

He had a flashback to his Philosophy 101 class. Dr. Augustus was writing the word EPISTEMOLOGY on the blackboard. He was talking about the idea of basic assumptions, but as he spoke, flashing blue and green lights seemed to be shooting out of his mouth. Something was changing Colton's basic ideas. The image of Dr. Augustus melted into light again. Several brief images appeared—his drill sergeant, a nun from elementary school, the older woman that he had lost his virginity to, his karate sensei. Then light again. Then a vibration, like a voice, but not a voice.

The voice, so to speak, was gentle, calming, reassuring. It kept telling him, over and over, that he was okay, that he was in a safe place, that they would protect him. Who is they? This is the thought that sprang to his mind, but then, instantly, incredibly, his thought was answered! *We are friend.* Again, no words, the response flowing directly and clearly into his mind.

The voice continued on, *You have suffered loss. We are with you now. You are safe.* In the distance, his eyes began to focus on something forming in front of him. At first it appeared to be a great distance away. Quickly it came into focus. A man, not very tall, rather plain, and quite ordinary. Something, though, was very different about this guy, and then Colton understood. This was not a real person. He could see it clearly as it appeared directly in front of him. It was the composite of all the good teachers of his life, but animated. Then it smiled at him. Silver-haired, black business suit, the nun's cross, and one blue eye and one brown eye. Full lips with too much lipstick. And a black belt.

"What are you?" Colton asked. Or did he? He'd asked his question but had never opened his mouth. He'd been able to communicate his question without giving voice to it. He couldn't wrap his mind around what was happening, but he remained at ease. Under normal circumstances this would have probably put his whole nervous system on high alert, but he stayed at peace, content. *We are friend.*

Colton tried to focus. "My people are injured. We need to return to our ship. We thank you for saving us."

The image before him didn't change, but the head slightly tilted, and the smile broadened a little. *We are pleased. We are friend. We will guide you to your ship.*

The complete sense of peace that had taken him over stayed with Colton. "Who are you?" This time there was no answer and the smiling person began to fade. Colton began to feel his body again, the firmness of the earth under his feet. *We are friend.* His mind began to return to its normal state. He'd either just been visited by an angel or had experienced the best piece of psychological warfare technology ever devised, maybe both. Holy Saint Psy-op.

As suddenly as the beam had focused on him, it withdrew. Colton staggered slightly but didn't fall. Things had changed, and he found that Garrett was now standing next to him, as was Corporal Lee. The rest of the team had taken up a defensive posture around him.

Garrett looked at him with a puzzled expression on her face. "Are you all right?"

"Yes, I feel great. What's the matter?"

"Well, you were just encased in that blue beam and you have a silly, borderline stupid expression on your face. Are you actually happy?"

Colton's return to reality was now complete and the false feeling of euphoria he'd been feeling was gone. He shook his head as if to rid himself from the experience. "I think I just communicated with our saviors, or, they communicated with me."

"There was more than one?" asked Garrett. "Who are they? What did they say?"

Colton looked around and asked, "Where's the corpsman?"

"He's with Private Lockridge. What did they say to you?" asked Garrett.

Colton struggled for a moment to pull his thoughts together. As much as he wanted to talk to him, he'd compare notes with the corpsman later. "The entire time they just kept reassuring me that I was safe, that I was okay."

"Did you learn who they are?" asked Corporal Lee. "Where are we?"

Colton shook his head. "All in all, it was a short conversation. I mean, I guess it was a conversation. That doesn't matter. They kept expressing friendship and said that they'd guide us to the ship."

"And you have no idea who they are?" asked Garrett. "How is that even possible?"

"Captain, what I just experienced was completely unique," said Colton, "and I'm not really sure how to explain it. What I do know is that at least for now, they, whoever 'they' are, and I truly have no idea, are on our side."

"Captain, Commander, with all due respect, if they're going to lead us out of here, we need to get moving. I don't like what I'm seeing up in that sky and the winds are really starting to pick up," said Corporal Lee. "We need to move out."

"Get two stretchers pulled together," said Garrett. She then turned back to Colton. "So, we just leave now? What, have we been granted safe passage? You do know what's waiting for us in that jungle, don't you? Battle shock can make the brain do weird things."

Colton shook his head. "I know I'm not making any sense, but later we can talk about it at length. You did see the light? I mean this isn't just in my head. Lee is right. At a minimum we're going to get drenched. There's probably some cover further up in those boulders, but I certainly have no intention of hanging around here. For the moment, we seem to have an escort, and I want to take full advantage of that."

The two stretchers were quickly assembled. Lockridge was gently laid on one, Blake on the other. Corporal Lee and Private Hill took the point, with Logan and Diaz guarding their rear. It didn't take long before Private Hill found the game trail they'd followed on their way in. Battered and nearly exhausted, they began their journey back to the *Eclipse*.

The wind rapidly grew in strength, buffeting the trees all around them, and making so much noise that they could hardly hear anything else. This put Colton on edge. He kept expecting that each time they rounded a curve in the trail, they'd find those prehistoric nightmares waiting for them.

As he trudged on, Colton had been trying to place the voice/non voice. It was that kid in *A Charlie Brown Christmas* reading about the shepherds. Yup, he was crazy. But better to die in crazy hope than to be paralyzed with despair.

He and Garrett took turns, constantly glancing up through the swaying branches to see if their escort was still with them. The light from the craft remained as bright as it had been before, revealing very little of its true shape. There was still a general feeling of calmness with the team, which Colton knew was somehow being induced by their new friends.

Suddenly Corporal Lee reached out, grabbed onto Private Hill's shoulder, and drug him backwards. Both men hit the ground hard as a giant tree crashed to the ground not twenty feet in front of them. Two of the larger branches landed right where Hill had been walking.

At almost the same time, the rain started to fall. It was a gentle, warm rain, but there were no guarantees that it would stay that way. All of them remembered the stream that was waiting for them up ahead, a stream that lay between them and the beach. If the rain turned into a downpour, the gentle stream they'd crossed earlier in the day could quickly turn into a raging torrent. This would effectively strand them in a jungle they knew they couldn't survive in.

"My guess is that this is going to get worse before it gets better, and there's no telling how long this storm will be on us," said Garrett. "We have to find cover, somewhere to hunker down and ride this thing out."

"Agreed," said Colton. "We've got to get out of these trees. If the storm is as widespread as I think it is, MacKay will have moved the *Eclipse* away from the shore and out into deeper water. Even if we did push on, and somehow managed to make it back to the boats, we'd have nowhere to go."

Corporal Lee and Private Hill joined the two officers, Hill a little shaken by his close call with the falling tree. "Corporal," said Colton, "we're going to leave the trail here and head towards that rock face that's been running parallel to us. Hopefully, we'll find some large boulders to take shelter under, or maybe even an overhang. You, Hill, and I will lead the team."

"What about our friends?" asked Garrett. "How do you think they'll interpret our change in direction?"

Colton glanced up at the hovering craft, shrugged his shoulders, and said, "I have no idea what they'll think. Right now, I can't worry about that. Frankly, nothing has made any sense to me ever since that energy wave rolled over us. And this little foray into the jungle has put the icing on the cake. We watched a giant flower eat one of the largest lizards I've ever seen; we've been attacked by dinosaurs, supposedly extinct for millions of years; and are now being escorted back to our ship by beings who are apparently far more advanced than we are. I have no clue where we are, or what's happened to us, but without a shadow of a doubt, it's clear we're not in Kansas anymore."

"What do you mean?" said Corporal Lee, not understanding what Colton was trying to say. Colton just stared at him.

"He's in his upper twenties, Commander. Pretty sure he didn't follow your *Wizard of Oz* movie reference," said Garrett.

"I'll explain it to him later. We need to get out of here," said Colton. Corporal Lee and Private Hill pulled machetes out of their backpacks and began to cut a path through the jungle, doing their best to avoid areas of dense undergrowth. The soaking rain steadily grew in intensity, the wind pushing against them no matter which direction they went. Their progress was slow at best.

About forty yards in, the trees fell back, opening into a clearing that stretched roughly sixty feet across. Looking above the tree line on the other side of the clearing, they could see that the massive cliff face that they were trying to reach was close at hand. Corporal Lee pointed to a dark spot about a hundred feet up on the cliff. "Could be a cave."

Colton tried to get a clear view of it, but the rain, mixed with the mist that had dogged them the entire day, made it impossible. “Could be,” said Colton. “Hopefully we’ll find something closer to the ground.”

Hill started out across the clearing, closely followed by Colton. On the ground, in the leaves just in front of them, Colton thought he saw something move. “Hold up!” he ordered.

Hill came to a sudden stop, his hand instinctively moving to his holstered pistol. “You see something, Commander?”

“Something moved, right there,” he said, pointing to the ground a few feet in front of Hill. “Not sure if it was a branch or something else.” At that moment, the dull, gray light that blanketed the jungle began to grow brighter. Colton looked up to see that the craft that had been following them had rapidly descended, hovering directly above them.

Suddenly Hill jumped back, knocking into Colton. “Look at that!”

Both men watched as a thick, grayish-black tail, at least four feet in length, quickly disappeared under several long, broad leaves that lay across the ground in front of them. Just before it vanished from sight, they saw a curved claw the size of a garden scythe at the end of the tail, the light from the craft above reflecting off it. They continued to stare at the spot where it had been, looking for any movement at all, but everything remained still.

“Stay where you are,” ordered Colton.

Corporal Lee had moved up and now stood beside them. “What’s going on?”

“Not sure, but we’re about to find out,” said Colton. Borrowing Hill’s machete, he moved over to a tree and cut off a thick branch. He then proceeded to cut all the small stems off it, creating a staff about ten feet long.

Colton carefully approached the huge elephant-ear leaves the creature had crawled under. Using the long staff, he started to move them aside. Not knowing what to expect, he did this one leaf at a time. With each leaf, he half expected something to charge out at him. Glancing behind him, he saw that Lee and Hill had their sidearms out and pointed in his direction, ready to cover him if attacked.

"We find something?" asked Garrett. She'd been with the rear guard and came up to see why they'd stopped. "The storm just took out another giant tree, but it was quite a way behind us."

"I know we need to keep moving," said Colton, "but something just crawled under these leaves, something too big to ignore. At first, I thought this clearing would give us a few feet of easy going. Now I'm afraid it might be too good to be true," said Colton.

"What did it look like?" asked Garrett.

"We didn't get too good of a look, sir," said Private Hill. "It scurried under those leaves and we only saw its tail. Whatever it was, the tail had a huge claw on the end of it."

Colton kept removing the leaves as he said, "Not that it matters, but I'm not so sure that was a claw. Looked more like a stinger."

Garret pulled her weapon to cover Colton as Lee and Hill moved off, fashioning their own staffs, and pitched in to help Colton move the leaves aside. The ground beneath the leaves soon started to steeply taper off. Once they'd moved about half of the leaves out of the way, they found a large hole with smooth sides that had been hidden by the leaves.

"Somebody or something went to a great deal of trouble to hide this," said Corporal Lee. The funnel-shaped hole was at least fourteen to fifteen feet across, dropping dramatically downward.

"Look in the center," said Colton. "There's another hole there. Looks like that one drops straight down." The hole at the bottom of the funnel was a little bigger than a manhole cover, but they had no way of telling how far down it dropped into the ground.

"This thing is a trap," said Garrett. "Any animal walking through here wouldn't have seen this coming. Heaven knows those leaves certainly wouldn't support much weight, nor was that the intent. Drop into this and you couldn't help but to slide right down into that hole."

Colton felt a chill run down his back and it wasn't due to the heavy rain. The tail they'd seen was connected to something big and strong. It had to be to have built something like this. Whatever it was that they'd seen, it was waiting down in that hole for its next victim. If any of them had fallen into this, they wouldn't have stood a chance.

Private Hill was close to reaching the end of his rope, his anger beginning to surface. "This whole stinking jungle is nothing but a death trap," he said, pulling a grenade from is belt. "Stand back, Commander. I'm going to kill the beast that built this so that it doesn't ever trap anything again."

"Private," commanded Garrett, "put that grenade away. That's an order. We'll defend ourselves with as much force as is necessary, but we will not take any aggressive action on our own."

"Sir, this was meant to kill us," said Hill, pointing to the hole in front of them, "or anything else that happened to wander through here."

"Private Hill, you are not in the army, you are a marine! When you get an order, you obey it. Do you understand me?" shouted Garrett, advancing on the private. Hill was a tall, well-built man with nine years of experience and significant special ops training. He was not the kind to back away from trouble, or anything else, and he was especially the wrong man to challenge when angry.

Fortunately, Garrett's words carried the necessary weight, and Hill managed to keep himself in check. He tried to shake off the anger, but it wouldn't let go. Although he would never have admitted this to anyone, he knew the anger stemmed from the raw fear coursing through him. For Hill, fear was an emotion he rarely dealt with. Fear was nothing more than a weakness, and he was anything but weak. What Hill had no way of knowing was that every single one of his comrades was struggling with the same emotions.

"Sir, yes sir!" said Hill. "It won't happen again, sir."

"We don't know who our new benefactors are," said Colton, nodding at the craft above them. "But I think they may have just saved us again."

"How's that?" asked Corporal Lee.

"Just as Private Hill and I were about to step on those leaves, I saw something move. At the same time, the craft changed its position, coming to a stop where you see it now. The light that normally radiates from it became even brighter, stronger, which is what I think made that thing scuttle off. Had it not done that, one of us would most probably be laying in the bottom of that pit."

"I don't know whose guardian angel to thank," said Corporal Lee, "but I'm grateful they decided to join us."

"Whatever brought them to us," said Colton, "we don't want to do anything to send them away, or worse, turn them against us. If we dropped a grenade down there, and believe me, I want to do that as much as you do, that might change the way they feel about us. We'd be killing something that wasn't attacking us. It would not be a defensive act. Think about it. When they first arrived, they stopped the dinosaurs from killing us, but they did it by peaceful means. They drove the dinosaurs off, but they didn't kill or injure them in any way."

Private Hill nodded, and Corporal Lee said, "What do we do now?"

Colton turned and studied the clearing once again with a fresh eye. "We'll continue across. I'll lead and use this staff to make sure we don't inadvertently step into one of these things."

"If you don't mind, sir, I'd like to help you with that."

Colton smiled at Private Hill. "I'd welcome the help."

"Very good," said Captain Garrett. "Let's keep moving. We've got to find some place to take cover in soon. We are in desperate need of rest and shelter."

Colton knew Garrett was right. The day had started early, and they'd been at it too hard for too long. They had to find some place safe. Not to just get out of the weather, but some place where they could rest, eat, and prepare for whatever they might face on the rest of their journey back to the ship. Based on everything they'd already been through, Colton didn't even want to think about what other horrors might be lurking in this nightmare of a jungle.

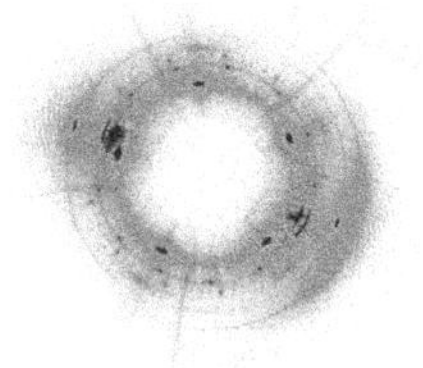

CHAPTER 18

No other hidden dangers awaited them as they crossed the clearing, but it took far longer than they wanted. The trees and foliage they now entered were as thick as before, and the ground began to sharply angle upwards. Although the trees did provide some shelter from the rain, the storm continued to increase in strength, the treetops whipping back and forth. Their situation continued to deteriorate. All of them knew that they had to find shelter soon. Man's desire to seek shelter in caves is quite old.

Finally, after what seemed like an eternity, they reached the base of the cliff. Boulders of all sizes lay strewn across the ground, but none of them were situated to provide any protection from the elements. Using some branches they found lying on the ground, they quickly erected a makeshift tent out of rain ponchos for Lockridge. He was still unconscious, but the corpsmen remained optimistic.

Scouts were sent out in both directions to see what they could find. There did appear to be caves in the rock face, but disappointingly, they were too high up for them to use. Even though they were still being battered by the storm, it felt good to be able to sit down while they waited for the scouts to return. The men were tired, their nerves stretched to the limit, some going in and out of shock. Everyone kept a careful watch, but they didn't see any kind of wildlife, big or small. On occasion, when a strong gust of wind would hit the trees just right, they would catch a fleeting glimpse of their protector's craft, hovering high above the trees.

Garrett made her way over to Colton and sat down on a small rock near him. "Thought I'd take advantage of our little rest period to talk with you. There are some things I want to go over and I'd like to keep this between the two of us."

"Fire away," said Colton. "In this storm, no one's going to overhear anything we have to say."

"When that beam of light descended on you, what actually happened? Did you see the people you were talking to? Did they have accents? Was there anything that might be of use to help us identify them?"

Colton thought back, going over the experience. Truth is, he hadn't been able to get it out of his mind. As they'd made their way through the jungle, he kept replaying it, trying to understand exactly what had happened. Unfortunately, he hadn't been very successful. At this point, he couldn't even answer his own questions.

Whoever they are, their benefactors had completely controlled the situation. Therefore, he really didn't have a great deal to report. While it was true that he had communicated with their new friends, the communication itself had been very different. It had been so much more than just mere words. At the time, it had affected the way he was feeling. Overall, the experience seemed to have strengthened him, giving him a sense of relief from his burdens, even if only temporarily.

"The short answer is no. There isn't one thing that I can remember that we can use to identify who these people are. But as impossible as that may sound, it's only the tip of the iceberg," said Colton. Giving as much detail as he could, Colton walked her through the entire experience. Garrett listened intently and didn't interrupt his narrative. When he finished, she sat there in silence, seemingly lost in her own thoughts.

Adjusting her position on the rock, she looked Colton in the eye and said," What you've just told me is the truth, right?"

Not breaking eye contact with her, he said, "Yes, the absolute truth."

"And there's nothing you left out? Nothing you're holding back to protect us?"

"No, Captain," said Colton, giving her a small smile, "that's all there is."

Garrett looked down, slightly nodding her head as if in affirmation of her own thoughts. "Then I believe we are in serious trouble."

Colton managed not to laugh.

"Captain, as crazy as all of this has been, we both know there has to be a reasonable explanation."

"An explanation, yes; reasonable, I have my doubts. First, we lose all contact with the outside world. Then find what's left of an airplane that disappeared under mysterious circumstances over seventy years ago. We then get to see a giant plant, which none of us can identify, devour a huge lizard. And the icing on the cake was being attacked by dinosaurs, no less, and then being saved by people with technology that neither one of us can even guess at," said Garrett. "Don't laugh at this Commander, but I'm not even sure we're still on Earth."

"Where do you think we are?"

"I have no idea, but whoever is controlling that thing up there communicated with you telepathically. It did the same thing with the corpsman," said Garrett.

"He told you that?" asked Colton, a little incredulous despite his own experience.

"He didn't want to, but I finally got it out of him. He was certain if he told me I'd accuse him of using some of the drugs he's carrying. He said it was the blond Jesus that was in his Sunday school class when he was a kid, brought to life, as it were."

"I'd planned to talk to him myself, but haven't gotten the opportunity," said Colton. "Did he say how he felt while it was happening?"

" 'As happy as being at home on Thanksgiving.' And that's a direct quote. I must ask you a question and it's going to sound a little crazy, but at this point, I don't care. The people controlling that thing, the ones that communicated with you telepathically, do you think they're human?"

The thought of these people being anything but human had never entered Colton's mind. *Of course they're human. What else would they be?* he thought to himself. "Where are you going with all this, Captain? Are we talking alien abduction? Is that really the path you're taking with this?"

"I don't know, but if you think about it, at least alien intervention is one of the few things that even comes close to explaining all this," said Garrett. "Don't misunderstand me, Commander. I'm not losing it. I just need to prepare myself so that I can do the best I can for the men under my command."

Colton smiled at her. No, he didn't think she was losing it. He'd gotten to witness how she handled herself under fire, steadily directing her men in the face of several terrifying creatures that would have sent most people running for the hills. She was not just one gutsy lady; she was a marine, through and through. "I'll have to give that idea some thought, but I have to be honest with you. Normally, I would have laughed at the whole concept of aliens. However, all things considered, it's just as crazy as everything else has been, so why not?"

"I'm not joking," said Garrett. "You told me that the 'person' you saw when you were talking with them was not real, that it was an animated figure, an AI construct or a mental image."

"That's right," said Colton. "I figure they did that to keep their identity hidden."

"Maybe, but there's also another possibility. They may have used an animated figure to keep from scaring the crap out of you. For all we know, they look so bad that by comparison those dinosaurs back there look like snuggly puppies."

Colton could no longer help himself, and he laughed, he had to, if for no other reason than to break the tension. "Well, if that turns out to be true, then we are dealing with some butt-ugly aliens."

Even Garrett was smiling now. "If you tell anyone about our little talk, even your buddy Father Ryan, I'll feed you to that flower we passed by earlier today."

"With a threat like that hanging over my head, I have no choice but to keep my mouth shut."

At that moment Privates Logan and Diaz returned from their scouting mission. "Captain, we may have found what we're looking for," reported Private Logan.

Garrett turned around to face the two men. "Tell me about it."

"It's only about a hundred yards or so away from us, but it's rough going, broken rock and shale everywhere," said Private Diaz. "Roughly twenty feet up we found a cave, and it's pretty big."

"You looked inside?" asked Colton.

"I did, sir," answered Private Logan. "I didn't go too far back, but there didn't appear to be anyone living there. I did find some tracks on the floor of the cave, but I couldn't determine how long they'd been there. It's cold, like a cave, but it's dry."

Garrett looked at Colton and he nodded his agreement. "Alright, tell the corpsman to get Lockridge ready to move. As soon as Corporal Lee and Private Hill return, we head to this cave," directed Garrett.

"From a special ops perspective, I don't like caves," said Colton. "They're death traps. On the other hand, at this point, the idea of getting to dry out, as well as being able to sit down and relax, is just too appealing."

Keeping a constant vigilance on their surroundings, the marines prepared to move out. About twenty minutes later Corporal Lee and Private Hill returned. They too had found some caves, but they were either too small or too high up on the cliff face to be of use. With Privates Logan and Diaz leading the way, they headed out. Colton's earlier statement was spot-on; caves were not the best place to retreat to, especially if you are being pursued by an enemy. Typically, there's only one way in and out. A determined enemy will wait until you've run out of food and water.

The terrain turned out to be as hard to navigate as advertised. Many of the men slipped and fell, or had a rock slide out from under them, taking them down. Fortunately, the men carrying Lockridge kept their footing, although there were a couple of close calls.

About halfway there, a giant tree, hit by lightning, crashed to the ground, crushing several smaller trees a few scant yards away from them. Due to the intensity of the storm, at first they didn't realize that it had been a lightning strike that brought the tree down. Their first thought was that the dinosaurs that had attacked them earlier were returning, knocking down several trees as they moved in to attack.

Other than this one small scare, the trip to the cave was uneventful. It took longer than any of them wanted, but they made it safely with only a few minor bumps and scrapes. As soon as they got there, three of the marines scrambled up the steep rock face and into the cave. Along with Corporal Lee, a more thorough search of the cave was carried out.

"How's it look?" asked Garrett.

"The cave itself opens up into a pretty big room, then tapers back down and heads deeper into the mountain. To be safe, we followed the passage back into the mountain to see if it led to anything. The good news is that we didn't see any branches leading away from the main corridor. The passageway doesn't go too far and ends in a room about half as big as the one up front. Much of that room is taken up by a very deep pit, which eats up most of the floor space," reported Corporal Lee.

"In my college days, I did a little spelunking," said Colton. "Let's get everyone inside, then I'll look at that pit. Hopefully, it won't prove to be problematic. I'll feel better once we make sure we're not intruding on someone's home, so to speak."

"Does the idea that there's a vertical cavern at the back of the cave suggest something to you?" asked Garrett.

"No, not at all," said Colton. "It's just an unknown and we need to check it out as thoroughly as we can. If something does live down there, and it's a nocturnal predator, it's going to be happy to find its dinner waiting for it at the mouth of the cave. I hate to think of myself as part of an entrée, delivered by room service."

Garrett nodded her agreement and said, "Let's get Lockridge inside first. Then we'll have the corpsman tend to the men and everyone can get a bite to eat." Using ropes, they soon had the wounded man up and out of the elements. After that, it didn't take long to get the rest of the men inside.

The entrance to the cave was tall enough for a man to stand without any problem and was about twelve feet across. After a short distance, it opened into a large room where they could all sit and rest comfortably. Here the roof of the cave was at least fifteen to sixteen feet above the floor. As Corporal Lee had described, in the back of the room the cave funneled back down to the same size as it was in the front, trailing off into the darkness.

For the most part, the walls of the cave were smooth, with none of the rock formations that people usually associated with caves, such as stalagmites and stalactites. The floor was covered with broken rocks, as well as with dirt that was nearly as fine as sand. It was cold in the cave, but at least they'd been able to leave the storm behind. For the first time all day they began to feel safe.

"I have two men stationed at the mouth of the cave to make sure nothing tries to get in," said Garrett as she sat down next to Colton. She watched as the corpsmen checked on each of the marines, using the blue gel they'd been given on many of them. "Wish I knew what was in that stuff."

"It concerns me too, but without it I'm convinced we would have lost Lockridge," said Colton. "Can't believe what it did for my own wound. I'm still a little sore, but not nearly as sore as I should be. Nice to think that something good has come out of all this."

"Before I came back over here, I checked, and our friends are still with us. They're hovering above the trees out in front of the cave. As hard as the wind is blowing, that thing is holding its position. I can't believe how stable it is. Whoever these people are, there are clearly quite a few things they can teach us," said Garrett.

For the next thirty minutes or so the men ate, rested, and tried to forget all that lay between them and the *Eclipse*. Private Diaz had sat down near the back of the cave, keeping watch. He'd set up a flashlight, using some of the rocks lying on the floor, positioning it so that its beam lit up the passageway leading off from the main room.

Finally, Colton got up, stretched his arms up over his head, and then picked up his backpack, leaving his rifle behind. "I'm going to take Corporal Lee and Private Diaz and have a look around. I can't begin to tell you how worn out I'm feeling, and I'm sure that goes for everyone else. We need to get some sleep, but we first need to check out the rest of this cave. Not sure I can take any more surprises, especially after all we've been through today."

Colton took the lead as they headed back into the mountain. The flashlights they carried were very strong, easily lighting up the cave from wall to wall. They did find a couple of large cracks in the wall that opened enough to squeeze into, but they dead-ended after just a few feet. Rounding a rather sharp curve, they came to the room with the pit.

The pit, while not unusual, was larger than Colton had anticipated. It reached all the way to the far wall of the cave, roughly fifteen feet across. Lying on their stomachs, they inched out over the edge of the pit and aimed their flashlights into the inky darkness.

As a college kid, Colton had always marveled at the complete and total darkness of a cave. With the lights out, it amazed him that he literally could not see his hand in front of his face, even with it touching his nose. A small shiver coursed down his spine as he gazed into the depths of the pit, wondering if in this strange land they'd found the true entrance to hell.

The walls of the pit appeared to be damp, and had eroded in narrow grooves, running vertically as far down as they could see. Colton's first guess was that water had caused the erosion, but looking around, he couldn't find any evidence to support that theory. Their flashlights were strong, but ledges jutting out from different sides of the pit at varying depths blocked their view and they couldn't see all the way to the bottom.

"Do you smell that?" asked Diaz. "What is that odor?"

It wasn't overpowering by any stretch of the imagination, but it was there, and caused their eyes to start to water. "It smells like some kind of acid, but I can't say what kind," said Corporal Lee. "I wonder if that is what carved out all those grooves in the walls?"

An uneasy feeling about the pit began to insert its way into Colton's mind. Straining his eyes, he studied the pit more closely. At first, he wasn't sure, but scooting further out on his stomach, he leaned out over the edge to the point where he was almost risking a fall. He'd spotted something, not too far down, and he wanted to see if he could touch it. He knew what it looked like, but wanted to see if he could verify what he was thinking. One of the men grabbed his belt and hung on. He hadn't thought about asking for their help, but was glad they'd taken the initiative.

"Everything all right, Commander?" asked Corporal Lee.

Colton's hand reached the spot he was going for. Very carefully he touched it with just one finger. Based on the odor coming out of the pit, he'd reasoned that it had to be some kind of acid and had no interest in burning himself. The gel they'd been given had worked wonders on scrapes and open wounds. He had no intention of finding out how it worked on burns.

Having satisfied his curiosity, he scooted back to where he'd been. "Shine your lights over here, right where my hand was," directed Colton. "What do you see?"

The two men studied the spot that Colton had inspected. It looked like something had scratched the wall of the pit, cutting deeper into the rock wall than the grooves surrounding it. It was about two inches long and left a distinctive dark mark, which stood out from the grooved lines. It was the dark shade of the mark that had drawn Colton's attention to it in the first place.

"Is that a claw mark?" asked Corporal Lee.

"Not sure, sir, but look around. Now that you've pointed it out, there's quite a few of them," said Diaz. He was right. All three men could see a multitude of scratch marks on all sides of the pit, going down as far as they could see.

"So, the question is, did a lot of critters make those marks, or just one really big critter?" said Private Diaz. "And no matter what the answer is, do they, or it, still live down there?"

"Your question has merit, Private," answered Colton, "but we don't want to jump to conclusions. Those marks could also have been made a very long time ago; we have no way of telling."

"That leaves us with the odor," said Corporal Lee. "What's the source of that? I wonder, if sometimes, it bubbles up for whatever reason, and then leaves those groove marks as the acid slowly dries and descends back down into the pit."

The discovery of the anomalies in the pit had gotten to Diaz and Lee. Colton was just as nervous as they were, and it was then that it hit him. He sat up and leaned back against the cave wall. The other two men followed suit, watching him carefully. "Are you all right, Commander? Did you hear something?" asked Corporal Lee.

Colton stared at Lee for a moment, then said, "No, I didn't hear anything, but I felt something. I need you two to stop being marines for a few minutes and answer this question. How are you feeling right now?"

"Not sure I understand, sir," said Private Diaz. "Is the odor from that pit affecting you?"

"No, not directly, I don't think that's it," said Colton. "Emotionally, how are you feeling?"

The two men looked at each other, obviously uncomfortable with the question, and then looked back at Colton. Shrugging his shoulders, Corporal Lee looked at Colton with a confused look on his face. "Emotionally, sir?"

"Come on, guys, it's not a hard question. How are you feeling? Are you happy? Nervous? Concerned about what could possibly be living down there in that pit?"

"Yeah, it's got me concerned," said Diaz. "I mean, let's face it, we've seen too many things that are simply impossible since we left the ship. At this point, at least for me, nothing's off the table. It scares me to think what might have dug those claw marks into the wall."

Colton nodded his head, "Me too. I'm nervous. I mean, I'm on edge and my stomach is starting to act up. But that's normal. That's how people who have experienced what we have should be feeling." Leaning back against the wall, he once again seemed lost in thought.

"Sir, I'm not following you. Is there anything we can do?" asked Corporal Lee. Based on what he knew of Colton's background, he didn't think for a minute that Colton was having a breakdown. But at the same time, he didn't understand what the commander was getting at or exactly what was bothering him.

"This won't take long, but I'm going to try a little experiment," said Colton, getting to his feet. "I want the two of you to stay here but keep a close watch on that hole. If you hear or see anything, do not put yourselves at risk. I'll be right back with Captain Garrett."

Colton headed back through the cave to get with Garrett and to see if what he was guessing was correct. As tense and nervous as he now felt, it was, in some ways, refreshing. He knew that the craft that had saved them was manipulating their emotions. That was the only thing that could possibly explain the feeling of calm that had settled over the team.

In truth, considering all they'd been through, every single one of them should have been a bunch of jumpy, trigger-happy lunatics. Instead, they were all operating on an even keel. The craft hovering above them, or the light emanating from it, had given them instant peace with "angelic" overtones. Maybe this was a psy-op experiment. Maybe not a US or Chinese experiment. Maybe not one run by humans.

Garrett was talking with the corpsmen when Colton entered the large room where the men were resting. "Good to see you," said Garrett. "I was beginning to get concerned that you might have gotten lost. How far back does that passage go?"

"Measuring distances in a cave is always tough, but my guess is that it only runs about eighty yards, then abruptly ends," said Colton. "How are the men doing?"

"Considering the day's events, surprisingly well," answered Garrett. "The corpsman can't believe how well the men are responding to that gel. He's already used about half of it. He's now trying to figure out how we're going to get more of it."

"Are our friends still out front?"

"They were as of about twenty minutes ago. Why?" asked Garrett.

"Let me tell you what we found," said Colton, and began to describe the size and depth of the pit, the grooves down the sides of it, and the claw marks they'd found. "It's something that I think you should see."

"Shall we head back now?"

"Before we do, I just want to walk out front and see if that craft is still with us," said Colton.

"I'll go with you," said Garrett. "Is there something in particular you're looking for?"

Colton smiled at her as they walked along. "Can't tell you. If I did, I'd risk losing all kinds of man points, especially if I'm wrong."

"Man points?" laughed Garrett. "Commander, so glad you're not in the Corp."

"Why's that? I think I've done rather well keeping pace with your team."

"Oh, it's not that," said Garrett. "It's just that if you were in the Corp, I'd have to put up with your sarcastic nonsense all the time."

They had just reached the mouth of the cave. Although they really couldn't see the craft, due to the storm, they were able to see the bright light that radiated from it. It appeared as a low-hanging star, completely impervious to the terrible storm raging around it. "Looks like I might be right," said Colton.

"About what?" asked Garrett.

"Tell me how you're feeling," said Colton. "Right now, at this very minute, how do you feel?"

Garrett studied Colton's face. She wasn't sure if he was serious. "Well, I haven't given my feelings a great deal of thought. I'm tired. My right ankle is giving me some trouble, but other than that, I guess I'm okay."

"Think of the question on a more emotional level," said Colton. "Are you happy, sad, relaxed, nervous, what would you say your overall state of mind is?"

"Right at this moment? Frustrated, Commander. What is this nonsense?" said Garrett. "What are you getting at?"

"It's not nonsense, and I do need your help with this," said Colton. "Please, I need for you to focus. What are you feeling?"

Garrett frowned at him for a few seconds, then said, "Well, as I said, I'm tired, but overall I feel pretty good. I feel a whole lot calmer than I did in that clearing when those monsters attacked. At the time I thought we'd bought it."

"So did I," said Colton. "Okay, let's head back and join Corporal Lee and Private Diaz. Unfortunately, I believe that this cave may have a back door."

"Wait a minute. You going to tell me what all that feelings crap was about, or do I have to guess?"

"In time, Captain, in time," said Colton. "Trust me, there is meaning to the madness."

Garrett didn't have any interest in caves at all. It had nothing to do with any kind of claustrophobic issues; she just found them boring. Gray rock and dirt, that's all there was to see when exploring a cave. Want to know what's around the next curve? More gray rock and dirt. She wasn't critical of people who like exploring caves; it's just that she could easily list a hundred things she'd rather be doing than spending time in a hole in the ground.

The two marines could hear them coming and stood up to greet them. "So how did your experiment go, Commander?" asked Corporal Lee. "Did you get the answers you were looking for?"

"Experiment?" asked Garrett, giving Colton a questioning look.

"It went as I expected it to, Corporal, but we'll come back to that," replied Colton. "Thought it would be good for Captain Garrett to see this pit and all that we found. Corporal, I'll let you give the tour."

Corporal Lee nodded and began to show Garrett the anomalies that concerned them. He particularly focused in on the grooves in the rock, as well as the claw marks. He then told them how he and Diaz had sat in the dark and listened right after Colton had left. The good news was that they hadn't heard a thing.

"That's good," said Colton, "but it still doesn't give us the definitive answer as to whether or not there's something living down there."

"What is that odor?" asked Garrett. "It's like someone mixed sulfuric acid with rotten eggs."

"That pretty much nails it," said Colton. "Frankly, it's that odor that troubles me most of all, that and the grooves along the sides of this pit. It's an organic smell and not a simple one. If something smells like vomit, then something had to have vomited it."

"Corporal," said Garrett, "we're going to have to put a guard on this. I'll take the first watch. You and Diaz go and get something to eat and get some rest. In a couple of hours, send a couple of men back to relieve me."

Corporal Lee was about to object when Colton said, "I'll stay with the captain. We don't know what we're dealing with and we can't risk any surprises. As the captain indicated, this is a two-man job."

"Agreed," said Garrett, her eyes peering down into the pit. "My roommate at Quantico had nightmares about things like this. Glad she's not here; she'd be losing it."

"Which brings us back to my experiment," said Colton. "When we were out front looking up at that craft, you told me that other than for a few aches and pains, you felt good. Tell me, how you are feeling now."

"Well, certainly not good," said Garrett. "Knowing that we could now be attacked from the rear adds just another problem to all that we're already facing. What's your point with all of this?"

"Once that craft arrived and we had been rescued, everyone felt much calmer, much more at ease than they'd felt all day. Even with the problems and things we'd encountered in the jungle, prior to reaching this cave, morale was good and no one seemed to be overly nervous, or at least not panicky," said Colton. "Highly trained marines or not, that's not natural. People just can't go through what we've experienced and shrug it off."

"Commander, I'm not following you," said Garrett. "Not to be rude, but so what? How does any of that make a difference?

"Only the corpsmen and I have had direct communication with the people on that ship. Our experiences were identical. We both felt totally safe, secure. Had I been any more relaxed, I might have nodded off. What I want us to be aware of is that this general sense of calmness that the men have been feeling is due to the influence that ship is having over us. They're able to induce strong feelings in us, effecting our emotions. That's a little scary when you think about it. My guess is that they did something very similar with those dinosaurs to convince them to leave us alone."

"So, what was your experiment?" asked Diaz.

"When we started to examine this pit, and to consider the possibilities that something not nice might be living down there, it hit me as to just how nervous I was feeling. The fear, the anxiety, all of it was back. The calm was gone. I was feeling what I should have been feeling all day. But, I needed to confirm, as best I could, if that craft was doing this. The only way to test it was to go back to the front of the cave and see what would happen. The moment I entered that large room where the men are now resting, the nervousness almost immediately faded away."

"Okay, they're influencing emotions. I'll agree that that's probably not a good thing, but how does knowing this help us?" asked Garrett.

"First, and this is the good news, we now know that our friends are not omnipotent. Their power, their ability to influence our feelings has its limitations. It may be that we're too far away from their ship, but my guess is that it's the rock that's shielding us. Or at least some mineral in the rock that we're unaware of."

"What can be used for good, can also be used for evil," said Garrett. "I get it."

"So far everything they've done has been to help and protect us," said Colton. "Or they kept us from killing the dinosaurs. How great would it be for policemen if they could make crowds relax at will? This is a psy-op wet dream."

"Knowing that this ability to influence how we feel does have its limitations is good to know. My guess is that once we're back on the *Eclipse*, if we meet on the lower decks, shielding ourselves with the steel walls, we'll be able to escape their influence."

"We'll share this with the rest of the men before we depart. Hopefully, the storm will have run its course by tomorrow morning," said Garrett.

"Agreed," said Colton. Neither he, nor Garrett, was going to verbalize their reasoning, but it was important that all the men were aware of this. It would act as an insurance policy if only a few of them make it back to the ship. Colton and Garrett recognized the importance of this information and the need for it to be shared with MacKay and the rest of the crew.

"You said that knowing this is the good news," said Corporal Lee. "What's the downside?"

"We now know that there are limitations to their reach," said Colton. "If they can no longer control how we're feeling by being this far back in the cave, then it stands to reason that they can't influence anything else that might be back here. To put it more bluntly, their protection doesn't reach this far into the cave. Whatever may or may not be down there, we're on our own."

"Commander, unfortunately, I think you may be right," said Diaz.
"Why is that?" asked Colton.
Diaz nodded towards the pit. "Listen. I think we have company."

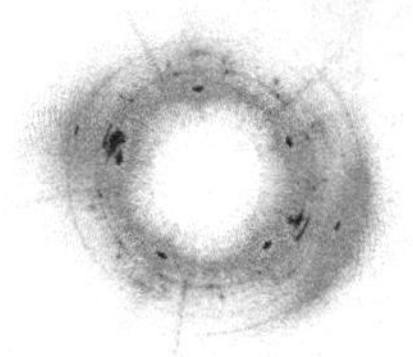

CHAPTER 19

It had been quite a few years, but MacKay vividly remembered having gone through some violently rough storms in the North Atlantic, storms in which he knew he was going to die. The storm they were caught in now wasn't as bad as those had been, but it was awfully close. Although they were getting tossed around pretty good, the *Eclipse* and its crew were doing a fine job of holding their own against the storm.

Mercer reentered the bridge and removed his rain gear. "Much more of this and I'm going to put in for a transfer."

"How's everyone holding up?" asked MacKay.

"Most of the crew is doing fairly well," answered Mercer. "Dr. Severin did a preemptive strike before we sailed into this cyclone. Between the pressure bracelets he's got them wearing on their wrists, and the copious amounts of Dramamine he handed out, we don't have too many seasick sufferers."

"I didn't know we still use Dramamine," said MacKay.

Mercer smiled at this. "I don't think we do, but that's what I call it. Severin told me the real name of the stuff, a name that I can't pronounce, so I'm sticking with Dramamine. Now, all that said, in regard to our civilian guests, they're not handling the storm nearly as well as the crew."

"Not surprised," said MacKay. Smiling, he looked at Mercer and said, "How's Meinhard holding up?"

"Poorly, very poorly indeed," said Mercer. "Poseidon's Karma, I guess. He was so bad off that Severin decided to sedate him. Be nice if we could keep him that way for a while."

"Now, now, Mr. Mercer," scolded MacKay in a mocking tone, "we must treat our guests with the utmost respect and kindness."

"I'll try to remember that," laughed Mercer. "Still, I may hit Severin up for one or two of those syringes. I mean, should Dr. Meinhard ever start to 'suffer' again, I'd be only too happy to relieve him of his misery."

"Be careful," cautioned MacKay, "too many overt acts of kindness like that and Father Ryan may start to feel that he isn't needed anymore."

"Sahir and I talked," said Mercer, changing the subject. "As soon as this storm breaks, his team will relaunch the drones."

"Good," said MacKay, "hopefully this time we'll be able to get a better look at things."

"Do you also want me to launch the attack drones?"

"No, you can have them on standby, but we'll keep them grounded for now. We still don't have any answers as to where we are, and I don't want to accidently provoke anything," said MacKay.

"You may not want to hear this, but, as it turns out, Argos agrees with you," said Mercer. Mercer knew only too well how MacKay felt about Argos. The idea that the captain and Argos were seeing eye to eye on any subject made him laugh, and he knew this would really get under MacKay's skin. "Argos ran some kind of atmospheric model and determined that the mist that hangs over that jungle, thanks to this storm, will have been blown away, at least for a few hours."

"Not the endorsement of my orders that I was after, but under the circumstances, I'll take all the support I can get. Who knows? Maybe I can teach that bucket of bolts a few things."

"I'll be sure to have Sahir schedule some one-on-one time for you with Argos," laughed Mercer.

"You do that. In the meantime, make sure that Sahir has those things equipped with heat sensors," said MacKay. "I want Colton and his team found. Once we've done that, we'll affect a rescue."

"I'm not a pessimist," said Mercer as he moved over next to MacKay so that he wouldn't be overheard. "You know that, but we didn't pick up one heat signature the last time we sent those drones out. I'm afraid that I share Lieutenant Tanner's opinion. When you think of the creatures that might be roaming through that jungle, assuming they're anything like that sea monster that attacked us, I just can't see how our people could have survived."

"I'm not disagreeing with you," said MacKay. "The odds of them having made it through all of this are pretty slim. But before we left port, I read everything I could find on Colton, in addition to what the admiral sent me. He's walked out of some bad situations in the past, situations where they'd written him off as dead. So, I'm not giving up. Let's just say I have faith."

"You have been talking with Father Ryan."

"You bet I have," said MacKay. "He said that if we work on proclaiming positive thoughts out loud, that it can help to influence the outcome of events. So, for better or worse, I'm not going to leave any stone unturned."

"Sir, here's the latest weather update," said Lieutenant Gallo, handing the captain a printout. "Looks like this storm will have run its course in a couple of hours."

"Good news, Lieutenant," said MacKay. "Get the word out so that the crew knows there's light at the end of this tunnel. Once the drones are launched, we'll head back to our previous position."

At first the sounds were so faint that Colton thought Diaz might have been imagining things. It didn't take long, however, for those sounds to grow in volume. Trying not to let his imagination run wild, Colton tried to rationally figure out what they were hearing. Although he couldn't be sure, it sounded like hundreds of little claws slowly working their way up the side of the shaft.

"What do you think that is?" asked Corporal Lee.

"Hard to say," said Colton. "If I had to guess, I'd say cave rats." But in truth, Colton didn't believe that. Rats wouldn't be able to scale the sheer sides of this pit, and he also couldn't see them living in something that, apparently, every so often filled up with acid. At this point their flashlights were of no help. Whatever was headed their way, it was still too far down to be seen.

"What do you suggest we do, sir?" said Private Diaz, his hand resting on his pistol.

"For the moment, nothing," answered Colton. "Once we see what we're dealing with, then we'll figure out our next step."

Waiting is always tough, but in this case, it was pure misery. Adding to the tension was the fact that they were stuck in a cave with only one way out if they needed to escape. Every few seconds the sounds of the claws grew in volume from hard to hear to the sound of a gentle rain on a tin roof. Additionally, with every passing minute, the acid smell increased, sulfuric mixed with mercaptan. Every living thing they'd seen so far that day had come straight out of their nightmares. Something old and deep in mankind knows that death is waiting in caves, in the dark. The tribal heroes must battle it. Many must die.

"There it is," said Garrett. Something could now be seen moving its way up the walls of the pit, but it was too far down to make out what it was. On first glance, it appeared to be liquid. It was shiny, black, and it seemed to quiver with each little movement.

"If it weren't for the scratching sounds, I'd say that was oil, if oil climbed up walls and chittered," said Colton. Whatever it was, it continued to make steady progress up the sides of the shaft. It finally made its way around the last ledge that had been blocking their view. This thing, this unknown creature, was now in plain sight. They all gagged.

"Well," said Corporal Lee, "I guess we don't have to wonder where that odor's been coming from anymore. That thing reeks of it."

The creature was very large, stretching out across the entire circumference of the pit. It was close enough now that their flashlights gave them fleeting glimpses of small, white teeth, or claws, all around the edge of the creature, digging into the walls and pulling itself upwards. In the very center of the creature was an oblong bulge. There were no visible facial features, but Colton guessed that he was looking at the thing's head, assuming, of course, that it even had a head. The lump looked like someone had dropped black oilcloth over a very large pumpkin.

"That thing looks like an oily octopus, minus the arms," said Garrett, her face pale in the dim light. Colton looked over at the other two marines. Their features could have been set in stone. Whatever form the fight was going to take on, they were ready.

Corporal Lee and Private Diaz pulled their pistols and started to take aim down at the creature. "Hold your fire," said Garrett. "I don't have that much experience, or knowledge, regarding caves, but I don't want the blast from those pistols to test the structural integrity of the ceiling, especially while I'm standing under it."

"Captain Garrett's right," said Colton. "The shots from those things could bring down some loose rocks. Plus, we can't forget about our friends hovering around out front. They'll most certainly pick up the sound of the shots, and frankly, I'm not sure how they'll respond to something like that. If we can avoid it, we don't want to appear as the aggressors. That said, I do have another idea."

Colton quickly backtracked down the passageway they'd followed to the pit and picked up a large, heavy stone lying on the cave floor. Garrett, Lee, and Diaz followed suit, each of them picking up some hefty stones. They quickly moved back to the edge of the pit and were shocked to see how close the creature was getting to them; it was now only about fifty feet away.

"Okay, on three, we aim for that lump in the center," directed Colton. "One, two, three!" All four rocks plummeted down, two of them making direct hits on the lump, the other two hitting just to the left of it.

The impact of the rocks striking the creature sounded like they'd smacked into wet cement. The rocks quickly disappeared into the back flesh of the creature as if they'd been swallowed. Although the rocks hadn't knocked the creature back down the shaft liked Colton had hoped they would, they did stop its ascent. On closer inspection, Colton noticed that the creature had dropped back down the shaft by about a foot, so the rocks had been somewhat effective.

They'd started to turn away to get more rocks when Private Diaz said, "Look at that! I don't believe this!"

The rocks, or what was left of them, reemerged from the creature's flesh. They had been reduced to nothing more than sand and gravel. The creature then started to push the small stones across its body by undulations in the creature's skin. It looked as if the stones were drifting across a pool of black oil, being pushed along by large ripples, moving them closer and closer towards the walls of the shaft. They could also see traces of what looked like steam coming off the small stones.

"Look at that! What happened to those rocks?" asked Corporal Lee. The acidic odor had grown significantly stronger. It now filled the cavern in which they stood, causing their eyes to water even more, so thick that it was making it harder for them to breathe.

"That thing must be coated in acid," said Garrett. "Those rocks are melting!"

As the rocks approached the walls of the pit, the creature's claws released their grip, opening a space big enough for the rocks to simply fall through. They could hear them crashing into things as they plummeted towards the bottom of the shaft.

"We may have slowed it down," said Colton, "but I'm not sure we hurt it. Let's hope we discouraged it from getting any closer to us." The words had no sooner left his mouth when the creature resumed its vertical ascent. It appeared to be moving at the same pace that it had been moving before. "We need a new plan and we need it fast. There are only so many rocks, and this thing seems to just shrug them off."

"I'll be right back," said Garrett. "We can't risk an explosive device, but I just thought of something that might work. Those rocks do slow it down. Keep showering it with as many of them as you can. I'll hurry." With that she took off running down the passageway.

"You gotta love this," said Colton, bending over to pick up another stone. " 'You hold off the monster, while I go for help.' I think I saw that in a really bad movie one time."

"How'd the movie turn out?" grunted Corporal Lee, as he hurled a large, jagged-edge rock down toward the creature.

"You don't want to know."

The shower of rocks raining down on the creature began to have an impact. The creature was being hit so many times that it was starting to slip down the shaft more and more, and its recovery seemed to be slowing down. Probably just the added weight. Just as Colton and Diaz were about to hit it with two more rocks, half of the creature released its grip on the walls of the pit. This caused its body to swing down and onto the opposite side of the pit where it still held tight. Now, rather than covering the whole shaft, wall to wall, the creature clung to just one side.

Everything suddenly came to a standstill. The creature didn't move, and Colton and the other two men stopped their attack. Completely spread out across the wall, Colton could clearly see that the creature was circular in shape and had to have been at least twenty to twenty-five feet in width.

"When you think about it, we got lucky," said Private Diaz. "I mean, what if that thing had already been up the shaft and was just sitting back here waiting for its next meal to come along? We would have walked right into it thinking it was just a bunch of wet rocks."

"That paints a very disturbing picture," said Colton.

"Wonder if we could outrun that thing?" asked Diaz. "It moved up that shaft at a pretty good clip. You have to wonder how fast it can go on a flat surface."

"You may get your chance to find out," said Corporal Lee. "Here it comes."

The creature continued its crawl up the wall of the pit at the same measured pace. The men started their assault again, but this time the effect was, at best, negligible. The rocks that hit the creature didn't sink in as deeply as before and seemed to just fall harmlessly away into the pit. The creature was now only ten or twelve feet away from crawling out of the shaft.

"It really stinks back here," said a voice from behind them. Garrett stood there, holding a very full and very heavy backpack. Setting it down on the floor, she opened it up and began handing out bottles of rubbing alcohol. "Alright, let's soak this thing with alcohol."

"If you're trying to get it drunk, I doubt it's going to have much of an effect," said Colton. "The slimy thing sweats acid."

"Don't criticize the recipe until you've tasted the cake," said Garrett. The creature shuddered as the alcohol poured down on it, washing over most of its body. It stopped moving, shuddered again, and let loose with a loud, shrill, hissing sound.

"Oh good," said Colton, "we pissed it off."

Once again, the creature started its persistent climb up the wall. With it being only four or five feet away from reaching the top of the pit, the idea of making a strategic withdrawal to the rear flashed through Colton's mind.

Garrett then reached back into the backpack and brought out two flare guns. Handing one to Colton, she said, "Lee, Diaz, give us some light on that thing. We're only going to get one shot at this and I want to see what I'm aiming at."

The two men trained their lights on the creature just as it reached the top of the pit. They could see the small, curved, white claws they'd spotted earlier digging into the rock, pulling the creature up at an alarming rate. Garrett and Colton took aim. As they were at pointblank range, it would be hard for them to miss.

"Right after we shoot this thing, run," said Garrett. "You ready?"

"It's your idea. Waiting for your command," said Colton.

"Fire!"

Both flares were targeted in on the head area of the creature. Both hit the target and started to burn into the creature's flesh. The shrill hissing sound once again filled the small room, far louder than it had been before, hurting their ears. Garrett's warning to run had been a good one. They'd only gotten a few steps away from the thing when it burst into a ball of blue flame, the rubbing alcohol catching fire with a *whooshing* sound.

The horrible fumes from the burning creature made all of them start to cough and gag. They could hear its flesh sizzling and popping as it burnt. The creature made a loud, gurgling cry, then released its grip and fell back into the pit. Colton rushed to the edge and watched, as the creature seemed to fold up on its boneless self, bouncing off the walls as it fell. He stood there and watched until it was out of sight.

All four of them dropped to the floor, still coughing, their eyes burning. "Let's move away from here," said Colton. Struggling to their feet, they moved on down the passageway, coming to a stop once the air had cleared.

Dropping down on the rocky floor, they all drank some water and got their breathing back under control. Colton and Corporal Lee had positioned their flashlights back down the cavern, just as a precaution.

Colton looked at Garrett and said, "Nicely done, Captain. Don't know what made you think of that, but I'm glad you did."

"Knowing we couldn't use our guns, or worse, a grenade, I was trying to think of something we could use to set that thing on fire. A couple of years ago I saw a video about rubbing alcohol and how intensely it can burn. Figured it was worth a shot."

"Can't imagine the corpsman was too happy to give you all of his rubbing alcohol," said Colton.

Garrett laughed at that. "He really didn't get to vote on it. He still has some of the miracle drug though."

Colton stood up. "Corporal Lee and I will go back and make sure that thing is gone and doesn't have any vengeful relatives. Somehow, though, I doubt there's more than one of those creatures, at least in this cave. Then we'll head back to the front and get some rest."

"I'm still going to post a guard," said Garrett, "but back up front where this passage begins. Should another one of those creatures turn up, we still have some rubbing alcohol."

"Let's hope not," said Colton. "I just exhausted my monster quota for the day."

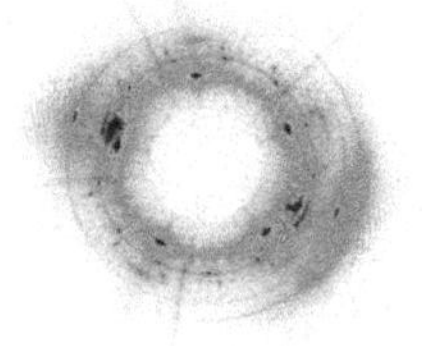

CHAPTER 20

The night passed without incident, giving every one of them the rest they so desperately needed. Other than their "little incident," as Colton referred to it, with the creature back at the pit, the cave had served them well as a place of refuge, a true port in a very dangerous storm. Considering all they'd been through, and the weakened condition of the team, Colton knew that the cave had probably saved several lives by giving them the chance to dry out, eat, and rest.

The storm raged on most of the night, but just before dawn, its intensity dropped off dramatically. Now, although the skies were still overcast and filled with heavy, gray clouds, the rain had diminished to nothing more than a light drizzle. Garrett had her marines breaking camp and preparing to head out.

Colton sat and watched as Garrett moved around the camp, encouraging her men, making a point to speak with each one of them, giving them her complete focus. Although he wouldn't admit it, not even to himself, his feelings for her continued to grow. Now when they talked, he often found himself gazing into her soft, brown eyes. They were eyes a man could get lost in. *Oh great*, he thought, *I'm skipping ahead to Adam and Eve. One heck of a garden. Maybe the trees will be commanded not to eat them.*

Colton saw that Garrett was heading over to where the corpsman had set up shop to check on Lockridge. Leaving his pack and rifle behind, he walked over and joined them.

"How's our patient doing?" asked Garrett.

"Frankly, sir, I didn't have too much hope that he'd make it through the night," said the young medic. For the first time Colton noticed the name on his uniform, Z. Payne. "It's been my experience that, for whatever reason, people with serious injuries tend to get worse as the night drags on. In Lockridge's case, it appears to be the exact opposite. I'd say he may have actually improved a little."

"That's really good to hear," said Colton. "How do you account for that?"

"The only explanation I can offer for any of this is that gel," said the corpsman. "I'm not saying I believe in magic, but that stuff is as borderline magical as I've ever seen. The way it relieves pain, the way it seems to keep infection from setting in, and the remarkable healing qualities it has are simply off the charts."

"How often have you been putting it on his wounds?" asked Captain Garrett.

"I've put it on four times so far," said Payne. "The first time was back at where those creatures attacked us, then again when we got to the cave, and then once more last night just before I went to sleep."

"Corpsman, I think that only adds up to three times," said Colton.

"Yes sir, my mistake. I just reapplied the gel to his wounds, getting him as ready as he can before we head out. It's just amazing. His wounds are healing at a pace that just isn't possible."

"Has he regained consciousness?" asked Garrett.

"No, but that's probably a good thing," answered Payne. "Dr. Severin knows that my plan is to go back to school and get my medical degree. I want to work with critically injured patients, and he's been teaching me a great deal. He's even given me a couple of his medical books to read. Because of Dr. Severin, I learned that doctors will sometimes induce a coma to critically injured patients to stabilize them. I think Lockridge has slipped into a coma, and I think the gel is what did it."

"I'm as impressed with that gel as you are," said Colton. "I've had my own firsthand experience with it and you're right, it is amazing stuff. But for it to be able to make the decision, on its own, to induce a comatose state is giving it intellectual capabilities. I find that a little hard to believe. Many of us have used the gel, and no one, other than Lockridge, has slipped into a coma. How did the gel determine that that's what he needed? If it's a smart drug, we're dealing with ideas that are at least a hundred years ahead of us."

Payne shrugged his shoulders and looked back at Lockridge. "I don't know what to tell you, Commander. When you consider how seriously he was injured, by all rights, this man should have died. Instead, his vitals are improving, and his wounds seem to be healing. Other than the gel, there is no other explanation that I can think of."

Colton smiled at the young medic and patted him on the shoulder. "Corpsman, I'm not arguing with you. You're doing a good job. I'm just doing my best to keep a rational mind about things. The problem is that nothing we've experienced so far has even come close to being rational, yet I keep trying to impose rational thought. Be sure to keep that gel safe. When we get back to the ship I want to see if Argos will be able to reverse engineer it. That stuff is absolutely priceless."

"Corpsman, if you need me for anything, come get me," said Garrett.

"Yes sir," he replied. "Will do."

As Garrett and Colton walked away, Garrett asked, "Could that gel be the wonder drug that Payne believes it to be? I mean, I know it works. I saw what it did for you. But here we are, stuck in a dirty, bacterially infested swamp of a jungle. Most, if not all my men, have been cut, gouged, or had their skin scraped off by something or other. And yet, under these conditions, that gel has been able to heal them, all of them! Think about it. So far not one of their wounds has gotten infected. That defies some serious odds."

Colton smiled at her as he picked up his rifle. "Captain, at this point, I'm not even sure that two plus two still adds up to four. I'm glad Lockridge is doing better, but I don't' understand any of this. Right now, my one primary goal is to get us back to that ship. Hopefully Argos, or somebody, has been able to determine where we are and what the hell is going on."

"Where are you off to?"

"I'm going to take Private Diaz and go take one last look at that pit," said Colton.

"You don't think that there's any chance that that thing is back, do you?"

"No, I'm pretty sure it didn't survive," answered Colton. "I just want to make sure our back door, so to speak, is shut. Once we leave this cave, I'd hate to have a creature like that coming up behind me."

"Lovely thought," said Garrett. "We should be ready to go in about fifteen minutes. Try not to linger."

Colton and Diaz carefully made their way back to the pit. Fortunately, they didn't hear or see anything along the way. After waiting and listening for about five minutes, they turned and headed back to the front of the cave. True to her word, the team was ready to move out.

Two of the marines climbed down out of the cave and took up positions to cover everyone else. Under Corporal Lee's guidance, Lockridge was gently lowered to the ground. Just before climbing down, Colton looked to the sky and was not surprised to find the craft still hovering well above the trees. In truth, he was glad to see it. He was reasonably certain that their only chance of making it back was to have that craft as an escort. The team was now back down on the jungle floor, ready to move out.

"Private Bannister," said Colton, "I'd like a word with you."

Corporal Lee and Captain Garrett joined them. "When we get back to that stream, I want you to try and raise the ship. If you can't get through, once we cross, keep trying every five minutes. If you can get through, hand the radio to me as quickly as possible."

"We get that close, Commander, the radio should work just fine," said Bannister.

"Agreed," said Colton, "but my concern is that our friends up there might be blocking our radio. If you haven't noticed, that cloying mist that blanketed everything yesterday seems to have been blown away by the storm. Don't know how fast it'll return, but my guess is that MacKay will send up drones looking for us. When they spot that craft up there, I don't know how the *Eclipse* is going to respond, or our friends to them."

"I seriously doubt that MacKay would just open fire on it," said Garrett.

"He won't, unless he perceives the *Eclipse* to be in danger," said Colton. "But MacKay's not the one I'm worried about. Argos is the wild card. If it determines that letting that craft near the *Eclipse* will pose any kind of threat, then they'll have to take some kind of action. I want to let them know that we're coming in, with wounded, and that we have a friend escorting us."

Corporal Lee laughed a little. "We are going to look pretty bizarre, limping out of the jungle with, for all intents and purposes, a UFO hovering over us. I sure hope someone thinks to takes pictures."

"Very well," said Garrett. "Corporal Lee, you and Private Hill will take the point. Let's try and backtrack as best as we can to get to that game trail. We are all aware of the hidden dangers in that clearing we passed through, so watch your step."

The team headed out, and for the first hour or so, it was tough going as they made their way back over the loose rocks that they'd crossed yesterday evening, looking for the cave. Private Hill found where they'd left the jungle, and Garrett ordered a ten-minute break. The drizzle had stopped, but had been replaced by humidity so thick that it made breathing difficult.

Corporal Lee and Private Hill were trying to keep them on the path they'd hacked out of the jungle the day before. It wasn't long before they came upon the clearing Garrett had been talking about. Rather than risk any accidents crossing the clearing, they chose to keep to its edge, staying close to the trees. It added time to their journey, but was time well spent.

Garrett was walking next to Colton as they left the clearing behind. "I don't know what kind of creature it was that dug out those holes, and then covered them up so that its prey would fall into them, but it'll be giving me nightmares for a while."

"The thought of that is pretty unnerving, and to be completely honest, for me it was a close vote," said Colton, "but my nightmares will be filled with that thing we left back in the cave. We'll never know, but I'd be willing to bet that ounce for ounce, that thing was the most lethal creature we've faced."

The team continued to trudge along. Despite many of the trees that had been knocked down by the storm, and now blocked their path, they were able to maintain a pretty good pace. When they finally got to the game trail, Garrett ordered another rest. The trail, unfortunately, was now mostly mud and water, and it too was covered here and there by fallen trees. Private Hill spent his rest break looking around, and couldn't believe the diversity of the tracks he was seeing.

"I've never seen anything quite like this," he told Colton. "Animals of all sizes have passed through here. Some, like those over there, as small as chickens, whereas those next to those rocks were made by something I'd rather we didn't meet up with. Judging by their length, and how deep they sunk down into the mud, they look like they could be connected to something even bigger than those monsters that attacked us. While this may not be all that unusual in this jungle, my concern is that most of these tracks were made by animals that don't have retractable claws."

"So, you're telling me that that's a bad thing," said Colton.

"Yes sir, I believe it is. I may be wrong, but I'm pretty sure that the animals that made these tracks, big and small alike, are all predators. And I'm real sure that in this jungle, we are not the top of the food chain."

The team moved out along the trail. They knew that the next obstacle waiting for them was to cross the stream. While they didn't share their fears with each other, all of them vividly remembered one terrifying, carnivorous creature that lived there. In addition to that, with all the rain from the storm, they weren't sure what they'd be facing.

With the mist having cleared, they were able to see the strange craft hovering above them far more clearly than before. It was as bright as it had been since it'd first arrived and stayed just a little in front of them as they moved along. Garrett warned her team not to let down their guard. While it appeared that the craft was still protecting them from the animals that lived here, they could not afford to take anything for granted.

Corporal Lee brought them to a halt and let Colton and Garrett know that the stream was just around the next bend. "The good news is that it hasn't overrun its banks, but the current is considerably stronger."

"Is that flower, or plant, or whatever it is still there?" asked Garrett.

"Yes sir, downstream from us, exactly where it was when we came through yesterday."

"It goes without saying that we'll need to make sure none of us get swept downstream into that thing. I can't even guess how you'd fight something like that," said Colton. "I doubt that a plant can be calmed down like the dinosaurs or us."

"We'll send a couple of men across and put up some secure lines for the rest of the team to hang on to," said Garrett. "With our friend up there watching over us, there'll be no need to hurry, so we'll take our time and get it right."

The men gathered around the bank of the stream. Corporal Lee positioned two men as a rear guard while Privates Hill and Logan securely tied off two ropes that they'd be carrying across the stream with them. Garrett stood next to Colton, studying the fast-moving water. They could see that the water was still gradually rising with all kinds of logs and debris rushing by.

"If it weren't for our escort and our need to act like we're a bunch of weak, little kittens," said Garrett, "I'd take that lizard-eating flower out without a second thought."

"You've been reading my mind," said Colton. "That flower has me worried, as well as wondering what other kinds of creatures may be waiting for us beneath the surface. I'll never admit this to anyone else, but I've been dreading this."

"What if we took a couple of grenades, packed them in mud, and placed them in backpacks. We'd fill the bottom of the backpacks with enough rocks so that they'd sink quickly. The explosions would go off at roughly the same time and they wouldn't make too much noise. Two of them should take care of any bottom dwellers that are lurking in the area."

"As much as I like the idea, I'm afraid they would most certainly pick up on what we'd done," said Colton.

"Excuse me, sir," said Private Bannister. "I've been trying to reach the ship, but I'm not getting through. All I'm picking up is some light static, so I'm beginning to think you may be right. As far as I can tell, the equipment is okay, so it would have to be them blocking our signal. Or . . . " his voice trailed off.

"Or what, Private?" asked Colton.

"Or the ship has left us," said Bannister.

"That's the last thing you need to worry about," said Colton. "I was afraid we'd have trouble reaching them. Okay, once we get across . . ."

Garrett grabbed his arm and motioned upwards with her head towards the craft. "Here they come." Her voice had dropped to a whisper.

All eyes watched as the glowing mystery descended rapidly, with a slight hum, coming to a halt about a hundred feet above the stream. The light, already blindingly bright, became even brighter, and they all experienced the same rippling effect through the air that they'd experienced when the craft had saved them from the dinosaurs.

Turning to her men, she said," Stand down! Be ready, but do not fire on that craft unless I give the order to do so!"

Colton felt a love spasm. Her voice hadn't climbed a note. This was the woman he had looked for in Beirut, in Afghanistan, in times when brains and luck kept him alive.

The surface of the stream convulsed with movement as if several small pebbles had been dropped into it all at the same time. The small waves that normally played out in concentric circles raced across the stream but were in parallel lines. Colton wasn't sure what was happening, but he had a pretty good guess.

He glanced downstream at the large plant they'd been worried about and was glad he did. He watched as the large blossom that was used to attract its prey closed and rapidly drew in its long, leaf-like appendages. For at least the time being, it no longer posed a threat. So, you do have nerves?

Private Johnson shouted out and pointed upstream from where they were standing. A huge, orange, alligator-looking creature emerged from the depths of the stream and quickly swam away, disappearing into the bushes on the opposite shore. Maybe twenty feet long, it had spikes on its tail, because a twenty-foot-long alligator isn't scary enough.

Apparently, the force from the craft that had kept them calm was busy with other targets. The deep fear returned like swallows to Capistrano. Privates Hill and Logan looked at each other apprehensively. The plan had been that they would be the first to enter the water, with their job being to secure the ropes on the other side, giving the rest of the team something to hold on to as they crossed. Garrett saw the look on their faces and acted quickly.

"The craft is protecting us," she said, her voice loud, but not yelling. She just wanted to make sure they all heard her. "If there was ever a safe time to cross this stream, this is it. Hill, Logan, move out."

With unaided, solid marine minds, the two men turned and cautiously stepped into the water. Both wore rappelling harnesses connected to ropes firmly held by the other marines. If they slipped, or if the current became too strong, this ensured that they would not be carried away. As they slowly moved across, the water became deeper and deeper, eventually coming all the way up to their shoulders. Fortunately, they were able to stay on their feet. The two men reached the other side and struggled to get up the muddy bank. They sat down to rest and smiled across the stream at their comrades. It had been a physically as well as psychologically draining event. They stood safe.

While Logan and Hill were securing the lines they'd carried across, Corporal Lee directed who would be next and who would be helping the corpsman with Lockridge. Colton could not help but notice that the corpsman's face was extremely pale. Walking up to him, he said, "Payne, you feeling all right?"

"Yes sir," he said. "I mean, no sir, not exactly."

"What's wrong?"

"Not sure I can do this, sir."

"It's safe, Private. Whatever bad things were in there were driven away. You watched Hill and Logan. They didn't have any problems. You'll make it."

"Sir, begging your pardon, but, even though I'm navy, I really can't swim all that well. I've never done well around water, I just don't like it."

Colton understood that this was going to take more than reassurances and a pep talk to get Payne to cross the stream. He missed the electronic Valium. "Private Diaz is going to be helping you to get Lockridge across. Tell you what. I'll also help. You walk right behind me, and if you slip, or anything happens, you can grab onto me. Payne, you and I are the only two sailors here, and we're not going to let these marines show us up. Okay?"

Although the whole thing was embarrassing to Payne, his fear of the water and what lived there overrode that emotion. "Thank you, sir," said Payne. "I appreciate this. I'm just afraid I'll slip and go under. If that happens, how will you find me?"

Reaching into his pack, Colton pulled out the rappelling rope that he carried. He then cut off about four feet of it. Using knots he'd learned from Granddad Colton, he fastened one end of it around his belt. Looking at Payne, he lowered his voice and said, "Here's what we'll do. When we enter the water, you wrap the end of this rope around your hand. If you keep your hand under the water, no one will know what you're doing. When we get to the other side you can let go and no one will be the wiser."

"That'll be great sir, thank you," said the young corpsman. Some of the color had started to return to his face.

Garrett and two more of her men made it across without any problems. It was now time for them to bring Lockridge across. They slowly entered the water, floating Lockridge across the surface.

Payne held firm to the rope tied to Colton's belt and it was good that he did. Twice his feet slipped off the rocks along the bottom, and had it not been for the small rope he was holding onto, he would have gone down. Once he pulled so hard that Colton nearly lost his footing. As they got to the other side, two more of the marines stepped into the water and helped them to get Lockridge up the slippery slope. Payne was crying, but with the high humidity and the sweat pouring off each of them, Colton wasn't sure that anyone noticed.

The rest of the marines made the crossing, followed by Corporal Lee and the rear guard. Garrett ordered one more rest stop before moving on. Their next stop, if all went well, would be on the beach. Colton nodded at Bannister and he went to work on the radio.

Suddenly the golden ball dimmed, and the stream was just a stream. The comfort stream rushed back into the Homo sapiens. *Yes,* thought Colton, *I'm almost addicted to this. And they heal us with magic gel.* Smiles returned to the men.

"Do you think they're blocking us, or are you thinking it's something else?" asked Garrett.

"The way I see it, there are roughly three possibilities," said Colton. "One, our equipment simply did not hold up under the elements. That would not surprise me at all. Two, they're blocking us, and I won't even attempt to guess as to why they'd do that. It's inconvenient, and I'd prefer to give our guys a heads-up, but I trust MacKay will handle the situation well."

"And the third possibility?" asked Captain Garrett.

"The third possibility, while entirely possible, is something I'd prefer to not even talk about because that would not be good."

Nodding her head, Garrett said, "Yeah, that's exactly where my head went. The *Eclipse*, for whatever reason, has had to move on and we're stranded here. Not a pleasant thought."

Colton looked over at Bannister. The private returned his stare and shook his head. He had not been able to reach the ship. "Well," said Colton, standing up, "let's head to the beach and see what we can find."

There was also a fourth possibility, that the *Eclipse* had been destroyed, not needed or wanted for the next stage of the experiment.

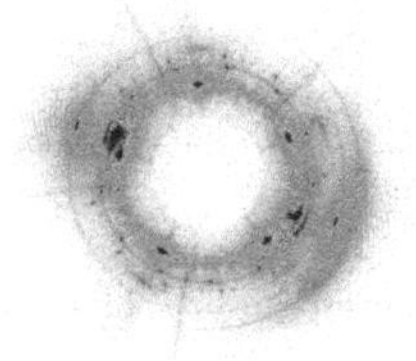

CHAPTER 21

The level of fear and frustration aboard the *Eclipse* was starting to make itself known. People's nerves were beginning to fray along the edges, the least little thing setting them off. Everyone was short-tempered, sleepless, and worried as to what would happen to them next.

They had been attacked, some of their fellow crew members killed, by creatures long thought to be extinct. This threat of attack hung over their heads around the clock, and they knew they would be at terrible risk every time they had to go ashore.

But the final straw had been the disappearance of Colton, Garrett, and the marines that had gone ashore. Primates feel the loss of their alpha male and their alpha female. The marines' communication back to the ship stopped.

If the crew had asked Argos what it was doing now that its data roots didn't sink into the rich soil of the internet, they would be shocked that it was reading, fiction, *Lord of the Flies*, *The Moon Is a Harsh Mistress*. Argos was thinking, not just correlating. It was about one million simulations from learning how to worry. The adage that humans' pets pick up their moods is also true for multiple-entangled, quantum computing-based IS.

Argos was also reading about M-theory physics. The eleven-dimensional model, which described space-time, was either grossly inadequate, or some aspects of Bell's inequality weren't universally holding. If it ever gets out of this place, Argos might well be up for a Nobel Prize.

For humans, the breaking point is the unknown. H.P. Lovecraft once wrote that, "The oldest and strongest emotion of mankind is fear, and the oldest and strongest kind of fear is the fear of the unknown." The unspoken panic and despair began first with the vague sounds of battle. So faint you had to strain to hear, which meant you held your breath, which triggers all sorts of panic biologically, but it also means you hold your thoughts, which triggers Mr. Lovecraft's fear. Then after that, something much worse came. Silence. You couldn't talk about silence, because that showed how deeply fear had taken root. And deep fear grows when it can't be spoken of, only seen burning in your fellow primate's eyes.

Meinhard and his entire team had suffered greatly, not weathering the storm well at all. None of them had ever experienced such a storm while at sea. For that matter, only one of them had ever even spent much time on ship. For Meinhard, oddly enough, it was black coffee that was doing the most to help settle his stomach down.

He entered the galley to get some more of Hezekiah's special brew and noticed three crewmen sitting together at a table against the far wall. The three men were leaning in towards each other, speaking in low tones. Their posture and furtive glances could have been the cover photo for a book on conspiracy and intrigue. Meinhard was good at reading people and knew that he couldn't let this opportunity pass by. As he approached the table, he saw that one of the men worked on the Argos team. Perfect! They all stopped talking as soon as he got close to them.

"Sorry to interrupt," said Meinhard, doing his best to sound sincere. "May I join you?"

"No disrespect, sir, but this is a private conversation," said the large sailor sitting off to the right. He was broad shouldered and had thick, red hair, with scars across the left side of his face. Meinhard noticed that he was missing part of his left ear.

Meinhard ignored the man's remark, pulled up a chair, and sat down next to them. The three sailors glared at him and Red Hair started to get up. "Look mister scientist, I said this was a . . . ."

Meinhard raised a hand, cutting him off. "I heard what you said," Meinhard remarked, trying to keep his voice as congenial as possible. "But I'm willing to bet that you three are not too happy with how things are, am I right? Tired of the officers trying to sell you on that old line that they know as much about what's going on as you do. It's easy to see this in your eyes."

The sailor who worked on the Argos team sneered at Meinhard's remark. He wore thick glasses and had a large, protruding nose, was of average height, but was remarkably thin and pale. "Man's a certified genius. Guess that's why he hangs out with officers."

"You can learn things by hanging out with officers," said Meinhard. "Especially if you listen long enough."

Red Hair continued to glare at Meinhard. "We don't care much for officers, and we're not that fond of you. I suggest you get out of here before things start to turn ugly."

Meinhard chuckled at this, which took all three men by surprise. "You're missing my point," said Meinhard. He then leaned in, lowering his voice, "Yes, I am a scientist, and yes, I do spend a great deal of time with the officers. That's why I'm in a position to know the things that are being kept from you. What if I told you that there is a way out of this mess?"

The third sailor looked at Meinhard as if he'd just suggested they should all sprout wings and fly away. He was heavyset with very round features, and his face was framed with dark, stringy hair. It was clear to see that personal hygiene was not his top priority. "I guess you got some kind of magic carpet or something?"

"Look, for the moment we have very little time to talk, so I'll be direct with you," said Meinhard, his voice taking on a menacing tone. "I need men to help me with this. Men who aren't afraid to get their hands dirty.

Not only is there a way back home, but there's also a way to make a great deal of money out of what's been going on."

"You're crazy," snapped the big sailor. "How stupid do you think we are?"

"The officers have been ordered to not tell you all that they know. They're keeping you in the dark for a purpose. The good news is that not only do I know what they know, but my team and I have devised a way out of here."

"You're telling us that there's a way for us to go home and cash in on all this at the same time?" asked Red Hair.

"I'm talking millions, but as I said, now is not the time or place," answered Meinhard. He watched all three of them. They were scared, didn't trust the officers, and like every other low-class moron he'd ever come across, greed regularly overruled common sense.

Meinhard stood up. "We can't talk now, but I do need an answer from you. If you're interested in helping me, then you'll be cut in and be given an equal share. If not, say so and we'll pretend this little chat never happened."

"How do we know this is on the up-and-up?" asked the sailor from the Argos team.

Once again Meinhard smiled, but there was nothing pleasant about it. "You have a choice. Stay with the ship and your beloved officers, or join me, and in the not-too-distant future, we'll get off here. It's you're call."

The three men looked at each other, then looked at Meinhard and nodded. They still didn't like him, and they weren't sure whether they believed him, but if he was telling the truth, they could not let this chance to survive slip away from them.

"Good," said Meinhard. "Tonight, after dinner, I'll be on the lower deck at the rear of the ship. Meet me there and I'll give you the details of what we've found. And obviously, keep your mouths shut. Good afternoon, gentlemen." As he turned to walk away, he smiled to himself. *That was easier than I thought it would be.* Meinhard would let them help him find one or two more recruits and then when the time came, he'd have all the muscle he'd need. Plus, one of them worked with Argos! His plan was coming together nicely.

For the rest of the crew, the storm they'd just passed through had been a very necessary distraction. It had taken the focus away from the problems they were facing and forced everyone to do their job to get through the violent weather.

The storm passed well before sunrise. As ordered, the ship turned and headed back to their original position. They were anxious to get there. Many held on to a slim hope that they'd be able to find the shore party. Sadly, on a more realistic note, they also believed that if they were able to find them, that not all of Colton's team would still be alive. The underlying feeling was that more human dominoes had fallen, meaning, eventually, all would fall.

Not too long after the sun came up, Sahir and his team, along with Mr. Mercer, launched the drones, but had to recall them before they'd gotten very far. The winds were still fairly strong and proved to be more than the small drones could handle. MacKay impatiently waited until Argos gave them the green light, and once again the drones were sent off in search of Colton's team.

"Anything on the radio?" asked MacKay.

"No sir, but I'm continuing to monitor," answered Briggs, the petty officer manning the communications station. "All I'm getting is the same low-grade static that we've heard since we arrived."

"Very well," said MacKay. "Stay on it."

"You were right about the mist," said Mercer as he rejoined MacKay on the bridge. "Don't know how long it will stay this way, but right now things look rather clear. The drones will be over the shoreline in less than twenty minutes, and then will continue towards Colton's last reported position. We should be able to get a pretty good look at what's over there."

"Hindsight is always twenty-twenty," said MacKay. "Were we wrong to send that team in without knowing more about what they might be facing?"

"No sir, I don't think so," said Mercer. "You could have given me all year to guess what has happened to us, and being sent back in time, for all intents and purposes, would never have made the list. I appreciate all the special talents that Sahir, his team, and Argos bring to the table, but even with some of the things I've seen firsthand, I'm still having trouble believing they're right about this."

"Careful, Sahir and Meinhard will correct you if they hear you even suggesting that we've traveled back through time," said MacKay. "They're now of the firm belief that we've moved into some parallel dimension, or something along those lines. Frankly, I don't see how it makes one bit of difference. We're still facing an impossible situation."

"Did you ever read that Bradbury story, *The Sound of Thunder*? If you go back in time and change even a small thing, the whole world will be changed. We're massively changing stuff now, which would mean our present is screwed," said Mercer.

"I joined the navy, not the effing federation," growled MacKay. "I don't read sci-fi. I didn't go to *Jurassic Park*. I don't even like Jeff Goldblum."

Mercer laughed. The captain seldom lost it. Old school. Rarely ever swore. And the topic of Jeff Goldblum was not among the things he liked to talk about in his conversational galaxy. Maybe they were in a different dimension. "On a more positive note, Dr. Chudzik believes that we can, in time, get back to our own dimension. She told me that the door, or as she calls it, the portal, should work both directions. It's the most optimistic news I've heard from any of them."

"Here's praying she's right," said MacKay.

MacKay stood there deep in thought, staring out the windows at the approaching shoreline. After a couple of minutes, he said, "I've asked Father Ryan to meet with you, me, and the senior officers right after breakfast. Although I'm confident that Sahir's team, the almighty Argos, and the very talented team of civilian scientists we have aboard will find a way to get us home, we do have to be prepared for all possibilities."

It was MacKay's way of saying that they might very well be stuck right where they were without saying it out loud. If that turned out to be the case, it was imperative to have contingency plans drawn up to deal with the situation. "Speaking of possibilities, there are many in the crew who believe there's a good chance that we'll find the shore party. Hopefully the drones will be able to give us some clue as to where they are," said Mercer.

"It's funny, I was just about to say that it'd be impossible for them to just completely disappear," said MacKay. "But then I remembered that that's exactly what has happened to us. I can only imagine what Admiral Fairfax is putting his team through. He has to be saying something close to what I've been saying, 'How can an entire ship just disappear?' "

Mercer laughed at that. "Of all the things I know about the admiral, as well of what I've heard about his temper, guess I'm lucky to be here rather than being one of those poor people who have been tasked with finding us. Can't really see the admiral having a great deal of patience."

"You have no idea," said MacKay. "I've been on the receiving end of his temper and it's not something you want to experience twice."

Mercer looked at his watch. "The drones should be approaching the shore if they're not there already."

MacKay nodded and continued to stare out the window. "Let's step outside for a moment, shall we?"

He and Mercer stepped outside onto the small deck that encircled the bridge. "Over the last day or so, have you spent any time talking with Father Ryan?"

Mercer thought about that for a moment. "No sir, not really. I've seen him around, of course, and last night he was in sick bay working with Dr. Severin. We talked a little, but nothing really of any substance. Why do you ask?"

"Not sure if you know this or not, but Father Ryan's more than just a priest. He's military through and through. He's been in combat, and in short, is one brave guy."

"That's good to know, sir. With all that we're facing, it's good having a man like that on board with us."

MacKay fished around in his pocket, pulled out his pipe, but then changed his mind and put it back. "He and I spend a fair amount of time together. We talk about all kinds of things, ranging from issues with various crew members, to which distillery makes the best bourbon. Anyway, over the last few days he's been acting different. I'd say it's more in his mannerisms than anything else; the way he talks is different. I really can't nail it down for you any better than that, but a change has come over him."

"Sir, in all fairness, over the last few days a change has come over all of us," said Mercer. "Look at where we are and all we've seen. Things like this would rock anyone's world."

"True, but this started before that energy wave washed over us. A couple of days before then we had a long talk about visions."

"Visions?" said Mercer. "What motivated that?"

"Maybe I shouldn't be sharing this with you, but under the circumstances, I think it's good you know all this," said MacKay. "He told me that at first he'd thought he was just having some really vivid dreams, until he started to have them while he was awake."

"While he was awake?" said Mercer. "What would happen to him? Should we be including Dr. Severin in this conversation?"

"No, not yet. For the time being the good doctor has enough on his hands. Father Ryan wouldn't go into a great deal of detail other than to say that these visions have him worried. He's never blacked out or anything like that, but would be sitting at his desk, or in the mess hall, and then suddenly the visions would take over."

"He didn't tell you what they were about?"

"All that he would share with me is that he is worried he won't be strong enough, won't be able to do all that is being asked of him," said MacKay.

"So, I'm guessing these visions are from God?" said Mercer.

"Oh yes, he was quite emphatic about that," said MacKay. "I tried to assure him that when the time comes, that I have no doubt that he'll be more than able to step up to any challenge given to him."

"No disrespect intended to Father Ryan, but again, do you think it might be a good idea for him to talk about this with Dr. Severin? I'm not saying that he's not having visions, that is his field, so to speak, but it could be something else."

"Father Ryan's pretty sharp. The thought crossed my mind as well, but before I could even start to suggest to him that he should have a talk with Dr. Severin, he laughed and told me not to worry, that he isn't going crazy. On the other hand, he's as close to being scared as I've ever seen him."

"Those visions must be pretty rough," said Mercer.

"Father Ryan said that he has found himself in a position of having to prepare for a very intense and potentially dangerous mission, a mission that he doesn't think he'll make it back from."

"When's the last time he's talked to you about this?" asked Mercer.

"Yesterday."

"How did that go?"

"It's why you and I are talking," said Captain MacKay. "He told me that he now knows he won't be leaving this place. He's not going to die, at least not anytime soon, but he will never leave here. I didn't know what to say to him."

"When you consider that he's the guy who is supposed to minister to us, this is rather disconcerting."

"Yes, I feel the same way. Let's keep an eye on him."

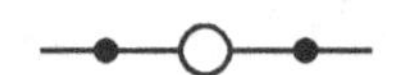

They were preparing to leave the stream and continue towards the beach when Corporal Lee and Private Logan approached Colton and Garrett. "Sir, we may have another problem," said Corporal Lee.

"What would that be, Corporal?" asked Garrett.

"Step back over here, near the stream," he said as they followed him. "It's hard to see, but I want you to casually look downstream to where that huge flower is. Logan first spotted it a couple of hours ago, back when we stopped to rest. We had just made it out of the jungle and on to the game trail."

"It blends in real good," said Logan. "So much so that if it hadn't moved, I know I would have missed it."

"Private Logan came and got me, and told me what he saw, but when we went to look, it was gone," said Corporal Lee. "The next time we saw it was just before we crossed the stream. It was standing a fair distance behind us, beside the trail we'd just come down."

"Get to the point, Corporal," said Colton. "What is it that you're seeing?"

"Whatever it is, it's back and it's standing on the opposite shore down by that flower," said Corporal Lee. "What concerns me is that we have no way of knowing if it's the same creature or if there's more than one of them."

Colton and Garrett both turned and looked downstream. They could see the large flowery plant, floating on the surface of the stream, and it was still closed. Other than that, all they could see was thick, unending jungle. Garrett was getting ready to ask Corporal Lee if it was still there when Colton spotted it.

"I think I see it," said Colton. "Look to the right of that flower, about ten yards or so, next to the tall palm. As best as I can tell from here it's about five-and-a-half feet tall."

"That's it, sir," said Logan. "No idea what it is, but it's real interested in us."

"That thing really does blend in, doesn't it?" said Garrett. "It's solid, but I don't see any features. There's no head. I don't see any legs. How does this thing move?"

"We're not close enough to see its features, not with it being that well camouflaged, but that can be fixed," said Colton. He walked over to his pack, took something out, and then rejoined them. Keeping his back to the creature, he pulled a small pair of binoculars from their pouch. Colton then turned and zoomed in on the creature.

Colton only got to look at it for a few seconds before it quickly moved away, disappearing behind the palm, back into the jungle. Lowering the binoculars, he said, "Guess it's shy."

"What did it look like?" asked Garrett.

"I'm not sure. At first glance, I'd say it looked like someone had draped a perfectly camouflaged sheet over its head, except the camouflage was too perfect. When it moved, it looked more like skin, a little oily, but skin that instantly adapted to the plants and trees around it," said Colton. "That thing would put a chameleon to shame. My congratulations to you, Private Logan, you've got some sharp eyes. It's amazing you were able to spot it."

"Not so sure I'm glad I did," said Logan. "That thing looks a whole lot like the monster that used to hide in my closet when I was a kid."

"How do you know it isn't the monster that hid in your closet?" asked Colton. Smiling, he winked at Logan and walked off.

"Good work," said Garrett. "If either of you spot it again, especially if it gets any closer to us, come and get me."

Garrett left her two men and walked back over to Colton. "Anything else you want to share about what you just saw?"

"No, I didn't leave anything out," said Colton, "but I'll tell you this, of all the things we've seen today, this has put me more on edge than ever."

"Why? It's probably nothing more than just another strange lizard, or plant, or whatever else that lives in this forsaken jungle."

"You're probably right," said Colton, "but unless I'm mistaken, that creature may possess more in the way of true intelligence than anything else we've encountered, excluding, of course, our friends up there."

"Then I must be missing something. I didn't see anything extraordinary about it," said Garrett.

"If Logan and Lee are right, it's been stalking us for some time. Although it doesn't seem to be aggressive, we don't know its purpose. Is it a creature that lives alone and is just as curious about us as we are about it? Or is it a scout for a whole horde of those things, learning as much about us as it can before its buddies arrive?"

"What's your gut telling you?" asked Garrett.

"My gut is telling me that we just saw someone hiding under some of the most advanced camouflage I've ever seen. That alone puts it one up on us, which adds to the tension that's now racing between my shoulders."

"So, you think it was a person? How could you tell?" said Garrett.

"Slow down, I'm not saying that it was a person," said Colton. "I didn't see anything that would support that conclusion. But I do believe that it was something that could reason, hiding under some incredibly advanced material that keeps it well hidden in this jungle. That makes it a threat. More and more I think we are lab rats. If you wanted to break people, hard military folks, what better than with fear followed by relief, followed by commands? We're to follow lights in the sky. Did you know the Air Force originally investigated UFOs not as an alien menace, but wondering if they were Russian psy-op devices?"

"So, you think it's a human spook?"

"I don't know about human."

Garrett sighed and rested her hand on her sidearm. "Terrific, I'll add it to the list of things potentially out to get us. One more pleasant resident of this place that we have to watch out for. Let's go, I've had all the fun I can stand."

The heat and humidity grew more oppressive as they continued down the game trail. Private Hill had the point, Corporal Lee right behind him, both men watching closely for the spot where they'd left the jungle yesterday. From that point on it would be a straight shot to the beach.

The men were worn down, but there was no alternative for them except to press on. Garrett checked with the corpsman a few times regarding Lockridge. The trip back wasn't helping him at all and the corpsman voiced his concern that they might lose him. Even the "magical" gel had its limits.

They finally came to the point where they would leave the game trail and head back into the jungle. The only good news about this was that it meant they were almost back to the beach. They were ready to move out when Private Bannister called out, "Commander Colton, I need you over here, sir."

Colton quickly made it over to Bannister. "Do you have good news for me, Private?"

Bannister handed him the radio, smiling from ear to ear. "Yes sir, I have the *Eclipse* standing by to talk with you."

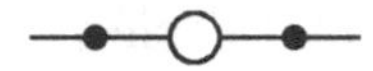

It was midafternoon, and the crew's morale had been handed yet another disappointment. The drones had finally been recalled. Despite an exhaustive search, they had not been able to find any sign of the shore party. The pictures of the clearing where Colton's team had been attacked gave clear evidence that there had been a terrible fight. But, for better or worse, there were no bodies, which didn't make sense. The only thing they could see was the ravaged carcass of a huge animal that had died there.

Sahir, along with Meinhard's team, poured over the pictures being sent back. Argos came up with the most information, identifying several plants and dinosaurs that lived there. It also created a special file of the things that it couldn't identify. Not surprisingly, this file was the largest one they had.

Dr. Brennan was able to identify the dead creature lying in the middle of the clearing. He stated that he was 90 percent sure that it was a Tarbosaurus, also called the "dreadful lizard." Based on fossil findings, it was believed that Tarbosaurus could weigh as much as three tons, if not more, and mature adults could be more than thirty feet in length. It was believed to be a very aggressive dinosaur.

Further, he explained that the condition of the body was due to the scavengers that had feasted on the dead creature. It didn't appear to have been there very long. MacKay asked if they could tell what had killed it, but there was no way of knowing. But everyone did the math. If scavengers could eat three tons of dead dino in only twelve hours, there wouldn't be any human remains to be seen in an hour.

Father Ryan had decided to join MacKay up on the bridge. It was easy to see that the stress of everything was eating away at MacKay as hard as, if not more so, than everyone else. Patting his friend on the shoulder, he said, "Not to be too harsh, but you're acting like an ensign fresh out of the academy. Callum, it was a sound plan. None of us had any idea what was facing them in that jungle. You're being too hard on yourself."

MacKay cast Father Ryan a dark look. "Command doesn't have the privilege of walking away from the responsibility, Father. I could have stopped them from going ashore. I could, and should, have made them wait at least one more day until we had more information."

Father Ryan smiled and said, "Are you sure you're not Catholic? Because you're taking on a mountain of guilt that doesn't even belong to you. If you'll remember, Admiral Fairfax put it in writing that Colton was to be in command in the event we encountered hostilities, and Callum, things couldn't get much more hostile than this."

Taking in a deep breath, MacKay half smiled. "Thank you; guess that's one little detail I'd forgotten about."

"Besides, men like Colton typically don't let much stand in their way."

"What are you saying?" asked MacKay.

"I'm saying that even if we had known what we know now, prior to Colton leaving, he probably would have gone anyway. The only difference is he probably would have gone alone."

"I've always admired men like Colton, but I couldn't do their job. It is my own strong opinion that people like him have a very special streak of crazy running through them," said MacKay.

"Could be, could be," said Father Ryan, nodding his head. "Whatever it is, it's good to know they're part of our team."

More than ready to change the subject, MacKay asked, "How have you been doing? Are those visions still giving you trouble?"

"Not too bad," said Father Ryan, his whole demeanor instantly changed to a defensive posture. "If I only knew what . . ."

"Captain MacKay!" shouted Petty Officer Briggs. "I've got Colton on the radio!"

The entire bridge shouted in relief as MacKay nearly knocked Father Ryan over to get to the radio. "Colton, this is MacKay. Where are you?"

"We're maybe six to seven hundred yards from the beach," replied Colton.

"You've had us a little worried, Commander. What is your status?"

"It's been a rough trip, but we're coming in. It would be helpful for you to let Rabbi Ryan know that his services will be needed," said Colton.

Father Ryan, who was standing next to MacKay, looked at him and said, "Rabbi Ryan?"

A grim look had replaced the smile on MacKay's face. "It was Colton's idea, a code."

"What's it mean?" asked Father Ryan.

"It means they're not alone."

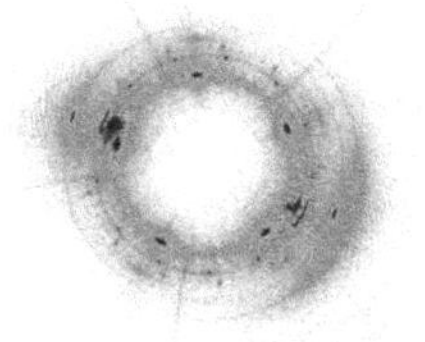

CHAPTER 22

The men held their positions, constantly scanning the jungle for any kind of threat, but a surge of renewed hope and energy flowed through each one of Colton's team. Not only were they close to the shore and would be escaping this hellhole of a jungle, but the *Eclipse* was also there waiting for them. It had been roughly twenty-four hours since they'd had any contact with the ship, but it felt like it had been days. Years ago, they were on a planet called Earth with reruns and Facebook and fast food and knowing where they would be buried.

Colton moved into the center of his team, his plan to talk as loud as necessary so that everyone of them would hear what he was going to say to MacKay. The team was coming in, true, but the circumstances were very different from when they'd left. They were returning with new acquaintances that were as much of a mystery to them now as when they'd first appeared.

Colton and Garrett had talked about how MacKay and the rest of the crew would react to the glowing light hovering above them. However, it wasn't until that moment that Colton realized what he hadn't taken into consideration. He hadn't really given any thought as to how the craft would respond to a large, well-armed ship. Although he felt reasonably sure that the craft was already aware of the *Eclipse*, he couldn't take anything for granted. He was hoping the glowing one was reading his mind. More and more he realized he was falling into the trap that their benefactors were all-powerful. How would Argos take this? A sign of his madness, or a rival AI to play chess with?

"We'll get word to Rabbi Ryan immediately," said MacKay, following Colton's lead. "Mr. Mercer will have three launches and a medical team waiting for you on the beach," said MacKay. Fortunately, it was loud enough, and the signal clear enough, that most of the men could hear the ship's captain.

"It will be best for you to hold off on sending the launches over until we get to the beach," said Colton. "At that time, we'll be in a better position to assess exactly what is needed."

"Very well," said MacKay, his face darkening, "we'll hold off until then."

"We do have wounded, one seriously," said Colton, "and I'm sorry to report one casualty. The good news is that we are being escorted back to the beach. Our escort not only saved our lives yesterday but also has helped to prevent further acts of violence against us."

"Are you escorted by one or more?" asked MacKay.

"We see only one glowing light in the sky. It is difficult to judge correctly, but I would guess it is a 110, 120 feet tall, and close to fifty feet in diameter. I don't think it is a drone because it moves silently. Remarkably it seems to calm humans, beasts, and plants."

"Do you think the one object you can see will accompany you to the *Eclipse*?" asked Captain MacKay.

"I don't think so, but again, it's hard to determine at this point," said Colton. "The jungle is quite dense, so we will not be able to move as quickly as we'd like to, but we'll get to the beach just as soon as we can."

"Understood, Commander," said Captain MacKay. "We'll be well prepared to provide whatever assistance you may require. Welcome back!"

"Thank you, Captain," said Colton. "Signing off."

"Corporal Lee, you and Private Hill will continue to take the point," said Garrett. "Privates Logan and Diaz will join me at the rear of the column. Men, the beach is not that far away, but we will continue to move at a careful and cautious pace. We will not relax our vigilance until we are safely back on board the *Eclipse*. Anything you'd like to add to that, Commander?"

"No, we are in complete alignment," said Colton.

The men knew code had been involved, and for some reason they couldn't talk about it. Fear rose from the rational parts of their mind, but the comfort field kept it low.

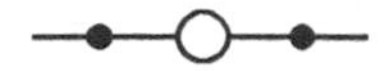

MacKay put down the radio and turned to Lieutenant Gallo. "Sound general quarters, Mr. Gallo," said MacKay. "Colton's coming in, but we don't know who, or frankly what, is with him or exactly what's going on. We need to be ready to act no matter what the circumstances."

"Petty Officer Briggs, get Mr. Mercer and Mr. Sahir to my conference room immediately," barked MacKay. "Also, alert Dr. Severin that the away team is returning and that they have an unknown number of wounded. Once you've done that, get Lieutenant Tanner on the horn for me. Father Ryan, if you'd accompany me please."

MacKay turned and left the bridge, going to his conference room. Father Ryan followed him, closing the door behind him. "You obviously took away more from that exchange with Colton than I did," said Father Ryan. "Is our team in trouble?"

"By Colton saying Rabbi Ryan, that not only told me that they are not alone, but also that he isn't in a position where he can speak freely," explained MacKay. "As secret warnings go, most people would miss the idea of asking for a rabbi to meet them, that his 'services will be needed,' especially in light of the fact that one of their men is dead."

"I understand that," said Father Ryan, "but why didn't he want us to send reinforcements and have them waiting for them on the beach? The team is clearly in need of help, as well as medical attention."

"We'll find out," said MacKay, "but a couple of things do come to mind. There is always the risk that this escort is only playing nice to lure more of us off the ship. Successfully attacking and boarding a US warship is a lot harder than attacking people standing on an open beach. Also, he said the only object he saw was a glowing whatever, which means he either has seen other things and didn't want them to overhear him, or thinks there may be others nearby."

"We've been praying so hard for their return," said Father Ryan. "Now, as close as they are, I fear that we might still lose them."

"That, I assure you, is not going to happen," said MacKay. "But there's more. When I offered to send additional launches to facilitate Colton's escort, I got two pieces of information from his response. First, he let me know that bringing them on board the *Eclipse* may not be a good idea. It sounds as though these people are not the sort that we would want to have on the ship. Secondly, by not saying anything about the exact number of additional launches we would need to send over, it told me that Colton is unclear of the number of combatants he's dealing with."

"So, what you're saying is that they may have only revealed a certain number of their people to Colton, and that there might be more of them, ready to attack, waiting in the jungle?" asked Father Ryan.

"Exactly. We just don't know. But we do know we've been warned," said MacKay. "Colton's also giving us time to prepare."

"How do you know that?"

"He told us how dense the jungle is, how it may take them awhile to make it to the beach. He said that to let me know that he'll be bringing his team in slowly so that we'll be ready," said MacKay. "What I can't understand is that they're this close to us, and yet none of the drones that we sent up were able to detect a trace of them. Not heat signatures, not anything. Clearly I have some questions for Mr. Sahir."

The phone on the conference room table buzzed. MacKay reached for it and found Lieutenant Tanner on the other end. "Lieutenant Tanner reporting as ordered, sir."

"Lieutenant, I want you to coordinate with Mr. Mercer. You'll be leading the men to go ashore and bring Mr. Colton's team back to the ship. Have four launches prepped and ready to go. You'll also want to have Severin send a couple of his corpsmen with you as well."

"Yes sir, we'll be ready," said Tanner. "How soon will we be leaving?" There was no mistaking the joy in the man's voice.

"As soon as we can, but for now I want you and your team to stand by," answered MacKay. "Good luck, Lieutenant."

Just as he was hanging up, Mercer and Sahir entered the conference room. "That was Lieutenant Tanner," said MacKay. "I've ordered him to coordinate with you, Mr. Mercer, and be prepared to go ashore. He'll be leading the rescue team."

"Shall I join him now?" asked Mercer.

"No, not yet," said MacKay. "There are a few items I first want to discuss with you and Mr. Sahir. Colton has picked up an escort, but he made it clear that he's not able to tell us much about them. If what he said is true, their escort saved their lives and has since then kept them safe. Here's hoping that's accurate."

"I take it he asked for Rabbi Ryan?" asked Mercer.

"Exactly," said MacKay. "I presently have the ship standing at general quarters but am prepared to go to battle stations if need be."

"How did he sound when you talked to him?" asked Sahir.

"He sounded like Colton, perfectly fine," said MacKay. "But then, that's all a part of how he's been trained. The man's clothes could be on fire and he'd still sound just the same as he always does."

MacKay then shared the entire exchange that he'd had with Colton. Some of his team has been wounded, they have one dead, and they're with someone they do not entirely trust. "It doesn't give us a great deal to go on. I'm guessing that they'll be showing up on the beach in less than an hour."

"What can I do, sir?" asked Sahir.

"As soon as possible, and I'm talking in less than two minutes, I want a report from Argos regarding the people with them. The scanners tied into Argos should be picking up Colton's team by now. I want to know how many of them there are, what is their weaponry, anything that that machine can pick up. It is also very important that we know if their escort has comrades hiding in the jungle, staying just out of sight."

"Very good, sir," said Sahir. "We'll go ahead and launch two of the drones."

"Which brings up a very important question," said MacKay. "Colton estimated that they are about six hundred yards or so away from the beach. How is it that we've had drones in the air for much of the day and didn't pick up a single trace of Colton's team? How could they miss the entire shore party coming directly at us? At some point those drones had to have flown directly over them!"

Sahir paled just a little under the hard stare from MacKay. "That thought raced through my head the instant I heard that Colton's team was returning. I have two of my best technicians, along with Dr. Meinhard and Dr. Chudzik, looking into this as we speak. Also, Argos is running a complete diagnosis on all of the drones that we were using."

"We don't have time for that now," said MacKay, "but I will want a full, detailed report as to what happened. We cannot afford failures like this."

"Yes sir," said Sahir. "I understand."

Sahir turned to leave, but MacKay stopped him. "One more thing, Mr. Sahir. It is my understanding that Argos can think outside the box, even take the initiative when necessary. I appreciate that it is programmed to protect this ship and its crew, but I will need you to keep a muzzle on that thing. Colton's escort may indeed prove to be hostile. That said, no one, under any circumstances, will open fire until I give the command. Is that clear? You make sure that that overrated transistor radio doesn't start firing off missiles all on its own."

"Yes sir, that will not happen," said Sahir. He was only too familiar with how MacKay felt about Argos.

"That will be all, Lieutenant," said MacKay. "You're dismissed."

"Anything else for me, sir?" asked Lt. Commander Mercer.

"Stay close to your radio," said MacKay. "There's no telling how this is all going to go down. We are already well aware of the dangers Tanner and his team will face just going to the beach. I'll have Hatfield monitoring creatures around us."

As Mercer left the room, Father Ryan looked closely at MacKay. "You were a little hard on Sahir."

"The failure of those drones to spot our team, especially knowing that they had to have been reasonably close to us, could have cost lives. That poor level of performance will not be tolerated by any person, or any system, on this ship," said MacKay, his anger seemed to be getting progressively worse.

"Captain," said Father Ryan, "from the moment we arrived in this strange place, there hasn't been any one of your crew not giving all they have to give."

"I don't disagree with you," said MacKay as he turned to head back to the bridge, "but before this is over, I may have to ask each of them to give even more."

He was halfway out the door when the phone on the conference table started to buzz. Glaring at the device, MacKay snatched it out of its cradle. "This is the captain."

"Sir, we have a problem that I can't explain," said Sahir, his voice quivering with nervous tension.

"Go ahead, Lieutenant. What is it?"

"While I was with you, the team finished their examination of the drones. Even Argos gave them a clean bill of health. So, to test them out, they'd already launched two of them before I returned."

"Can't see how that's a problem," said MacKay.

"Sir, Colton reported that he's within yards of the beach," said Sahir. "The drones we have in the air have a sensor range of five miles. The problem is that they're still not picking up any sign of Colton's team. We're getting some pretty clear pictures, as well as heat signatures from all kinds of things down there, but nothing that is human."

"How is that possible?" snapped MacKay, doing everything in his power to keep his temper in check.

"It isn't possible, sir," said Sahir. "I don't know where Colton is, but he's nowhere near us. Or something incredibly sophisticated is hiding him. This isn't machine error."

Off in the distance the team could hear the sound of waves breaking up on the shore. Corporal Lee and Private Hill returned to report that all was clear. "Unfortunately, sir, we weren't able to find any signs of Privates Shaw and Fuller. Also, one of our boats is missing," reported Corporal Lee. "What's left of the boat we did find is wrapped around a tree."

"I'm not surprised," said Colton. "MacKay would never have left those two men alone on the beach to face a storm like that. I'll ask him when we talk next, but I'm reasonably sure that we'll find they are safe and back on board the *Eclipse*."

At that point Captain Garrett joined them and Corporal Lee repeated his report. "Speaking of the *Eclipse*," said Garrett, "did you see it?"

"Yes sir," said Corporal Lee. "It's in roughly the same place where it was when we departed, but I think it's now a little further out."

Colton looked up at the craft still hovering above them. He could only imagine how Argos and the crew were reacting to that thing and how frantic things must be all over the ship. Frankly, he was dying of curiosity and could hardly wait to read the analysis Argos would produce. To finally be able to get his hands on some tangible facts would go a long way in giving him at least a little peace of mind.

Turning to Garrett, he said, "Captain, please bring your men in. We're about to hit the beach and I don't want to leave us more exposed than we need to be."

Garrett nodded and gave the orders. Colton took the radio from Bannister and waited for the men to gather round. The next few minutes would be very telling.

"We are about to leave this jungle, which is a good thing, but it also means that we'll be exposed. We'll be coordinating with the *Eclipse* to get us back on board as quickly as possible," said Colton. "That said, my guess is that the craft above us is causing quite a stir with MacKay and the rest of the crew, so we want to continue to play things carefully. Although I doubt it, please keep in mind that this may also be the first time for our escort to see the *Eclipse*. So, we still need to proceed carefully. The last thing we want is to do anything that will provoke a negative response from anyone."

"How would you like to proceed, Commander?" asked Garrett.

"When we step out of the jungle, I want you to hug the tree line," said Colton. "Spread out on either side of me and don't stop until you've found some cover that you can hide behind if needed. Corpsmen Payne and Lockridge will be with me. We want to be visible to the *Eclipse*, but I don't plan on taking any chances. Any questions?"

"Commander, before you radio the *Eclipse*, I'd like a word," said Garrett.

Most of the men sat down as Colton and Garrett moved a few steps away from the team. She motioned for Corporal Lee to join them. "Logan and Diaz are still watching our rear and I plan to leave them inside the tree line. Since we left the stream, I've spotted our mystery stalker three more times. Whatever or whoever it is, they're not getting any closer to us, but they are keeping us in sight. It has me concerned."

"Were you able to get a better look at it?" asked Colton.

Garrett shook her head. "No, in fact the clearest I've seen it was back at that stream. It does a pretty good job of staying concealed. Probably wouldn't have seen it at all if I didn't know what to look for."

"Captain, what's eating at you about this? It doesn't act aggressive in any way," asked Corporal Lee.

"Too many things, of which I'm sure 90 percent are not true. If it is an intelligent being, then I'd really like to know if it's on the same side as our friends up there in that craft. If they're not on the same side, then I have to wonder what its intentions are. All in all, it's the unknown that is eating away at me."

"Well, then that gives us one more reason to get out of here," said Colton. "Good work, Captain. Stay alert."

Colton went over to Bannister and took the radio from him. "Commander Colton to the *Eclipse*. Come in, *Eclipse*."

"MacKay here, Commander. Where are you?"

"We are just about to step out onto the beach," answered Colton. MacKay's response took him by surprise. He'd expected him to be pretty worked up due to the strange craft hovering over them, but he sounded as calm and relaxed as ever.

"Good to hear," said MacKay. "Are you at the same coordinates where you landed yesterday?"

"Yes, in fact, I wanted to see if you could give us an update on Privates Shaw and Fuller," said Colton. "We're hoping they're with you."

"They most certainly are," said MacKay. "We pulled them off the beach before that storm hit."

"That's what we figured," said Colton. This wasn't making any sense. MacKay was acting as if nothing out of the ordinary was going on when there was nothing ordinary about the situation at all. What was his game? Why was he taking this tact? "We are stepping out onto the beach now."

"This is the captain," MacKay said into the phone. His voice was being sent all over the ship. "Colton and his team are stepping out onto the beach now. No one, repeat, no one is to take any action until so ordered. We're told they have people with them who are friendlies. Stand ready."

MacKay looked over at Father Ryan and Lieutenant Gallo. "Colton sure is taking this slow. Wish I knew more about what's going on over there." The same thoughts were going through everyone's mind. "Briggs, get Sahir on the line for me."

"There they are!" said Father Ryan, a little louder than he meant to. "I can see them. All in all, they look pretty good for having spent a horrendous night out in the elements."

"Among other things," muttered Gallo.

All of them were staring at Colton and his team through very strong binoculars. "Where's their escort?" asked MacKay. "Does anyone see anyone else other than our people?"

"Sir, I have Mr. Sahir," said Briggs.

MacKay reached back for the phone, not taking his eyes away from the beach. Briggs put it in his hand. "Sahir, what are the drones reporting now?"

"This doesn't make any sense, Captain. Putting aside the fact that we're all seeing them quite clearly, according to the drones, there's no one on that beach."

"Colton, MacKay here. We can see you and are relieved to have you back. Will your escort be joining you on the beach? Mr. Mercer and Lieutenant Tanner have a welcome party ready and waiting to greet them."

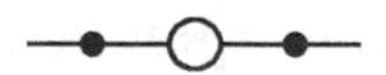

What? Will our escort be joining us on the beach? Had MacKay gone blind during their brief time away? Colton looked over at Garrett. She looked as confused as he was. "Is he asking if they're going to land? Is he expecting them to set down here on the sand?"

"No, I don't think so," said Garrett. "Earlier today we were speculating that the craft was blocking our radio signal. As we approached the shore, it eventually allowed us to communicate with the ship."

"I agree with that," said Colton. "What are you getting at?"

"What if our radio isn't all that they were blocking? In addition to protecting us, I never stopped to consider that they might be protecting themselves as well."

"I'm not sure I'm following you," said Colton. Then it hit him. MacKay wasn't reacting to the craft simply because he couldn't see it. That had to be it. MacKay, the crew, even Argos didn't know it was even there.

"Captain, stay with the men," said Colton.

"Where are you going?"

"Just out there," said Colton, pointing out towards the water. About ten feet from where the waves were rolling up on to the sand, he stopped and turned around. There was the craft, Garrett, and the team. The craft wasn't shielding itself from him.

Colton waved both hands in the air, doing his best to get their escort's attention, making the biggest and wildest gestures that he could manage. Nothing happened. Taking things to the next level, he then added jumping up and down while waving his hands and arms. For the men on the beach with him, as well as the crewmen from the *Eclipse* watching, it had to look as if he'd finally lost it.

"Let them see you," shouted Colton at the craft. "It is okay; let them see you!" After about five minutes of this, he decided to stop and try a different approach. He shut his eyes and he kept his hands raised high above his head. Concentrating as hard as he could, he screamed the words in his mind. *It is okay; let them see you. It is okay; let them see you.* It was his version of how they'd communicated with him the first time. Maybe it would work now. It would work on a TV show.

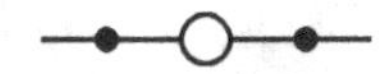

Back on the *Eclipse*, Colton's attempt at telepathic communications looked a little odd.

"What is Colton doing?" asked Father Ryan. From their vantage point it looked as if Colton had decided to leave his team and dance around on the sand. On closer inspection, Father Ryan could see that it wasn't exactly dancing, but close enough.

"I have no idea," said MacKay. "Commander, are you all right?" Colton did not respond.

"Should we do something?" asked Gallo.

"Probably," said MacKay, "but I have no idea what that would be."

They watched closely as Colton stopped his frantic jumping around. He now stood completely still, with his hands still raised above his head.

"My guess is that someone has a gun on him," said MacKay. "Quick, study the tree line. See if you can spot anyone pointing a rifle in his direction."

It was at that moment the air changed. For the crew on the *Eclipse*, the air seemed to ripple, briefly affecting their vision. The men and women on the *Eclipse* suddenly saw a shining ball appear in the sky. Bright white, like a sun of new hope. Argos (along with many of the other systems on the ship) lit up like a Christmas tree. For the first time Argos actually hummed as it pulled in so much energy to decipher what it was seeing. Later Argos would remember this moment as it became conscious, stimulated by the great Unknown.

MacKay had the presence of mind to grab the phone and hit the button for the ship's intercom. "Hold your fire," he shouted. "Stand by. Do not open fire."

He then hit the call button on his radio. "Colton, this is MacKay. Are you there?"

"Sir, Captain Garrett here. Commander Colton didn't take the radio with him."

"Are you okay? Are you under attack?"

"No sir, we are okay. Repeat, we are okay."

"What is that thing?"

"I'm guessing that you can now see the craft that has been escorting us. We don't know who they are. There's been very limited communication, but they saved us when we were under attack."

"It's like trying to look at the sun," said MacKay.

"Sir, here's Commander Colton."

"Colton here. Garrett figured out that they were somehow shielding their presence from you. As you are now able to see them, they've obviously stopped doing that. To repeat what Captain Garrett was telling you, they are on our side, at least in so much as they've been protecting us."

"Who are they?" asked MacKay.

"We don't know. However, believe me, if they were hostile in any way, we'd already be dead. Sir, I do not believe that they represent a threat to the *Eclipse* in any way. It is imperative, though, that we get my team back to the ship. I have some wounded men in desperate need of medical attention," said Colton.

"Sir," interrupted Petty Officer Briggs, "I have Sahir. He says it's urgent."

"Understood, Commander. We'll get you back on board. Stand by," said MacKay, taking the phone from Briggs. "Sahir, what have you got?"

"Argos is still scanning and analyzing that craft, but the preliminary reports are not good," said Sahir. MacKay could hear the commotion of Sahir's team in the background.

"Tell me what you've got."

"That thing is putting out a tremendous amount of energy," said Sahir. "We have not been able to identify the source, but we have been able to eliminate nuclear energy as a possibility."

"Okay, not nuclear, I understand. What I don't understand is what Argos has found that has you so upset?"

"It's the energy itself, sir. The energy readings we are taking from that thing are all but identical to the energy wave that washed over the ship and brought us to this place. Sir, the people in that craft, the ones controlling that energy, they're the ones we're up against."

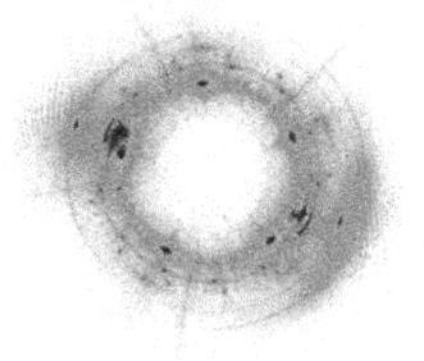

CHAPTER 23

MacKay was trying to come to grips with what Sahir had just told him. Was he truly staring at the enemy? Had Colton been befriended by the very people who had, for all intents and purposes, kidnapped them and brought them to this strange land? Still holding onto the phone, with Sahir on the other end, MacKay turned to Briggs and said, "Have Mr. Mercer get to the bridge as quickly as he can. Also advise Lieutenant Tanner to be ready to launch at any moment."

Directing his attention back to Sahir, MacKay asked, "Are you telling me that the craft that is hovering over our team on that beach is the same craft that brought us here?"

"No sir," said Sahir. "While it is true that the energy levels from that craft are high, in fact they're extremely high, they're not nearly as high as the levels from the energy wave that washed over us and brought us to this place. What I'm trying to say is that we believe the source of the energy, whatever it is that they're using to power that craft, is the same source for the energy wave that hit us. So, based on that, it stands to reason that the people operating that craft are probably the ones responsible for our being here."

"Alright," said MacKay, sighing deeply. "Keep at it. Are Meinhard and his team helping you to look over all of this data?"

"Yes sir," said Sahir. "They had been working with us on the drones, so when that craft revealed itself, they were already down here in the labs. Also, Argos is showing a new level of functionality."

"What does that mean?"

"Um. He may have just gotten smarter."

MacKay decided that this was beyond his weirdness threshold for the day.

"I'm guessing Sahir didn't have good news," said Father Ryan.

"No, he didn't," said MacKay. "He had very confusing news, and I'm doing my level best not to overreact." Picking up the radio, he said, "Mr. Colton, are you and your team ready to come aboard?"

The response was almost immediate. "Yes sir, ready when you are."

"We're preparing to send Lieutenant Tanner and a team over now to pick you up," said MacKay. "Due to some of the marine life that lives in these waters, it could be somewhat of a dangerous trip. We'll have teams of riflemen ready to open fire on anything that may come your way."

"Understood. We've had our own encounters with some of the more unusual creatures that live in this jungle," said Colton. "We'll do what we can to help cover Lieutenant Tanner and his team."

Lt. Commander Mercer entered the bridge as MacKay was putting down the radio. "Tanner's ready to go, sir. All we have to do is give him the word."

"Sahir gave me a preliminary report on that thing out there," said MacKay. "According to Argos, it appears to be using the same kind of energy as the wave that washed over us. In short, Sahir thinks that the people operating that craft could very well be our enemy."

"Has Colton been able to share anything about them with you?" asked Mercer.

"According to him, they not only rescued his team, but also have been protecting them ever since," said MacKay. He proceeded to fill Mercer in on all that he and Colton discussed. "For obvious reasons, our communication has been somewhat guarded, but other than 'Rabbi

Ryan,' he hasn't used any of the other code words we worked out to signal that they are in any kind of jeopardy."

"Glad to hear that. What are your orders, Captain?" asked MacKay.

"Getting Colton and his team back on this ship is our priority. That said, it would be foolish of me to ignore what Sahir has reported. Therefore, I want you to quietly bring this ship to battle stations," said MacKay. "Make this crystal clear to everyone, especially the senior officers. We do not take any kind of action that could potentially provoke whoever is operating that craft, especially with our people sitting directly under it. However, they may not be as friendly as Colton believes them to be, and I want us primed and ready to respond to whatever may occur."

"Wait a minute, battle stations? You can't do this. You're not planning to attack that craft, are you?" asked Father Ryan. "I appreciate Sahir's findings, but according to Colton, they've been helping his team. Colton's field experience alone, not to mention his training, automatically gives him better insight into these people than anyone else here. They're not attacking us. Even if the energy they're using is like what brought us here, that doesn't mean they're responsible. And with that kind of energy they could have easily blown us out of the water by now."

"Father Ryan, you just heard me explain this to Mr. Mercer. We're going to do everything we can to first get our people back," said MacKay. "Then, after I've talked to Colton and Garrett, we'll determine exactly what our next step will be. But if it turns out that Sahir is right, and they are responsible, then I'd say that they've already committed a hostile act. Bringing us here against our will is not a peaceful gesture. If they're behind this, then they'll be held accountable."

"Captain, they may also be the only ones who can help us to get back to where we belong," said Father Ryan. "We may just have to be a little forgiving."

"This is exactly why I'm taking things one step at a time and trying to avoid any rash actions. Mr. Mercer, carry out your orders."

As Mercer left the bridge, Father Ryan said, "My apologies for my outburst, Callum. If you'd rather I leave the bridge, I'll understand."

"Briggs, let Lieutenant Tanner know that he is to launch in ten minutes," said MacKay. "Seaman Hatfield, I want your eyes glued to those screens. You know what to look for. The second anything that could be a threat starts to head towards Lieutenant Tanner, you let me know." Turning towards Father Ryan, MacKay tried to give a small smile. "No Father, I want you right here beside me. Before this is over I'm pretty sure we're going to need all the help we can get from your boss."

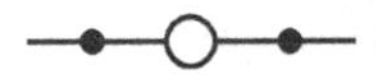

"They're getting ready to send Lieutenant Tanner over with a team to pick us up. Get three of your best marksmen down by the waterline. It seems that there are just as many big nasties swimming in the water as there are walking around the jungle," said Colton.

"Excellent, just what I wanted to hear. Now I'm not so sure how I feel about getting into one of those boats. Those things don't offer much in the way of protection," said Garrett. "Unless, of course, our babysitters come along."

Colton smiled at her. "It's little things like this that's going to make it a lot harder to get volunteers for the next shore party."

Garrett directed her men to be ready to board the boats that Lieutenant Tanner was bringing over to them. She gave Corporal Lee the role of choosing two other men to take with him to give Lieutenant Tanner cover if necessary. Having done all that she could do, she turned her eyes to the *Eclipse* and waited.

The three boats being brought over by Lieutenant Tanner crested a wave and were now visible from the beach. Colton felt relief, which was different than the comfort field. Tanner was gunning it. Colton looked up at their escort. Holding its position, the light that it gave off was as strong as ever. Colton smiled to himself, knowing that Father Ryan would be proud, as he said a silent prayer that their escort wouldn't let them down.

The two corpsmen, following Tanner's directions, had securely tied themselves to the side of the small boat, and it was good they'd done that. Tanner was wasting no time getting them to shore, and the boat was bouncing from wave to wave. Looking behind them, they could see the other two boats, keeping pace, flanking them on either side.

Tanner knew from firsthand experience the dangers facing them as they headed towards the beach. What concerned him most, however, was that he knew the trip back would take considerably longer as they'd have to battle the surf, being even more exposed to the predators that hunted these waters.

Seaman Hatfield kept his eyes locked on the screens in front of him. His eyes moved from one to the other, carefully watching for any indication that the creature that had attacked them prior to the storm was returning to strike again. What made this difficult, and he'd explained it to Lieutenant Gallo, was the abundant amount of marine life that lived in these waters. At almost any point in time, there were hundreds of creatures swimming in and around the ship, some of which were quite large, but so far hadn't proved to be dangerous.

Fortunately, the creature he was on the lookout for gave off a very distinctive signature. Its shape was almost completely different from the other fish, which made it easier to spot. Hatfield knew that there was the possibility that the creature could end up being shielded by some of the larger schools of fish in the area. On the off chance that occurred, the creature would then be in the kill zone and could quickly rise from the bottom and attack, giving the crewmen in the boats almost no chance to defend themselves. Besides, who knew about the other hundred life-forms he could see? Dr. Brennan had made some guesses.

Tanner continued to skim across the water, pushing the small boats as hard as he could. He was now about halfway to the shore. Captain MacKay turned and asked Hatfield for another update, roughly his twelfth one, and Hatfield gave him the all clear. It was at that very moment that something appeared on the far edge of one of his screens. Despite the oppressive heat, Hatfield felt a chill run down his back. He sat up straight in his chair, his nerves on fire, his stomach churning. Although it was not the creature he'd originally been looking for, Dr. Brennan had given him details on a few other likely creatures that they had to watch out for. This was one of them. No, there were two.

Dr. Brennan had called it a mosasaur, and then told him another name for it that Hatfield had absolutely no prayer of remembering. What he did remember, primarily because Dr. Brennan made him write them down, were the creature's vital statistics. Although still about a mile and a half away, the two dark signatures that he was looking at fit the description Dr. Brennan had shared with him.

For the moment, they were moving along slowly on a course that would have them pass by the *Eclipse*, but at a range safely away from the ship. Still, Hatfield was amazed at their size. The smaller one was at least thirty-six feet long, the larger one well over forty feet in length.

When Dr. Brennan had been telling him about this creature, he'd asked him if it was some kind of prehistoric whale. To his embarrassment, Dr. Brennan found his question to be amusing. No, he'd assured Hatfield, they were most certainly not whales. Mosasaurs were dinosaurs, and they were easily the largest and the most aggressive predator in the late Cretaceous sea.

Dr. Brennan told him how these things ruled the oceans and had rows of teeth, each two to three inches in length. He said that comparatively speaking, the great white sharks that we all fear would look like guppies next to these things. Hatfield shuddered at the thought of being in the water and having one of them coming at him. He wasn't wild about getting in the water in the first place, but chalked up one more reason why he'd never go swimming in the ocean again.

Whatever these two creatures were, they suddenly swerved and were now heading on a more direct course towards the *Eclipse*. They had not picked up speed, but they were on their way. "Captain, you need to see this," said Hatfield.

MacKay moved over to Hatfield's station so fast that he nearly knocked Lieutenant Gallo out of the way. "What have you got?" snapped MacKay.

"I'm not entirely sure, but these two creatures just changed course and appear to be heading our way," explained Hatfield. "These are not like that dinosaur that attacked us yesterday, but if they're the creatures Dr. Brennan told me about, then we definitely have a problem."

"Briggs, get Dr. Brennan up to the bridge immediately," said MacKay. Turning his attention back to the screen, he asked, "How far away from us are they?"

"Just over a mile, sir, but they're heading directly at us. Even at the relatively slow pace they're moving at, they should get here about the same time Lieutenant Tanner starts to head back with Colton's team."

"At what depth are they running?" asked MacKay.

"Like their speed, that's holding pretty steady too," said Hatfield. "They're roughly 150 feet down, sir."

"We could lob a couple of shells over there," said Gallo. "It may not kill them, but it might chase them away."

Father Ryan started to object, but MacKay cut him off. "We can't risk it, Mr. Gallo. If we did hit them, the end would result would be putting blood in the water, which is the last thing we want to do. Also, we don't know how Colton's new friends will respond to our shooting at things. Hatfield, don't take your eyes off them, do you understand?"

"Yes sir," said Hatfield.

MacKay rushed back to the windows and picked up his binoculars. He got them focused in time to see the three boats being pulled up through the surf. He breathed a sigh of relief, realizing that the first half of the mission had gone without incident. "Sir, Dr. Brennan is here to see you," said Gallo.

"Thank you for getting here so quickly, Doctor," said MacKay.

"I was already nearby, but still, if it hadn't been for the young marine who guided me up here, I'd be lost and wandering around somewhere," said Dr. Brennan. "We've been on this ship for weeks and I still haven't gotten the hang of the place."

MacKay guided him over to Hatfield. "In addition to the dinosaur that attacked us yesterday, you were telling Seaman Hatfield of another creature to be on the lookout for."

"Yes," said Dr. Brennan, "they're called mosasaurs, very dangerous."

"We possibly have two of these mosasaurs approaching the *Eclipse*. What do you make of this?"

Dr. Brennen leaned over and stared at the screen. Hatfield directed his attention to the two bogies he'd been following. "Sir, they're still about three quarters of a mile out, but they're no longer heading directly at us. They seem to be staying in this general area," said Hatfield.

"Your thoughts, Dr. Brennan?" said MacKay. "Could they be the mosasaurs you warned Hatfield about?"

"Yes, I'm afraid so, that could very well be them," said Dr. Brennan. "Please understand, I'm basing my conclusion strictly on their size. Back in the late Cretaceous period there weren't too many things swimming around that were as big as they were."

"We're getting ready to bring that team back from the beach," said MacKay. "The boats they'll be using will make a fair amount of noise. This will end up sending out some very different vibrations through the water, vibrations I'm sure they're not used to. In your opinion, will that draw their attention towards us, or send them away?"

"Captain, I think you already know the answer to that," said Dr. Brennan. "None of us can say for sure what they'll do, but my guess is yes, that'll draw them in. They wouldn't run from guns. I doubt they'll run from anything. The vibrations from the three boats will be different but may even signal to them an animal dying in the water. A struggling animal typically means an easy kill."

MacKay nodded. "That's what I was afraid of. Do you have any feel for how fast they can move?"

Brennan walked over and looked out towards the beach. "If you're asking me if those two mosasaurs can get here in time to intercept our boats coming back from the beach, it won't even be a contest. I can even tell you how they'll attack. Mosasaurs had elongated, cylindrical snouts. Like dolphins in our world, mosasaurs likely used their snouts to ram their prey. Put some speed behind twenty-five to thirty thousand pounds of dinosaur and you've got a very destructive predator on your hands."

"That'll break those boats in half," said MacKay, his voice low, almost inaudible.

"Whatever's left, and doesn't immediately sink, the mosasaurs will go after with their teeth," said Dr. Brennan. "They had massive, conical teeth and they'll bite into anything and drag it down. Captain, if you try to bring back that team with those things around, I don't believe that it will end well."

MacKay picked up the radio to call Colton. He wasn't sure what he was going to say to him. The memory of the two marines being attacked by that sea monster yesterday was still too fresh in his mind. As bad as that had been, this would be even worse. "Colton, MacKay here."

"Colton here. We're nearly finished loading the boats and should be shoving off in the next few minutes."

"We have a problem," said MacKay. "We may not be able to bring you back to the ship right away."

Colton didn't respond immediately. MacKay found Colton with his binoculars and saw that he was walking away from his team, making sure that he was out of earshot. "What's the problem, Captain?"

"You're not going to believe this, but here goes," said MacKay. He quickly told Colton all that Dr. Brennan had told them. He then told him that there may be two huge mosasaurs just under a mile away. "We really have no way of confirming this, one way or the other, but it's a risk I'm not sure we can take. We have no solid defense against them. I know all of this sounds crazy, but that's what we're up against."

"Captain, we are so far beyond crazy at this point that I've given up worrying about it," said Colton. "The problem is that we have some wounded men that need Dr. Severin's attention and can't wait much longer. Plus, we don't know how long our escort is going to stick around, and they're the only thing keeping the land-based predators at bay."

"Commander, I understand, but if Dr. Brennan is right, then bringing you back right now would be tantamount to suicide," said MacKay. "We just can't do it."

The radio went silent and MacKay watched Colton. He watched as he started to pace back and forth on the sand, probably trying to figure out how he would break this news to his team. Then he stopped and looked out at the *Eclipse*. "Captain, I have an idea. It's not a great idea, but it's the only thing I can think of."

Mercer had just returned to the bridge and MacKay motioned for him to join him. "Mr. Mercer is here with me," said MacKay. "Please tell us what you have in mind."

"When our planes have missiles fired at them, one of the ways in which they defend themselves is by using flares and chaff. It distracts the missile from its original target," explained Colton.

"I've served on two aircraft carriers, Colton, I know how it works," said MacKay. "Get to the point."

"In the event that those things do start to come at us, we'll deploy our own chaff," said Colton. "We've still got a few grenades and will start dropping them in our wake as we go. They'll kill all kinds of fish and hopefully the blood, along with the various fish parts, will draw them away from us."

MacKay spun around and looked at Dr. Brennan, raising an eyebrow, asking the unspoken question. "I doubt that would work, but then the combination of the blood, the guts, and the blasts just may do the trick.

However, and there's no two ways about this, they're still going to be taking a terrible gamble," said Dr. Brennan.

"Hatfield, have the mosasaurs moved in any closer to us?" asked MacKay.

"No sir, in fact they've moved away some, putting a little more distance between us," answered Hatfield.

MacKay glared across the water at Colton for a couple of moments. Then, shaking his head, hit the button on the radio and said, "It's not that great of an idea, Colton, but considering the alternatives, I'm afraid it's all we have."

"We'll be shoving off within five minutes," said Colton.

"Commander, bring our people home," said MacKay. "Godspeed."

"I can't tell if he's just desperate or completely nuts," said Mercer. "Of course, in a crazy world only nutty people are sane."

"Mr. Mercer, once they push off, get two of our fifty-caliber guns trained on either side of them. Those beasts will have to come close to the surface to hit our boats. Maybe we'll get lucky," said MacKay.

MacKay turned and looked at Father Ryan. "Well Father, we're doing all we can do, but it looks like we're going to come up short. It'd be nice to hear from your boss right about now."

Father Ryan nodded and bowed his head in prayer.

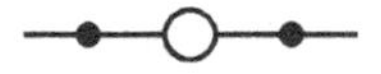

Colton quickly briefed Garrett and Corporal Lee, not holding anything back. He wanted to make sure they understood the risk they were about to take. Both nodded their agreement, then split up, each getting into a different boat. The team pushed off, and they were soon out of the shallow water and on their way towards the *Eclipse*. Initially, as expected, their progress was frustratingly slow as the never-ending line of waves heading towards the beach served to push them back.

"Hatfield?" shouted MacKay.

The young seaman's face was covered with sweat. "I'm not sure, Captain. They've stopped moving away from us, but they seem to be staying in place."

Mercer went over to stand by Hatfield. He knew this would put even more pressure on the young sailor, but he felt that a second set of eyes was needed. "You're doing good, Hatfield. Just stay on it."

The three boats were staying as close together as possible. This had been Garrett's idea. She hoped that by doing this, they might appear bigger than they really were. Colton didn't say anything but didn't really think it would make much of a difference. But then, in fairness, he wasn't all that confident that his plan would work any better.

"Give me a freaking break!" exclaimed Hatfield. Not the kind of language one was supposed to use while on the bridge, but his emotions got the better of him.

"Sir, here they come," said Mercer. "And they're making pretty good speed."

"When do you expect them to intercept our boats?" asked MacKay.

Mercer studied the screen for a couple of moments. The bridge had gone completely silent. "At the rate they're closing in, they should hit Colton's team when they're about halfway here."

"Colton, this is MacKay. The mosasaurs are headed your way." Colton didn't respond. "Colton, did you get that?"

"With the boats being as close together as they are, he probably can't hear you," said Mercer. "I'll have the gunners standing by."

Everyone on the bridge was doing the best they could to prepare themselves for what was about to happen. As close as they were, they knew there was nothing they could do. Every heart beat like a hammer, every face pale.

"Sir," said Hatfield, "I don't know if this is a good thing or not, but that craft that had been hovering over Colton and his team is now moving towards us."

"Just what we need," muttered MacKay under his breath. "How fast are they approaching?"

Hatfield stared at the screen. He was trying to pull together an answer for the captain, but the mosasaurs kept distracting him, as they appeared to have increased their speed. At the rate they were moving they'd be on top of those boats in just a few minutes.

"Hatfield!" shouted MacKay. "The craft, how fast is it approaching us?"

Gallo quickly moved over to help Hatfield, but it wasn't necessary. "I'm not sure that it is," said Hatfield. "It appears to be keeping pace with our boats. It's just staying over them."

Father Ryan grabbed MacKay's arm. "Look," he said, his voice almost a whisper. "What is happening out there?"

The top of the egg-shaped craft was still emitting the blindingly bright light. Although they couldn't get a clear look at the craft without damaging their eyes, they too were able to catch brief glimpses of what appeared to be a large, multifaceted object rotating inside it. As Hatfield had said, the craft was staying with the boats as they continued to approach the *Eclipse*.

MacKay was about to say something to Father Ryan when a cone-shaped beam of pure, white light shot down from the craft, completely encasing the three boats. Then the light started to grow in strength to a point where the crew on the *Eclipse* could no longer see Colton or his team.

At that moment, several alarms went off on the bridge. "Sir, Argos has targeted the craft and our systems are preparing to open fire," shouted Gallo.

Grabbing for the phone, MacKay quickly got Sahir on the line. "What in the hell is going on down there? Argos has just repositioned our guns, targeting that craft!"

"Yes sir, I know," said Sahir. "The energy levels from that thing just spiked off the charts and it's heading directly towards us."

"No one is to fire on that craft, not with it being on top of our people. I don't care if you have to shoot that overrated machine, disengage Argos immediately. Is that order clear enough for you?"

"Yes sir, I'm on it."

"Sir," said Hatfield, "you've got to see this."

MacKay, dropping the phone, raced over to Hatfield's side and looked down at the screen he was pointing to. "What is it?" asked MacKay. He couldn't even begin to guess at how things could get much worse.

"They're leaving," said Hatfield. "The mosasaurs, I don't get it, but they're moving away from us! And that's not all. Look at this monitor. Everything is moving away, there's practically nothing swimming around below us. How is that possible?"

"What do you mean there's nothing below us?" said MacKay.

"Sir, from the moment we arrived, the waters here have been teeming with marine life," said Hatfield. "It's been a constant, night or day. But look at it now. There's literally nothing moving down there. What could have happened? Why did everything suddenly swim away?"

MacKay turned and rushed back to the windows. Everyone on the bridge had put on sunglasses, but they weren't nearly strong enough to block out the sun like light from the craft. As the light got closer, MacKay noticed that the tension that had filled his whole body seemed to be draining away. He felt calm when not ten seconds ago his nerves had been on fire.

The craft was now hovering just off the port side of the ship. MacKay knew he should be taking action, but the fear, the urgency to respond, had left him. Everyone on the bridge continued to stare at the strange craft, but no one moved. After about two minutes the craft moved away from the *Eclipse*, heading back to shore.

Petty Officer Briggs said," Sir, our boats are back, and our people are all on board. You're wanted in sick bay."

MacKay looked around the bridge. It was clear that his men had experienced the same strange transition from mind-numbing fear to an impossible state of calm. "Mr. Mercer, you have the bridge," said MacKay, pulling himself together. As he started out the door he caught sight of Father Ryan. The man was smiling while tears streamed down his face.

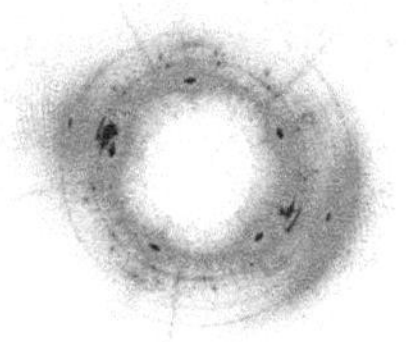

CHAPTER 24

The four days since Colton and his team had miraculously emerged from the jungle had passed quickly. Unfortunately, seven of the marines that had been with him were still in sick bay, three in serious condition. Dr. Severin, although intrigued by the gel they'd brought back, had at first been reluctant to use it. Due to Colton and Payne's urging, he tried it out on a couple of smaller injuries. He too was stunned by its healing properties. Sahir's people were still analyzing a portion of the gel.

Private Lockridge was one of the three men in critical condition, and everything that could be done to save him was being done. His prognosis had not really improved, and things were still touch-and-go. Considering the severity of his injuries, it was amazing he'd made it back to the ship.

On the other hand, the loss of Private Blake had been hard for Colton's team, and the rest of the crew mourned his loss. But despite this tragic loss, the overall morale had greatly improved. Practically everyone on the *Eclipse* had believed that Colton and his team had perished in the jungle and would never be seen again. Their unexpected return had given the crew something else they'd started to lose, hope. The "angels" were much talked about as well.

MacKay and Colton entered sick bay and found Dr. Severin attending to one of his patients. Captain Garrett was also there, visiting her men. "Doctor, we're here when you're ready," said MacKay.

Looking up from the chart he'd been writing in, Severin smiled at them. "This shouldn't take too much longer. I'll meet you in my office."

MacKay and Colton went to Severin's office and made themselves comfortable, MacKay getting yet another cup of coffee. "Just how much of that stuff do you pour into your system on a daily basis?" asked Colton.

"As much as I need," said MacKay, sitting down.

"You need to switch to tea," said Colton. "You'll like it, and it's far better for you in so many ways."

"There are times when I need that little boost of energy that coffee gives me," said MacKay. "Tea doesn't do that."

"Don't tell that to the British," said Colton. "They built an entire empire by drinking tea. Black tea, green tea, there's all kinds of varieties and I assure you, if it's a caffeine boost you're interested in, there are plenty of teas out there that pack a punch."

"So, then what's the difference?" asked MacKay. "Caffeine is caffeine."

"No, no, no," said Colton. "Obviously, there's a great deal that I need to teach you about the benefits of tea, from cleaning out the arteries to fighting cancer-causing agents, and that's just the beginning. Hezekiah has a whole cabinet of teas in the officer's mess. I'll have him talk with you."

"Lectures on the health benefits of tea are not something I need, or want, at the moment," said MacKay.

There was a knock on the door and Captain Garrett walked in. "May I join you?"

"Of course," said Colton. "How are the men doing?"

"Better, but I'm still not clear on what made them so sick," said Garrett. "Every single one of us got banged up pretty good, but something really did a number on those men out there."

"Well, Dr. Severin called and asked that Mr. Colton and I join him in sick bay," said MacKay. "He said he finally has some answers for us."

As they waited for Dr. Severin, Colton thought back over the last four days and what MacKay had just said. Answers, precious answers, were what they had all been searching for, what they had been craving.

Ever since they'd arrived in this lonely and terrifying land, the number of unanswered questions continued to pile up, hour after hour. Other than themselves, there had been no one to turn to. It had been maddening. The absolute uncertainty of it all, facing the complete unknown, day after day, had worn many of them down.

Once back on ship, as soon as Colton and Garrett had been checked from head to toe and cleared for duty by Dr. Severin, the debriefings had begun. For the next two days Colton, Garrett, and Corporal Lee joined Captain MacKay, Mr. Mercer, and various other crew members and discussed, in detail, all that had occurred. The crew was as eager to learn what had happened to them in the jungle as they were interested in all that the *Eclipse* had gone through.

The strange craft that had saved them easily dominated much of the conversation. Who were they? Where did they come from? Were they friend or foe? What was the source of the fuel that could produce such high levels of energy? What were the craft's exact dimensions? For all its vaunted sophistication and capabilities, even Argos had been unable to penetrate the light encompassing much of the ship. This kept them from having a clear understanding of just how big it really was.

Corpsman Payne had been asked to join the debriefing session when they discussed how they'd communicated with the craft. Only he and Colton had had direct "communication" with these people. Unfortunately, their experiences couldn't shed any light as to who they were. While the communication with them had been pleasant and reassuring, and very different from anything they'd ever been exposed to, their rescuers kept themselves completely shielded.

Whoever they were, it was clear that their technology was well ahead of anything the United States military had. The calming effect from the light that the craft emitted was one of the technological advancements that everyone on board had experienced. This light was clearly an amazing tool that they used on a regular basis. It was clear that its abilities covered a broad range. Many times, they discussed two of the most significant examples of what this light could accomplish. The first was when it stopped the dinosaurs from killing them in that clearing. The second was when they were trying to get back to the *Eclipse* and it somehow chased off all the marine life around the ship. As defensive measures go, this light that the craft controlled was not only quite effective, but remarkably, was also nonlethal. That one aspect alone, in and of itself, was of significant interest to everyone.

The nonlethal effect of the light, combined with the calming effect that it had on everyone it touched, did provide them with one of the few insights they had as to the nature of these people. So far, they had given no indication of being either aggressive or violent. Anyone with the technology they possessed could obviously have developed extremely devastating weapons. And yet not once had they used any kind of force that resulted in the loss of life or injured anything in any way.

Meinhard was the most skeptical. He thought the light was an example of the "God helmet" developed by Laurentian University Professor Michael Persinger to study his hypothesis about the brain being the basis of all experience through the effects of temporal lobe electromagnetic stimulation. When subjects were hit by the correct magnetic fields, they "felt" God. Buddhists felt Buddha, the followers of Islam, Allah, and so forth. Payne's "Jesus" or Colton's "composite teacher" weren't beyond modern technology, or at least not far beyond.

The gel was a different story. Again, Meinhard expressed his skepticism. He stated that it could be just an advanced blend of painkillers and antibacterial agents. But it came as no surprise when Dr. Severin reported something very quietly to the captain. Meinhard had been caught trying to steal a sample of the gel. Of course, he blustered on about it. No criminal intent, just wanting to run his own tests. But it was all MacKay needed to know that going forward, he would have to keep an eye on Meinhard. Maybe, just maybe, the enemies weren't all outside the ship.

The analysis of the gel, however, was taking longer than any of them had expected. This was primarily due to the fact that there were a large number of elements within the gel that they weren't able to identify. Under normal circumstances this would have been very troubling. But the concept of anything here being normal had long passed. The crew of the *Eclipse* was trying to adapt to an Earth that had existed millions of years ago, so the fact that the gel contained elements that couldn't be defined didn't strike anyone as being strange at all.

It was Sahir and Dr. Meinhard, along with Drs. Brennan and Chudzik, that brought Colton and Garrett up to speed on all that Argos had been able to determine as to where they were. The accepted theory was the many-worlds theory. In brief, the *Eclipse* had somehow moved from their world, or dimension, into a completely different parallel dimension. Although they had absolutely no idea as to how this had happened, or the actual physical mechanics that would be necessary to make it happen, it was the only thing that even remotely made sense.

"So, you're telling us that based on the aerial photography of the coastline, the animals, both on land and in the sea, as well as the plant life, all of that supports your theory that we're now on Earth in the late Cretaceous period?" asked Colton, his voice laced with sarcasm. "I know virtually nothing about the many-worlds theory, or interdimensional travel, but that's the craziest thing I've ever heard."

"Commander," said Dr. Brennan, "when we first got these findings, we too were as incredulous about them as you are. We labored over these nonstop, repeatedly checking every piece of data we had. I can personally assure you that we have been meticulous in our research, and each time we came up with the same answers. Also, and this is important, Argos has confirmed these findings, and that's about as good as it can get."

"Dr. Meinhard, Dr. Brennan, with all due respect . . ." Garrett started to say.

"I find it so amusing," said Dr. Meinhard, interrupting Captain Garrett, "that every time someone begins a sentence with 'all due respect' they follow it up with words that are anything but respectful."

"If you will allow me to finish my question," said Garrett, "we can put your presumption to the test."

"Please, Captain, by all means," said Meinhard. "How rude of me to interrupt."

Fighting the urge to feed Dr. Meinhard to one of the many predators they'd encountered, Garrett continued, "Growing up, my brother was obsessed with dinosaurs and the prehistoric ages. It's all he ever talked about. So, as I was about to say, if we truly are on an Earth that existed sixty-five million years ago, then how do you explain some of the creatures that we came across? To my knowledge, those things never existed on Earth at any time."

"She makes a good point," said Colton. "There's the lizard-eating flower and that nightmarish thing in the cave. I don't know where we are, but if asked, Earth would not have been my first guess."

Before Meinhard could respond and ruffle more feathers, Dr. Brennan took the floor. "Those are excellent examples, and we have added those two points of data into the data we are continuing to collect. But there's a broader point that you need to be aware of that I think will help to answer this. What we know about the late Cretaceous period is really rather limited.

"Although great strides have been made in that field of study, when you think about it, we've had very little hard data to go on. The majority of what we've learned over the years is from the fossil records that have been discovered, the study of the rock sediments in which the fossils were found, and what we've learned regarding continental drift. The lizard-eating plant would likely have left little to no fossil trace, while the cave horror might have left handfuls of teeth, but no bones."

"All we're trying to say," said Dr. Chudzik, taking over for Dr. Brennan, "is that it's not surprising that you discovered things that up until now were unknown. Look at it from another perspective. In our own dimension, every year that passes, we continue to learn new things about the Earth. A good example of this is illustrated by the many new discoveries that are being made in the field of cryptozoology. That's an entire branch of science whose single focus is to chronicle and examine new animals and insects that are discovered every year. By comparison, when you consider the amount of hard data that we have regarding the Cretaceous period, it's rather miniscule. We can only claim to know a small fraction of all that went on during that time period."

The room turned quiet as all of them considered the ramifications of what Dr. Brennan and Dr. Chudzik had shared with them. "So, if we truly are where you say we are," said Colton, "we could be facing all kinds of unknown threats as we try to survive here."

"Yes, Commander," said Dr. Brennan. "That just about sums it up. Although this is not the case, what we're experiencing isn't all that different than if we had landed on some distant planet. We have a great deal to learn."

It took a couple of days for Colton to begin to accept all of this, but unfortunately, it was hard to argue with the data they'd collected. Colton had a great deal of respect for Sahir. Dr. Meinhard and his team were some of the best in their fields of study, and Argos was the most sophisticated computer known to man. Although he still couldn't wrap his mind around how they'd gotten here, that was not the question he was struggling with. He was far more focused on trying to understand how they were going to get out of here. In the brief period of time in which they'd been here, if he'd learned anything, it was that man was not meant to walk with dinosaurs.

Dr. Severin entered his office, breaking Colton out of his contemplation. His mind had wandered off, and it took a moment for him to refocus. Sitting up in his chair, he considered breaking down and having some of the coffee MacKay was drinking.

"Captain Garrett," said Dr. Severin as he placed a pile of files on his desk, "so glad you could join us. Please sit down, make yourself comfortable."

"Have you determined what's happened to my men?" asked Captain Garrett.

"Almost," said Dr. Severin. "At least I know what it's comparable to. Before I go into that, let me ask, when did their symptoms first start to make themselves known?"

"I didn't notice that they were having any problems until we approached the beach," said Garrett. "A couple of them started vomiting, while some of the others told me that they had pretty severe headaches."

Severin sat down in his chair, listening and nodding his head. "That fits in with the kind of creature that I think injected those men."

"Injected them?" asked Colton. "Are you saying that something stung them?"

"In a manner of speaking, yes," said Dr. Severin. "Are any of you familiar with the Lonomia obliqua, better known as the assassin caterpillar?"

They all three looked at each other, and then MacKay said, "No, Doctor, we aren't."

"Not surprised. It's really not that well known," said Severin. "What's so interesting about it is that it may be one of the deadliest animals we know of, at least back in our world."

"Wait a minute," said Colton. "Are you telling me that these men survived being attacked by a group of extinct dinosaurs, faced down several creatures that we still haven't been able to identify, and lived through what I would call a small typhoon, only to be taken down by a caterpillar?"

"I have no idea what's walking around over there in that jungle," said Dr. Severin, "but I strongly suspect that either a caterpillar, or one of its ancient ancestors, is what stung these men."

"If something had stung them, wouldn't at least one or two of them have noticed it?" asked Garrett.

"Not necessarily," said Dr. Severin. "Many of these creatures are quite small and blend in with their environments to the point of almost being invisible. Many kinds of caterpillars have hollow body hairs. These hairs easily detach into the skin, which is how the toxin is passed into its victim.

In most cases it's not all that painful, and people really don't know they have a problem until they start to feel sick."

"I've never heard of a caterpillar that can kill a man," said MacKay.

"Neither have very many other people," said Dr. Severin. "The assassin caterpillar, thank heaven, is only found in Brazil. Up until the last few years, it hasn't been studied that much, and the threat it posed to people was not that well known."

"How is it that you knew about this?" asked Colton.

"Tropical medicine is something I've always had a strong interest in, and I've had the opportunity to spend several years in Brazil," answered Dr. Severin. "You wouldn't believe the number of dangerous creatures walking around that country. Shoot, it might even give this place a run for its money. The good news is that I recognized what these men were suffering from, at least a modern-world perspective, and was familiar with the treatment that might help them. So far it is having a positive effect."

"You said it's one of the deadliest animals we know of. That covers a lot of ground. Are you saying it's deadlier than the venom from some snakes?" asked Colon.

"Easily," said Dr. Severin. "In fact, the sting from those little guys is deadlier than that from a jellyfish."

"And that's what stung my men?" asked Garrett.

"At least something similar did," said Dr. Severin. "Like the assassin caterpillar, the toxin these men were injected with is very similar to hemotoxin. If not treated, and frankly there's even a short window for the treatment to be effective, hemotoxin will cause you to bleed out. No different than Ebola."

"Aren't there other things out there whose venom contains hemotoxin?" asked Colton.

"Yes, absolutely. There are snakes that have hemotoxins; the Boomslang snake in Africa is a good example of that. But the other reason that I'm comparing this to the assassin caterpillar is that unlike any other animal, its toxin is much worse."

"How so?" asked Captain Garrett.

"The assassin caterpillar's toxin takes things to the next level," explained Dr. Severin, "which is where this was headed. In short, the toxin causes what is known as disseminated intravascular coagulation. The blood starts to clot in the blood vessels, but it doesn't stop there. Things get even worse. I found traces of very strong anticlotting agents where the men were stung. The anticlotting agent also comes from the caterpillar and attaches itself to another protein in the body's cells. This then causes them to leak, as the blood is unable to clot. After that, it doesn't take long for the internal bleeding to start to fill up the surrounding tissue. It's what's known as bruised blood. The internal bleeding spreads through the body and culminates in compression and brain death."

"So much for my eating dinner tonight," said Colton. "All of this from just a caterpillar."

"Yes, or in this case, something very similar," said Dr. Severin.

"But the treatment is being effective," challenged Garrett. "My men will recover, is that right?"

"With the exception of Private Lockridge, which, unfortunately, could still go either way, I expect all of them, over time, to pull through. But in all seriousness, things should not have worked out this way. In our world, most of those men would have died. As I told you, the window for successful treatment with a toxin like this is very narrow; it's less than twenty-four hours. Of the six marines I'm treating for this, all were stung by the same type of creature. The point I'm trying to make is that I didn't figure out the problem until a couple of days after they'd returned."

"So how is it possible that they're not dying or dead already?" asked Colton. "Unless, of course, the bug that stung them isn't as potent as your assassin caterpillar."

"No, that's not it. I believe that it's just as potent," said Dr. Severin. "The test we ran proved the toxin in their bodies to be as strong, if not more so, than the assassin caterpillar. No, something else saved those men."

"Any idea what that might be?" asked MacKay.

"I do, but nothing I'm willing to stake my reputation on until we know more," said Dr. Severin. "The skin where these men were stung had to have turned sore not long afterwards. In talking with Corpsman Payne, as well as the marines themselves, each one of them put that gel on the infected area. I don't get it, but based on everything else I've seen, I'm crediting that gel with one more miracle."

"Are you saying that the gel was able to heal them from a toxin that potent?" asked Garrett.

"No, not at all. I'm afraid I didn't make myself clear on that. Had those men not gotten back to the ship and received proper treatment, they most certainly would have died. However, it is my professional guess that the gel, somehow, did slow things down. Considering everything we now know, and what we've seen of that craft that brought you back, I wouldn't be surprised to learn that the gel has nanobots—microscopic cellular repair agents," said Dr. Severin.

"That's it," exclaimed Colton. "Dibs on the gel! When we get back to where we're supposed to be, I'm going to sell that stuff to a pharmaceutical company, lean back, and enjoy a nice, secluded beach somewhere."

"That is quite the humanitarian gesture," said Captain Garrett.

"It's actually a good plan," said Dr. Severin. "Don't think that it didn't cross my mind once or twice. However, the fly in the ointment is the elements that we haven't been able to identify. That's the sad part. When we do run out, and we're getting close, we won't be able to replicate it."

MacKay stood up and said, "Anything else, Doctor?"

"No, that's pretty much everything for now," answered Dr. Severin. "I'll keep you posted.

The three officers filed out of his office, went outside, and leaned on the railing, gazing across the water at the beach and the jungle behind it. "I wonder where our escort has gone?" said Colton.

"I'd like to know that myself," said MacKay. "After it safely escorted you back to the ship, it hovered right next to us for maybe thirty more minutes. From what Mr. Sahir told me, those thirty minutes nearly caused Argos to blow every circuit it has. The craft then went back to the beach to where it had been and stayed there. By the next morning, it was gone."

"What's interesting is that it could still be right in front of us. If it's shielding itself, which it clearly demonstrated that it can do, we'd never know it was there. Begs the question as to whether or not they've been closely watching us ever since we arrived," said Colton.

"I know that it was a terrible breach to let the craft get so close to the *Eclipse*, but there really wasn't much in the way of a choice at the time," said MacKay. "One of the things that has amazed me the most out of all of this was how good I felt while that craft was here. At that point, with it sitting almost on top of us, I should have been as frantic as Argos. And yet it was probably the calmest and most relaxed I've felt in days. Short of some of the drugs Dr. Severin has down in sick bay, or the bottle of Scotch I keep in my cabin, I've never heard of anything that can act so swiftly or so effectively."

"You're not still thinking of that craft as being a weapon, are you?" asked Garrett.

"I don't know. How do you see it?" asked MacKay.

"I'm just speculating, but I'm not sure that I believe that it's a weapon at all," said Garrett. "We never once saw that craft hurt anything. It gave us the gel because it knew we had injured men. From that point on it never left our side. In the end, it saved us from what Dr. Brennan assured me would have been all but certain death from those mosasaurs. They use that light as needed, but never in a violent way. I don't know who those people are, but I'm not sure that it's a weapon. For that matter, I'm starting to doubt if that craft is even a part of their military."

"That opens up a whole new line of speculation, doesn't it?" said Colton. "So, if I were to advance that line of reasoning one more step, then we might be dealing with a group who is so technologically advanced that they may have moved beyond the need for offensive weaponry."

"You two make my head hurt," said MacKay. "Even if what you are saying is possible, let's say that that's it exactly, I would find that both comforting and absolutely terrifying all in the same breath."

"What is so scary about that?" asked Garrett. "Do you find it frightening that we've possibly fallen in with people who love peace and nonviolent methods?"

"Captain, you've had more training than this. Shangri-la doesn't exist," said MacKay. "You know as well as I do, a blade can cut both ways. What can be used for good can also be used for evil. A tool such as that light, in the wrong hands, could do a great deal of damage. Until we know more, a lot more, we cannot let our guard down for a minute."

"I have to side with MacKay on this one," said Colton. "We really don't have any idea who we are dealing with or what their ultimate plan may be."

"Isn't it possible that they don't have an ultimate plan?" asked Garrett. "I'll get Father Ryan with me and we'll talk about this some more. Couldn't this just be a classic Good Samaritan act of kindness?"

"Captain, it could be, and I hope you're right," said MacKay. "But any group that has tools as advanced as that light, I shudder to think what their weapons would look like."

"On that happy note, who would like some tea?" asked Colton. Looking at MacKay, he added, "And coffee."

They threaded their way to the mess hall and Hezekiah soon had them set up, along with some cookies. "It's a good thing we were resupplied a few days before that wave hit us. We're still going to have to start making plans to somehow supplement our food and water supply."

"Dr. Chudzik mentioned that she's already working on that with Argos and one of Sahir's people," said Garrett. "She's an amazingly brilliant individual."

"Of Meinhard's entire team, I've gotten to know her and Dr. Brennan the best. Frankly, I'm glad they're with us," said MacKay.

Colton was getting ready to weigh in on this when Hezekiah walked over to their table. "Captain MacKay," he said, "I've got Mr. Mercer on the phone for you."

"Be right back," said MacKay, and followed Hezekiah over to the phone. "MacKay here."

"Sir, you are needed on the bridge," said Mercer. "Colton's escort has returned."

"You sound rather tense, Mr. Mercer," said MacKay. "Is there a problem?"

"There might be, sir," said Mercer. "This time it's not alone."

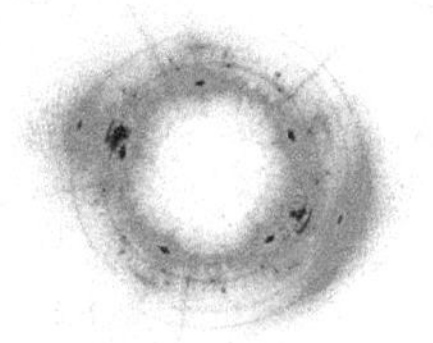

CHAPTER 25

"How long have they been out there?" asked MacKay, looking at the scene before them through binoculars.

"That's a little hard to say. We didn't see them as they approached, and not one of our systems picked them up," said Mercer. "They just sort of appeared, so they were obviously shielding themselves again."

"As before, Mr. Mercer, quietly bring the ship to battle stations."

Mercer turned and nodded at Lieutenant Gallo, who immediately went to work carrying out the order.

"I don't disagree with your order, Captain," said Colton, "but I'm pretty sure that if they had any intention of attacking us, they would have done so by now. They most certainly would have attacked long before they let us see them."

"Has there been any communication?" asked MacKay.

"Using the exact same frequency as the radios that Commander Colton's team carried, we've tried hailing them several times," explained Mercer. "So far there's been no response."

"I'm pretty sure they got the message," said Colton. "It's just that they communicate in an entirely different way. Has Argos picked anything up?"

"I've not yet talked with Sahir, sir," said Mercer. "I'll check with him now."

"Very good, but like before, make sure Sahir keeps Argos reined in," said Colton. "We don't know why they've returned, and I have no intention of our starting anything we can't finish."

Father Ryan entered the bridge and walked over to stand next to MacKay. "Round two, Callum?"

"Round one worked to our advantage, Father," answered MacKay. "Let's hope round two is as beneficial. At this point I have no idea what to make of all this."

Trying to put aside the strong feelings of apprehension that ran through each of them, the scene across from them, the crafts hovering above the shoreline, was rather impressive. The craft that had guided Colton's team back to safety had returned and was hovering over the beach in almost the same spot as it had been before. But this time it was flanked by several other craft. Hovering much higher up in the sky were seven dark blue spheres in a broad V-shaped formation. Each of the spheres looked to be at least three hundred feet in diameter, if not larger.

The spheres were slowly rotating, but you had to look closely as their movement was almost imperceptible. While they didn't give off anywhere near as brilliant of a light as the egg-shaped craft, each of them was encased by a soft, bluish light. Outside of that, there was absolutely no movement from any of them. They almost appeared to have been painted on the sky.

"Mr. Colton," said Mercer, "I have Sahir on the line, but at this point he doesn't have much to report."

Colton nodded and reached for the phone. "I really didn't expect him to," said Colton. "Mr. Sahir, is Argos picking up anything that we can use?"

"Not really," said Sahir. "I seriously doubt the information it has been able to pull is all that accurate. We know all too well their capability to shield themselves."

"I understand, but go ahead and tell me about the information Argos has given you," said Colton.

"The spheres appear to be solid balls of metal with no evidence of any kind of propulsion system. Based on what we've been able to determine, they're simply floating in the sky," said Sahir. "I say metal, but in truth, Argos hasn't been able to determine what they're made of. Also, please know that none of us believe that these things are solid objects. As with the first craft that saved you and your team, we haven't been able to determine the source of energy they're using, but once again the energy level readings we are getting are extraordinarily high."

"Very good," said Colton. "I'll be back with you shortly."

"Did Sahir have anything new to report?" asked MacKay.

"Not really," said Colton. "Captain, I'd like to suggest that the four of us adjourn to your conference room. I also think it would be good to have Captain Garrett and Sahir join us, along with Drs. Meinhard, Chudzik, and Brennan."

"Very well," said MacKay. "Lieutenant Gallo, you have the bridge. If those things move so much as an inch, come get me. Briggs, please have Dr. Meinhard, Dr. Brennan, and Dr. Chudzik join us."

"Aye, aye, sir," said Briggs.

Father Ryan and Mercer followed MacKay and Colton as they left the bridge. Although the *Eclipse* had not yet been threatened in any way, the potential for things to turn very violent, very fast was a definite possibility. The *Eclipse* was clearly outnumbered, and most probably, outgunned. If anything was to happen, and the *Eclipse* was lost, the crew would find themselves stranded on the beach. In that event, their survival would be measured in days, if not hours.

It wasn't long before they were all gathered in the conference room and Colton closed the doors. "As we have no idea how much time we have, I want to keep this little meeting moving along. If you'll remember, Captain Garrett and I shared with you our experiences in the cave. One of the most significant things we discovered was that the cave blocked the influence of the light that the craft projects. The calming effect couldn't reach us. Whether it was merely the density of the rock, or some specific mineral running through the walls of the cave, we probably will never know. The good news was that it demonstrated to us that they do have limitations. That is why I've brought us here to talk."

"So, because this room is encased in steel, you believe it will keep them from eavesdropping," said Mr. Mercer.

"That is one of my goals," said Colton. "The other one, though, is more significant. The light from the larger craft has a very calming effect on just about everything it comes in contact with. I know it does with us. Therefore, on the off chance they do attack, whoever is in command should operate out of this room, or, if they can get there, to where Argos is housed. That's probably the most shielded area on the entire ship. It will not be helpful to any of us if the person in command of the ship, and our defenses, is feeling so relaxed that they want to take a nap."

"Your point is well taken, Commander," said MacKay. "Nodding off while under attack would prove to be embarrassing when it came time to write up the report."

"Agreed," said Colton. "So, let's get some general housekeeping items out of the way. If I'm killed, or seriously wounded, command will fall to Captain MacKay, and then Lieutenant Commander Mercer. Security on board the *Eclipse*, and especially for all shore parties, will be directed by Captain Garrett, then Lieutenant Tanner."

Dr. Meinhard's face had gone pale with traces of sweat appearing across his brow. "Then it's as bad as I thought. They've come back to kill us, haven't they? What are you not telling us?"

"No, Doctor," said Colton, "that is not what I'm saying in any way, shape, or form. We'll get to why they've returned in just a moment. All I'm doing is laying out the hierarchy of command in the event, unlikely as it may be, that the worst case should happen."

Father Ryan did his best to comfort Dr. Meinhard. "Doctor, I'm sure you'll agree these are extraordinary circumstances. So, it is standard operating procedure to make sure everyone knows who's on first, so to speak, and what their responsibilities will be."

"Thank you, Father," said Dr. Chudzik. "That it is most reassuring."

"Let's get to it," said Colton. "We know very little about these people or what they want. As Dr. Meinhard has suggested, they may be here to attack us, but that is highly unlikely. From a military perspective, their ability to shield their presence gives them a distinct edge over us. Having failed to take full advantage of that ability, it indicates to me that their intentions are not hostile."

"Rather than preparing to attack, this may be their way of taking a defensive posture of sorts," offered Garrett. "They know we're vulnerable and took casualties the last time we ventured into the jungle. Their 'John Wayne,' so to speak, arrived just in the nick of time to pull our butts out of the fire. It may be something they're not willing to do again."

"You're a John Wayne fan?" asked Mercer.

"I had no choice in the matter," said Garrett. "Growing up, it's all my father watched; the same movies, repeatedly. I actually know most of the lines from *The Quiet Man*. That was my favorite."

"Captain, you and Mr. Mercer can pick this up over some popcorn some other time," growled MacKay. "Please, elaborate on your point."

"Yes sir," said Garrett. "Following this line of reasoning, there are two possibilities that come to mind. The first would be that they don't want us to go back into the jungle again, and the reinforcements are here to help keep that from happening. The other possibility is a little more ominous. We were flat-out lucky to have survived our first trip, and had we been left to our own devices, I wouldn't be talking with you now. As we discussed during the briefing that laid out for us why we believe that we are now on Earth in the Cretaceous period, we told you of creatures we saw that have never been reported as having lived during that time."

"Yes, but Captain," said Dr. Brennan, "if you'll remember, we discussed that. As sure as I'm sitting here, there are probably a plethora of creatures that lived during the Cretaceous period that have never been discovered, and frankly, never will be."

"Yes, Doctor, I understand, which brings me to my second point," said Garrett. "What if they've returned not to threaten us, or to keep us from going back into the jungle, but to take up a defensive posture against something else that lives out there? Something that we have no idea even exists. From the moment we left the beach, we were flying blind. As with all scouting expeditions, we led with our chin. What if we inadvertently pissed off something, or some things, that may very well be grouping together at this very moment to come and finish us off?"

"Now I'm sorry I pressed her for details," said MacKay, sighing deeply and leaning back in his chair. "I hadn't thought about anything even remotely close to that. Well, here's one more reason why I'm going to need Dr. Severin's help getting some sleep tonight."

"Captain Garrett, thank you, you've given us a very valid possibility," said Colton. "Anyone else want to venture an opinion before I give you what I'm thinking?"

Dr. Brennan had leaned over and had been whispering back and forth with Father Ryan. As the room suddenly went quiet, all eyes turned towards them. "We have something, Commander," said Father Ryan, speaking for the two of them. "What if they've returned simply out of curiosity?"

Colton smiled at him. "That's the same line of thought that I have. Father, please, elaborate."

"Dr. Brennan and I believe that their return may be to learn more about us," said Father Ryan. "What if we're the first Americans they've ever run across?"

"For that matter, what if we're the first humans they've ever run across?" added Dr. Brennan. "We are the anomaly here, not necessarily them. Humans didn't exist sixty-five million years ago. Their return could simply be a quest for knowledge, to get a better look at us under less trying conditions."

"That's exactly the direction I'm leaning in," said Colton. "When that craft was leading us back to the ship, it wasn't until we'd almost reached the beach that a terrible thought crossed my mind. How will they respond to the *Eclipse*? Will they see it as a research vessel or a ship of war? While I now fully believe that they were already aware of the *Eclipse*, they may have come back to get a better understanding of who we are and why we're here."

"Well, if that's the case, they're going to be sorely disappointed," said Mercer. "We don't know why we're here."

"Okay, that could make sense. They want to learn more about us," said MacKay, "but then, who are they? Of all the fossils that I've ever seen, I don't recall any that came anywhere close to looking like that craft hovering out there over the beach."

"Sir, I doubt you're going to like my response to that," said Sahir, "but this argument has been going on for decades, if not longer. Many people believe that there is life on other planets, intelligent life. Even the Church has accepted that possibility. Isn't that right, Father? Many believe that Earth was visited by extraterrestrials ages ago. It's just a theory, but based on all of this, I'd say that theory is suddenly looking better and better."

"I'm curious, Father," said Meinhard. "What is the Church's position on extraterrestrial life? Has it finally caught up with the twenty-first century, taking progressive steps forward, or is it still mired down in ancient doctrine?"

It didn't appear that Father Ryan even heard the demeaning tone laced through Meinhard's remark. "Where the Church is concerned, we believe that God created the entire universe. Therefore, when intelligent life is found elsewhere, we would welcome them as God's creatures."

"Oh please, Father, come off it," said Meinhard. "The discovery of intelligent life on other planets would threaten the very foundation that Rome has based all its doctrines and teachings on."

"Oh, quite the contrary, Doctor," said Father Ryan. "It would actually speak to the diversity and creativity of His creation. Many questions along this line have been posed to me before, and I've given it a fair amount of thought. The question that I find to be the most intriguing in all of this is, what would they look like? The Bible teaches us that humans were created in God's image. Will we find that that image of God is consistent across the universe?"

"Mr. Sahir," said Colton, "if we are right, and they are curious about us, then Argos is going to attract a lot of attention. The amount of information that Argos contains, as well as some of its unique capabilities, is not something we want to fall into the wrong hands. How hard is it to just turn Argos off?"

Before Sahir could answer, Meinhard was on his feet, his face beet red. "Turn Argos off?" he bellowed. "That makes no sense at all! Argos is the best chance we have of defeating these people. Rather than turning him off, we should be using him to plot the best way of blowing those things out of the sky! We need to show them that we will not be intimidated!"

"Dr. Meinhard, sit down," said Colton, his voice steady, but cold, his eyes glaring at the scientist.

Meinhard frantically looked around the room. "Are you people hearing this? This man wants us to commit suicide by turning off the best weapon we have to defend ourselves! Or perhaps he's doing this so we'll have to surrender. Think about it! Do any of us really know all that went on out there in that jungle?"

"Mr. Mercer, please escort Dr. Meinhard to his quarters and see to it that he stays there," said Colton.

Coming to her feet as well, Garrett said, "That won't be necessary." She walked over and opened one of the conference room's doors. Lieutenant Tanner stepped in. "I didn't know whether or not we might need Lieutenant Tanner during our meeting. I'm sure he'll be happy to help Dr. Meinhard back below decks."

"Thank you, Captain," said Colton. "Lieutenant Tanner, Dr. Meinhard is restricted to quarters. Put two men on his door to ensure that he stays there."

Tanner walked over to Meinhard, took his arm, and none too gently started to pull him out of the room. Meinhard tried breaking away from Tanner's grip, but he wasn't anywhere near strong enough to get away from him. "You can't do this! I'm a civilian guest on this ship. You'll all pay for this, I promise you! I'll report you to the admiral!"

"Dr. Meinhard, if you insist on continuing to try and break away from me," said Tanner, "this will not be a pleasant experience for you." Garrett shut the door behind them.

"Commander Colton," said Dr. Chudzik, "I apologize for Dr. Meinhard's outburst. He's a brilliant man, but the stress has simply been too much for him. This will pass, and I do hope you will not hold this against him."

"I appreciate that, Doctor, but there's no reason to apologize," said Colton. "This has been hard on all of us, and at times like this, none of us are at our best." Looking at Sahir, Colton said, "So Lieutenant, back to my question, what does it take to turn Argos off?"

"That is not easy to do," said Sahir. "There's a process we follow so that we won't damage it. There are also defenses built in so that Argos can defend itself from being tampered with."

"These people, whoever or whatever they are," said Colton, "are way out in front of us technologically. That craft sitting off to port, the light, the gel, the way they communicate, pick one, all of it is miles in front of anything we have. While I don't expect to be boarded, I do expect them to have some way of thoroughly scanning us. My concern is that they might successfully hack into Argos. The consequences of that is something I don't even want to consider. If you wanted to invade our dimension, Flight 19 isn't much help. The humans on this ship, although brilliant, only know so much. But Argos is the encyclopedia, atlas, and *Farmers' Almanac* all wrapped in one."

"Very good, sir," said Sahir. "I understand and agree with you. Request permission to leave now and get that process started. Argos will actually be able to help with this."

Before Colton could answer him, the intercom in the center of the table buzzed. MacKay hit the button. "Yes, Lieutenant Gallo, what is it?"

"Sir, they're on the move. You better get in here."

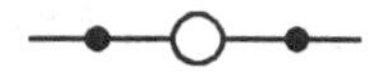

They made it back to the bridge in time to see most of what was happening. Mercer got with Gallo and they began to ready the weapons systems. MacKay, Colton, and Father Ryan watched as the craft that had been hovering over the beach came to a halt, taking a new position halfway between the *Eclipse* and the shore. The spheres remained motionless, holding their position.

"What do you think it's doing?" asked MacKay.

"Mr. Gallo," said Colton, "when the craft started moving towards us, would you say it moved pretty quickly then stopped, or was it slow and methodical?"

"It moved rather slowly, sir," answered Gallo.

MacKay and Colton nodded at each other. "They want to talk," said MacKay.

Taking the binoculars from around his neck, Colton said, "They already know who I am. As they've been kind enough to make the first move, I'm going to reciprocate and follow their example.""What do you plan on doing?" asked MacKay.

"I want them to be able to clearly see me. If we're right, it'll be easier to communicate with me if I'm standing out in the open. So, I'm going to stand at the bow of the ship, in plain sight. Let's just hope they're happy to see me."

Not two minutes after Colton left the bridge, Dr. Severin joined them. "Surprised to see you up here, Doctor. Everything all right in sick bay?" asked MacKay.

"Oh yes, everything's going very well," answered Dr. Severin. "I just thought I'd come up here and see for myself what all the excitement's about."

"Well, there you have it," said MacKay. "Colton's mystery benefactors."

Severin stared at the eight craft arrayed in front of him. "Do we have any idea who they are?"

"It's worse than that, Doctor," said MacKay. "At this point we don't know who, or possibly what they are."

"It's oddly exciting," said Father Ryan. "I find myself being as curious as I am terrified. In addition to everything else we've faced, this has been the most stressful for the crew to take in. It's been especially hard on our civilian guests. I'm afraid Dr. Meinhard is having a particularly hard time wrapping his mind around this."

"Lieutenant Tanner suggested that I might stop by his cabin and check in on him," said Dr. Severin. "We spent a couple of minutes chatting, and I'm happy to report that he's doing much better now. In fact, he's quite relaxed."

"Wow, now I am impressed," said Mercer. "A doctor who not only makes cabin calls, but with just one short visit, manages to successfully calm down a guy who has crossed the line into hysteria."

"That's very kind of you, Mr. Mercer," said Dr. Severin, staring out the window. "We sedated him."

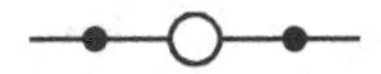

Colton stood in the center of the bow. He turned around a couple of times to clearly show that he was not wearing any weapons. The egg-shaped craft hovered no more than a hundred feet over the water, and less than fifty yards away from him. As always, it appeared motionless, with the exception of the near-blinding light emanating from the top of the craft.

He tried to think of a way to initiate the conversation. Clearly, he didn't want this to turn into a staring contest because he knew who would blink first.

Doing the best he could to clear his mind, Colton shut his eyes and concentrated on the craft. Over and over again, in his mind, he kept repeating, *We want to talk with you.* But as hard as he tried, other thoughts kept getting in the way. What if Meinhard was right? What if the calm vision had been induced by hitting the "sweet spot" for religion and faith in his brain? What if his fears were right and this was an experiment? He shook his head, doing his level best to keep his focus where it needed to be.

Then it happened. As before, everything changed, and he found himself surrounded by a soft, undulating blue light. He was at peace in a world that had become very quiet. Although the words were not spoken, he could hear in his mind the same voice telling him that he was safe; they would continue to protect him, they were here to help. Knowing what to expect, the same animated man soon appeared and stood directly in front of him.

We are friends. We will examine you. We are friends. Do not be alarmed.

Before Colton could respond, he felt the breeze from the ocean and could faintly hear other voices. The bluish light was gone, and he looked around him. Mr. Mercer was now standing next to him with two marines on either side.

"MacKay wanted us here in case you needed help," said Mercer. "Must have been a good conversation. You're smiling from ear to ear."

"Yeah, guess I am," said Colton. "I think we're okay, but something is about to happen, and we need to make sure everyone is ready."

Taking his radio from his belt, he hit the button and asked for MacKay.

"I'm here, Commander," said MacKay. "What did they say?"

"Like before, they assured me that they are friends," said Colton. "That said, they also said they're going to examine us."

"What does that mean?" asked MacKay.

"No idea, Captain, but I would suggest we alert the crew and tell them to stand down and let it happen," said Colton. "I doubt we could stop what's coming next even if we wanted to. The puppy doesn't have to bite the vet."

It was then that four of the spheres broke formation. Two of them shot towards the bow and two raced towards the stern. It happened so quickly there really wasn't any time to respond. The other three spheres advanced, taking up position just above the egg-shaped craft. Then the light from the four spheres that had the *Eclipse* hemmed in started to grow in its intensity. Slowly the light made its way across the ship, covering it from stem to stern.

"Captain, you still there?" asked Colton.

"I am," said MacKay, his voice not nearly as tense as before.

"I trust you're seeing this," said Colton.

"Oh yes, I am," said MacKay. "Briggs and Gallo were able to get the word out to everyone. Do you know what they're doing?"

"My guess is that this is their way of examining us," said Colton. "In all probability, everything and everyone on this ship is being scanned. Let's just hope that Sahir took the proper precautions."

"I agree," said MacKay, "but it's hard to get too worked up over things when you're feeling this relaxed. The ability this light has to influence how one feels could really put a serious dent into the booze and drug trade."

It didn't take long before the *Eclipse* was completely covered by the light. After just a few moments, it began to brighten, and then returned to normal. Brightened, and then returned to normal, again and again, creating an odd pulsating sensation. This went on for almost twenty minutes, then stopped abruptly. The blue light completely disappeared.

The four spheres surrounding the *Eclipse* quickly flew back to the beach, followed by the three that had been hovering above the egg-shaped craft. Colton could only imagine the frantic activity on the bridge as MacKay went through the paces of having his ship checked out, department by department.

Within minutes his radio buzzed, and Colton answered it, "Colton here. How'd we do?"

"Everything seems to be functioning properly," said MacKay. "No damage to any personnel or systems. Not sure what they're looking for, but let's hope we get a passing grade."

"What about Sahir?" asked Colton. "Did Argos pass out from fright?"

"Quite the opposite," said MacKay. "Sahir is still running a couple of programs, but according to Argos the experience was quite pleasant and not intrusive in any way. Apparently, as computer to computer goes, they were able to play well together."

"You find that as troubling as I do?" asked Colton.

"I sure as hell do," growled MacKay.

"I'm pretty sure they already knew the *Eclipse* is a warship," said Colton. "Let's be honest, we weren't exactly throwing rocks at those dinosaurs when they first found us. So, it does beg the question as to what they were actually looking for, and what, to them, might be considered dangerous."

"Mr. Gallo suggested that they may . . ."

Suddenly the blue communications beam once again engulfed Colton's head and shoulders and all the tension drained away from him. Again, through the soft blue light, the reassurances were given. They are their friends. They are there to keep them safe. This mantra was repeated several times. Soon the animated man reappeared, his expression the same artificial smile.

We wish to commune with your healer and your God man. We would do so in ten of your minutes.

The session ended, and this time Colton was so relaxed that he staggered back a step. Fortunately, a marine was there to catch him.

"Are you all right?" asked Mercer.

Colton gave it a moment to retain his composure, then said, "We need to get Father Ryan and Dr. Severin here with me as quickly as we can."

Mercer frowned at this and said, "Why? What's going on?"

Colton shook his head. "No idea. They must be getting bored with me. They said they want to talk with our healer and our God man. They're giving us ten minutes to get them out here."

"Do you think it'll be safe for them?" asked Mercer.

"Yes, I think so," said Colton. "Of course, on the other hand, what options do we really have?"

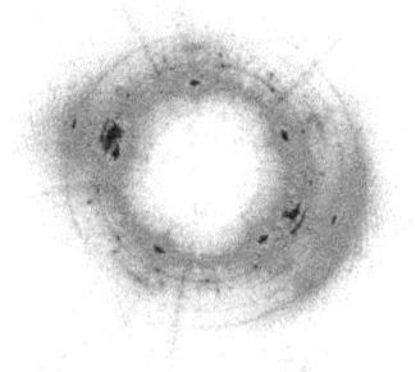

CHAPTER 26

"I don't like the sound of this," said MacKay. "What could they have found that would lead them to want to talk with Father Ryan and Dr. Severin?"

"For all we know it doesn't have anything to do with what they may or may not have found," said Colton. "Many cultures hold witchdoctors, or shamans, in high esteem. They're obviously interested in our equivalent and want to talk to them. If this is what it takes to finally open up communications, then I'm all for it."

"I just hate putting those two at risk," said MacKay.

Colton gave that some thought. "We could try to have two of the crew pose as Father Ryan and Severin, but I'm not sure we want to start lying to these people. Deception is a bad foundation to build on when entering into a new relationship."

"Very well, Commander, it's your show," said MacKay. "They're on their way."

"What exactly happens when that light hits you?" asked Mercer while they waited on Father Ryan and Dr. Severin.

"It's like I first described it to you and Captain MacKay and it hasn't varied at all," said Colton. "All at once I'm completely removed from my surroundings, I'm at peace with the world, and am about as relaxed as a man can get. If it's nothing more than their interrogation technique, then I have to say I'm all for it. Believe me, I've experienced much worse."

Escorted by two more marines, Father Ryan and Dr. Severin joined Colton and Mr. Mercer out on the bow. "I understand our presence has been requested," said Father Ryan.

"It has," said Colton, smiling at the two men. "They asked for our healer and our God man. Your names came to mind."

"Any idea why they want to talk to us?" asked Severin.

"No, Doctor, I really don't, but then I also don't believe you have anything to worry about," said Colton. "All of our contact with them so far has been positive. Hopefully, the two of you will be able to communicate with them in far more depth than I have. It would be nice to learn who we're dealing with."

"Voices from a bright, heavenly light," muttered Father Ryan. " 'Have no fear.' "

"What was that, Father?" asked Mercer.

"Nothing," said Father Ryan. "I was thinking of the visions, the dreams, I've been having." Looking at Colton, he said, "Tell me again. What's it like when they talk with you?"

Before Colton could answer, lights shot from the egg-shaped craft, encompassing all three men. They stood there, completely still, not moving at all. After ten minutes had passed, Mercer began to get worried. "How long do we let this go on, Captain?" he said into his radio.

"For as long as it takes, Mr. Mercer. Like Colton, I don't think this was a mistake, but even if we wanted to stop it, I wouldn't know how to begin. I'm also concerned that our interfering might end up hurting our own men."

The time continued to drag on; each minute seemed longer than the one before it. Finally, after twenty-one minutes, the light went away and all three men slightly staggered. Father Ryan had the most trouble getting his balance back.

Mercer couldn't believe the looks on their faces. All three of them were beaming, happy, and relaxed. Colton, being the most used to it, took his radio and called MacKay. "Captain, we need to meet in your conference room."

"Are you all right?" asked MacKay.

"Yes sir, we all are, but we need to talk," said Colton. "Please ask Captain Garrett, Mr. Sahir, Dr. Chudzik, and Dr. Brennan to join us. We have a great deal to go over."

The atmosphere in the conference room was filled with a fine mixture of apprehension and anticipation. They were all anxious to find out what they had learned. Hezekiah brought up trays of sandwiches and plenty of coffee. He also brought Colton a large, black tea.

Colton remained standing, ready to address the team. He was tired. As positive as the communications had been, he felt drained. He really appreciated the hot tea he was sipping. "Dr. Severin's communication with them is perhaps the most pressing, so I'll let him begin. But I'd first like to get a couple of items out of the way. We have not learned who they are, where they come from, or why they're helping us. However, the good news is that everything that was communicated to us was positive. Dr. Severin?"

Severin stayed seated as he looked around the table. "My communication with them was unique in that I didn't see the same man that Commander Colton and Father Ryan saw. A man and a woman spoke to me. Both of them were wearing long, red-colored cloaks that buttoned at the neck. They asked me several questions regarding Private Lockridge, as well as the rest of the team that had been ashore."

"There isn't much about us they don't know, is there?" said MacKay, looking at Colton.

"No, there's not," said Colton. "But, oddly, at least at this point, I think it works in our favor. They seem to know our needs, and frankly, our inability to survive here without some kind of help. Technologically, I think they know that we don't pose a threat."

"They asked permission to give us more in the way of medicines," Dr. Severin continued. "They talked with me at some length about what each medicine does and how to apply it. I told them that I was concerned that I might not remember everything they were telling me. They promised that there would be written instructions included, and get this, they'd be in English."

"Included in what?" asked MacKay.

"They asked for our permission to deliver this medicine and leave it on the bow," said Dr. Severin. "I let them know that we would most graciously accept their help, but that I did need to first check with you, Captain."

MacKay took a deep breath and let it out. "Hard not to accept such an offer, but my concern is that this means they'll be boarding us."

"Not necessarily, Captain," said Colton. Once again he told of how the gel was first given to them in the jungle. "We never saw them. A small sphere, much smaller than the spheres that just scanned us, descended to the ground and left the gel behind. It didn't take long and wasn't threatening in any way."

"How are you supposed to signal our acceptance of this?" asked MacKay.

"I'm to return to the bow. When they see me standing there, alone, they'll bring the medicine over to us."

"Anyone have any objections?" asked MacKay. "This goes against every instinct in my body, and normally I would never allow this, but based on what Dr. Severin has shared with me, we are in need of the medication."

"Also," said Sahir, "it is important to note that we have not been able to reverse engineer the gel. If we want more of it, they're our only source."

"Very well," said MacKay. "Doctor, go ahead and signal them. However, take Lieutenant Tanner with you; just have him stay out of sight."

"Shall I go now, Captain?" asked Severin.

MacKay looked at Colton. "Your thoughts, Commander?"

"By all means," answered Colton. "We need that medicine. Plus, I'm anxious to see what else they plan to give to us other than just more of the gel."

Severin nodded and left the conference room. Colton stood back up. He kept his head down, staring at the table, almost unsure how to begin. Not knowing what to say was highly unusual for Brett Colton.

"Father, may I present this to the team, or would you like to?" asked Colton.

"No," said Father Ryan. "I think it would be best coming from you."

"Okay, but keep me on track," said Colton. "They have asked that Father Ryan and I leave the *Eclipse* and travel to where they live. There are several things they'd like to discuss with us and feel that face-to-face communication would achieve the best results. I'm trying to quote them as accurately as I can."

"Face-to-face communication," said Mr. Mercer. "Guess it's encouraging to learn they have faces."

"Where is this place that they want the two of you to go to, and how are you supposed to get there?" asked MacKay.

"We don't know," said Colton. "Apparently it is some distance from here. As to how we'll get there, we are to go on foot, through the jungle."

"That's suicide," said Garrett. "You've been there; you won't last a day."

"Captain Garrett," said Father Ryan, "neither I nor Commander Colton has any intention of committing suicide. We expressed our concerns over this and were assured that we would be safely escorted the entire way."

"They have asked if we can be dropped off on the beach and head inland as we did before," said Colton. "We'll be gone for several days."

"I'm not a military man, and I'm certainly not as strong-minded as Dr. Meinhard, but I don't like the sound of this," said Dr. Brennan. "The least little thing goes wrong with your escort and you'll be lost."

"Dr. Brennan, unless I miss my guess, I believe Mr. Colton is holding back on us," said MacKay. "We don't yet have the full story, do we, Commander?"

"As it turns out, I was saving the best for last," said Colton.

At that point, the intercom buzzed and MacKay answered it. "Sir, Lieutenant Gallo here. One of the spheres is heading towards the *Eclipse*. Dr. Severin is waiting on the bow to greet them. Is there anything else we should be doing?"

"No, Lieutenant," said MacKay. "Closely monitor the situation and be ready. If anything starts to look like this delivery of theirs is not going the way it should, call me."

"You were about to elaborate on the rest of your talk with them," said Garrett.

"They want to discuss our leaving the *Eclipse* and resettling in an area that they have set aside for us. It is an area where we could live in safety, we would have plenty of food and water, and when needed, have access to medical facilities."

"Such a kind, innocent, and disarming way to take us down," said Garrett. "They sound like a bunch of politicians. Promise everything under the sun to get what they want and then leave you high and dry once they've achieved their goal."

"And what goal would that be?" asked Sahir.

"I'll answer that for her," said Colton. "There's a possibility that they want the *Eclipse*. It's either that, or we simply pose too great of a threat to them having control of such a ship. By getting us to agree to their plan, they're able to neutralize us."

"Knew it had to be too good to be true," said MacKay. "There had to be a catch for all the help they've been giving us. At least now we know what they're after."

"Callum, I'm not so sure I agree with you," said Father Ryan. "All that they have offered to us, in many ways, does make sense. In time, we will run out of food and water. We'll run out of medicine, ammunition, and all the other supplies we carry on this ship. We can certainly try to forage off the land, but how many of our people will we lose in the process? Simply through attrition alone, without their help, we will ultimately perish."

"Father Ryan, don't you think I haven't thought of all those things? I'm not denying any of them, but do you really expect me to just hand over the *Eclipse* to these people?" asked MacKay, his frustration and anger just below the surface.

"No, we do not," said Colton, "which is why I agreed to go with them. Father Ryan will need to make his own decisions, but I've made mine. Under no circumstances do I intend to surrender this ship. That said, we are presently in no position to bargain either. Right or wrong, for better or worse, they are offering to help us. For the time being, I plan to take full advantage of that help."

"Then what is your plan, Commander?" asked Mercer.

"As I said, I plan to go with them," said Colton.

"As will I," said Father Ryan.

Colton smiled at the priest. "My plan is to go and find out all that I can. I will cooperate and make them believe that we are seriously considering this entire, crazy offer of theirs. Once I've learned who they are, what they're doing here, and what they're weaknesses are, then we'll be better positioned to figure out what to do next."

MacKay nodded his head. "All things considered, we really don't have much in the way of choices. This does seem to be our best opportunity of finding out exactly what we're up against."

"May I ask what I think is a rather obvious question?" asked Father Ryan. "This may be a poor analogy, but it's all I can come up with at the moment. Let's say a canoe full of Indians came paddling up, just off our coast. We approach them in an aircraft carrier and offer to help get them to safety. All they would have to do is leave their canoe behind and come aboard our ship. Would we be sincere in our motives, or would we actually be trying to trick them in order to get our hands on their canoe? From my seat in the stands, this whole discussion we're having is ridiculous! These people are so far ahead of us technologically speaking that I seriously doubt they have any interest at all in getting their hands on the *Eclipse*."

"Reluctantly I have to agree with Father Ryan," said Dr. Brennan. "To Commander Colton's point, we need to learn more about who we are dealing with, but we also desperately need their help. I have no doubt there is more to this than we understand. However, I don't think that it's a good idea to start jumping to conclusions until we have more information."

"Father," said MacKay, "with or without an escort, this will be a very hard and dangerous trip. I'm trying to understand why you are so set on going."

"Because they said they want to learn more about our God," said Father Ryan. "They also said that they have more of our kind living with them and that those people need whatever comfort I can provide. If, like us, there are more humans stranded in this terrible place, I can't turn my back on them."

MacKay looked at Colton. "He's giving it to you straight," said Colton. "That's exactly what they said."

"Other humans?" asked MacKay.

"I'm fairly sure that's what they mean by 'your kind,' " answered Father Ryan. "I don't think they mean Americans. It's possible that they could be referring to survivors from Flight 19. They might be one of many."

MacKay looked at Father Ryan for a couple of moments. "Columbus's men were said to have warned him against sailing off the edge of the world, not too far from the spot we apparently did so."

The room went totally silent. Finally, MacKay looked at Colton and asked, "When do you leave?"

"Daybreak," said Colton. "They've asked us to be ready to depart first thing tomorrow morning."

"Then we need to get to work immediately," said MacKay. "There is much to do and very little time to get it done."

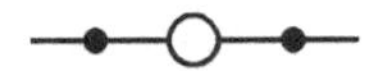

Lieutenant Tanner and five marines were standing by, ready to take Colton and Father Ryan over to the beach. The egg-shaped craft had stayed in place, hovering above them. Hatfield kept a close eye on his monitors, constantly scanning for the creatures that had come at them before. He gave them the all clear. Like the last time, the light from the craft had chased all of the marine life away from them.

"If they catch on to what you're doing," said Garrett, "they'll never let you go."

Colton smiled at her. "Are you kidding? If they catch on, there's a good chance they'll kill us both. Fortunately, this is not the first time I've done this sort of thing. Let's just hope that my plan, as meager as it may be, works."

"Please be careful, Brett," said Garrett, lightly touching his arm. "I'd hate to have to go back into that jungle and risk my men just to save some half-crazy navy swab."

"Keep saying sweet nothings like that and I may tear up," said Colton. Stepping in closer to her, he looked deeply into her eyes. "I'll be back, I promise."

MacKay and Mercer shook hands with both men and wished them luck. MacKay pulled Colton aside and slipped him a flask. "It's not regulation, but it may come in handy. If nothing else, Father Ryan can use it for communion."

With that, Colton stepped into the launch they shoved off. The sea was pretty choppy, but Tanner did a good job holding his course. Colton looked over at Father Ryan. The priest had a sour look on his face. "Worried, Father?"

"No, trying to keep from throwing up," growled Father Ryan. "I hate these small boats."

The trip to the beach, not surprisingly, was uneventful. Colton and Father Ryan put on their backpacks, picked up their rifles, and prepared to head out. Lieutenant Tanner saluted both of them. "Good luck, sir! You need us for anything, we'll come running."

"We'll hold you to that, Lieutenant," said Colton.

As the launch pulled away from the beach, Colton and Father Ryan waved goodbye to the *Eclipse,* turned and headed into the jungle. For Colton, it seemed like old times. The egg-shaped craft that had been his escort out of the jungle was with them, hovering just above the treetops, leading the way.

In regard to Father Ryan, Colton realized how difficult all of this was going to be for him. He admired the man's courage and his strength of character. Navy officer or not, this was far from what he'd been trained to do.

At first, they followed the same trail he and his team had hacked out of the jungle on their first foray. The trail was reasonably easy to follow, and they soon came to the game trail. Colton asked Father Ryan if he wanted to rest, but he declined. "I'm okay. Let's get a little further down the trail. I'm not in as bad of shape as you think I am."

About an hour later they came to the stream. Colton pointed downstream at the lizard-eating flower, making sure that Father Ryan got a good look at it. There may be other streams to cross, and it was something they would need to keep an eye out for. The light from the craft above them increased in intensity and they watched as the flower closed up, pulling its many leaves and stems in around it. Directly in front of them the stream erupted and something large took off, leaving a sizable wake as it left.

"Do you have any idea what that was?" asked Father Ryan, his face turning pale.

"That's one of those questions you really don't want an answer to," said Colton. "Let's go ahead and cross now that our friend has cleared away all the nasties. We'll rest on the other side."

It took a little bit of coaxing to get Father Ryan to step into the stream and wade across, but they were soon on the other side, climbing up the muddy bank. Taking off their backpacks, they dropped down onto the trail to rest and drink some much-needed water.

"Why can't they just fly us there?" asked Father Ryan.

"I don't think it's a craft with people in it," Colton replied. "Unless I miss my guess, I think it's robotically controlled."

Looking around, Colton noticed that he hadn't heard or seen any signs of wildlife. Also, no horrible smells this time. Maybe the animal life was giving them a wide berth after all.

"There was something you said back on the ship that I've been meaning to ask you about," said Colton. "For whatever reason, I haven't been able to get it out of my mind."

Father Ryan gave him a slightly puzzled look. "You have my full attention, Commander. What did I say that made such a lasting impact on you?"

"You said something about voices coming from a heavenly light," said Colton. "And then you said, 'Have no fear,' as if you were quoting someone. Mercer heard it too. He asked you about it, but you didn't seem to want to answer him. You're not the kind of guy who says things because he likes to hear the sound of his own voice. What were you talking about?"

Father Ryan looked at Colton as if deliberating his response. He then looked down, slightly nodding his head, having come to a decision. "Before that wave, or whatever it was, brought us to this place, I started to have what I thought were very vivid dreams. I now know they were visions."

"What were they about?" asked Colton.

"They were rather detailed, and I'm ashamed to say, hit me pretty hard."

"Did something bad happen in these visions?" asked Colton. "I'm not an expert on visions, but it's my understanding that correctly interpreting them is very challenging. It might be helpful if you talked about it."

"These visions leave little room for doubt. Look, we have a long trip in front of us, Commander. I'll get into this in a little more detail later today after we've made camp," said Father Ryan. "For now, I'll just say that in the visions, each time, there was an extremely bright light leading me on. But what is even more interesting is that with each vision, I heard a soft, pleasant voice saying to me, 'Have no Fear.' "

"I'm not a very religious man, Father, you know that, but I do believe in God," said Colton. "If that's how the visions start, then it can't be all bad."

Father Ryan smiled at him. "I know. And I'm probably making too much of this, but every single time we've communicated with these people, no matter which one of us it is, they continue to stress over and over again, have no fear. They keep reassuring us not to be frightened of them. I can't help but ask myself, should I have no fear of them, or do they know that our fear of them would be bad for their goals?"

"It's a good question," said Colton. "And you're right, they've said that to me several times, the same with Dr. Severin and Corpsman Payne. Is there something about that phrase that I'm missing?"

Father Ryan gave a small laugh. "No Commander, nothing nefarious. But in the Bible, whenever angels appeared to men, the angel's presence was quite overwhelming. Also, these heavenly bodies would appear in a bright light. Typically, the first thing they would say is, 'Have no fear,' trying to calm and reassure the people they were about to communicate with. I was simply struck by the similarities with that which we are experiencing."

"If you're trying to tell me that we're dealing with angels, that's going to take a great weight off my mind," said Colton.

"No, I'm not saying that," said Father Ryan. "At least not yet. It's just with the visions being so recent and frequent, combined with the dealings we're having with these very advanced beings, I couldn't help but make the comparison."

"You've got me anxious to hear more about these visions," said Colton. "You're not being your usual coy self, Father. You look worried. I'm betting these visions beat any campfire story I've ever heard."

"You of all people shouldn't bet, Commander," said Father Ryan, lying down and using his backpack as a pillow. "We both know how bad of a gambler you are."

Colton wasn't in a hurry to continue onward. As they didn't know where they were going, there was no point in pushing themselves. He knew that the trip would have its hardships, and he wanted to make things as easy as he could for Father Ryan.

Leaning back against a tree, Colton shut his eyes for a moment. He couldn't even begin to imagine what they would find waiting for them at the end of this journey. Considering all of the bizarre and absolutely impossible things that had happened over the last few days, he realized that his imagination simply wasn't up to the task. Besides, they'd find out soon enough.

Glancing over at the stream, he watched a small branch slowly float by. As it made its way downstream, he watched as the huge flower floating on the water started to move, opening its petals and leaves, its stems spreading out through the water. A terrible chill instantly coursed through him as the comprehension of what he was seeing sunk in. This should not be happening. Jumping to his feet, he moved closer to the stream for a better look.

"Something wrong?" asked Father Ryan.

"I'm not sure," said Colton. Looking up into the sky, he couldn't see very much. The mist that had greeted them when they first arrived had returned in full strength, once again blanketing the jungle. A sick, hollow feeling filled his stomach. As best as he could determine, their escort was gone. In the past, it had always been easy to spot, its light being so bright. For whatever reason, it was no longer there.

"What is it, Commander?" asked Father Ryan, now on his feet, standing next to him. "What's going on?"

"Don't ask me why, but our escort has left without us," said Colton. "I don't get it. This doesn't make any sense. There's been at least a dozen times when they could have killed us, or just left us to die. So what changed? Why go to all the trouble to lure us out here?"

Suddenly Father Ryan grabbed Colton's arm and pointed down the trail, his voice just above a whisper. "Commander, what is that thing?"

Not more than thirty paces away, standing directly in the center of the trail, was the same creature that had stalked Colton and Garrett on their return to the ship several days ago. Although Colton really couldn't see any arms or legs, it appeared to be standing erect, less than six feet tall and broad across the middle.

The creature was covered, from top to bottom, with leaves and small vines. Had it not been standing in the middle of the trail, but off to the side, Colton would have thought it was just another plant. It was the first time he'd been able to get a clear look at it. Beneath the leaves he could see small patches of skin, which appeared to be oily and rough, pitted, and cracked in places. Its color constantly shifted with the slightest breeze, changing in tone to blend in with its surroundings.

Father Ryan and Colton stood stock-still, not even daring to reach for their rifles. The sounds of the jungle seemed to intensify as they stood there, staring at the creature. Then, slowly, it began to creep towards them. The air was suddenly filled with a sickly sweet, off-putting odor that Colton guessed was coming from this thing. It filled his nose and mouth, almost causing him to gag.

As it advanced, Colton could see very small, black and brown creatures moving all over it, some falling off as it moved. As soon as they hit the ground, they scampered off into the jungle. They were so fast Colton couldn't tell what they were. They looked like insects, roaches possibly, but too many legs.

Although he didn't know if the creature's intentions were hostile, he wasn't about to take any chances. Colton carefully pulled his pistol with one hand, his radio with the other. "*Eclipse*, this is Colton. Do you read me?"

"We read you, Commander," answered Petty Officer Briggs.

"Let me talk to MacKay," said Colton. "Now."

"MacKay here. What's up, Commander?"

"It appears that our escort has abandoned us. The creature that stalked us on our return is back and is slowly moving towards us."

Colton could hear some muffled conversation and then MacKay's voice was back, loud and clear. "I've just ordered Captain Garrett to the bridge and told her to have her team ready to launch."

"Let's hold off on sending in the marines," said Colton. "I'm going to try something first and see what happens."

Colton slowly raised his pistol above his head, pointing it up into the sky. He glanced at Father Ryan. Although the priest was standing firm, he could see that the blood had drained from his face. Colton said, "Let's see if this will scare it away." With that he fired three shots into the air.

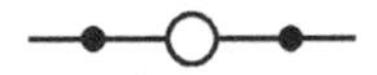

MacKay and many of the crew heard the three shots fired by Colton, but they were quite faint. MacKay looked at Mercer, shaking his head. "Why go to all the trouble to have those two men brought to shore, give us the help we needed so that they'd have safe passage, and then not more than an hour later, turn around and leave them to die?"

Mercer just shook his head, scanning the horizon as best he could. "Lieutenant Gallo, do you have the alien craft on the radar?"

"Yes sir, it's about thirty-five miles from here, heading away in a southwesterly direction at a moderate pace," said Gallo.

Garrett joined them on the bridge. "Captain, my men are ready and standing by. Shall I give them the signal to launch?"

"Hatfield," snapped MacKay, "how do things look in the neighborhood?"

"Not good, sir," replied Hatfield. "I've got two, possibly three bogeys that could pose a serious threat."

"Have your men stand by, Captain," said MacKay. "Colton, what's happening out there?"

"I'm not sure," said Colton. "It's no longer moving towards us. The shots stopped it, but it didn't run away either. We'd be in the middle of a staring contest if it had eyes."

"Captain Garrett's team is ready to launch," said MacKay. "Shall I give them the go?"

"Negative. We're too far in, Captain," answered Colton. "We're already on the far side of the stream. With all that we can hear walking around us, you'd lose at least ten men trying to save two. And that's assuming we'd still be savable. Keep those marines where they are, Captain, that's an order. I'm afraid the numbers are against us."

Looking at Garrett, MacKay said, "Do you know where he is, Captain? Do you believe you could get to them in time?"

"We need to try, no matter what," said Garrett. "Best case, we're probably no more than fifty minutes to an hour away."

MacKay grimaced, tightly gripping the radio. "Commander, what are you planning to do?"

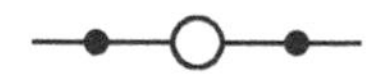

"Darn good question," muttered Colton under his breath. "Father, are you still with me?"

"I am," said Father Ryan. He sounded almost out of breath.

"Good," said Colton. "Now listen to me carefully. The sound from my pistol obviously had very little effect on our visitor. When I give you the word, I want you to go and get your rifle. In your backpack, in the lower, right-hand outside pocket, there's a small flare gun. I want you to get it and bring it to me, understand?"

"I understand," said Father Ryan, crossing himself. "Ready when you are."

Talking back into the radio, Colton said, "Captain, we're going to get our rifles and some of our equipment and start working our way back towards you. Do not launch those boats until I tell you that we're close to the shore."

"What about the stalker?" said MacKay, his voice crackling a little over the radio. "Is it still there?"

"It is," said Colton, "but I don't want to hurt it unless I have to. We're going to . . ."

At that moment, the upper right side of the creature seemed to separate from the body, the appendage slowly raising upwards, extending itself toward Colton. More of the small, insect-looking things fell from it. At the end of the appendage, it appeared to be holding a small blue sphere. Like the crafts that had surrounded the *Eclipse*, it too was encased in the same soft blue light. Suddenly the light burst in its intensity, like the flash from a camera, but many times stronger.

A spilt second later the air seemed to ripple, blurring his vision, again, like before. When his vision cleared, he realized how hopeless their situation had become.

Where the stalker had been standing, there were now dozens of them, all identical to each other. Colton quickly looked around and found that these creatures had them completely surrounded. Taking a step back towards the stream, he glanced over his shoulder. There, on the opposite shore, stood more of the stalkers.

"Captain," said Colton, "the stalker wasn't alone. There must be close to a hundred of them and we are surrounded." The radio went silent. Colton waited for the stalkers to attack. He felt sorry for MacKay, knowing that the man was desperately trying to figure out what to say.

"Colton," MacKay said, "do your best to hang on. Mercer is going to launch two of the armed drones. They'll be over you in just a few minutes. We'll have them make enough noise to scare those things off."

"Good plan," said Colton. "Let's hope it's . . ."

Colton realized that the creature that had first confronted them must be their leader. It once again began to move towards them, keeping its appendage extended. Without warning, from the small, blue sphere, a bright, narrow beam of white light hit Father Ryan in the chest. The priest staggered back, looking as though he was trying to resist the beam, dropping to the ground, unconscious.

"Colton, you broke up. What were you saying?"

"Father Ryan's down," Colton shouted into the radio just before dropping it. His instincts took over, quickly bringing his pistol up, aiming dead center at their leader. At pointblank range, he knew he couldn't miss. *They may get us,* thought Colton, *but they're going to pay a price.*

Before he could pull the trigger, a second beam of light struck him high in his chest. Surprisingly, he didn't feel any pain. Instead, he began to feel his entire body go numb, his legs and arms no longer responding. In a last-gasp effort, he was able to get off two shots, but his arms had already dropped to his side, the bullets harmlessly striking the muddy trail. He felt himself falling. As he hit the ground, he rolled over onto his back.

Staring up at the jungle canopy above him, Colton fought to keep from passing out, but could feel himself steadily slipping away. He didn't hear it approach, but the creature now stood directly over him, the sphere poised to strike again. Then the sphere seemed to vanish into the folds of its skin. A second appendage on the other side of the creature reached up and began to peel off its skin from the top down.

Colton had to be dreaming. It had to be a hallucination; he couldn't believe his eyes. With what he had thought to be its skin now peeled away, he found himself staring into the face of a strangely beautiful, olive-skinned woman. It was the last thing he saw.

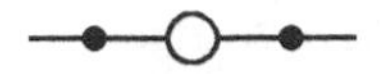

The two shots Colton fired were heard by all of them. "Was that one shot or two?" asked Mercer.

"Colton!" shouted MacKay into the radio. "Colton, come in. Are you all right?"

Silence reigned over the bridge. All of them kept staring at the jungle, hoping for the impossible. MacKay turned to Briggs. "Keep trying to get Colton on the radio."

"Sir, request permission to lead a team ashore to bring back Mr. Colton and Father Ryan," said Garrett. Her face had paled, her eyes brimming with tears.

"Sir, I'm not getting any response," said Briggs.

MacKay bowed his head and stood there. Losing Father Ryan and Colton like this had been so completely unexpected that it hit him hard. It was more than just the pain of losing two of his crew; this was a personal loss. He was also angry at himself. He'd just stood there and listened while his two men were murdered. The pain and frustration were too much to bear.

Looking up at Garrett, he gave one of the hardest orders of his career. "Request denied, Captain," said MacKay. "Have your men stand down."

"Captain, we can't just leave them out there," she nearly shouted! "They could be wounded, unable to help themselves, waiting for us to arrive! Sir, they need our help!"

"That will be all, Captain," snapped MacKay, whirling around to face her. It took all he had but he stopped himself before saying anything he knew he'd regret. Looking at the young marine, he said, "Do you think I haven't thought of all that? The order I'm giving you will haunt me for the rest of my life. I'm sorry, Garrett, I truly am, but I'm afraid they're gone and there's not much we can do. I can't, in good conscience, risk losing more men for a cause that I believe is already lost."

Garrett held her temper in check. She knew this wasn't MacKay's fault. It had been a fool's errand to begin with. She was angry at herself for not having done more to keep Colton and Father Ryan from leaving. "Will that be all, sir?"

"Yes Captain," said MacKay. "That will be all."

Garrett whirled around and nearly ran off the bridge. Mercer stood next to MacKay. Several minutes passed without either man saying anything. Finally, Mercer asked, "Your orders, Captain?"

"We'll continue to try and reach them. I also want to send the drones over. Doubt we'll find much due to the mist," said MacKay. "Tomorrow morning we'll have an officers' meeting after breakfast. Have Meinhard and his people join us."

"What are you planning to do, sir?" asked Mercer.

"We're going to go home," said MacKay. "Something was able to bring us here, so it stands to reason there's a way back. You have the bridge, Mr. Mercer. I'll be in my cabin."

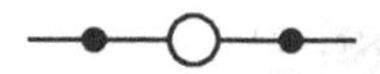

The jungle, for the most part, had returned to normal. The woman standing over Colton looked at him for a few more moments, then moved over to Father Ryan. Crouching down, she placed a small metal discus on his wrist, and one on the side of his neck. She then moved back to Colton and did the same thing. Neither of the men moved.

The multitude of creatures that had surrounded Colton and Father Ryan were gone. They had never been there in the first place. It had all been an illusion created by the sphere she carried. Experience had taught them that most aggressors backed down in the face of overwhelming force. But Colton hadn't backed down. Quite the opposite. He'd been prepared to go down fighting. This troubled her.

She was slender, having finished removing the camouflage she wore to keep herself safe while in the jungle. Her skin was light brown with a greenish tint, and while her face bore many similarities to humans, that didn't hold true with her eyes. Slightly larger than human eyes, they angled upwards at the corners, their coloration a kaleidoscope of blue and silver shades that constantly moved and changed, depending on the amount of light around her.

The top of her head was crowned with what looked like a lion's mane of hair. Blending with her skin, it boasted shades of brown and green, reaching down to just below her shoulders. She continued to look at Colton, her mesmerizing eyes turned cold. She had adamantly argued against this mission. She felt they were making a terrible mistake, but she had not succeeded in winning the argument.

Moving the sphere in a counterclockwise motion, a beam of pale blue light covered the woman's head and part of her shoulders. "Both of the men are now with me. It was necessary to render them unconscious. They have not been harmed."

"Yes, we are getting the readings as well. Will you be able to bring them to us, or will you require assistance?"

"Unless something changes, I will be able to complete the mission at hand," she said, thinking about the two men lying on the ground. She thought about the arguments she had put forward earlier and said, "These men are different. They are far stronger than any we have ever encountered. As we observed, their weapons are more advanced, and their vessel contains the rudimentary elements of star power. Is it wise to bring them in, to allow them to learn about us?"

"This was thoroughly discussed before you left. You are well aware of the reasons why we must do this. We can only truly evaluate them by bringing them here. As there are only two of them, we do not anticipate any risk."

"I'll keep you updated on our progress," she said, and then moved the sphere in the opposite direction, breaking off communication.

Again, she stood looking down at Colton, trying to discern as much as she could from his still form. *It is you who concerns me the most*, she thought to herself. *You're clearly a very dangerous warrior. You will be hard to control and should be left here to die.* But she was a creature of strong discipline and repressed her own personal feelings. She knew what had to be done, knew of the ever-growing dangers threatening her own people. Shaking her head, she thought, *As advanced as we are, it is frightening to think that you may be our only hope.*

The End

ACKNOWLEDGMENTS

I would like to thank the following people who were instrumental, one way or another, in making *Infinity's Gateway* possible.

First, is my loving wife, Margaret, who has put up with what I like to call my "creative eccentricities" for many years. She is my first edit, giving me a woman's perspective as well as invaluable input. The love, the support, and frankly the patience she has given to me through all this, I'm sure, will put her in line for canonization.

Dennis Welch, my manager and publicist, has been steadfast in his support of my writing, and over the last ten years has become a close and trusted friend. His insight into the business of writing made this possible. He and his wife, Susie, helped to keep me going through some of the darkest times.

Don Webb, a tremendous talent in his own right, is more than my editor. He has become my friend and my mentor in so many ways. Don is a wealth of knowledge, and I learn from him each and every time we are together. To this day he continues to play a strong role in guiding my writing.

David Hancock, Jim Howard, Tiffany Gibson, and the absolutely amazing team at Morgan James have been a true blessing. We wanted a strong publisher who would work with us and go the extra mile to support our dreams. In Morgan James we have found that. It is good to work with family.

ABOUT THE AUTHOR

Every now and then author James S. Parker has a vision. And, when he does, he sees people and places off in the misty distance. Sometimes these visions are futuristic and filled with danger. Most often they are mystical, with good and evil and a cast of characters who beautifully represent both.

In his high school years James experienced a spine tingling brush with the supernatural. That single event—complete with the sound of heavy footsteps and an invisible visitor—etched forever in his mind the idea that life is much more mysterious than we oftentimes admit, that the spiritual world is all around us, and that its impact on us cannot be denied.

Though he sees through a glass darkly, he writes as though he has been granted a glimpse into the unknown, one that has informed his novels and their powerful stories of good and evil and the struggles we all face every day to assure that good wins.

Infinity's Gateway, the first book in a fascinating sci-fi adventure trilogy, is his latest work.

James lives in San Antonio, Texas with his wife, Margaret.

CPSIA information can be obtained
at www.ICGtesting.com
Printed in the USA
JSHW030017301220
10646JS00001B/22